PRAISE FOR DONNA GRANT'S
BEST-SELLING ROMANCE NOVELS

"Grant's ability to quickly convey complicated
backstory makes this jam-packed love story accessible
even to new or periodic readers."
–Publishers' Weekly

"Donna Grant has given the paranormal genre
a burst of fresh air…"
–San Francisco Book Review

"The premise is dramatic and heartbreaking;
the characters are colorful and engaging;
the romance is spirited and seductive."
–The Reading Cafe

"The central romance, fueled by a hostage drama, plays
out in glorious detail against a backdrop of multiple ongoing
issues in the "Dark Kings" books. This seemingly penultimate
installment creates a nice segue to a climactic end."
–Library Journal

"…intense romance amid the growing war between
the Dragons and the Dark Fae is scorching hot."
–Booklist

SKYE DRUIDS SERIES

Iron Ember ~ Shoulder the Skye ~ Heart of Glass
Endless Skye ~ Still of the Night ~ Blood Skye
After Midnight ~ Kiss of Skye ~ Between Twilight

DARK KINGS SERIES

Dark Heat ~ Darkest Flame ~ Fire Rising
Burning Desire ~ Hot Blooded ~ Night's Blaze
Soul Scorched ~ Dragon King ~ Passion Ignites
Smoldering Hunger ~ Smoke and Fire
Dragon Fever ~ Firestorm ~ Blaze ~ Dragon Burn
Constantine: A History, Parts 1-3 ~ Heat ~ Torched
Dragon Night ~ Dragonfire ~ Dragon Claimed
Ignite ~ Fever ~ Dragon Lost ~ Flame ~ Inferno
A Dragon's Tale (Whisky and Wishes: *A Holiday Novella*,
Heart of Gold: *A Valentine's Novella*, & Of Fire and Flame)
My Fiery Valentine ~ The Dragon King Coloring Book
Dragon King Special Edition Character Coloring Book: Rhi

DARK WARRIORS SERIES

Midnight's Master ~ Midnight's Lover
Midnight's Seduction ~ Midnight's Warrior
Midnight's Kiss ~ Midnight's Captive
Midnight's Temptation ~ Midnight's Promise
Midnight's Surrender ~ A Warrior for Christmas

CHIASSON SERIES

Wild Fever ~ Wild Dream ~ Wild Need
Wild Flame ~ Wild Rapture

LARUE SERIES
Moon Kissed ~ Moon Thrall
Moon Struck ~ Moon Bound

WICKED TREASURES
Seized by Passion ~ Enticed by Ecstasy
Captured by Desire
Books 1-3: Wicked Treasures Box Set

★.° ☼★.◉˙ᥫ.°

☆ HISTORICAL PARANORMAL ☆

THE KINDRED SERIES
Everkin ~ Eversong ~ Everwylde
Everbound ~ Evernight ~ Everspell

KINDRED: THE FATED SERIES
Rage ~ Ruin ~ Reign

DARK SWORD SERIES
Dangerous Highlander ~ Forbidden Highlander
Wicked Highlander ~ Untamed Highlander
Shadow Highlander ~ Darkest Highlander

ROGUES OF SCOTLAND SERIES
The Craving ~ The Hunger
The Tempted ~ The Seduced
Books 1-4: Rogues of Scotland Box Set

BURNING SEA

ELVEN KINGDOMS
BOOK FIVE

NEW YORK TIMES & USA TODAY BESTSELLING AUTHOR
DONNA GRANT

Puma Land
Dragon Land
Shecrish
Neron Lake
Ghris Mountains
Orgale
Ferdon Woods
Stonemore
Belanore
Flamefall
Iron Hall
Ravula Canyon
Cairnkeep
The Doorway
Corrial Plateau
Silver Falls
Ever Reaching River
Dangerous Peaks
Rannora
Argares
Zora
Highvale

— ⋆·☆·⋆ —

7 RACES OF ELVES

— ⋆·☆·⋆ —

SUN ELVES (GOLD ELVES)

– recognized by their golden complexions.
Known for their levelheadedness, think things through.
Have long memories. Maintain a love of
freedom and personal expression.

Skin: golden brown
Eyes: amber, copper, gold
Hair: golden blond, tawny
Ability: Readers
Magic Color: yellow/golden

⋆⁺₀°⋆˙⁺ ☽ ○ ☾ ₊˙⋆°₀⁺⋆

MOON ELVES (AKA SILVER ELVES)

– Isolated race who prefer only themselves.
Moon elf society values individual
accomplishment and rights.

Skin: very fair, silver tint
Eyes: various shades of blue (icy blue)
Hair: blue, silvery white
Magic Color: silver

STAR ELVES (AKA PEWTER ELVES)

– Nomadic, often interacting with other elves.
Have a knack for perceiving inner beauty.
Curious and adventurous. Can be focused and relentless.

Skin: fair skin
Eyes: violet/shades of purple
Hair: lavender, purple, silver
Homeland: nomadic
Ability: Healers
Magic Color: purple

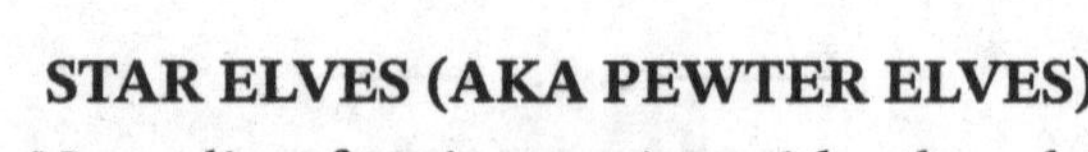

SEA ELVES (AKA BLUE ELVES)

– Have webbed fingers and toes. Gills hidden behind
their ears. AKA as mermaids without the tails.
Among their own, delight in song, dance, and magic.
Toward others they are slow to bestow the gift of
their voice/artistry.

Skin: Blueish/greenish
Eyes: iridescent blue to silver white
Hair: bluish-black or greenish-black (oil slick)
Homeland: bodies of water
Ability: animals in the water
Magic Color: blue

WOOD ELVES (AKA COPPER ELVES)
– guardians of all things in the forest.
They live in complete harmony with the woods and
its inhabitants. Can be judgmental, but take time to
consider everything before passing judgment.
Once won, a Wood Elf's friendship is deep and lasting.
Some of the best fighters.

Skin: coppery skin
Eyes: Green or Hazel
Hair: Brown or Red
Homeland: forests/woods
Ability: good with animals; can sense truth/lies
Magic Color: green or copper

★⁺₀°★˙˖⁺☽ ○ ☾₊˙★°₀⁺★

MOUNTAIN ELVES (AKA BRONZE ELVES)
– prefer the highest peaks. Rarest of the elves.
Cautious and aloof. Understand the importance of
community. Suspicious of strangers. Best weapon crafters.

Skin: white or brown
Eyes: Black
Hair: Black, Dark Brown
Homeland: mountains
Magic Color: bronze

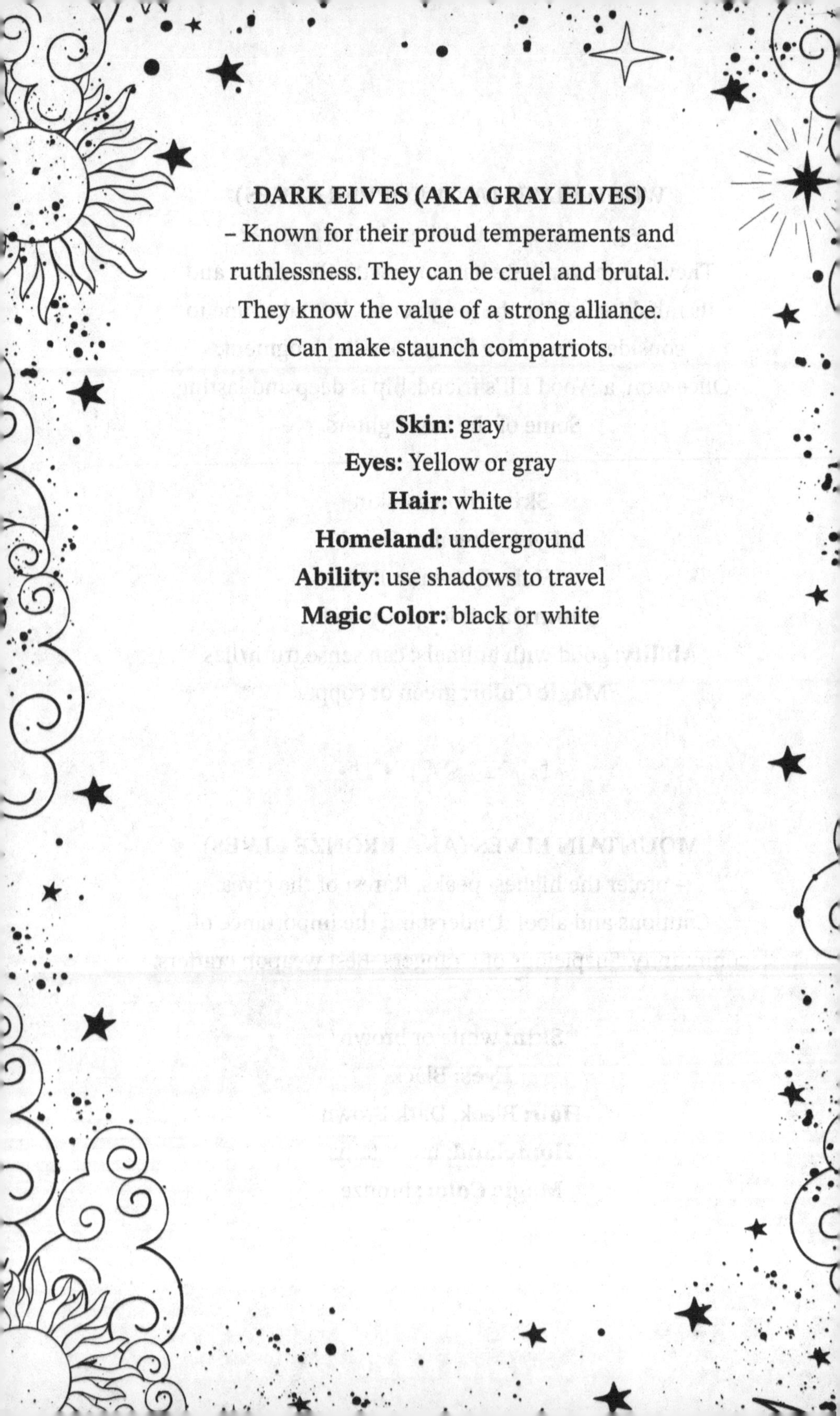

DARK ELVES (AKA GRAY ELVES)

– Known for their proud temperaments and ruthlessness. They can be cruel and brutal. They know the value of a strong alliance. Can make staunch compatriots.

Skin: gray
Eyes: Yellow or gray
Hair: white
Homeland: underground
Ability: use shadows to travel
Magic Color: black or white

BURNING SEA

ELVEN KINGDOMS
BOOK FIVE

1

Somewhere in the Amrata Ocean

A low hum whispered in the vast quiet of the deep. It stirred Varum's senses and wrapped soothingly around him. The world narrowed to shades of sapphire and shadows—endless and alive. He hung on to the *mareth* as its enormous wing-like fins stirred, quickly cutting through the cold ocean waters. As Varum scanned the bottomless blue ahead, he could just make out the faded images of the two Sea Elves he followed.

The *mareth* drew closer to the surface, and light began to fracture above him, breaking into ribbons of molten blue. The currents flowed in all directions—some swift, others gentle, but all dangerous. Off to his right, a group of *nairu* rippled past, their silver scales scattering light like shattered glass.

There was no time to enjoy the serene beauty around him. Not when he had the chance to find the rogue elves rumored to be aiding the Masters. He had been urging the High Tide Assembly to take the reports coming to Tarangarh seriously, but they repeatedly dismissed his concerns. They cared not that humans were being taken. The Assembly couldn't even muster shock at the knowledge that other elven races were also being kidnapped. To most Sea Elves, the land dwellers got what they deserved.

Except Varum knew of at least three Sea Elves who had gone missing from other cities.

His unease grew at the Assembly's inaction. If they wouldn't heed the reports making their way to them, then he would bring them proof. Starting with the duo of elves he now trailed. They had left Tarangarh by way of a passage that should have been guarded. That meant someone in the city must have aided these elves. He had no idea how far up the betrayal went, but he intended to find out.

Varum leaned closer to the *mareth* and telepathically told it to go faster. The colossal beast beat its wide fins quicker in response. He kept the animal in deeper waters to watch everything unfold. It would also allow him to spring into action should the need arise. He wouldn't allow the Sea Elves to be tainted by the depravities of the Masters and their sycophants.

It was bad enough that the Masters' influence had grown too fast and spread too far. The first hint of the group had reached Tarangarh a year past. No one had heeded the gossip at the time. That was the way of Sea Elves. Nothing mattered but their world beneath the water. They kept to themselves and rarely interacted with other elves.

Yet Varum worried that his kind's dismissive behavior could very well be their undoing.

A dark shadow marred the rippling surface as a ship headed in his direction. Varum narrowed his eyes as the two elves headed straight for the vessel. He'd hoped he had been wrong about them, but this clearly wasn't a chance meeting. Even from his depth, he could hear the cries of fear from those on the ship, mixed with the deep voices of those tormenting them.

He kept his gaze on the pair of Sea Elves as they poked their heads above the water. Try as he might, he was too far away to hear their exchange with the boat. He urged the *mareth* to head toward a coral outcropping. Varum patted the animal and said his thanks before sliding off to hide. This area of the ocean had treacherous currents that could—and often did—cause ships to lose their way.

His worry doubled when one of the Sea Elves swam to the front of the craft while the second went to the back. He caught flashes of blue magic as they drove the vessel through the roughest currents. Fury coiled tightly inside Varum. He didn't know how long his kinsfolk had aided the Masters, but it stopped today.

He shoved away from the coral and headed toward the ship. He was halfway there when movement out of the corner of his eye caught his attention. Varum did a double-take, his mind refusing to believe what he saw. It wasn't another Sea Elf coming up from the depths, but a woman. She swam calmly, deliberately. Swiftly. As if the ocean were hers to command.

No human could swim at such depths without drowning. Their fragile bodies weren't built to sustain a held breath for that long. And yet, this female was doing just that. Long, dark hair billowed behind her like streamers as she swam straight for the vessel.

She didn't slow as she came up behind the elf at the rear of the ship and whacked him on the back of the head. His hold loosened, and he sank into the abyss, unconscious. Varum's gaze jerked back to the woman. The craft began to slow, and she used that time to grab a rope floating in the water.

He moved closer for a better look, being sure to stay out of sight of the other Sea Elf. It wasn't long before he realized that the boat wasn't a large transport ship as he had thought. It was a sloop, designed for speed and maneuverability. The female pulled herself up and out of the water with ease.

Varum broke the surface to get a clearer view of the action and counted twenty humans shackled together, with five elves manning the boat. Each of the elves had their attention focused on their destination as the sloop glided smoothly through the waves, all while the woman managed to unlock the prisoner's chains.

One of the humans, a man, slipped soundlessly into the water and beneath the surface. Varum watched him for a moment. He hadn't gone very deep, and his strokes were sloppy and frantic. He was using too much energy, which meant he wouldn't get far before his body gave out and he drowned.

The next to go over was a middle-aged woman. Her foot slipped on her way into the water, causing her to splash. That caught the attention of the Wood Elf nearest her. There was a second of silence as the female, unchaining the prisoners, locked eyes with the elf. Then, the Wood Elf bellowed a warning, and chaos erupted as desperate humans fled overboard despite still being restrained. The ship dragged them along in its wake. A few were able to raise themselves up enough to catch a breath, but most succumbed quickly.

Varum had thought the female would jump into the water to escape. Instead, she *charged* the kidnapper. She went low, aiming for the Wood Elf's knees, letting out a battle yell that made his brows rise in surprise. The elf aimed his hand, ready to launch a round of magic, when the human twisted and fell onto her back, taking the elf with her. He toppled over, his head slamming into the side of the vessel.

When Varum spotted a Moon Elf rushing toward her, he nearly called out a warning. He stopped himself in time. He might sympathize with what was happening to them, but he also knew there wasn't anything he could do to help the ones here. His focus was on ending whatever connection the Masters had to the Sea Elves. He certainly didn't care about a woman, no matter how heroic—or perhaps idiotic—her efforts.

A strangled yell cut off mid-cry and caught Varum's attention. He turned to see the large fin of a *vorash* before it vanished beneath the waves, and the blood pooling in the water. With a flick of his wrists, Varum slipped beneath the surface and turned in a slow circle. The torso of a young man floated lifelessly in a cloud of bloodied water, but it was the sight of the Sea Elf surging fast from the deep, his face mottled in fury, that drew his gaze.

Varum rushed toward the elf with two kicks of his feet, intercepting his quarry before the elf could reach the boat. He rammed a shoulder into his kinsman and knocked him off course. The younger male turned silvery white eyes to Varum and peeled back his lips in a sneer. The elf attacked in a burst of magic and bubbles, but Varum had expected such an assault and easily moved to the side, hitting the elf in the back as he passed.

The younger elf tumbled head over heels before catching himself and hurriedly swimming back into the dark depths of the ocean instead of continuing the fight. Varum glanced back at the sloop. The remaining Sea Elf was farther away now, and he'd have to fight the other elves to get him. It would be easier to go after the one trying to escape. He flipped down and started swimming.

The sleek body of a *vorash* glided below him. Suddenly, the animal spun, flicking its tail as it hurried away. Varum looked over his shoulder to see the woman sinking quickly. She kicked her feet, but there was a chain locked around her arms, preventing her from moving them. And billowing in her wake was a cloud of blood from a wound.

He almost felt sorry for her becoming the *vorash's* next meal, but it was the way of the sea. Just as he started to swim away, something made him hesitate. He watched her sink deeper and deeper. Behind her, the *vorash* gained ground quickly. Yet Varum still held back, unsure why he couldn't seem to do anything. He tried to look away when the animal opened its huge mouth, but his eyes wouldn't obey. Just before the *vorash* slammed its jaws closed around her, it suddenly jerked away, swimming off into the blue.

Varum's gaze swung back to the human. She continued to fight against the chains binding her, even as blood continued to darken the water around her. One *vorash* might have left, but others would soon come to feast. They couldn't resist the smell of blood, and there was a lot of it in the water.

She plummeted toward the reef without realizing it. Finally, she twisted so she was facing downward and just managed to shift to the side to prevent striking the coral. But by doing that, she set herself on a course toward a rockier area. She attempted to rotate again, but it was too late. Her knees struck a section, causing her to spin. Within moments, her head hit another. Then, there was no more movement as she tumbled to the bottom.

Varum looked toward the fleeing Sea Elf, finding him long gone, then looked back at the vessel. It, too, was gone, leaving dozens of dead floating in its wake. If the rumors about what happened to those kidnapped were true, death was a blessing. He searched the water for any sign of the second Sea Elf, but he was nowhere to be seen. The only link to any of what had occurred was the human.

He sighed as he descended to her. His gaze locked on her chest, watching it rise and fall steadily. Surely, his eyes were deceiving him. A human couldn't breathe underwater. They had never been able to. Never would.

The light was dim this far down, but Sea Elves were made to see in such murky depths. Once he touched the sandy bottom beside her, he held her close and unwound the chain. She floated back and forth with the current, her dark hair moving like seaweed about her head. He watched as several strands clung to his arm.

He had only heard humans described. This was his first time seeing one up close. Her face might be what her kind called pretty. Her features were symmetrical and pleasant to look upon. As her head lolled to the side, he caught sight of something. Gently, he gripped her chin and turned her head away. He moved aside her hair and saw three small slits—gills—behind her ear.

Varum jerked back in shock. How was this possible? He needed to know more—about her *and* her knowledge of the Masters. The blood bloom around them was swelling and getting larger. He glanced up to see dozens of *vorash* feasting on the dead above. He could hold them off if he had to, but it would be better to get away while they were occupied. Her wounds needed tending. The cut along her hairline from striking the coral bled profusely, but it was the injury to her side that threatened her life.

He couldn't tend to her here, but he couldn't take her back to Tarangarh. It was forbidden for anyone other than Sea Elves to enter the city—not even the other elven races were permitted. Regardless, she had answers that he needed to keep his people safe.

There was nowhere he felt comfortable taking her, though. He couldn't chance any other Sea Elf city, and going ashore was out of the question. There was only one answer. Tarangarh.

Defying the oldest law of Sea Elf civilization would mean death for him *and* her if they were caught, but if he could prove to the High Tide Assembly about the Masters, then maybe the punishment wouldn't be as harsh. For him, at least. They wouldn't be lenient with a human. He looked down at her floating before him.

She had answers he needed. If her life saved tens of thousands of elves, then he would find a way to deal with it. That was *if* they got caught. He would just have to make sure that didn't happen.

2

The hollow, biting pain ruthlessly dragged Kalyani to consciousness. Every breath was like a million tiny razors slicing into her lungs. She gasped and moved a shaky hand to her side, feeling strange material. It was then that it hit her. She was no longer in the water.

Immediately, she panicked, thinking that Rohan had found her. But that wasn't possible. He had no idea she had gone out—no one did. So, who had her? On the heels of that question, she picked up the sound of voices.

"...know what they'll do to you if anyone finds out?" came a nervous male voice.

"They won't." The second man's voice was deep, his words decisive.

And yet, the first argued. "They will. It's just a matter of time."

"I didn't have a choice."

Kalyani tried to focus on the conversation, but her head was pounding. Though she was sure she had heard elvish. The accent was different from what she had heard before. Lyrical. Refined.

She wheezed as she peeled open her eyes, but all she saw was blue before they fell shut again. She rolled her head toward the voices, which sent agony prickling through her neck. Her desperate attempt to hold back the moan was for naught.

Suddenly, someone was beside her. She tried to see who it was, but her eyes wouldn't obey her, and the pain was mounting by the second. A soft *whoosh* met her ears before a light cloth was placed over her mouth. Large hands held her chin, keeping her head in place. She wanted to fight the person off, but she had neither the will nor the strength. When sleep called again, she willingly went into its arms.

The next time she woke, the pain was much more manageable. She was able to take a breath without thinking she might die. Her side still ached, but it wasn't the debilitating agony from before. Even the throbbing in her head had diminished. Yet she still couldn't string two thoughts together. She touched her face, but there was no cloth over her mouth. She frowned, sure she hadn't imagined it.

Her eyes were so heavy that it took everything she had to pry them open. Each time she did, she saw blue. Not the deep indigo of the ocean, but a pale aqua shimmer that moved against the ceiling and walls in gentle, rhythmic waves. It was altogether different and otherworldly.

A pulse of violet caught her attention. She turned her head toward it and found herself staring out a window. Except it wasn't a window, exactly. She wanted a better look, but she couldn't keep her eyes open. Kalyani rolled onto her good side and pushed herself up with her hands. The room spun wildly as she clung to the bed.

When it finally stopped, and she could open her eyes, she saw another pulse of violet outside in the velvety darkness beyond the window. The long tendrils of a massive *lunai* glowed a soft azure as it idly floated past. She rose on unsteady legs to get closer to the animal. She'd been stung by a few over the years, but she had never seen one so big. Or one that glowed.

She took a tentative step, only to find herself pitching forward. The floor came up too swiftly for her to stop herself. The jarring drop stunned her, but only for a moment. If she couldn't walk, she'd crawl. She had to know what kind of strange dream this was.

Within moments, Kalyani was out of breath, her body shaking from the exertion. She glanced up, expecting to find herself at the window, but it seemed as far away as it had been before. That didn't stop her, though. She didn't know how to give up on something she wanted, and she really wanted to get a closer look at the *lunai*.

When she couldn't crawl and keep her eyes open, she crawled with them shut. That ended up being a bad idea, though. She fell over twice, and it took extra effort to get back on her hands and knees again. But she kept moving until, finally, she was at the window.

Her body wanted sleep, but she wasn't giving in so easily. She peeled open her eyes. The *lunai* was no longer in sight. Kalyani blinked and focused her gaze on the glass. Except, it wasn't glass. She squinted, trying to make out what it was, when something shimmered above her. She lifted her head toward the ceiling to see what it was and overbalanced. She toppled to the side and rolled onto her back.

Sleep sounded so good. Just as she was about to give in, she caught sight of the shimmer again. She sleepily blinked while attempting to follow the movements of the aqua waves without bothering to get up again. Each time she blinked, her eyes stayed shut for longer. She should be scared, but she wasn't.

She opened her eyes to see the waves again. Instead, she found a face peering down at her. She tilted her head to the side and blinked to see if he would disappear. When the face remained, she raised a hand and attempted to move it out of her way. He was blocking the pretty shimmers.

"You shouldn't have gotten out of bed."

Her eyes widened at the deep voice. It sounded familiar, but she couldn't remember why. He reached for her hand, but she yanked it away. At least, she thought she did. Her body wasn't responding as it should.

"Don't you want up?" he asked.

"You're blocking the view."

His dark brows snapped together before he lifted his gaze. He released a sigh and stepped back. Kalyani smiled when she had her view back once more. It was so pretty and calming. Her eyes drifted shut again.

"Your wounds aren't quite healed. You shouldn't be moving around. I must admit, I'm surprised you're able to heal as quickly as you do."

His voice was nice. She could listen to the deep resonance all day.

"My...voice?"

She grimaced. Had she said that out loud?

"Aye. You did."

Kalyani blinked up at him in confusion.

"Human, you need to get back into bed."

She grinned at the way he called her *human*. Aye. His voice was very nice. Even when he was grouchy. He reminded her of Rohan.

"Who's Rohan? Your mate?"

Kalyani rolled over and found her head cushioned by something a bit hard but comfortable all the same.

"My boot won't make a good pillow, human."

"Shhh," she murmured.

3

Varum blew out a frustrated breath as he stared down at the female curled on her side with her head on his boot and one arm wrapped around his ankle. He had taken a chance giving her the *thalorine* to dull her pain as she healed— only a tiny drop of paste in each of her wounds. Seeing her as she was now made him glad he hadn't given her more.

He couldn't leave her on the floor. Once more, he cradled the woman in his arms as he carried her back to his bed. For the last two nights, he had slept on the couch. He wanted his bed back, but it looked like he had at least one more night on the uncomfortable furniture.

The female weighed nothing. He wasn't sure she'd even come to his chest when she stood. He placed her on the bed and checked the wound at her hairline, liking the healing he saw. Then, he carefully felt around the broad *serynth* leaf on her side. The naturally occurring adhesive film not only sealed the skin but also released natural antiseptic oil. It was working well to heal her injury. Even better than he had expected.

Varum covered her with the blanket and sat on the edge of the bed. Her hair, once dried, had become a riot of curls as dark and rich as kelp roots. Her eyes, however, had startled him. He'd seen every color the ocean could birth, but never had he glimpsed brown laced with copper, gleaming like the heart of a shell.

Even though he knew what he would find, as he had already looked several times before, he gently moved aside her hair to see the back of her ear. There was still no sign of any gills on either side, yet he knew what he had seen. He moved his hand away, only to have a curl wrap around his finger. He froze, his eyes glued to the thick strand. Something about the sight of it held him captivated. Slowly, he slid his finger loose.

He returned his attention to her and stared for a long time, taking in her oval face, high cheekbones, and dark brows. Her skin was the color of sun-warmed sand. She had rushed to help the humans seemingly out of nowhere. Who was she? How could she breathe in the water? And why had she been out in the ocean alone?

His gaze dropped to her mouth, and he recalled the way she had smiled while staring at the ceiling. The sight of the grin had been so unexpected that it had disarmed him. He didn't want to be surprised by her or her actions. She was a means to an end.

Varum turned his head away and spotted the wide leather belt he had removed from her waist and discarded while tending to her wounds. She wore simple, bleached gray garments—the kind of clothes favored by those who worked the land. Or the sea.

Sighing, he leaned his forearms on his knees and stared at the floor. Was Nirav right? Had he made a mistake? When he made the decision to bring the human to Tarangarh, it had seemed like the right thing to do, regardless of the consequences. He'd heard Nirav's arguments and still believed his actions would be worth the risk in the long run.

Varum surged to his feet and raked his hand through his hair, shoving the long strands away from his face. There were things he needed to see to, but he was hesitant to leave his quarters should the human wake again while he was out. She hadn't made it far from the bed this time, but the *thalorine* would wear off soon, and it would be better for everybody if *he* were the one here instead of Nirav when it did.

He looked around his room before striding into the living area. His home might be where he lay his head and rested, but he didn't usually spend much time here. He plopped down on the chair at the head of the two couches and stretched his back. Not only were the sofas uncomfortable, but he was also tired of having his legs hang over the arm.

His gaze was drawn through the open bedroom door. The woman was tiny enough that she could fit on the sofa without issue. He shook his head and leaned back in the chair. As tempting as that sounded, he couldn't. For the moment, he could shut the door to his room and keep anyone from seeing who was inside. It would be problematic to move her should someone knock on his door.

And they would.

His absence was bound to raise eyebrows soon. He toyed with the idea of asking Nirav to sit with the human, but that meant putting him at risk. Nirav would do it without question, though. That was just the kind of elf he was.

The silence threatened to do Varum in. He was a doer,

someone who rarely stayed still. Sitting idly was the worst kind of torture. He shot another quick look toward the human. It was really too bad that she was still out of it from the pain reliever. If she weren't, he could be getting the information he needed. Unfortunately, he had to wait.

He slid lower in the chair and stretched out his legs. After a moment, he laced his hands over his stomach and closed his eyes.

4

Consciousness came to Kalyani sluggishly, like surfacing from a great depth. She opened her eyes to find everything around her fuzzy and distorted and quickly shut them again. There was a dull ache in her side—slight but constant. Her mouth felt as if someone had stuffed a rag into it. She tried to swallow and managed a little saliva on her second attempt. Her tongue stuck to her chapped lips when she made the mistake of licking them.

The next time she tried to open her eyes was easier. After two blinks, her vision cleared. She stared at the pale aqua light moving on the ceiling. Something about it was strangely familiar, as if she had seen it before. She frowned up at it, trying to figure out when that might have been. She gave up when her head started to throb.

Kalyani was desperate for a drink. She couldn't hear anyone moving about, and she had no idea where she was. It was only while studying the slightly domed ceiling and the etched reliefs of sea creatures there that her foggy brain registered a niggling worry and a directive to be careful.

She rolled to her side and winced as a bolt of pain shot through her. Her arms worked, but not well. It felt as if she were moving against the tide. As if something else fought with her over control of her body.

It took some doing, but eventually, she got a hand beneath her and pushed herself into a sitting position. That little bit of movement made her breathless. Her side throbbed again, but she was loath to move any more. She sat with her eyes closed and waited for the pain to subside, until her arm began trembling from the effort of leaning on it. She drew in a shaky breath and opened her eyes, her gaze landing on the broad, arched opening of a window. It wasn't just any opening. Beyond it was a luminous expanse of deep blue water, growing darker the farther she looked.

The sight of the enormous *krelite* drawing near had her on her feet, but it quickly ducked out of view. She shuffled across the floor on wobbly legs, intent on getting to the window as quickly as she could manage—which wasn't that fast at all. When she reached the opening, she got as close as she dared and looked out, but the *krelite* and all eight of its tentacles were gone.

She stared out at the water for a beat before focusing on the window. It wasn't glass between her and the ocean. It appeared to be some kind of transparent membrane that glistened faintly like oil on water and flexed with the ocean's movement. But nothing penetrated the film. Unable to stop herself, she lightly pressed a finger against it, gasping when it gave slightly. But it was the warmth that met her skin that truly astounded her. If she had felt this with her eyes closed, she would've sworn it was alive.

Kalyani dropped her arm to her side and started to turn away when the window structure itself caught her attention. Her lips slackened in amazement as she spotted the faint traces of silver coral filigree along the window edges in a wave motif. She smoothed her finger along the inlaid silver, her eyes tracing the engraved motif up the tall, elegantly curved opening designed for both light and view.

Her gaze shifted to the walls then. It took her a moment to realize that the smooth, iridescent material was living coral. Within it were faint veins of bioluminescent light that shifted like currents through stone. It was the most beautiful thing she had ever seen. She reached toward a vein of light, but it shifted before she could touch it.

Something tugged at her side. Kalyani looked down to see a gaping hole in her tunic, stained dark with dried blood. A memory of one of the elves striking her with magic rose. In an instant, she was taken back to the battle and the fury she had seen on the Wood Elf's face as he launched his green magic at her. The pain had been instantaneous, snatching her breath even as her body tried to move away.

The memory faded, and she focused on the mosaic of shell, pearl, and stone at her feet. The colors varied, going from a deep blue to silver and sand white. She lifted her bare toes against the slightly cool texture. There was no distinct pattern, but that was part of its beauty.

Her perusal eventually brought her to a woven rug that faded from indigo to black next to the bed. She hadn't remembered walking on it, but then again, her attention had been focused outside the room. She returned her gaze to the rug and ran her foot over the geometric pattern. The tightly woven sea-grass fibers were something she had never seen before. Her people knew how to soften the *shrava* stalks to create mats, but this went beyond their skills. She leaned closer and saw what looked like thin strands of kelp silk threaded through it, creating subtle color shifts.

Kalyani then noticed the bed on the raised coral platform. Atop it was layered kelp-fiber bedding in the same indigo and silver as the rug. She rubbed the material between her fingers, marveling at its silky feel. Next to the bed was a low table, empty save for a book, its spine creased from many reads, and a bioluminescent crystal sphere that illuminated the room with soft light. The only other piece of furniture was a tall wardrobe made out of polished coral.

The room itself was quiet, the comfort noticeable through the craftsmanship, and very masculine. She looked up at the ceiling again, then turned around to follow the wavy, aqua lights down the wall. She found herself looking into iridescent blue eyes that watched her like a predator observes its prey.

And with that realization came another.

She was with a Sea Elf.

She stopped herself from taking a step back just in time. She hadn't heard him approach. She didn't know how long he had been standing there, silently scrutinizing her. The one thing she *did* know was that he was possibly the tallest male she had ever seen. He had at least four inches on Rohan, and that was saying something, because her brother was tall.

The elf wore a sleeveless tunic of midnight blue that showed off muscular arms and his blueish-green skin. The top molded to his wide chest like a second skin before opening diagonally down his torso. His pants were a dark teal with faint silver piping at the seams, and a broad belt of braided kelp encircled his trim waist, secured with a carved rune belt clasp. His feet were bare.

She studied his webbed toes for a moment before slowly running her gaze back up his intimidating frame, taking in the polished drift-leather wrist guards and the torc necklace made of interlinked shells, before returning to his face.

The minute she did it, she knew it was a mistake. His eyes were piercing, cutting through her like the sharpest blade. His blueish-black hair held a slight wave, and he'd gathered the top portion behind his head while the rest fell past his shoulders. She couldn't tell how long it was, but she suspected it was longer than hers.

He had a jaw cut from stone, a square chin, and wide lips that were neither full nor thin. Just right. Dark brows cut over his penetrating eyes, and his pointed ears held no ornamentation. He held himself like an elf who went after—and got—what he wanted.

The question was: What did he want from her?

Meeting a Sea Elf had been Kalyani's dream for so long. Her first experience with them had been fighting against them to save her own kind, which hadn't turned out well. This second encounter wasn't shaping up to be much better. She wasn't sure whether he was friend or foe. She would have to tread carefully until she knew where she stood.

She shifted, her arm brushing against her ripped tunic. Something scraped softly against the inside of her arm. She wished to see what it was, but she didn't want to take her eyes off the elf for too long. Kalyani searched for the offending culprit with her fingers and found the edge of something that seemed stuck to her side. She grasped the corner and tugged.

"I wouldn't do that."

His voice was as smooth as a fish cutting through water, and as deep as the ocean behind her. Something about it tugged at a memory. She was sure she had heard it before. Why couldn't she place it?

"You aren't fully healed," he said.

She stilled as the memory of the chain being wrapped around her filled her mind. Her heart raced as she recalled struggling against the pain from her wound and her arms being bound. She had been sinking. She'd noticed a shadow in the water out of the corner of her eye right before she struck something.

Her hand rose to her temple. The spot was still a little sore. Kalyani looked closer at her side to see a broad, translucent, pale jade leaf with golden veins that pulsed faintly.

"It's a *serynth* leaf," he said. "It's used to stanch bleeding and draws out toxins, among other things. It secretes an adhesive film that seals the skin and releases antiseptic oils."

She immediately released the edge and slid her gaze to the elf. Then she shot a quick look over her shoulder out the window. "Where am I?"

"Safe."

"That depends on who you're talking to. And you didn't answer my question."

"I have questions of my own," he replied.

She had almost put him in the *friend* column, since he'd obviously helped her. The longer she talked to him, the more she realized he might be anything but a friend. "Answer mine since I asked first."

His nostrils flared, and those iridescent blue eyes turned frosty. "You're in a Sea Elf city. That's all you need to know right now."

"Says you. Why did you bring me here?"

"You were injured," he stated slowly, as if she were a child who couldn't possibly understand.

Kalyani bristled at his arrogant tone. "I would've been fine."

"A *vorash* was coming for you."

She rolled her eyes. "She wouldn't have hurt me."

His eyes narrowed as he tilted his head, his body going rigid. "Oh? And how do you know that?"

Kalyani inwardly kicked herself. She kept a great many secrets for a great many reasons. Mostly not to worry Rohan because her brother took on the weight of everyone's problems like it was his duty to solve them. No one knew her secrets. *No one.*

And it was going to stay that way.

"What I meant was that if she had wanted me for a meal, she wouldn't have swum away."

The elf eyed her for several tense seconds before relaxing. "And how were you going to get out of the chains?"

"I would've found a way," she replied with a shrug. "I always do."

"So, you find yourself chained often?"

She stopped short of rolling her eyes. Did he take everything literally? "Of course not."

"How do you explain your connection to the sloop and its occupants?"

He was really getting on her nerves now, but he also had her at a disadvantage. She was weak and disoriented. Going up against him now would be unwise. "If you were there, then you saw what happened. I was trying to save them. They had been kidnapped. Or do you not realize what's going on out there?" She studied him, her eyes narrowing as another thought took root. "Unless you were there because you work for the Masters. You do, don't you?" Kalyani took a step back, her mind racing as she glanced around for an escape. The window was the closest. "I won't be locked away, tortured, or sold as a slave."

She spun to race to the window. She only got one step before her knee buckled, and she dropped heavily to her hands and knees. Pain radiated through her body, coalescing at her side to throb in time with her heart.

Kalyani looked behind her. The elf didn't rush to stop her or to offer help. He hadn't moved from his spot. She clenched her teeth against another wave of pain as irritation slid alongside it. Even Rohan had helped Farah when they were enemies. Then again, her brother had feelings. This Sea Elf was obviously as stony and unmoving as the coral that surrounded them.

A sound at the windows drew her attention. She swung her head around and watched some coral lattices slide closed.

So. He was definitely in the *foe* column.

5

Varum stared at the human after she fell. He settled back into place and motioned his hand to the side, so the shutters closed to prevent her from escaping. She was still injured and feeling the effects of the medicine he'd given her, so he hadn't actually thought she might try to leave. He wouldn't make that mistake again.

He hadn't anticipated her bravado. Or was it stupidity? She had no idea where she was, but she would rather chance the ocean than stay in the room with him. Ironically, it was the same move he would've made. The difference was that he would've gotten free.

"What do you know about the Masters?" he demanded.

She didn't answer as she slowly climbed to her feet, her curls tangled at the back of her head. She stayed facing away from him, her gaze on the windows. He'd woken to the sound of her moving about the room, and when he entered, had found her at the window, looking out with wonder and excitement. Everywhere she looked around his room, her eyes had been bright, her lips parted in astonishment—and she'd had to touch everything. Almost as if it weren't real unless she felt it. Her actions had surprised him—again—holding him to the spot as he watched her discover her surroundings.

"Are you preventing me from leaving?" she finally asked.

Her words were clipped and edged with fury, though her accent wasn't as harsh as he had thought it would be. The dialect was grittier but not unpleasant. But that wasn't what got his attention. It was the way her body trembled with anger. Varum drew in a breath and released it. It was better to be honest about what he could. "I am."

"So, you *do* intend to hand me over to them."

He didn't like the resignation in her voice. Where was the fiery spirit he had just witnessed?

Suddenly, she whirled around, her dark eyes sparking with outrage, her hands clenched in indignation. Her wrath was palpable. "I will fight until my dying breath. There won't be anything left of me to give them."

The conviction in her words warned him that she meant what she said. He had no intention of giving her to anyone, but she didn't need to know that. For all her outrage, her body was about to give out. He watched the sweat running down her face as she swayed.

"What do you know about the Masters?" he repeated.

Her lips peeled back in a sneer. "I know they're the lowest, vilest beings to walk Shecrish. I know that their time will come to an end soon. And while I might not be there to see it, they will be dealt with swiftly. And painfully."

"You honestly believe that you, a human, would be able to confront them?"

She laughed, the sound hollow and mocking. "You have no idea what I can do."

"Then tell me."

The female crossed her arms over her chest and raised her chin, defiance radiating from her.

Varum was getting nowhere with this tactic. He needed answers, but she wouldn't tell him anything as long as she believed him the enemy. Unfortunately, there was no way to back up and start again. Or was there? He turned on his heel and walked out of the room. After counting to five, he returned.

The human hadn't moved, but her arms were now at her sides, and a frown marred her forehead. Confusion crossed her face as she studied him.

"I see you're awake. You were injured, so I brought you here and tended to your side and head," he said, motioning to both with his hand.

She considered him for a long minute before comprehension dawned. Her tone was softer, the anger banked but not gone. "Why didn't you bring me to shore?"

"We were too far out for that."

"And the others who managed to get off the boat?"

His gut twisted at the hope that flashed across her face. "There were no other survivors."

"No," she stated with a firm shake of her head. "I saw many of them get into the water."

"Do you have any idea how far out you were?"

She started to reply, but her hesitation was answer enough.

"Only a couple of them could swim. They used up too much energy trying to get away."

"Why didn't you help them?"

The fury in her dark eyes made them burn brighter. He almost wished he were closer to see if the color changed. "It was you or them."

"You should've gone for them."

"They had a chance. You were chained and bleeding."

She turned her head away. After a moment, she whispered, "At least they got free of their captors."

"Why did you go after the boat alone?"

"There wasn't time to get help. I thought..." She shook her head and walked to the window.

Varum took two steps toward her. "You ventured that far out into the water on your own?"

"I do it often, though no one knows. I wanted to help, to do my part, but I couldn't save even one."

"You took the captors by surprise. Had there been others with you, you might have been successful."

Her head swung to him, and then she faced him fully. "What were you doing there?"

"Following two of my people, who I suspect of aiding the Masters."

"Then why didn't you help me? We could've saved the entire ship."

He couldn't look away from her. "I was collecting information."

"Oh," she said casually. "Collecting information, huh?" Her expression hardened as she glared daggers at him. "I'm so happy to hear the lives of humans mean so little to you. I'm surprised you deigned to help me."

"You have a right to your anger."

"You're bloody right, I do," she retorted as she cut him with a single look.

Varum clasped his hands behind his back. "We're led by the High Tide Assembly here, and none of them thinks the Masters' reach has found us. I believe otherwise. I needed proof to bring to them."

"You'd better not tell me *I'm* that proof."

"You are not." He held off telling her that humans were forbidden from entering the city.

She glanced down at her side again, moving her ruined tunic to look at the leaf. "You really expect me to believe you aren't helping the Masters? I saw two Sea Elves doing just that."

"Did you not hear what I just told you?"

"Oh, I heard." She lifted her head to meet his gaze. "That doesn't mean I believe you. The Masters' reach is long. I know what they can do and the power they wield. I also know just how little the elves think of humans. Well," she paused, her face scrunching up slightly. "Most elves."

He quirked a brow. "What does that mean? Most elves?"

"It means there are a few decent ones."

Her tone made it clear that he wasn't one of those. "If I were working with the Masters, would I have brought you here? Would I have tended to your wounds?"

"If you thought I had information, aye, you would."

"I'm not working with them. I'm trying to keep them from my people."

Her eyebrows shot up. "What about the rest of us who have been fighting against them? I know you don't care about my kind, but what about the other elves being taken?"

It was true that Varum had never interacted with a human before, but he didn't recall ever hearing about them being so outspoken or brash. This female was both, despite being detained.

"Ah. I see," she said before he could comment. "Things that happen on land don't concern you and yours. Well, I hate to be the bearer of bad news, but a Sea Elf was recently freed from the Masters."

Varum was in front of the human in a blink. He towered over her, not bothering to hold back his annoyance. "How do you know about that?"

She tilted back her head to meet his gaze. Instead of being frightened, she smiled. "I heard about the group that saved her. I also know that some Sea Elves came to the aid of that same group as repayment."

What she said was true. He had learned it from Nirav, who had heard it from the female who had been kidnapped. "Do you know those who helped the Sea Elf?"

Her smile slipped as she swallowed and looked away. "Why would someone like me know them?"

He sighed and took a step back. If she were affiliated with the group, she wouldn't have been out on her own. They would've been there to help her. That put him back at square one.

"Can I go now?" she asked.

It would be wise to release her. She wasn't cooperating. But he still suspected she had more information that could help him. There was also the fact that he would have to explain to her how he had gotten her into the city—and how he would have to get her out.

"You claim not to be working for the Masters, yet you're

holding me against my will. I don't see much of a difference between the two," she replied acerbically.

"I'm not beating you. Nor do I intend to sell you into slavery."

She snorted. "Captive is captive, no matter how you look at it. I'm sure the female Sea Elf who was recently freed would be happy to explain that. Though I'm not sure your small brain could handle it."

Varum raised a brow at her biting remarks, though he didn't comment on them. She was angry, and she had every right to lash out at him. "Is there anything else you can tell me about the Masters?"

"Why don't you leave your precious home and go walk around on land to mingle with the other elves? You'd learn everything you need to know about what's happening."

"If you could save your city and those within it from the Masters' reach, would you?"

She rolled her eyes and huffed. "Aye."

"That's what I'm trying to do. I risked a lot to save you, and I'm asking for your help."

The seconds stretched as she held his gaze. Finally, she said, "If I give you what you want to know, will you release me?"

"Aye. I never intended to keep you here."

Those dark eyes narrowed slightly. "I want your word."

"You have it."

She dipped her head once. "I don't know where to start."

"How about with names? I'm Varum."

That seemed to startle her as she blinked up at him. "I'm Kalyani."

"Are you hungry?"

"I...um, a little."

Varum was buying time. If he allowed it, Kalyani would dump what information she thought he needed and demand to be released. It wouldn't be that easy. She would object once she realized what he was doing, but he would deal with that when the time came.

"Come. Let's eat," he bade and turned on his heel.

6

Serenia

Rohan fought to control the irritation rising within him. He spun away from the water and stalked to Kalyani's hut. He threw open the door, not bothering to knock or announce himself, because he had already been inside and knew it was empty. Dread curdled his gut as he scanned the sparse interior, searching for anything that might tell him where his sister had gone.

Hurried footsteps approached. He looked over his shoulder to see Farah running up, her red hair woven into a thick braid, showing off her pointed ears and hazel eyes filled with concern. The setting sun reflected off her coppery skin, announcing her as a Wood Elf. She shook her head.

That unsettled feeling churned in his gut again. He'd lived with it for weeks after his youngest sister, Lata, had been kidnapped.

Now, he was experiencing it again. "I never should've let her come here with us."

Farah placed a comforting hand on his back. "We don't know what happened to her."

"The fuck we don't." He whirled around and stalked back outside, his gaze pausing on the water that stretched from one end of the horizon to the other. Nothing could keep Kalyani out of the water. "Did I ever tell you how she ran to the water as soon as she learned to walk?"

"Aye," Farah replied softly as she came up beside him.

"That's where she is."

"Then you needn't worry. You said it yourself. She's the best swimmer around."

Rohan looked at Farah. "She promised to tell me when she was going out for a swim."

"Maybe she forgot," Farah said, shrugging.

He faced his lover. "No one has seen her since last night, and there are only a handful of us in Serenia. Kalyani knows how dangerous things are. She wouldn't just go off. She wouldn't do that to me."

Farah took his face in her hands and held his gaze. "We'll find her, my love. I promise. We found Lata, remember?"

He yanked Farah against him and held her tightly, wishing he could dispel the fear that clutched his heart. Part of him had hoped that Farah would tell him he was worrying for nothing, but he knew that wasn't true. Something had happened to his sister. It reminded him of waking and discovering that Lata and several other youths were gone from their village.

"I never wanted to feel this again," he said.

Farah lightly skimmed her nails over his back. "I know."

She was one of the few who actually understood what he was going through since her sister had also disappeared. The difference was that Farah's sister had decided to work with the Masters. Rohan buried his face in Farah's neck and inhaled the salty, sun-bleached scent of the ocean on her skin.

"I'm going to look for her," he said as he pulled out of Farah's arms.

Her brows snapped together, and she grasped his arm, drawing him back. "Is that wise? It's getting dark."

"I can't stay here for another moment. I have to *do* something."

"You're not in this alone this time. I'm here. Jai, Arya, Ravi, and Yasmin are here, too. Dain should return soon. They will help."

"Have you not found Kalyani?" Ravi asked as he walked toward them.

When Rohan looked at her, Farah shrugged and said, "We're a team, remember? Of course, I told them."

Rohan squeezed her hand in thanks. He was used to leading his people, to taking on everything by himself. His village was no more. Most of his people had moved away from the coast. Only a few lingered. It was out of a need for safety for them that he and those who had been actively fighting against the Masters had moved farther north and up the coast into a secluded cove. There wasn't a leader in Serenia. Farah was right. They were a team.

"She's gone," Rohan stated to the Sun Elf.

Ravi's lips compressed a moment before he let out a long whistle. Shadows came out of nowhere as the two Dark Elves, Arya and Jai, stepped out of them. The wind whipped Ravi's shoulder-length blond hair about as he searched the area where their huts were.

"I'm here!" called Yasmin.

Everyone turned toward the water and saw her climbing up the rocks from the opposite side of the cove. Yasmin might be human, but apparently, she was also something called a Druid. Rohan was still trying to figure out exactly what that was. All he knew was that the rocks and stones seemed to communicate with her.

That's when it hit him. She might be able to figure out what'd happened to Kalyani.

"You're going to be the death of me," Ravi told Yasmin as he hurried to her. His words might be harsh, but there was a smile on his face as he held out a hand to safely help guide her to land.

Yasmin dusted off her hands and shrugged her long, black hair over her shoulder as her deep blue eyes landed on Rohan. "I should've told you what I was doing, but I didn't want to get your hopes up in case there was nothing to learn."

"But you found something," Arya said, a knowing gleam in her gray eyes.

Yasmin nodded and glanced at Farah. Her hesitation brought another wave of panic to Rohan. His palms started to sweat, and his heart raced. He couldn't seem to catch his breath as he waited for the inevitable bad news. The Masters wouldn't just sit back and let Lata and the other villagers they had found go without some form of retribution.

Finally, Yasmin's voice reached him. "The stones told me she went swimming before dawn."

"See? I told you she was fine," Farah said, a smile curving her lips.

But Rohan knew by Yasmin's voice that there was more. He held his breath, anxiously waiting. Then...

"She went past your marker."

They had argued heatedly about that marker. Kalyani wanted the option to go anywhere she wanted. He, on the other hand, didn't want to worry about something happening to her. Rohan reminded her that she was in Serenia by his will alone, and if she wanted to remain, she needed to abide by his rules.

Jai's light gray gaze searched the water. The sinking sun wasn't as bright as during the day, but it still forced the Dark Elf to raise a hand to block the light. "How far out did Kalyani go?"

"Far," Yasmin replied hesitantly.

Blood drummed loudly in Rohan's ears. "Just tell me what happened."

"She saw a ship and attacked it."

Ravi jerked back. "She did *what*?"

"She wouldn't have done that without reason," Farah stated.

Yasmin wrinkled her nose. "It took some doing, but I eventually figured out what the stones were trying to impart. The boat was loaded with kidnapping victims."

"She wouldn't do that," Rohan said with a shake of his head. "She wouldn't do that on her own."

"The stones don't lie to Yaz," Ravi said.

Arya asked, "Did she free them? Or was she…?"

Taken. Rohan knew Arya didn't say it for his benefit, but it didn't matter. They all knew what she meant. The word hung in the air as he clutched Farah's hand in a bid not to spin out of control. It was a losing battle.

Through the haze, he heard Yasmin say, "She surprised the crew and managed to free several prisoners before she was seen. There was a scuffle, and she got hit with magic before they bound her arms against her with chains and threw her into the water."

Rohan's knees buckled. The water was supposed to be

Kalyani's playground—the one place she excelled and could be herself. It was never meant to be her doom.

Farah dropped down beside him and wrapped her arms around him. He kept seeing Kalyani sinking to the bottom of the ocean floor, looking up at the surface, waiting for him to find her. He hadn't been there for Lata, and he hadn't been there for Kalyani. It didn't matter what he did or what lengths he went to for the safety of those he loved. Danger still found them.

"Rohan, love, look at me. I need you to focus on me. Right here, sweetheart. Look at me."

He heard Farah's words and followed her voice until his vision cleared, and he found himself staring into her beautiful, hazel eyes. "She's gone."

"You need to hear the rest of what Yaz has to say," Farah urged.

It took a second for her words to penetrate the thick fog in his brain. He frowned, and she gave him a firm nod as her hands fell away. Rohan slid his gaze to Yasmin, who had lowered herself to her haunches. He didn't dare allow hope to get a foothold. He was barely hanging on as it was. Instead, he braced himself for the worst.

"Kalyani was rescued and taken to a Sea Elf city," Yasmin said.

"Taken to a..." He trailed off and shook his head. He couldn't have heard that right. "Kal can hold her breath longer than normal, but she'd never survive underwater for that long." He jerked his gaze first to Ravi and then to Arya and Jai, before finally landing on Farah.

Ravi shrugged. "I've never seen a Sea Elf city."

Arya and Jai shared a look before shaking their heads. "Us either," Jai answered.

"I've never heard anyone talk about them," Farah said, lifting a shoulder. "I wouldn't know where they are."

Yasmin caught his attention. "The point is, Kalyani is alive."

Rohan shifted his gaze to watch the waves roll onto shore and become foam before sliding back out into the ocean. "Why would they take her? Why not bring her to shore?"

"And are they working for the Masters?" Ravi asked.

He grunted as Yasmin hit him in his shin and shot him a dark look.

"He's right to ask," Rohan said. "She went up against a ship full of kidnappers. Who's to say the Sea Elves weren't working with them?"

Arya shot Jai a pointed look. "We know a Sea Elf."

"We don't even know her name. Once we saved her, she was gone, remember?" Jai said.

Arya grimaced. "How could I forget? Not even the Sea Elves who boarded the ship and tended to my wound spoke. I wish we had tried harder to get her name—or *any* of their names—for just such a reason as this."

Farah stood and faced the water. "Maybe we go out and see if one finds us."

"It could be a trap," Rohan said, climbing to his feet. "Admit that you're all thinking it. Why take Kalyani? They would know we'd go looking for her."

"I don't—" Yasmin began.

Jai said, "I don't care if it is a trap. Kalyani is family. We'll do whatever we need to do to bring her home."

Tears pricked Rohan's eyes. He would never ask any of them to do such a thing, but Jai's words were a reminder that he didn't have to.

"Wa—" Yasmin tried again.

Ravi rubbed his hands together eagerly. "Any excuse to bring the Masters and those working for them to their knees."

"Enough!" Yasmin yelled, leveling Ravi and then Jai with a pointed look. Her face was drawn, her color pale. She inhaled deeply and then slowly released the breath. "If you could hear them, you would know the stones have been screaming—and they're exceedingly loud."

Rohan looked around him, noting the number of rocks and stones. If each of them had a voice, it must be deafening. "What are they yelling?"

"Kalyani wasn't taken for the Masters. The Sea Elf in question —and aye, it was only one—saved her," Yasmin explained, color returning to her face.

Arya smoothed back strands of her long, white hair that got caught in the wind. "I have so many questions about that."

"We all do," Rohan said.

Yasmin gave him a quick, sad smile. "That's all the stones said. There might be more later, but that's all I know."

"She's alive," Farah said as she faced him. "Let's be happy about that."

"I won't be happy until she's home." And Rohan would do whatever was necessary to ensure that happened.

7

There was something extraordinarily relaxing about hot water. Kalyani reclined in the shallow coral basin, soaking in the water heated by current vents. She had only ever bathed standing up with water coming from a hollowed shrava stalk overhead, but after soaking in the tub, she never wanted to wash standing up again.

She had been so excited to get in the water that she hadn't looked at the bathing chamber that closely. It was directly connected to the bedroom with a door that kept things private. Another first she enjoyed. The walls were inlaid with pale shell tiles that caught and scattered the light from bioluminescent orbs embedded in the upper wall. Three small alcoves near the tub held cleansing oils, kelp soap, and sea-herb cloths.

On the opposite wall, at waist height, was a carved coral basin grown directly from the wall. Its edges were smooth, while the inside was scalloped like a giant shell. Water flowed into it continuously in a thin, elegant stream from a spout shaped like a curled fish tail. Above it was a vertical mirror in a pearlstone frame. Alcoves on either side of the mirror held sea-salt scrubs and additional cleansing oils.

Not far from the basin was a toilet, seamlessly integrated into the architecture. Its elevated seat had been grown from pearlstone, then polished smooth and shaped for ergonomic comfort. She had never seen anything so pretty in a bathing area.

The scents of salt and something light and floral only added to the room's allure. She never wanted to leave. Especially now that her belly was full. She had tried to talk while she ate, but after the first bite, her body had demanded nourishment. She had stuffed her face, all while Varum sat across from her watching. Not once had Kalyani asked what she was eating, because she hadn't cared. She was starving, and the food was delicious.

The moment she pushed her plate aside, Varum had suggested the bath. She had been happy to get out of her ruined clothes. But no matter how great it felt, she couldn't remain in the water forever. She had to get out and give Varum everything he needed so she could return home before Rohan realized she was gone.

She wrinkled her nose. How long had it been since the battle? That should've been something she'd asked Varum. Kalyani sat up. It had probably been hours, which meant Rohan had discovered that she was gone. He was likely beside himself with worry.

Grabbing the first soap she found, she lathered one of the small towels and washed. The leaf was still adhered to her side, but at least she only felt it when she touched it. Next, she washed her hair. It felt so good to scrub her scalp, but she wasn't looking forward to working out all the tangles. She really needed to start braiding her hair before she swam.

Kalyani reluctantly rose from the water and found a large

towel to dry off. She was looking around, trying to figure out how to drain the water, when it suddenly disappeared. She stood over the tub, inspecting every detail before finally giving up with a shrug.

She wrapped the towel around herself and used another to soak up water from her hair. Unable to help herself, she put a finger in the washing basin. The cool water warmed beneath her touch as if by magic.

"Well, I'm in a Sea Elf city," she murmured.

Did all elves live like this? She had never asked Farah what the Wood Elf cities were like, but now, she wanted to know if they had the same kinds of things. Kalyani eyed the toilet before walking over and touching it. To her surprise, the seat was warm.

A soft knock on the door made her jump. Before she could respond, Varum's deep voice came from the other side. "There are clothes for you on the bed when you're finished."

She stared at the barrier separating them. He confused her. Their first interaction hadn't gone great, but then he had left, only to return and begin again. That had baffled her, at first. It hadn't taken her long to catch on to what he was doing, and then she went along to see how things played out. She still wasn't sure if he was friend or foe.

When she was sure he had gone, Kalyani walked to the door and turned the pearlstone knob. It opened, allowing her to peer out. She opened it wider, and when she didn't see Varum, she stepped into the bedroom. The door to the living quarters was closed.

Her head swung to the bed that had been made up, the covers pulled tight. She raised a brow at that. Varum certainly seemed the type to like things tidy. At the foot of the bed lay the clothes he had mentioned. Her mouth fell open at the sight of the finery before her. She crossed to the bed and immediately reached over to feel the cloth.

The long, soft, turquoise tunic gleamed like moonlight underwater. The sides had high slits for ease of movement, but it was the neckline, embroidered with pearl-colored thread, that dipped slightly in both the front and back, that drew her attention. She smiled in relief at the sight of the trousers with their tiny pearl buttons to fasten at the waist. Lying next to the pants was a braided belt of silver kelp fibers.

Kalyani dropped the towel and reached for the tunic, but paused at the sight of a short top with wide-cut armholes. She thought it might be an undergarment, but the embroidery at the hem and the exquisite feel of the shimmery material made her doubt that. Then she spotted the matching briefs. Just as elegant as the top, the garment had high-cut legs.

She wasted no time trying on both. The material was even softer once on. She moved her arms about as if she were swimming and was amazed at how much better the top felt than what she was used to. Her hands smoothed over the briefs, knowing they would feel the same.

Her gaze snapped to the clothes. Kalyani slid her legs into the trousers to find that they tapered at her ankles. The tunic was next. She pulled it over her head, and the material skated down her body to stop at her knees. She wound the belt around her waist and tied it before hurrying back to the bathing chamber to get a glimpse of herself in the mirror.

She shifted from one side to the other, admiring the color against her skin. How would she ever go back to wearing her old-style clothes when she went home? She put that out of her mind as she caught sight of her hair. Kalyani winced at the tangled mess. She did a quick search, looking for a comb. When she didn't find anything, she resorted to using her fingers. It wouldn't be the first time she'd had to work through her hair in such a way.

But she had tarried for long enough. It was time to get things underway with Varum so she could go home. Kalyani took one more look at her reflection before walking out to find the Sea Elf.

Varum sat in the largest space of his home. There were two low, driftwood couches with sea-silk cushions in a deep teal, along with a matching chair. Sitting between them was a coral table carved like a spiral and inlaid with bits of shell. Beneath the furniture was a large, circular, teal rug with a silver center design that mimicked a nautilus shell.

Glowing spheres hung suspended from the ceiling by fine cords. The décor itself was minimal, consisting of wall shelves grown from the coral for storing books and other keepsakes she was dying to investigate.

"This might help," Varum said and held out something to her.

She walked over and reached for what he offered. It was a comb, but it wasn't just any comb. This one had fine, smooth, slightly curved teeth. When she turned it over, the spine was engraved with delicate wave motifs and inlaid with silver coral threads. At its center rested a small opaline gem. She ran her fingers over the smooth, luminous material of the comb. She didn't know how something so common could be so beautiful.

"What is it made of?" she asked, still stroking the item.

He studied her before leaning back on the sofa, his arms spread along the back. "Pearlstone."

"It's beautiful."

"Consider it yours."

She jerked her gaze to him, suddenly wary. "Why give me such a gift?"

"Why not?" he retorted with a shrug.

It would be rude to refuse a gift, and while she wanted the comb, she was also suspicious of Varum.

"I'm glad to see the clothes fit. I took a guess on the size," he said.

She looked down at herself before slowly lowering to the opposite couch. Try as she might, Kalyani couldn't hold his gaze for long. She didn't know if it was because the unique color was so distracting or because he unnerved her. Maybe a little of both. She decided to focus on her hair and began the tedious process of untangling it.

"They do, thank you," she replied. Then she said, "I think we should begin. Do you need to get something to take notes?"

The silence stretched for long enough that she glanced at him to find his brow quirked. "Do you have that much to impart?" he asked.

She had to be better at thinking about what she was going to say instead of just blurting things out. She had become adept at it with her brother, but for some reason, she was having a hard time now with Varum.

Kalyani shrugged. "There might be something important in what I share."

"Let me worry about that."

"Suit yourself." She winced as she hit a large tangle. In order to reach it, she had to turn her head and twist her arms. "Let me see where the best place to start would be."

"How about where you live?"

She cut him a look. "Why do you need to know that?"

"My guess is along the coast."

"I'm sure that was obvious."

He stretched out his legs and crossed his ankles. "It wasn't, actually. It was a guess based on how well you swam."

"You know Shecrish is filled with rivers and lakes. I could've learned to swim anywhere."

"Aye. Of course."

Something in his voice caught her attention. She paused her combing and looked at him, her suspicions growing. "I have a particular fondness for Trudia. The city is so clean and beautiful," she lied, waiting to see what he said.

"That it is."

She dropped her arms to her lap. "There is no city called Trudia. By the gods. You've never ventured onto the land, have you?"

He laughed softly and shrugged. "You caught me. I've not."

"How is that possible?"

"How many Sea Elves do you run into?"

Kalyani almost blurted out that she hadn't encountered *any* elves until Farah came into their lives, but she stopped herself just in time. There was no need to have him throw that back at her after her outburst. "None. Though I know some are walking around Shecrish."

"Very few. We prefer to remain in the ocean."

"Away from the goings-on that the rest of us are dealing with, right?"

His iridescent blue eyes hardened slightly. "Would you care to explain how you're able to swim to such depths as a human?"

8

There was only a slight stiffening of her body, but Varum had been looking for it. He had wanted to catch her off guard, and he had done just that. Now, all he had to do was sit back and wait for the lies to fall from her lips.

"My arms were bound, remember? I sank," Kalyani answered.

Varum nodded slowly, his lips twisting. "All right. Tell me how you were able to swim so far from shore? And don't try to tell me you were on a boat and fell overboard. There were none around, other than the sloop you attacked."

Her brown eyes never left his as she drew in a breath and calmly released it. She sat serenely. The only indication that she was bothered by his questions was the way she gripped her hands so tightly that her knuckles turned white.

This time when she spoke, her voice held a slight tremor. "I swim every day. I've built up an endurance."

"So it would seem. Do you have any idea how far out you were?"

Her lips parted, but no words came out. Instead, she gave a single shake of her head.

"The fact that you don't know raises questions. Who would swim out so far that the shore was no longer in sight? Unless, of course, you were certain you could return without issue."

"I'm a strong swimmer. You make it sound like that's some kind of crime."

He quirked a brow at her. The human was in a foreign place with no friends in sight, yet she remained defiant. He would think her brave if he knew she wasn't hiding a secret that could get her killed. If other Sea Elves learned about Kalyani's skills, they would swiftly end her life. The sea was their home, and there was no way they would share it with other elves, much less humans. If Kalyani had gills, it was likely that other humans did, as well.

"Why not just tell me the truth?" he pressed. "It'll be easier that way."

"I have no idea what you're talking about."

Varum leaned forward and braced his forearms on his knees as he stared at her. "I cannot abide liars."

"You wanted information on the Masters. I agreed to give it to you. And in return, you gave me your word that I could leave. Are you going back on that?" she challenged.

He slowly sat back. It had taken everything he had to get her inside the city unseen. Getting her out would be even harder. What if another Sea Elf came across her? It would come back that he had found her and didn't immediately bring her to the Assembly. He still wasn't quite sure *why* he hadn't done that yet.

"Ah. I see," she replied with a sneer. "Heal me, feed me, and give me some clothes. Am I some kind of pet? A plaything to entertain you until you're finished with me, and you can hand me off to someone else? Did you really want to know about the Masters? Or was that an excuse? You gave me your word. I took you for an honorable elf."

Damn her for striking him where it stung the most. He had never gone back on his word. Ever. He shouldn't have promised her anything, but what was one human's life over that of every Sea Elf?

"I didn't lie about needing information on the Masters," he said.

She rolled her eyes and crossed her arms over her chest. "Just everything else."

"I have an opportunity to keep the Masters from getting to more of my people. What would you do if given that chance?"

"I'd do whatever it took."

"Then you understand," he said hopefully.

She rose to her feet, her hands fisted at her sides as she glared daggers at him. In a heartbeat, he was on his feet, facing her with the table between them.

"If you had no intention of freeing me, the least you could've done was be honest. How can I trust anything you say now?" she demanded.

He raked his gaze over her. "And you've been just as truthful?"

"You should've kept up your charade a little longer. You would've learned all you needed to know." Rancor laced each syllable and flooded her gaze.

Varum parted his lips to reply, but a knock on his door stopped him. It was followed by a feminine voice calling his name. He didn't have time for Tanira today, but he knew from experience that she wouldn't go away until she said what she had come to say.

His gaze moved from the door to Kalyani, whose lips turned up in a smile as she sensed an opportunity.

Blue magic shot from his outstretched hands toward Kalyani, lifting her over the table and against him as he backed her into his bedroom. Her eyes widened, a spark of fear in the deep brown color. Her hands were braced against his chest, but she didn't cower. He was beginning to think the human feared nothing.

Varum pressed her against the wall next to his door and leaned his face close to hers. "I'm only going to say this once, so listen carefully. If anyone learns of your presence, they'll kill you, and me right after. Humans are not allowed here. Even other elves are refused entry."

Her brow furrowed in response.

"While I see to this guest, you'll remain in this room and stay quiet. That is, if you want to see your home again. And before you say you have no reason to do what I'm telling you, let me say that you have no desire to experience Sea Elf torture. They will draw it out for days until they wring everything they want from you."

"You're bluffing," she countered.

There was another knock, louder this time. "Varum!" Tanira called.

"Coming!" he threw over his shoulder. He dug his fingers into Kalyani's arms. "I want to stop the Masters. If you believe nothing else, believe that."

Varum released her and stepped back. She remained quiet as he straightened his clothes and closed the bedroom door behind him. He wound magic around the handle so it couldn't be opened by anyone but him, then strode to the front door and swung it open.

Tanira stood with a warm smile, the seductive curves of her

body clothed in luxurious, deep sapphire sea silk that appeared black until the light hit it. Then, it burst into ripples of turquoise and silver. The enchanted fabric was weightless and moved as if alive. Her sleeveless, fitted crop top had a high neck but was open along the sides. He knew from the countless others she had worn before that it would close at the spine with thin, silver clasps shaped like shells. To denote her status, her family crest was embroidered in a drift gold and pale pearl wave pattern across her shoulders.

Skilled coral artisans had created layers of sheer finsilk that fell from her waist to her ankles, creating an illusion that she was surrounded by moving water. The narrow, jeweled belt rested low on her waist, while a nearly transparent scarf of woven sea lace, edged with threads of pearl and shell, rested on one shoulder and lay across her chest.

She knew how to dress her body to draw the eye, using the garments to proclaim her heritage, beauty, and power, but it was her attention to detail that kept all eyes on her. The top portion of her blue-black hair was pulled into a loose braid studded with pearls. Her silvery white eyes were lined with kohl made from crushed pearl dust.

Long spirals of white coral tipped with teardrop pearls brushed her shoulders, while silver filigree caps covered the points of her ears. Polished shell armbands etched with curling motifs encircled each arm, and delicate silver sandals adorned her feet.

Tanira's beauty, wealth, and rank made her highly sought after by every male in Tarangarh. She had left a trail of lovers behind her, each one completely ensnared by her magnetic charms. Varum had known for some time that she wanted him in her bed, but he had managed to stay out of her clutches by using their family connection.

She raised a perfectly arched brow. "Aren't you going to invite me inside?"

He didn't want her in his home, but his other option was to be seen with her in public, and that simply wouldn't do. He would have to take the chance that the human would keep quiet.

"Forgive me," he said and stepped aside to allow her entry.

As she glided past, the soft chimes of her anklets floated between them, followed by the subtle, lingering fragrance that was unmistakably hers: salt lotus and sea jasmine. He shut the door and faced her as she walked to the sofa and sat in the exact spot Kalyani had previously occupied.

"Come sit," Tanira beckoned as she patted the spot beside her.

It wasn't that he was immune to her charm. She was stunning to look at, and she had a sharp mind. Perhaps if he hadn't seen her rip so many of his friends' hearts to shreds, he might have found his way to her bed. But he *had* seen. And so, he kept his distance. Much to her chagrin.

Varum took the opposite sofa. As he sank into the cushion, he asked, "What brings you here?"

"No one has seen you in a day and a half. It isn't like you not to be at the Assembly. I was worried."

He studied her pale eyes, looking for deceit. Though he didn't find any, he knew it was there. It wasn't exactly Tanira's fault. Her mother had taught her manipulation and seduction on a level that couldn't be touched. "No need to concern yourself with me."

"Varum," she replied with a serene smile. "We've known each other our entire lives. Why wouldn't I be worried about a friend?"

"You know why."

She waved away his words. "Surely, you can't be thinking of what Mum said ten years ago."

It was impossible to forget the way Tanira's mother had proclaimed, in the middle of Assembly, that he was only good enough to be the Currentspeaker and not on the Assembly itself. Which made him lacking in every other way—including as a husband for anyone of rank.

"Hard to forget something done so publicly."

"Mum often speaks out of turn. You may also remember that she apologized."

To him. In private. It wasn't done publicly as her scolding had been. Yet he had accepted the apology because he had no other choice. Tanira's family was too powerful to have them as enemies.

Tanira smiled and adjusted her shawl. "Why bring up the past? I came by to see for myself that you were well and in good spirits."

"I am that."

"Then why haven't I seen you about?"

Varum glanced at the bedroom door. "I've been working some longer hours, and I wanted a few days off."

"Oh, yes. The nasty business with the Masters. The rumors circulating that we Sea Elves are involved are getting out of hand. Have you found anything to support the gossip?"

"Not as of yet."

Tanira rose and walked around the table to sit beside him. "A Wavecaller position is opening soon. You've more than proven yourself in your current role. It's time for you to move up."

"You think because my father and grandfather were on the Assembly that I, too, wish for a seat?"

"I know you do."

It proved how little she knew of him. "There is power in the

Assembly, but there are also limits. I can do more as a Currentspeaker."

She said nothing for a long moment as she stared at him. Then she grinned. "Right. You can't go off investigating as easily as a Wavecaller. I know if there is anything to discover, you'll find it. That will put you in the spotlight. No more will you be able to hide all that you do, and then you won't be able to shy away from moving up politically."

"I guess we'll have to wait and see."

"I can help you."

Varum looked down to find her hand covering his. "You do help."

"I mean, in your investigation. I believe you, even if the Assembly doesn't."

"If I need something, I'll let you know." There was no way he would bring her into this. Not just because he didn't want to worry about her safety, but because he didn't trust her.

She smiled and sighed. "I guess I'll have to accept that. For the moment."

"Was there anything else?" he asked as he stood.

"My worry has been appeased. I shall leave you to your solitude."

Varum walked her to the door and held it open. She paused at the threshold and swung her silvery white eyes to him. Unease rippled through him at her determined look.

She picked something from his tunic before smoothing her hand along his chest. "My door is always open for you. Anytime."

He dipped his head in response. Her hand lingered for another moment before it fell away, and she walked out. Varum closed and locked the door before breathing a sigh of relief. Then he spun around to look at his bedroom. Thankfully, the woman hadn't made a sound. It was what he had demanded, but he hadn't actually expected her to do it.

His strides quickly ate up the ground. He recalled the magic he'd set to lock his bedroom and threw open the door. There was a startled squeak followed by a thud. He hurriedly stepped inside to find Kalyani on her backside on the floor.

"You couldn't have just told me to come out?" she asked sharply. "Did you have to open it with such force?"

He snorted as he crossed his arms over his chest. "I take it you were listening."

"Of course, I was bloody listening," she bit out angrily as she climbed to her feet. "You'd do the same in my place. And, by the way, I'm not hurt."

"I know."

That got him an icy look. "How could you possibly know that?"

"You had anger shooting from your eyes, not pain."

She glanced away and dusted herself off. "Oh."

"How much did you hear?"

"Enough to know that whoever that woman was, she wants you."

Varum laughed. "*That's* what you got out of the conversation?"

"Are all males as dumb and blind as you?"

"Excuse me?" She was forever surprising him.

Kalyani shook her head, her look saying he was slow. "How pretty is she?"

"Very. What does that matter?"

"Wow. So, a very beautiful woman comes to see if you're all

right, offers her help, and then tells you that her door is always open to you... That's an invitation if I've ever heard one."

Varum didn't like his romantic life being discussed. "And you have a lot of such experience?"

"It's okay if your interest is in males, but it would be good to tell her, so she doesn't waste time with you."

He was so shocked by her statement that he could only stare at her for a full minute. Even when he found his voice, his words sounded strangled to his ears. "My interests, as you put it, lie strictly with females."

The corner of her mouth lifted in quiet triumph, betraying her amusement. He gaped at her, utterly taken aback by the barb he hadn't seen coming.

"Rather proud of yourself for that one, aren't you?" he asked.

If she heard the irritation in his words, she never let on. "I have no idea what you mean."

"Two can play that game," he challenged.

In an instant, the grin vanished. "Game? This isn't a game. This is my bloody life!"

"It's mine, too. It's everyone in this city."

"And what about my village? My family? My friends? Do none of them matter? I suppose not since we aren't in your precious city!"

Her chest was heaving in outrage, her eyes ablaze with indignation. The annoyance he'd felt at being the butt of her jest evaporated. Whether he liked it or not, the human was right. Few would dare to speak to him in such a way. Yet this mere slip of a female stood with her shoulders back, giving as good as she got. She was fervor and fury, blazing brighter than the sun. A stark contrast to the emotional restraint, discipline, and propriety that were valued within Sea Elf culture.

She was fire.

He was ice.

A volatile combination in every regard. He thought she held clues to learning about the Masters and their plan, but she might very well be his end. It would've been better had he left her on the ocean floor to bleed out or become a meal. He'd been out of his mind to think he could bring her to Tarangarh.

But she was here. He had two choices. Kill her and dispose of her body. Or...continue with his plan.

He'd already broken their highest law by bringing her to the city. The only way to save himself now was to pry every bit of knowledge from her. It had worked earlier when he left the room and returned to start over. It wouldn't hurt to try that again.

9

Kalyani watched as the elf spun around and left, only to return moments later. As if he could reset their conversation again. He stopped before her, his eyes locking with hers. Earlier, when he had pressed his face nearly against hers, threatening her to remain quiet, she had barely heard him after getting lost in his eyes.

Like his hair that shifted from black to blue, and his skin from blue to green, his eyes were just as mysterious and mesmerizing. There were multiple layers of blue and silver, alive and shifting as if lit from within. Iridescent and too vast to behold. She had seen their color from afar, but once she witnessed the unusual hues up close, she found herself drawn to his eyes again and again.

She tried to hold on to her anger, but it flowed out of her as if someone had turned on a spigot. He was too close. She needed to back away, but her feet wouldn't obey her.

"It seems we need to begin again," he replied in a soft voice.

The spark of ire she had glimpsed was banked once more.

Kalyani thought back to the exchange she'd heard between the woman and Varum. It had been restrained, composed, as they danced around their intent instead of just saying what they really wanted.

"Stop," she told him, holding up a hand. "What I need from you right now is the truth. No matter how you might think it will upset me, I need to have it."

"And what truth would you like?" He clasped his hands behind his back and patiently waited.

"Will you keep to your word and release me?"

He lowered his gaze to the floor for several moments before looking at her again. "If I can, I will."

"That isn't an answer."

"It's the truth you seek. And all I can give you at the moment."

"Explain," she demanded.

He huffed and walked past her to the window. With a wave of his hand, the lattice slid back, giving her a view of the ocean. "If you're discovered here, they will kill you exactly as I described. And then do the same to me and anyone else who came into contact with you. There won't be a chance for any of us to justify our actions, because no one will listen. It is our oldest and highest law. I broke it. Every moment you're here makes it more dangerous for us both."

"Then why bring me? I know it wasn't because you wanted to heal me. You care little about me."

He turned his head to look at her over his shoulder before facing her. "You asked for the truth, so I'll give it. You're right. I don't care much for humans. I healed your injuries because I need to discover what you know about the Masters."

"Asking about my village and my swimming has nothing to do with the Masters."

"Doesn't it?"

Kalyani could feel her annoyance growing. Perhaps she should take a page out of his book and attempt to restrain herself. "It doesn't."

"If you say so."

She walked to the window. He turned with her, his body tense. She had endeavored to dive out the window earlier. It would likely come to that, but not right then. She swept her gaze around, looking for the city he kept speaking of.

"Look down," he urged.

She lowered her gaze and saw lights flickering below them. Some pulsed, others blinked slowly, and more moved in a wave pattern. She spotted other formations that looked like the tops of buildings. The more she looked, the more she saw. Walkways, columns, and stairs. If she squinted, she even glimpsed Sea Elves in the water.

"I see elves swimming, and I see some walking on what look like paths."

Varum touched the window, and it bent against his finger as it had done with hers earlier. "Long before the other elven races created their Conclave on land, the Sea Elves founded Tarangarh in the vast, coral-lined walls of Sagaris Trench. We didn't build the city. We grew it."

"Grew?" she repeated.

He glanced at her, their eyes meeting briefly. "We coaxed the coral with magic to create the city. It is a living, breathing organism. The trench plunges farther than any light can reach. No ships sail above it either. The surface waters seem calm, but storms can gather without warning."

"That's why the Sea Elves were helping the boat," she said.

He sighed, nodding. "For us, this area is sacred. Our ancestors chose the heart of the trench for the city, suspended between the cold darkness of the abyss and the filtered light from above. You could jump out the window right now, but you'd be crushed by the pressure. If you somehow managed to survive that, you'd have to know how to navigate the Hidden Currents. Get caught up in one of them, and you'd be lost forever."

She looked to the side again as he spoke, seeing the walls of the trench expanding into the blue.

"Tarangarh is a vow to live in harmony. Canals weave through the city, connecting air-filled districts to submerged ones. These windows are actually living membranes of magic and coral essence that we call *nehras*. They flex like water itself while resisting the pressure of the ocean beyond." He pointed to the right. "Look there. You'll see one of the larger *nehras* form the outer walls and domes of the Assembly Hall."

Kalyani craned her head and saw a towering dome of living coral and embedded pearls. "What happens there?"

"That's where the High Tide Assembly meets. If you look down and to the left, you'll see the dome of the Coral Galleries. You might even spot the dome for the Hall of Tides."

She straightened and turned her head to him. "Why tell me all of this?"

"Why not?" he asked with a shrug.

"I'm forbidden to be here."

"Aye. But not forbidden in the knowing of it." He swung his head to her.

Kalyani looked at the *nehras*. Maybe she wouldn't be jumping out anytime soon. "I have people searching for me."

"Rohan, you mean."

She frowned and shot him a look. When had she mentioned her brother? "Aye."

"Tell me what I want to know, and I'll figure out a way to get you home."

Kalyani wanted to believe him. It would be easy to do, but she wasn't sure she could. Friend or foe. Maybe Varum was neither. Perhaps he was just someone trying to save his people. She had been in his shoes not that long ago. In fact, she was still there. Not that Rohan would let her do much, but she was trying. She was just as capable as everyone else.

"I should've told him where I was. I promised I'd tell him before I got into the water." She imagined him pacing the shore, bellowing her name. He'd run himself ragged after Lata went missing. He was just getting back to his old self thanks to Farah, and then Kalyani had to go and do this.

"Why keep such things from your mate?"

She jerked her head to Varum. "Mate? Rohan is my brother."

"I see."

"I kept it from him because he worries too much. Also, because he never really understood." She could've told him. All of it. Including the secrets she had never shared. She should've confessed everything long ago. She sucked in a breath and faced Varum. "We should get comfortable. There's a lot to catch you up on."

He stepped to the side and swung his arm out for her to go first. Kalyani walked past him into the living area. She took the sofa, but the instant she sat, she smelled perfume. She waved her hand around and wrinkled her nose.

"Tanira always did wear too much," Varum said.

She raked her hair out of her face and realized she hadn't finished combing it. Nor did she remember what she had done with the comb.

"It's in the bedroom."

Her gaze clashed with his again before she jumped up to find the comb on the floor and hurried back. She returned to the chore of untangling her hair. "I'm taking a chance that you aren't working with the Masters."

"I'm not," Varum stated.

"That's exactly what you'd say if you were."

He shrugged one shoulder. "It is. You'll have to take a chance. Just as I'm taking a chance by believing whatever you tell me."

"I have no reason to lie."

Both his brows rose as he shrugged.

She told him about her younger sister being kidnapped and how it had changed things for her village. When she got to the part about Shaldorn, she paused.

Kalyani tugged out a knot and took a breath. "The Masters know the names of my friends anyway, so I don't suppose it matters. It all began with Ravi and Yasmin."

"Who are they?"

"Ravi is a Sun Elf who works for the Defense Intelligence Agency. Yasmin is human and was duped as a child into going to Shaldorn, where they enslaved her."

Varum sat up at the mention of the stronghold. "*The* Shaldorn?"

"The very one. She escaped."

"I heard that was impossible."

Kalyani grinned. "I know. But when you're desperate, I suppose you'll take any chance you get."

"Aye," he murmured before sitting back. "Go on."

"Ravi was sent on a mission to the stronghold, and they blackmailed Yasmin into taking him there."

Varum made a shocked sound verging on incredulity.

"I don't know what they had on her, but they got Yaz to do it. They completed the mission, and in the process, shut Shaldorn down."

"So, that was who did it."

She nodded. She knew more of the specifics, but she had no intention of telling him everything. "They weren't alone, though. A Mountain Elf, Manu, helped Yasmin when she first escaped. Arya, an undercover Dark Elf working for the Counter Corruption Division, joined them."

"Even we heard about the shuttering of Shaldorn. I didn't know of its existence until then. The stories that came out of there were..."

"Horrific." Kalyani nodded. "Yasmin nearly died." She paused, recalling Arya's retelling of what Yaz had looked like when they found her.

Varum's voice was soft when he asked, "Were you there when they found her?"

"It was described to me. And the distress on Arya's face when she talked about it told me how dire it was. It took days and several Healers to save her."

"It must have been very grave, indeed, for it to take so much."

Kalyani ran the comb through the hair on her left side several times before moving to the right. "While Yaz and Ravi tried to live a normal life, Arya was abducted."

"By the Masters?"

"Sort of," she said with a twist of her mouth. "Years before, Jai —a Dark Elf in love with Arya—was taken on the night they were supposed to meet and run away together. The Masters forced him to work for them as a slave ship captain. He believed he had been betrayed, and that his capture was Arya's doing, so he plotted to bring her in and claim the reward the Masters had put out on her."

Varum watched her closely, his brow furrowed. "Did he?"

"He discovered someone else had turned him over to the Masters and set Arya free."

"Wait. You said captain? Was he sailing these waters?"

She shook her head. "It was the Lotus River in the Dark Elf territory. That's how the Masters are transporting the kidnapped to their compounds. Once at places like Mortham, the people who were taken are broken. Arya and Jai went to Mortham, looking for the elf responsible for Jai's imprisonment. They found her and killed her. When they were making their escape, they found a female Sea Elf."

10

Varum was sure there was more to the stories Kalyani told, but he wouldn't press her yet. He needed to show her that he could be trusted. She had asked for honesty earlier, and he had given it. As he spoke the truth, he hadn't known how she would react. To his surprise, she'd faced it head-on. Things would be easier now that he knew how to approach her.

"What happened to the ship Jai commandeered?" Varum asked.

Kalyani set aside the comb. "I'm not sure. I never asked about it, but if I know Jai, he still has it somewhere."

That might come in handy later. Varum set that aside for the moment. "How did the Masters learn the names of those involved in Shaldorn and Mortham?"

"No one seems to know."

"They've not looked into it?"

"Dain said—"

"Dain?" he interrupted. That was a new name, and the way she smiled when she said it caught his attention.

Kalyani's brow furrowed as she tilted her head to the side. "Have I not mentioned him yet?"

"You've not. Who is he?"

"Dain is...well, Dain." She laughed softly. "He's unlike anyone I've met before."

Varum tapped a finger on his thigh. "What makes him different?"

She looked around as if struggling to find words. The longer she took, the more intrigued he became. Who was this Dain who could make the feisty Kalyani lose her words? His gaze moved to the dark strands of her hair curling around her face as they dried.

"He's dangerous."

Her words snapped him out of his thoughts. "Plenty of people are dangerous."

"Not like Dain. He exudes a different kind of danger."

"And your brother allows you to be around such a male?"

She grinned. "Dain is a friend. He was there at Shaldorn. And at Mortham—twice."

So, this Dain, who made her smile so secretively, was an elf. But which race? "Twice how?"

Kalyani's expression turned serious. "I told you how my sister and others were taken from my village. What I didn't tell you was that Rohan was the leader. Losing our people was killing him, but Lata's disappearance broke him. He was desperate, and in that desperation, he came up with a wild plan."

She paused, and Varum caught himself before he pressed her for more. Her gaze was on the floor, and she gripped the edge of her tunic, absently fiddling with the hem. He knew without asking that she was reliving painful memories. He didn't like that he had pushed her there, but he would do it again if it meant saving others.

Suddenly, she drew in a breath. "He and some others were taken as prisoners bound for Mortham. They were working with insurgents within the compound to set off a bomb to cause chaos. That would allow Rohan to capture one of the guards and force them to bring him to Lata."

"I take it things didn't go according to plan if your brother is with you."

"Things went as well as they could. The bomb exploded, and Rohan found his prisoner in a Wood Elf named Farah."

Varum vaguely remembered Kalyani mentioning that name earlier. He waited, impatient to hear the rest.

"The bomb worked as planned, but Farah was badly injured. He brought her to the village to heal her, unaware that she was an undercover DIA agent, who was at Mortham looking for *her* missing sister."

"Incredible," he murmured.

Kalyani's dark eyes lifted to his. "It was. They worked together and got back inside Mortham. Turned out Farah's sister had aligned with the Masters. She captured Rohan and tortured him to lure Farah there. The sisters battled, and Farah was the one who walked out. Rohan and Farah got Lata and a large number of our people out that night with Dain, Jai, and Arya's help. But that put Farah's and Rohan's names on the Masters' list."

"Why speak so highly of Dain if all he does is help at the end?"

"Dain does much more than that. He's also part of the CCD."

So, he was a Dark Elf. It was unusual to find three aligning with other elves and humans. Unexpected. At least from what he knew of the Dark.

"He has connections," Kalyani continued. "He's the one who brought the intel about Stonemore to the DIA. In some ways, he's the leader in all of this."

"Forgive me, but it is odd to hear that a Dark is close to others outside of his race."

She gave him a flat look. "You mean humans. Just say it."

"I mean exactly what I said. The Dark are similar to us in that they prefer their own kind. And they don't function well in sunlight."

"Yet Dain, Arya, and Jai are with us."

While she might believe it, Varum wasn't convinced. "Could they be undercover for the Masters?"

"Nay," she answered firmly and quickly.

"You sound very sure of that."

She tucked one leg under the other. "I am. Everyone has put their lives on the line against the Masters time and again. They're looking for me."

Perhaps she hoped that Dain would find her. Varum knew she would be disappointed. Dark Elves kept away from the water just as Sea Elves kept out of the underground. "All you've told me so far is that you know people who have stood against the Masters."

"There is one more story. Manu and Inej's. One of the Masters' favorites, a Moon Elf named Gita, once ran Shaldorn. She sent Inej to the Dangerous Peaks to kill Manu. None of the Masters' mercenaries survived in the peaks, so they sent a human, knowing Manu would help."

"And did he?" Varum pressed.

Kalyani nodded.

"Did this human...what was her name? Inej? Did she succeed?"

Kalyani chuckled and gently shook her head. "They ended up defeating more mercenaries together. They remain in the Dangerous Peaks, where Manu continues to thwart the Masters. It also gives us an ally in the mountains, should we need it again."

"Are there any more stories?"

"Nay. That's it."

He stretched his arms along the back of the sofa. "A Sun Elf, three Dark Elves, a Wood Elf, and now a Mountain Elf. I'm impressed that such a grouping would come together."

"You left out the humans. Yasmin, Rohan, and Inej."

"What about you?"

Kalyani flicked her hair over her shoulder. "What about me? I'm fighting with them. Or I try. Rohan is...protective."

"As he should be. He already lost one sister. The gods smiled upon him and allowed her to return. Knowing that, you still ignored his wishes to tell him when you went into the water."

"I don't need you to remind me of that."

He snorted. "Seems someone should. I cannot imagine what he's going through right now."

"I can," she murmured as she looked away, regret filling her eyes.

"It's amazing that none of you has been found by the Masters yet. But it's only a matter of time."

Her head snapped back to him. "We have allies."

"Who?"

"As courageous as Ravi, Yaz, Arya, Jai, Rohan, Farah, Manu, and Inej are, they didn't do anything alone. They always had help.

If it wasn't Dain directly, he sent someone to them. Others in the DIA are also involved."

Varum quirked a brow at the way she continued to set Dain on a pedestal. "The larger your group gets, the easier it'll be for the Masters to infiltrate it."

"We know that. Only certain individuals know where we live. The point of those stories was to tell you that the Masters aren't impossible to get to. The group got into Mortham twice. And they got out twice."

"I doubt that would happen again."

She shrugged. "So what? They shut down Shaldorn."

"And another is being built. From the rumors I've heard, it's somewhere in the ocean."

Her lips twisted as she nodded. "We heard another was being built, but we didn't know where. Do you have its location?"

"I'm attempting to gather that information."

"Can they even do something like that without the Sea Elves' permission?"

He looked at the ceiling. "Did the Masters get permission from the Mountain Elves to build Shaldorn?"

"Point taken," she agreed softly.

Varum lowered his gaze to her. "Why disregard your brother's wishes about the water?"

"It isn't just Rohan. I did the same to my father. The look of disappointment on their faces never goes away. Rohan loosened the restrictions, thinking I would adhere to them, but I can't."

"Why?" Varum asked, his voice a whisper.

She looked away and returned to fiddling with the hem of her tunic. "Rohan used to tell me that I headed to the water the minute I could walk. A wave struck and pulled me out into the bay before Dad could reach me. He was frantic, terrified that I would drown. Rohan said that when Dad managed to bring me to the surface, I was smiling and none the worse for wear." Her shoulders lifted as she drew in a deep breath. "I can no more stay out of the water than I can still my own beating heart."

"Are there others like you in your village?"

Her sad smile was fleeting. "I know of no others like me."

Varum should probably stop questioning her, but he wanted to see if she would share more. He kept his voice soft, his words gentle as he asked, "How deep do you swim?"

"I don't know. Deeper than Rohan knows about. I go where I'm pulled." Her gaze slid back to him. "Sometimes, I'm drawn to animals. Other times, it's the currents themselves."

Varum's brows snapped together as he stared at her. "The currents? You hear them?" he asked incredulously. That couldn't be possible. Only the Sea Elves could discern such a thing.

"I don't know what I hear, or even if I hear anything. It's more what I *feel*."

"You...*feel* it?" Feeling the currents was even more special. That meant the ocean was communicating directly with Kalyani. He thought again of the gills he had seen and felt behind her ears—the same gills that seemed to have vanished.

Who was this human? What made her so unique from others of her kind?

"You're staring," she said and looked away nervously.

Varum dropped his arms and scooted to the edge of the cushion. "Do you have the names of anyone involved with the Masters besides the Moon Elf, Gita?"

"One."

"What is their name?"

"One."

He flattened his lips. "I heard you. I need a name."

"And I'm telling you the name that he goes by. It's One."

"His name is One?"

Kalyani's distaste for the individual was obvious. "He worked at Shaldorn under Gita. One, Two, and Three. They were known as the Trinity to Yasmin and the other enslaved. They carried out Gita's orders and dished out their own kind of cruelty and torment. Ravi and Dain killed Two and Three at Shaldorn, but One actually helped Ravi."

"*Helped*, you say?"

"Odd, I know. I doubted it, too, but he did. He was also in Mortham and healed Arya when she was injured."

"He's a Star Elf?"

She grimaced. "I must have left that out. Aye, he's a Star Elf."

"If he aided Ravi and then Arya, he must be trying to get in with your group to work undercover for the Masters."

"He's not asked for anything."

Varum made a noise at the back of his throat. "He will. It's simply a matter of time. You can't trust him."

"I never would."

"One isn't a name I can track. He's likely using that so no one can find him. He has a name, though."

Kalyani grinned. "Dain said the same thing. He's been searching for him since Shaldorn. They know what he looks like, but so far, they have come up empty."

"It looks like I'll have to focus my attention on Gita."

"How?" Kalyani asked. "It isn't like she's visiting Tarangarh."

Varum hated to admit that she had a point. He might not get to the surface, but he knew someone who did.

11

Rannora

All he needed was one look. Just one. Dain pressed against the side of the building, surrounded by the shadows of the night, as he sought the one he couldn't stop thinking about.

He scanned the occupants of The Crossing, his gaze pausing each time he spotted dark hair. But none held the depth of color Reva's possessed. He had already been by her flat. She only ever went to the pub and home. Unless... Had she gone to dinner with that bastard? They were coworkers. That should be frowned upon. What was Sidiq doing, allowing them to be together in such a way?

His fingers curled into fists as he thought about Darshan and Reva dining together. Dain imagined punching the human in the face. Nay. That wouldn't be enough. A hit to the ribs might do. Then again, if he really wanted to cause damage, he could just castrate the pile of dung.

The fantasies of how much he could hurt Darshan fizzled when he saw the object of his hatred walking up to the bar for another order. If the man was at work, then where was Reva? Fear seized Dain's heart. He took a step forward, ready to barge into the pub and...

The laugh, soft and tinkling, reached him. He forgot all about the carnage he had been about to exact as his panic eased at the sound of Reva's laugh. Then he saw her beside a table of women, taking their orders. Her hair was gathered at the base of her neck by a red ribbon, while the wealth of her brunette tresses fell down the middle of her back. Her red tunic was new, as were the black trousers. He followed her with his gaze as she walked to the bar. Her smile was easy, her stride relaxed—if a bit hurried.

He watched as she and Sidiq exchanged words as the elf filled glasses with ale. How Dain envied him. Dain had once been able to talk to Reva any time he wanted, but he had given up that right. Nay, that wasn't true. He had walked away from her to keep her safe. Sidiq had been right to question him about it.

Dain stilled, suddenly aware of someone directly behind him. He palmed a dagger with one hand while gathering magic in the other. Then he spun and came face-to-face with Salil. The Wood Elf had the gall to smile, his hazel eyes filled with amusement.

"I knew I'd find you here," Salil said.

Dain pressed the tip of his dagger into Salil's side. "Sneak up on me like that again, and I'll slit you open."

Salil's gaze slid past him to The Crossing's doorway before he looked at Dain again. Dain waited for a sarcastic comment. They might be fighting on the same side, but that didn't mean he would listen to any comments about Reva.

In the next breath, the smile vanished from Salil's face. "Durga has been looking for you."

"I don't have any more information than I did two days ago," Dain said as he sheathed his blade and recalled his magic.

"This isn't about that. We have a problem."

"With?" Dain demanded.

Salil held his gaze. "Let's get to Durga's so she can fill you in."

Dain stepped back and gathered his shadows. As he was leaving, he heard Salil say, "I knew you'd leave me, you bastard."

It was Dain's turn to smile. Salil deserved that for sneaking up on him. No one snuck up on him. At least, not usually. He forgot everything else when it came to Reva. Just one more reason he had been right to sever her working relationship with him.

Dain checked Durga's office at the DIA headquarters. When he found that empty, he went to her house. Dain parted his shadows inside Durga's home office to find her and Arya bent over a table, looking at a map.

Arya's head snapped up first. "Where have you been?"

Durga lifted hazel eyes and slowly straightened. Her brown hair was in its usual bun, but she had removed her earrings, ear caps, bracelets, and rings and set them off to the side. Stress caused her mouth to form a hard line.

"I got here as soon as I could," Dain said as he looked between the two women. "What's going on?"

It was Arya who answered. "Kalyani is gone."

"What?" Dain must not have heard that right. "Are you sure?"

Durga nodded, the light catching on her coppery skin. "We're sure."

Dain strode to the table and saw a map of Shecrish and the surrounding terrain, including the Amrata Ocean. He found the location of Serenia along the coast and then peered at the vast water beyond.

"As you can imagine, Rohan isn't handling this well," Durga said.

Dain raised his gaze to the Wood Elf. No matter how many times he had asked, Durga wouldn't tell him her exact title in the DIA. Whatever position she held, it was one of extreme importance, because she always got what she needed—that and the fact that there was always one elf with her, and about a dozen more nobody ever saw.

He turned to his protégé. "I need details."

"There aren't many," Arya said. "We don't know what time Kalyani went into the water. It was hours before any of us realized she was gone."

Dain looked at the map again. "Are we sure she went into the water?"

"She doesn't go anywhere else," Arya stated. "And we're sure. Yaz told us."

He nodded, understanding exactly what she wouldn't put into words in case anyone was listening.

"No one found us," Arya said, knowing his next question.

Dain quirked a brow as he looked between the females. "Tell me everything."

It didn't take long for Arya to spill everything. He ran a hand down his face as he sighed.

"You know as well as I do that if the Sea Elves took Kalyani, she's dead," Durga said.

He did know that. Everyone called the Dark bastards, but the Sea Elves were the most brutal of all the races.

Arya shook her head. "Yaz said she wasn't in danger."

"Things could've changed," Durga argued.

Dain thought about the Sea Elf they had released from Mortham. "I think they'll take anyone. I'll head to Serenia now."

"Good. Maybe you can stop Rohan from trying to swim out to find her," Arya said before vanishing into the shadows.

Durga grabbed his arm before he could follow.

He met her gaze. "What is it?"

"Something feels off. Be careful," Durga said before she released him.

Dain dipped his head. "I always am."

12

Hours. That's how long Kalyani had repeated the stories. Varum asked her the same thing twenty different ways to see if he could trip her up—and she'd nearly stumbled a few times. But he hadn't relented. Not even when they shared another meal. She could hardly keep her eyes open. She had no concept of time since she couldn't see the sky, but it was getting harder to ensure that she didn't accidentally say more than she already had. Since she had kept the stories to the basics, it made it easier.

Kalyani didn't care if she'd forgotten to mention something she might have said in the numerous times she had repeated them to the tyrant across from her. Nay, her worry was letting something slip. Because if she did, Varum would become even more relentless in his interrogation. If only she could close her eyes....

She heard him demand that she repeat Yaz and Ravi's story, but it sounded as if the words were coming down a long tunnel. Kalyani tried to shake herself awake. She propped her elbow on the arm of the sofa and rested her head in her hand as she relayed it once more. Her eyelids grew heavier. She let them close for just a heartbeat. That was all she needed. Just a little rest.

"Jai and Arya's now, please."

It was too bad that he wasn't rude about it. If he were, she'd be tempted to tell him to shove it. Instead, his voice was gentle, almost compassionate. It was a ruse, of course. All she needed to do to dispel that image was open her eyes and find his iridescent blue orbs narrowed on her as he listened. It was one of the reasons she refused to look at him anymore.

Her mind started to wander as she repeated yet another story. Kalyani caught herself just before she mentioned Reva. She hadn't revealed her for many reasons, but the most important was how magic didn't work on her. Kalyani wasn't even supposed to know that. She had overheard it one night when Dain was talking with Arya and Jai. Kalyani had vowed to all three that she would never repeat what she had heard, and she intended to keep that promise.

Reva's abduction when Arya was taken had been a mistake. Dain had righted it, though. And that's where Reva's story was supposed to end. There was no need to drag her into the thick of things now that she was safe.

"And no one has seen the Masters?"

Kalyani chuckled at the question. "Of course not." She'd feel a lot better if she could just lie down. "Arya talked to them."

The minute the words were out, Kalyani jerked upright with a start, now completely awake. She swung her head to Varum to find a knowing grin curving his lips.

"I knew you'd eventually let something slip," he said.

"That was rather devious."

He slowly sat forward, his gaze locked on her. "I warned you that I would do whatever it took to get the information. Why didn't you tell me sooner?"

"I guess it slipped my mind."

A grunt followed her words as he reclined once more. "Tell me about the interaction."

"There isn't much to tell."

"Let me be the judge of that."

Kalyani wanted to kick herself for letting her attention slip, her words following soon after. It was a good thing she hadn't said more. In all honesty, she had forgotten about Arya and the Masters. "Arya was caught while in Mortham. They hung her in a dark room with her ankles and wrists bound. The Masters interrogated her there. She never saw their faces. She only heard their voices. They were going to cast her in with the others who had been kidnapped, but she offered to sway her parents into joining the Masters."

"The only reason for her to do that was if her family has influence."

"Oh, they did," Kalyani said with a nod. "Her family was very well respected, before they were killed."

Varum nodded for her to continue.

"Just as Arya had hoped, the Masters fell for her lie. They released her, but she was injured in the interrogation. As she walked the halls trying to find Ini and Dain—"

"You said nothing about Dain being with them before."

Kalyani forced a smile, barely holding back the tirade she wanted to deliver. But she managed to hold it in. Varum was her way home. She had to play by his rules if she wanted to see her family and friends again. "I told you he was in Mortham twice."

"You're making me wonder how many other things you left out."

"Do you want the rest of this story or not?" she bit out.

He motioned for her to proceed.

"It was during her wandering that Arya ran into One. She didn't know who he was, and she was so weak that she had no way of refusing his help to heal her."

"What did he ask for in return?"

Kalyani shook her head. "Nothing."

"I find that odd."

"We all did. I think he'll want some kind of repayment in the future."

Varum grunted again. "Without a doubt."

"That was it. One healed her and left."

"How does Arya know it was him?"

Kalyani shifted on the sofa, trying to get comfortable as she smothered a yawn. "She described him. Both Yasmin and Ravi said it sounded like One."

"Interesting. Both Yasmin and Arya had an encounter with One."

"Inej did, too."

Varum's laugh was cold, cutting. "You don't say."

Kalyani got to her feet in one motion. "You have what you need. I want to return home now."

"You keep leaving out things. I'm going to need you to stay longer so I can make sure I have it all."

Fury ripped through her, making her see red. "You have no right to keep me here against my will."

"I'm trying to save my people."

"I don't think they want to be saved if they're so keen on joining the Masters."

He calmly rose to his feet, unaware or unconcerned that she was incensed. "What was the exchange between Inej and One?"

"She thinks it was him, and based on the description she gave Arya, it was."

"You still haven't told me what he said to her."

Kalyani threw up her hands and growled. "It didn't make any sense. He was in an alley she was walking down, and he commented on her going on a long journey and the fact that she packed light. Then he told her he wasn't a threat to her. He made that distinction."

"How, exactly?" Varum questioned.

Kalyani closed her eyes and thought back to the conversation Arya had relayed. "His exact words, if I'm remembering right, were, *'I'm no threat.'* He then added *'to you,'* almost like an afterthought."

Her eyes opened to find Varum's brow wrinkled in a deep frown. "Was that all between them?"

"Nay," Kalyani said. "She asked for a name, and he said he had many. She said, 'Give me one.' That's when he laughed and said something along the lines of names not being as important as we think. He then wished her luck."

"Your friends are sure that was One?"

She shrugged. "As sure as they can be."

"Anything else you left out?"

"Probably. These stories were relayed to me. I wasn't there for any of them, and I doubt I heard everything. You can grill me some more, but I'm going to sleep now."

Amusement lit his face as he watched her fluff a pillow. "Do you even know what time it is?"

"Nay!" she bellowed and swung around to him. "I can't see the sky. Do you know how confounding that is?"

"I do not."

She rolled her eyes as she sank onto the cushion. "Of course not."

"You plan to sleep out here?"

"I do unless there's another bed, but since you put me in yours, I'm guessing there isn't." There was a long stretch of silence as she lay down and turned her back to him.

She jerked when something suddenly touched her and lifted her head to find a soft, silver and navy blanket covering her. Her gaze lifted to find Varum standing over her, his expression unreadable.

"Don't bother trying to get out through the door. It's locked with magic," he warned.

She adjusted her head on the pillow and closed her eyes. "As if I'd run around for other Sea Elves to find me."

"The lattice is also shut over the *nehras* again."

"I get it," she snapped. "I'm a prisoner. You made that abundantly clear earlier."

Just when she thought he had walked away and she could sleep, his deep voice said, "I'll have to go out tomorrow."

"Fine." Why couldn't he leave her be? Then it struck her that it would mean more hours of being kept in the city while Rohan searched for her. Kalyani opened her eyes and rolled her head to look at Varum.

She thought about pushing him again to release her, but he was a stubborn bastard. There was no way he would relent until he thought he had all he needed. The fact that she had spilled a couple of extra things meant that they would be back at it again tomorrow. Why had she told him about Inej and One?

"Does your family know?" Varum asked.

She frowned at him and flopped onto her back. "Do they know what?"

"What you can do."

Kalyani stared up at him, a fissure of dread swirling in her gut. "As I've stated, they're aware of my love for swimming."

"They don't know the rest, though, do they?"

"The rest of what?" she asked evasively.

Varum lowered his gaze to the floor for a heartbeat. "I'm beginning to wonder if even *you* know."

"It might be helpful if I knew what you were talking about."

"Get some rest," he replied as he turned on his heel and strode to his room.

She rose up on her elbows to watch the door to his room shut behind him. She glared at it for a long time while trying to ascertain what he had been trying to say. Riddles exasperated her. The wordplay and hidden meanings made her want to pull her hair out. Varum hadn't actually delivered her a riddle, but his vague questions might as well have been one.

Kalyani dropped onto her back and glared at the ceiling. The lights had dimmed, going almost completely dark, and she hadn't even noticed. She was surrounded by magic, deep in the heart of the ocean, and yet it was the infuriating, tenacious Sea Elf who dominated most of her attention.

Despite spending hours with him, she still wasn't certain if he was friend or foe. If she did anything to harm his people or his city, he would likely cut her down without hesitation. And she would do the same to him if their roles were reversed.

But who was he? She had a few more facts about the city and its workings, but not enough to know where he fit in. It had to be a position of note, or the female wouldn't have paid him a visit.

Her gaze returned to his door. As captors went, he had been kind. Not only had he seen to her injuries, but he'd also fed her and given her clothes. She wasn't in some tiny room being starved. But she was still prevented from leaving. A prison was a prison, no matter how pretty it was.

"I'm sorry, Rohan," she whispered into the night. "I should've told you I was going out. I never should've gone after the ship by myself."

She moved an arm beneath her head and sent up a prayer to the gods that Rohan wouldn't do anything rash.

13

Varum stared down at the human sprawled on his sofa, her arms above her head, one leg out of the blanket, and those dark, wild curls spread around her like roots trying to find purchase. Her face was turned away from him, giving him a view of her neck and her ear. Once again, there was no sign of the gills he had seen in the water.

He drew in a breath and lifted his gaze, wondering if she had the ability to hide them. It was the only explanation he could come up with. He wanted to shake her awake and demand that she tell him, but he knew it would be futile. She'd only agreed to tell him about the Masters. Besides, he didn't need her to tell him again that his promise wasn't worth anything. There was also the fact that he couldn't keep her here forever. Eventually, she would be found.

His night had been plagued with nightmares about Tanira or someone else discovering the female. He hadn't exaggerated about what his people would do to her—and him. His death would be slow and agonizing. Everything he'd worked for, all he had sacrificed, would be for nothing. He needed to get Kalyani out of the trench as soon as possible.

It would be difficult, but he was good at finding ways out of impossible situations. He had no choice but to do it now.

Varum turned and headed toward the door to leave. As he did, Kalyani turned in her sleep. He spun around the moment he realized she was about to roll off the sofa and caught her with his magic. His hip cramped at the odd angle he found himself in, lunging on the floor. He carefully lifted her back to the cushions and gently turned her so her back was to him. It was only then that he let out the breath he'd been holding. He shook his head and covered her with the blanket once more.

As he turned, he looked down at the coffee table she had missed smashing her head against by a hair's breadth. He liked that table. It was an irreplaceable gift. He took the time to move it closer to the other sofa to give the human room to fall if she rolled off again. After he straightened, he looked around his home. The lattice was in place, there was plenty of food, and he would bind the lock when he left, so he and Nirav were the only ones who could open the door.

Not only would that keep Kalyani shut away, but he also wouldn't have to worry about anyone else stopping by and getting in. No one had ever done that in the past, but he hadn't ever hidden a human before. There was a lot at stake, and if he had to take extra measures, then he would.

There were perks to living away from the crowd. He was glad he had chosen this location for his home. Few came his way—just the way he liked it. Varum walked out without another look at

Kalyani and closed the main door behind him before using magic to bind the lock.

After a short walk down a coral-columned walkway, he dove into one of the numerous canals that wove through the city, connecting the air-filled districts to the submerged ones. He glanced toward the Residential Arches. Once, long ago, his family had carved their own dwelling out of the trench wall to grow their family coral.

He swam past it toward the Assembly Hall, where he was expected—and also where he would find Nirav. Varum swam up to a *nehras* and stepped through. The magical membrane dried him immediately, without even a single drop of water falling. He looked around him as he stood in the busy corridor. No suspicious looks were cast his way, and no whispers met his ears. It looked as if his secret was safe.

For the time being, at least.

The only way to get through the day was to put Kalyani out of his mind and act as if nothing that was happening was out of the ordinary. He adjusted the sleeves of his tunic and headed to his office. It was small, and he was rarely there, but it was also the place he was expected to visit after missing work the day before.

He opened the door to find a stack of files on his desk. Varum sighed and closed the door before walking to the front of the desk and shifting through the files. Most were requests from citizens, which were delegated to all Currentspeakers, but since he hadn't been here yesterday, he'd been given more than his share.

Varum tossed the files back onto his desk and walked around to sit. It was better to get these looked over than to leave them. He got comfortable and opened the top file. Except it wasn't words he saw, it was dark curls. He squeezed his eyes shut and shook his head. The next time he looked, there were words once more.

"She needs to tame that mess of hair," he murmured as he began reading.

One after another, he read the requests, complaints, and applications for each file. It took him all day, but he got through them before handing the files—and his decisions—off to one of the clerks to put into motion. Varum rubbed his eyes with his thumb and forefinger.

"I know that look well."

His head jerked to the side at the sound of Nirav's voice. He smiled at the sight of his friend. "Are you telling me I look how I feel?"

"Only if you've been in your office all day going through files," Nirav answered with a grin.

"You know that because you've been in my shoes."

Nirav threw his head back and let out a booming laugh that caused others to look their way. "And I don't miss it. Come," he said, motioning for Varum. "Let us get some dinner."

Varum's smile slipped. "That sounds good, but I should get back."

"We won't be long," Nirav replied. "You look like you need to talk. Would you rather go to my place or somewhere else?"

There were too many servants at Nirav's. They couldn't take the chance of one of them overhearing. Same with any restaurant. However, they couldn't go to Varum's either.

"Come on. I know just the place," Nirav said.

He fell into step with the man he had grown up calling *uncle*. Varum trusted Nirav. And if anyone could help, it was him. Varum would have to be diligent in making sure nothing could ever be tracked back to his friend.

As usual, Nirav kept idle banter going as they walked. It wasn't until they sat down in a secluded room at an out-of-the-way eatery that Varum had never been to before that all pretenses fell away.

"How are things going with your guest?" Nirav asked, shooting him a pointed look.

Answering about Kalyani was difficult. "So far, so good right now."

"I'm too old for you to be worrying me in such a way," Nirav chastised.

"Please. You're going to outlive us all."

It was usually a jest that brought a smile to Nirav's face, but not that day. His silvery white eyes were locked on Varum. "I'm worried," Nirav whispered.

"I know."

"Your parents left you in my care. I'm responsible for you."

Varum adjusted in his seat and nodded. Out of all the people his parents could've chosen to step into that role, Nirav had been the best. "I'm not that little kid anymore."

"Believe me, I'm well aware of that. Tell me what's going on. Did you get anything?"

"A lot, actually."

They were interrupted by a discreet knock at the door. Nirav bade them to enter, and a man came in, carrying a tray. Once the two glasses and a bottle of tidewine were placed on the table, the man bowed and left the room, closing Nirav and Varum within.

Nirav poured some of the tidewine for each of them. Varum took a drink of the soft green liquid. The fermented sea fruits sealed in coral pods slid smoothly down his throat. When he looked up, Nirav's eyes were on him once more.

"How are her wounds? Is our medicine working on her?" Nirav asked.

"It seems to be. She's healing faster than I expected."

Nirav's eyes lit up as he sat straighter in his chair. "Have you spoken to her, then?"

"I have."

"What did she tell you?"

Varum relayed what he had learned about the Masters and those fighting against them. The bottle of tidewine was empty by the time he finished.

"I've never heard of this Gita, but that doesn't surprise me. She would've moved in different circles than I did when I was on land," Nirav said.

Varum took another longer drink. He was disappointed but not surprised. "It was a long shot that you'd know her, but I needed to ask."

"Do you think Kalyani knows anything else?"

"Without a doubt."

Nirav reclined in his chair. "You gave her a promise."

"That's part of the reason I'm here."

"You want my help getting her out."

A grin pulled at Varum's lips. "You always were smart."

Nirav snorted as he smiled. "And you were always cheeky."

"I'll be the one to take her out," Varum said, growing serious.

"You barely got her into the city and your home. You said it yourself. It nearly killed both of you."

Varum rubbed the back of his neck. "I need help in finding a way out so we won't be discovered. I took a longer route to get inside, and when it became too painful, I headed straight for my house. I'm amazed we weren't seen."

"I am, as well. Let me think this over and get back to you. You'll need to get her out soon."

Varum nodded. "I'm aware."

"I didn't say this the other day, but you could've taken her anywhere to tend her wounds and talk to her. Why bring her here? You've never done anything reckless like this in your life."

"I've been asking myself that. And I wish I had an answer. All I can tell you is that Tarangarh seemed the best place."

Nirav drank the last bit of tidewine from his glass. "We have some new intel on the Masters, which is good. I'm not sure it's enough to take to the Assembly, though."

"I don't think so either. They'll want to know how I got it, and I won't be able to provide that without revealing that Kalyani was in the city."

"They don't need to know she was here. Say you took her ashore and spoke then."

That was a possibility—and one Varum should've thought of. What was it about having the human around that clouded his judgment? "That's what I need to do if I'm to protect our people."

"And yourself."

Varum shook his head as he thought about the Assembly. "I wonder if they'll believe anything I tell them. They'll want proof, and they know I can't give them anything."

"You saw the two Sea Elves."

"I only saw one's face, though. And without recognizing them or having their names, it's only my word."

Nirav crossed his arms over his chest. "I'm wondering if you're purposely not speaking about the gills because you don't want to discuss it, or because you don't know anything."

"Perceptive, as usual. I have tried to nudge Kalyani in that direction, but she doesn't want to talk about it. Even when I stated how deep she had been in the water, she disregarded it. Yet I have to wonder if she knows."

"Knows what?" Nirav asked.

Varum scratched his jaw. "She claims to be able to hold her breath for a long time."

"That's when you told her you saw the truth, right?"

"That's the thing. When I checked after seeing to her injuries, the gills weren't there."

Surprise flashed over Nirav's face. "Isn't that interesting? This is why you believe she doesn't know?"

"It is."

"You need to press her."

Varum twisted his lips. "The deal we made was for the Masters."

"I think you need to make a new deal."

"I can try, but what good will it do for her to admit she can breathe underwater like us?"

Nirav lowered his arms and sat up. "For one, we need to know if there are others like her. Tarangarh is hidden, even from other Sea Elves. From what I remember about humans during my time on land, they go where they shouldn't."

"I don't think there are others like her in the village."

"She's proof that it's possible. And if there is one, there are more."

Varum had to agree. "I was hoping to get her out tonight."

"I'll need at least tonight to find you the best and shortest route. Use the time to pry into who she is."

"I'll do what I can."

Nirav rubbed his hands on his thighs. "Perhaps I should meet her."

A jolt of shock ran through Varum. "Is that wise?"

"I already know about her."

"Even so, there's nothing specifically linking her to you."

A brow arched on Nirav's forehead. "Do you not want me to meet her?"

"It isn't that. I'm trying to keep anything from blowing back on you."

Nirav rose to his feet. "Let it. I can handle whatever comes."

"Not if she's discovered. You know what they'll do to her. And me."

"Then we make sure that doesn't happen." Nirav slapped him on the shoulder. "However, if you would rather I didn't, I'll accept that."

Varum stood and let out a sigh. "I would never turn you away."

"Good. I'm curious to speak to this human."

"You may regret it. She's not what you would expect."

Nirav chuckled as he grinned. "Oh? Why is that?"

"She's stubborn."

"A female with a mind of her own," Nirav murmured in amusement. "That isn't a rare thing. Just uncommon around you."

Now Varum was offended. "What is that supposed to mean?"

"Never mind. Let's go," Nirav said as he tossed some coins onto the table.

He was out the door a moment later. Varum lengthened his strides to catch up to Nirav. "Please explain your comment."

"Must I? Surely, you know."

"If I knew, would I be asking?"

Nirav tsked as he cut a quick look at Varum. "As I said earlier, you always follow the rules."

"They're there for a reason." Yet he had broken one. And not just any rule.

"Other youths pushed against them to see how far they could go. But you, my dear boy, never bothered."

Varum grunted. "What good does it do to act in such a way?"

"Perhaps you should ask yourself that."

Nirav had never scolded or shouted. He had merely laid things out and waited for Varum to step into the ruse before revealing some wisdom. It seemed that he had yet to learn, because he'd plowed straight into this latest one.

"Shouldn't you tell me all the ways I've mucked this up?" Varum asked.

The older man shook his head. "You're doing enough of that for both of us. And before you ask, I know because it's all over your face. Stop worrying. We'll get this sorted and come out the other side better for it."

"You really think so?"

"I've not let you down before. I won't now."

Of all the people in his life, Nirav had been the only one who hadn't disappointed him. The weight on Varum's shoulders lightened a little. And he knew it wouldn't dissipate until Kalyani was far from the city.

"In case you're wondering, I probably would've made the same decision regarding her," Nirav said.

14

Serenia

Chaos reigned behind Dain as he stood at the edge of the water, staring out at the expanse that stretched as far as the eye could see. Just as he had expected, Rohan was a wreck. Dain couldn't imagine what the human was going through with the disappearance of yet another sister.

"We have to get to Kalyani," Rohan stated for the third time.

And for the third time, Farah answered calmly, "We're trying to find a way."

"We know Kalyani was taken by the Sea Elves," Dain said as he turned to face the small group. He looked at each of their faces. "Do we know where?"

Yasmin shook her head. "All the stones would say is that it was deep."

"Meaning we can't reach it," Jai said.

Dain eyed Rohan. Exhaustion pulled at the human from lack

of sleep and food. His light green eyes were filled with the kind of pain that burrowed into the soul. His cheeks were sunken, and his shoulder-length, dark brown hair was disheveled. He was a man who had barely come back from the brink before and had been shoved there a second time.

"I can't just do nothing," Rohan said, his voice soft, as if it had taken every bit of energy he had just to get the words out.

Dain glanced at the water. "We require a Sea Elf to get us where we need to go. Without one of them, we'll die."

"Why didn't the elf bring Kalyani to shore?" Farah asked.

Ravi rocked back on his heels, his arms crossed over his chest. "That's what I've been trying to figure out."

"The Sea Elves aren't exactly welcoming to other races," Arya said.

Dain snorted as he looked between Arya and Jai. "And the Dark are?"

"Is there no way to contact the female Sea Elf you rescued?" Yasmin asked.

Jai turned his head to Dain. "There might be. The ship we stole from the Masters is hidden."

"That would get us *on* the water, and with Yasmin's help, we could pinpoint where Kalyani tried to rescue the others," Ravi said.

Rohan anxiously looked around at the group. "How do we find the city she was taken to?"

"We won't be able to," Dain said.

Arya nodded. "He's right. The Dark keep most of the entrances to the underworld hidden, but the Sea Elves take things to another level. We could swim the depths of the ocean for eternity and never locate a single city if they don't want us to."

"They can't keep Kalyani. She's human," Farah stated.

Dain yanked a strand of hair from his face, tired of the wind teasing him. "I understand she's a good swimmer, but if what Yaz heard from the stones is correct, Kalyani was taken to depths that shouldn't be possible for a human."

"Or anyone but a Sea Elf," Ravi added.

Rohan hung his head, clearly not wanting to share anything. It was Farah who spoke while holding on to one of his hands with both of hers. "Kalyani loves the water the way I do the trees. But her ability goes further than just being able to navigate the currents easily."

"How so?" Dain pressed.

Rohan shook his head as he lifted it. "I'm not sure. She won't tell me much, but I saw her tame a *kythi* near a cave which held plants I needed for Farah's wound. I've witnessed Kalyani cutting through currents that would've torn another person in two. And..." He trailed off, the silence broken only by the crash of the waves onto the shore. "She can hold her breath for an unfathomable length of time."

"Could that be why the Sea Elf took her?" Yasmin asked.

Farah nodded. "Maybe."

"We won't know until we find her," Jai added.

Rohan asked, "Then what are we waiting for? Let's get to the ship."

Dain faced the water as the three couples ironed out specifics. Jai was the only one who knew how to sail the vessel, but he, Arya, and Dain would be all but useless in the water since they couldn't call their shadows there. None of their group would be able to dive deep enough to make a difference, either.

These were facts that everyone but Rohan was aware of, but no one wished to state. Because, if their positions were reversed, each of them knew they would want the others' support. Rohan would comprehend things eventually, but all that mattered now was taking some kind of action.

Arya moved to Dain's side. "I keep wondering if this is somehow tied to the Masters."

"You mean to get us out in the open since they've not been able to find any of us?" Dain stated.

"Exactly that."

"It has crossed my mind."

She glanced at him. "It would make sense. We would all be out on a ship and easy to pick off."

"Only if the Sea Elves are working with them."

"The other races are. Why wouldn't they?"

Dain blew out a breath and shook his head. "Shaldorn was hidden for years without anyone knowing. We recently learned they were building another stronghold. You know where a good place to hide it would be?"

"Of course," Arya murmured. "The ocean. And if only Sea Elves can transport visitors, it would ensure that only those they want in would get to visit the new Shaldorn."

Dain hoped he was wrong, but the more he thought about it, the more it made sense. "The bounties on us have continued to rise, too."

"You think this is a trap?" Jai asked loudly from behind them.

Dain turned to face the group. "We should also expect that."

"I agree," Ravi said.

Rohan's brow furrowed deeply. "Do you think they're torturing Kalyani to get our location?"

Dain waited for one of the others to answer, but no one did, leaving it to him. "It's something we should keep in mind."

"I knew I never should've let her stay in Serenia," Rohan mumbled.

Farah gripped his hand tighter. "She's not a child. She makes her own decisions."

"If this is a trap, it's a good one," Jai said. "They had to know we'd go looking for her."

Yasmin asked, "But what if it isn't? What if she was taken for another reason?"

"Did the rocks tell you more?" Farah questioned.

Yaz shook her head, tossing her black hair. "I just think we need to consider everything."

"That's a good point," Ravi added.

Jai threw up his hands. "What's the decision? Are we going out to sea?"

"Let's split up," Dain suggested. "If it's a trap, we don't want to make it easy for them. Arya, you stay with Jai, Rohan, and Farah. I'll remain here with Ravi and Yasmin."

"What if Yasmin learns something new?" Rohan asked.

Dain softened his lips into what he hoped was a smile. "I'll relay that to you immediately, should that happen."

"And either Arya or I can make it back here if something comes up while we're on the ship," Jai added.

Dain watched Rohan, Farah, Jai, and Arya hurry away to gather supplies as Ravi and Yasmin stayed with him.

"What are the chances that we'll find Kalyani?" Yaz asked.

Ravi shook his head. "Slim."

"It depends on why she was taken," Dain said. "She's a fighter. She'll stay alive for as long as she can."

Yasmin glanced toward the newly built huts. "I know it's better for us to split up, but I hate that I won't be on the ship if something happens. Not that I'd be much help. I'm a decent swimmer, but I can't hold my breath for very long."

"Not many can," Dain pointed out.

Ravi caught his gaze. "You think there's more to it?"

"I think if the Sea Elf isn't working for the Masters, something caught his attention."

Yaz shrugged. "Maybe he thought Kalyani was pretty."

"Even if he did, he wouldn't do anything about it," Ravi said. "There's a reason you don't see many Sea Elves in Shecrish. And it isn't just about preferring the water."

"It's about keeping separate from everyone else," Dain said.

Yasmin frowned. "And by separate, you mean they don't like other races."

"All the infants found in Shecrish are supposed to be brought to the Domestic Ministry. Any Dark Elf babies are handed to the Dark, same with the Mountain and Sea Elves, while the rest of us intermingle," Ravi said.

Dain nodded when Yaz looked his way. "It's how it's always been."

"What about us humans?"

"You saw for yourself with Manu. The Mountain Elves don't take in humans," Ravi said. "The climate in the peaks is too harsh."

Dain grunted. "Underground would be a death sentence to a human since you're unable to see in the dark and can't survive well without sunlight. Same with breathing underwater."

"All that makes sense, I suppose." She sat there for a moment.

"Dain, how do the Dark feel about one of their own marrying outside of your race?"

He shrugged as he shifted his feet, moving once again from the wind. "It isn't well received, but those Dark aren't ostracized. Inej seems to be doing all right with Manu. However, I know that the Sea Elves refuse such unions."

"How sad to be so close-minded," Yasmin murmured.

Ravi took her hand in his. "Think of it as being because only one of their own can exist in their cities."

"Then I'm even more worried about Kalyani." Yasmin shifted closer to Ravi, the two exchanging a look.

Dain had to admit that he was concerned, as well. Kalyani might be able to hold her breath for a long time, but she wouldn't be able to descend to the places the Sea Elves lived. Not even another elf could do that. So, where had they taken her? And for what purpose?

It wasn't long before Rohan and Farah returned to the beach. The moment Jai and Arya joined them, Rohan was impatient to leave. Jai, with the help of Yasmin and the stones, drew a rough map of the direction he needed to sail.

Jai's excitement to be back at the helm of a ship was tempered by the reason for sailing. Arya looked ill at ease at being back on a boat after her bout with motion sickness the last time.

"Be safe," Dain told the two couples as they huddled together.

Rohan dipped his chin. "You, too."

The four clustered together as Arya and Jai gathered their shadows around them before vanishing. Dain let out a sigh, ill at ease with what was happening. The Masters had been too quiet, and that made him wonder what they were hiding.

"I need to report in to Durga," Dain said.

Ravi nodded. "I have some reports for her. Would you hand them off?"

"Of course."

"Let me get them," Ravi said and hurried off.

Yasmin remained behind, her gaze on the horizon. "I can tell you're as uneasy about how quiet things have been as I am."

"Is it that obvious?" Dain asked.

"Nay," she said with a grin. "We're all feeling it, but no one wants to talk about it."

Dain nodded slowly in agreement. "Shall I return to the Dragon Kings and check on the children for you?"

"You were just there," she said as she turned to him. "I miss them so much. But knowing the six of them are out of harm's way is a relief. What you and Manu have done for us is—"

"What friends do for others," Dain said, interrupting her.

She rested a hand on his arm. "Thank you, just the same."

"I'm glad the Kings were able to take them in. The children miss being with you and Ravi."

"They have other kids to play with, and there, they can be children. They aren't going hungry anymore."

Dain chuckled as he patted her hand. "Nay, they are not."

"Have you seen Reva?"

The quick change in subject startled him for a second. Dain was searching for a reply when Ravi returned with the reports. Dain grabbed them, thankful that he wouldn't have to answer. "I'll return soon," he said as his shadows enveloped him.

15

All day. That's how long Kalyani had been on her own. At least she thought it was day.

"Bloody hell," she ground out as she tried to move the lattice over the windows.

She needed to see the sky. It didn't matter if it was the moons or the sun that cast her in light. No amount of pulling, yanking, or pushing moved the lattice even a little, though. Kalyani balled her hand into a fist and slammed it against the covering.

"Problems?"

Her entire body went still at the sound of that deep, rich voice. To her surprise, a flicker of exhilaration sparked, but thankfully, it was extinguished quickly as irritation flared as bright as a raging fire. She spun around and found Varum standing in the living area just outside the bedroom door.

"You could say that," she retorted.

One dark blue brow arched on his forehead. "And why is that? You had the entire area to yourself, and I left plenty of food."

"Am I some kind of pet to you?"

He released a long sigh. "Perhaps if you told me what the problem is."

"I don't know what time it is. I can't see the sky!"

Varum's brows drew together as he stared at her after her outburst. Even she was shaken at the emotion cracking in her voice. She had yearned to encounter the Sea Elves and see their realm. Now, all she wanted was to return to Rohan and see the sky.

"It's evening," Varum said into the silence.

He held her gaze for another heartbeat before shifting to the side. Kalyani's gaze landed on an older Sea Elf about four inches shorter than Varum. He had a muscular frame with wide shoulders that filled out his pale aqua tunic. The newcomer's greenish-black hair was short, emphasizing his handsome face and startling silvery white eyes—that were locked on her.

Kalyani took a step back before she realized it. Varum had told her that no one could know of her existence, or they would both perish. Had it all been a lie?

"There's no need to fear me," the Sea Elf said.

She eyed his warm smile, unsure of what she should believe. Waking up alone had frightened her, and the more hours she spent on her own, the more time she had to think about what Rohan was going through.

"It has been many years since I last laid eyes on a human." He cleared his throat and swung his head to Varum. "Did you leave her all alone?"

Varum's lips flattened as he met the man's gaze. "Kalyani, this is Nirav. My friend, mentor, and family. Nirav, this is Kalyani."

Nirav bowed in her direction. "It is a pleasure to see you awake. I was here while you were recovering. May we talk?"

His manners were impeccable, but how would he react if she refused?

"You can trust him," Varum stated after another loud sigh. "I wouldn't have brought him otherwise."

Kalyani shot a longing look through the lattice as she made her way to the men. Nirav motioned to one of the sofas. She found herself sitting on the couch she had claimed earlier while Nirav took the other, and Varum sat in the chair.

"I know how disorienting all of this must be," Nirav said. "I remember the first time I walked the streets of Rannora. Everything was loud, the colors wrong. The people strange. The difference is, I went there willingly."

She cut her eyes to Varum to find him watching her. Kalyani returned her attention to Nirav. "I'm guessing you got to leave when you wanted, too."

"Actually, I didn't. I was forced to remain for a period of time." Nirav frowned as if searching for a word. "Call it a request by our ruling body."

Well, now she was curious. "Why?"

"That is the nature of politics, isn't it? One side giving something for the other. I was sent to spend some time with the Conclave."

The Conclave was Shecrish's ruling body, and they were known to be vipers. Kalyani didn't want to feel sorry for him being sent into the viper's nest, but she did. "How did that turn out?"

"I survived," Nirav said with a shrug.

"Are you saying I'll survive this?"

"Do you want to?"

Kalyani felt Varum's gaze on her, but she kept her eyes locked with Nirav's. "I must return to my brother. He shouldn't be suffering the disappearance of another sister."

"Varum relayed your stories to me. I agree that his anguish shouldn't be drawn out. I intend to help find a safe way to get you out of the city, but I requested to meet you first."

She scooted closer to the edge of the cushion as hope blossomed. "Will you really help?"

"Of course. I will always protect Varum."

Right. Varum was why Nirav was here, not her. Kalyani needed to keep that in mind. She had no allies in the city. It was her against everyone. The only way she would continue living was by the benevolence of the two males in the room with her now.

Her stomach chose that moment to growl. She tensed, but neither of the elves said anything.

"Would you mind if I asked some questions?" Nirav requested.

Kalyani had been expecting this. It wasn't enough that Varum had grilled her incessantly the night before. He had brought someone else to continue the interrogation. If she angered them, would they slide back the lattice and toss her out to be crushed by the force of the water? Would her death be over quickly, or would she linger as her bones were slowly pulverized to dust?

Her stomach growled again.

Varum surged to his feet and looked down at her with annoyance. "Did you not eat the food I left?"

"I ate some," she answered and cast him a quick look.

He said nothing more as he stalked into the kitchen and checked the sealed compartments. Kalyani swallowed and looked up to see Nirav watching her with a peculiar expression.

"You hardly touched any of it," Varum stated as he returned to stand beside her. "Is it your intention to starve yourself?"

"It is not," she fired back, her anger getting the best of her.

Nirav's voice was soft as he said, "Perhaps you should ask her why she hasn't eaten."

Varum looked away. When his iridescent blue eyes landed on her again, his emotions were once more in check. "Why haven't you eaten?"

"What little I attempted to eat refused to stay down," Kalyani grudgingly admitted. She hated being ill. It made her look weak, and she had already been injured. It was embarrassing.

"The food yesterday settled fine," Varum said.

She shrugged, wishing she could disappear between the cushions. "I know."

"What did you use to treat her injuries?" Nirav asked. "That could be causing the issue."

Varum sank back into the chair. "*Serynth* leaf to bind the wound, *thalorine* for the pain, and *morasyl* to keep her sedated during the initial healing."

"None of those have ever been used on a human before," Nirav replied.

Kalyani itched her side where the leaf was still stuck to her. "Speaking of the leaf thing, can I remove it?"

"I'll do it," Varum said, leaning toward her.

She jumped up and to the side, out of his reach. "I can handle it."

"Actu—" Nirav began.

"What's wrong?" Varum demanded, his jaw set as he stared at her.

Kalyani took a step back. "Nothing. I can take care of it."

"Well, it mi—" Nirav tried again.

Varum snorted. "Is it difficult for you to ask for help?"

She gaped at him. "I have no problems asking for help."

"Then ask now," he pressed.

Those uncanny eyes swirled dangerously, as if a great beast were waking. Then he blinked, and the anger was banked. Or maybe she had just imagined it. "I don't need to."

"Come here and lift your tunic. I'll remove it," Varum directed.

But she didn't budge. She couldn't. The thought of baring her skin to him made her heart race uncontrollably.

"Kalyani."

The sound of her name in his accent actually sent chills racing over her skin.

Varum released yet another loud sigh, his disdain clear. "Are you afraid I'm going to see something?"

"I'm sure you'll just rip another hole in these clothes to tend to me," she fired back. "You left me in bloodied garments."

"Would you rather I have stripped you?"

He didn't raise his voice, but contempt laced every syllable. Yet it was an image of her naked in his bed that lodged words in her throat.

Nirav cleared his throat to get their attention. Then, in a soft but firm voice, he said, "If I may. Kalyani, removing a *serynth* leaf needs to be done carefully so as not to reverse the healing that has taken place. If a female was present, she would tend to you. I know we just met, but I promise to remove it quickly."

She was mortified that her temper had shown itself so dramatically. Her mouth had run away with itself, making it impossible for her to meet either of the elves' eyes now. She might not have been raised among the elite, but she knew how to act properly. For some reason, she let Varum rile her at every turn.

Both males were staring, and she was getting nauseous again. Maybe it would stop once the leaf was removed. She started in Nirav's direction.

"I'll do it," Varum said.

He didn't give her time to decide, just dropped down on one knee before her. She found her eyes moving to his, but he wasn't looking at her face. His attention was on her left side. Kalyani swallowed anxiously as she gathered the hem of her tunic, then lifted the fabric enough to reveal her side and the leaf.

The first brush of his fingers against her skin made her suck in a breath. He jerked his gaze to her, but she quickly looked away. Gently, he pulled back the edge of the leaf. She felt the tug of the adhesive as it slowly peeled free. A tremor went through her when she felt Varum's warm breath flowing over her skin.

She closed her eyes and turned her head away, but she felt the pad of each of his fingers and the warmth of his palm. Little by little, he detached the leaf until it was gone. Her breath caught in her chest when he smoothed a finger along her skin.

"The leaf worked well. You'll have a scar, but it'll be minimal," Varum said.

She wanted to back away. Yet she also wanted to stay as they were. Her mixed feelings were confusing.

Suddenly, he stood, towering over her. "You can breathe now. I'm finished."

Kalyani's fingers loosened their hold on her tunic as she drew air into her starved lungs. She felt flushed, her heart raced, and her legs were wobbly. Somehow, she made it the couple of steps to the sofa and plopped down right as her knees gave way.

Varum and Nirav started talking, but she couldn't make out their words with her side still tingling from Varum's touch. That couldn't possibly be the reason, though. It had to be the removal of the leaf. That was it. Her body was still absorbing the residue. Magic was long-reaching. It made sense that it would continue to work, even after the leaf's removal.

She found her gaze on Varum as he listened to something Nirav said. He didn't make her skin tingle. He was too rigid and aloof for her to feel anything. It was definitely the magic.

As for Varum, she still hadn't decided if he was friend or foe. He should've been firmly slotted in one column or the other by now. Every time she thought he might be a friend, he did something reprehensible. Same as when she was sure he was a foe—he'd be kind out of nowhere. How was she to figure anything out when he kept doing that? It was infuriating.

16

Everything around him became fuzzy, and Nirav's voice faded as all Varum's attention was on the pulsing in the fingertips that had touched Kalyani's skin. He had been so close. He could've pressed his lips to the puckered area of her wound.

And he nearly had.

He had no idea what had come over him. He rubbed his thumb over his fingertips, imagining that he was once more stroking her skin. Soft. Alluring. Her quick intake of breath had matched his when he first brushed against her bare side.

If only his heart would quit racing. If only he could stop pondering her inviting warmth, maybe he could think straight once more.

He wouldn't need to touch her again now that the *serynth* leaf had been removed. Perhaps he should've drawn out the process even longer. Yet he had taken it off because she couldn't keep food down.

And just like that, the room and its occupants snapped into focus around him. Varum turned his head to Kalyani. "Are you feeling better?"

"My side no longer itches," she answered.

Nirav asked, "Would you like to try some food now?"

She waved away his words, shaking her head. "Not yet."

"Let me know when that changes." Varum waited until she inclined her head before relaxing into the chair.

Nirav settled more comfortably on the sofa. "I was curious about the Moon Elf you mentioned in your stories."

"Gita," Kalyani replied immediately.

Nirav gave her another friendly grin. "That's her. What else can you tell me about her?"

Varum waited to see if Kalyani would stick to the stories she had told him or disclose new information. He really hoped there was nothing new to add.

"What else is there to say about someone like her?" Kalyani replied. "She bestows anguish and misery wherever she goes, which makes her a perfect match for the Masters."

"Are you telling me no one really knows who they are?" Nirav pressed.

She shook her head. "None of my friends have seen them. As I told Varum last night, the only one of us to get close was Arya when they spoke to her. She never saw anything about them."

"They could be a group of two or two hundred. We can't know," Varum said.

Nirav nodded thoughtfully. "Too true. It will take much to uncover who they are. The first step is finding those like Gita. Can you tell me how she swayed Yasmin to get her to Shaldorn?"

"She tricked her."

Kalyani shoved her wealth of curls over her shoulder, drawing Varum's gaze. He remembered how the strands had moved in the water as if reaching out for him. Even when he had tended to her while she slept, those curls had found their way to him like a living entity.

Varum had spent the previous evening listening to every word that fell from her lips and her voice's inflections, searching for lies or deceit. This time, he let Nirav do the talking as he watched her. She finally scooted back against the sofa and tucked one foot under her. Color was filling her cheeks, so her skin didn't look so sallow.

"Yaz's parents were elves. Her mum intentionally poisoned her to get attention from others. One day, Yaz had had enough and ran away," Kalyani said.

Disappointment filled Varum at this new part of the story. He had hoped that Kalyani had shared everything, but he'd known deep down that she hadn't.

Nirav frowned. "Other family kept Yaz away from the mother?"

"She didn't want to chance being returned, so she lived on the streets." Kalyani slid her gaze to him. "And before you get upset that I didn't tell you this last night, these are specifics that don't pertain to the Masters."

"I disagree. Yasmin's story is tied to Gita, who is a part of the Masters." Varum waited for a rebuttal, but none came.

Kalyani pressed her lips together. "You're right. I was tired of repeating everything, so I shortened some stories."

"That's understandable, and you're sharing now. Please, continue," Nirav insisted.

Varum stretched out his legs and crossed one ankle over the

other. "I have a difficult time believing a child would choose to live on her own without protection, shelter, or food."

"Because you've never known hardship," Kalyani replied stiffly.

Nirav jumped in before Varum could reply and said, "Yasmin escaped one kind of horror, only to end up in another. I remember the streets of the city well. They aren't kind or just."

"She scraped by, but that's how Gita found her. When Gita offered to give Yaz a home, clothes, and food, she took the opportunity. It wasn't until they arrived at Shaldorn that Yaz learned her fate. By then, it was too late."

Nirav made a sound at the back of his throat. "How long was Yasmin there before she escaped?"

"If Yaz ever told me the exact number of years, I don't recall. I know it was a long time. I've never asked what she endured there, and I won't, not after hearing Arya talking about the depravity that went on there." Kalyani wrapped her arms around her middle as she curled her toes against the rug.

"Nay, it's best not to ask someone who has sustained such trauma to relive it." Nirav drew in a breath and released it. "She lived to tell the tale, however. Then she was able to return and get some revenge."

Kalyani shrugged, her head tilted to the side. "I suppose. Gita got away, though. She had been living in Belanore the entire time."

"Did your friends check to see if she was there?" Varum asked.

Kalyani shot him a flat look. "Of course. They're good at what they do. She had long since vacated the flat."

"So. She could be anywhere," Nirav murmured. He shook himself and asked, "What about the Moon Elf, One?"

She twisted her lips, her nose wrinkling. "He's even more of a mystery."

"So it seems." Nirav rubbed the back of his neck.

It was a signal that he was troubled and needed to think things over. Varum glanced toward Kalyani to see her looking his way. How much more was she withholding? Did she have a clue that could protect his people? She might not even know what it was. It was why he needed her to tell him every detail.

Nirav slapped his hands on his legs, his expression taut. "It has been many years since I've walked on land, and I've met many people. I might have encountered Gita if she went by another name. It's difficult to say."

"I hope that what I've shared helps," Kalyani said.

Varum nodded. "It was more than we had before."

"I do have one more question, if you'll allow it," Nirav said.

Kalyani smiled and placed both feet on the floor. "Of course."

"Are there others like you who can swim so well?"

Kalyani stiffened the moment the words registered. Her warm smile turned frosty as she fought to keep it in place. Varum wasn't yet sure if it was fear that kept her from saying anything, or something else. He wanted to ask, but he knew she wouldn't answer. And even if she did, it likely wouldn't be the truth.

"No one can swim like I can," she replied.

Nirav laughed softly. "Bold words, but I bet you're right."

His lighthearted response wasn't enough to break the tension in the room. Now wasn't the time to press her on the gills. She was like any wild, unpredictable animal that had been cornered. Varum was getting ready to steer the conversation in a different direction when Nirav got to his feet.

"It's been a long day, and I need to look over some charts to find a way out for Kalyani." Nirav turned to her and bowed once more. "It was a pleasure to meet you."

Varum walked Nirav out the front, intending to have a private word, when he spotted Tanira headed their way. He cursed under his breath, even as Nirav grinned.

"Tell me why you don't make her yours?" Nirav whispered.

Varum subtly locked his door with magic. "You know why."

"There you are," Tanira said as she made her way over. "I was hoping to run into you."

Nirav couldn't stop smiling. "It was bound to happen since you were headed to his place."

Tanira turned her silvery white eyes to him and gave him a smile.

"That's my cue to leave," Nirav murmured.

Varum grabbed Nirav's sleeve, hoping to keep him there, but his friend slipped away and hurried off, leaving Varum with Tanira. "What brings you here tonight?"

"I thought we could have dinner."

"I ate with Nirav already."

Her smile widened as she stepped closer and touched his hair. He leaned back out of her way.

"That was an early meal. We can have a drink first and then dessert," she offered suggestively.

Varum had repeatedly refused her advances, but Tanira wouldn't give up. "I'm afraid I'll have to disappoint you tonight."

"Invite me inside."

"Excuse me?"

She looked at the door. "Invite me inside, Varum. I want to be with you."

"All you have to do is snap your fingers, and you can have any man you want."

Tanira snapped them. "Done. Now, let's go inside."

"I've already told you that I'm not the one for you."

"But you're who I want."

He dodged her hands when she attempted to grab him. "You want me because I turned you down."

"That's not true," she stated in outrage. "I know what I feel."

"It's late, and I've had a long day. I'm going inside. It's time for you to go home," he urged.

She dashed at her face to swipe away a tear. "I can love you if you would only let me."

Varum tried to find a way to respond to that, but he must not have done it quickly enough, because Tanira whirled around and walked away. He waited until she was out of sight before slipping back into his home and locking the door behind him once more.

He found Kalyani at the table with a cup of something hot in her hands. She met his gaze, and he was surprised to see there was no hostility there. "How are you feeling?"

"A little better. I'm hungry, but every time I smell food, my stomach revolts."

He looked at the sofa. "Take the bed tonight. I'll sleep out here."

"I'll be fine. This is your home."

"One I brought you to without your consent."

She lifted one shoulder in a shrug. "You're going to release me."

"I am."

"When that's done, we'll call it even."

He took a step, then halted and faced her. "I know you think I went to extremes last night, and I did. There's a lot riding on what you know."

"Take me home, and you can talk to the others yourself. You can hear their firsthand accounts of things."

"Maybe. Maybe not."

She raised the steaming cup to her lips and took a sip as she looked at the table. "You're going to waste an opportunity to get information because you can't stand the sight of those of us who walk on land."

"That isn't it at all."

"Really?" She cut her eyes to him.

"Really."

Kalyani sighed. "Maybe you're right, but I don't think so. You could've taken me anywhere to tend to my wounds and talk to me, but you brought me here. A place I can't escape. A place I'm not supposed to be."

"I did it at great risk."

"Because you're scared of leaving the water or actually encountering humans and other elves."

17

There was something inherently wrong with being simultaneously hungry and nauseous. Kalyani had been elated when Varum disappeared into his room, leaving her to face the awkward discomfort alone.

She sipped the...she didn't even know what it was. Soup? Tea? Whatever it was, it was something her stomach could handle, and that was all that mattered. She didn't acknowledge the passage of time, just the rise and fall of the nausea that kept coming like waves crashing onto the beach. It was only in those brief moments of respite that she became aware of the other aches in her body—like her knees from sitting cross-legged in the chair.

A few times, she had contemplated standing to walk to the sofa, but she wasn't sure she could make it. Why chance a losing battle? It was bad enough that she was feeling so poorly again. So, she remained in the chair.

The ache in her knees was eventually overshadowed by her feet going numb, followed by a twinge in her lower back. Yet through it all, she forced herself to sip the liquid, expecting that her stomach would finally settle.

She lifted the cup to her lips for another drink, only to find it empty. Kalyani stared into it, hoping that more would miraculously appear, but fate wasn't on her side that night. No matter how hard she stared, hoping for more of the liquid, the cup remained empty. She slowly looked over her shoulder to the cabinet, where Varum had pulled out the tin. It was only a few steps away. First, though, she needed to heat some water.

Her stomach was feeling pretty good, which meant it was the perfect time to stand. She didn't rush anything, however. Kalyani took her time getting to her feet and crossing to the sink. She filled the kettle and set it to heat. Then, she went to the cabinet to get another sachet of whatever it was she had been drinking. Just as she opened the door, a wave of intense queasiness assailed her. She gripped the door in one hand and the edge of the cabinet in the other until the worst of it passed.

"I just might be getting better," she murmured with a grin.

She grabbed the tin and opened it, but it wasn't the soothing scent from before. This was something strong and bitter. She immediately replaced the lid, but the damage had already been done. Her stomach roiled violently. Kalyani hastily replaced the tin and turned to the sink, just as everything came up.

Sweat soaked her skin, and her legs shook so badly she had to grip the edges of the sink to stay upright. Then, suddenly, her hair was pulled away from her face, and a cold cloth pressed against her forehead. She tried to straighten once her stomach had emptied, but before she could, Varum lifted her into his arms.

"Stop," she told him when she saw that he was headed toward his room.

"You need the bed."

Her head dropped onto his shoulder despite her best efforts to keep it up. "Sofa is fine."

There was no reply as he laid her out on the side nearest to the bathroom. He then placed the cold, damp cloth on her forehead once more, covered her, and strode out. Kalyani rolled onto her side. Another wave of nausea hit her as she listened to Varum moving about the kitchen.

She must have dozed because when next she opened her eyes, there was nothing but silence.

"Stay still," Varum said when she turned her head. He gently wiped her heated face as he urged, "Go back to sleep."

She let herself be soothed by his voice and the cool cloth as she succumbed to exhaustion.

Kalyani opened her eyes to find herself on her side again. There was no queasiness this time, but she was afraid to move in case it returned. The soft sounds coming from outside the bedroom got her to gradually roll onto her back. A shadow filled the door, and her gaze landed on Nirav. To her surprise, she felt a thread of disappointment that it wasn't Varum.

"You're finally awake," Nirav said with a relieved smile. He moved to the foot of the bed. "How are you feeling?"

"Weak. But better," she admitted.

He nodded thoughtfully. "Varum sent for me this morning. He was called away and didn't want to leave you alone in case your condition worsened."

She rolled over and managed to push herself up with her arm. The older elf was immediately by her side.

"Easy, easy," he cautioned.

With his help, she got herself propped up against the head-board. That little effort left her winded and her limbs shaking.

A frown creased his forehead as he regarded her. "I looked through some material last night. I think it's the *serynth* leaf that caused the issue. While there is no record of it ever being tested on humans, there have been cases where it affected elves with queasiness—just not at the magnitude you felt."

"Is there a way to make it stop?"

"Removing the leaf was the first step. It takes some time for the remnants of the medicine to leave the body. I believe that's what is causing the issue. The elves who experienced such nausea were given a mixture to drink."

The thought of putting anything in her stomach made her grimace. "Please, tell me there's another way."

"I suspected you might feel that way after Varum told me how sick you were last night. My next suggestion is *ashal* moss. It's one of the ingredients for the brewed concoction, but it is also used alone as an anti-nausea tonic. I've crushed some. If you'll allow, I'll spread it over the inside of your wrists."

It sounded much better than drinking anything. "What will it do?" she asked.

"The moss is found on the underbellies of large shells. It releases vapors that will ease and quiet your stomach. It's a gentle, safe remedy that has been used by my people for generations."

Kalyani nodded. If she wanted to return home, she needed to be healthy. As it was, she was so weak she could barely lift her arm, and that meant she couldn't leave until she built up her strength again.

Nirav returned within moments. He held a palm-sized orange shell as he approached her. She held out her arms, wrists up. He dipped his fingers into the shell, and when he lifted his hands, they were covered with a silvery green substance. The first contact was cold and somewhat slimy, but within moments, she started to feel better. She closed her eyes and waited for Nirav to finish.

"There now," he said and lowered her hand to her stomach.

She looked up at him as he stepped back. "Thank you."

He flashed a smile. "Rest. I'll return later to look in on you."

"Do you have somewhere you need to be? If so, please go. I'll be fine."

"My days of moving in political circles are over, and I'm happy about that. I'm quite enjoying having you to care for. It's been a long time since I've had someone to look after."

It suddenly dawned on her that Nirav was a way for her to learn more about Varum. All she had to do was ask the right questions. "I don't want to sleep right now. Will you sit with me for a bit?"

"I'd be delighted," he beamed. "Let me put this away. I'll be right back."

True to his word, he returned with some water and bread that he placed on the table next to her. "For when you're feeling up to it."

She waited until he was settled in the chair before asking, "How long have you known Varum?"

"Since the day he was given to his parents." Nirav chuckled and shook his head. "My, that was some years ago now."

"You were close to his parents then?"

Nirav nodded. "Very close. His mum was so excited to finally have a child."

"His father wasn't?"

Nirav twisted his lips and glanced to the side. "His political career and wife were the important things. If she wanted something, he gave it to her."

"But he didn't want children."

"He didn't have a thought about it, one way or another."

Kalyani brushed back a curl that had fallen into her eyes. The way he said the words made her realize he wouldn't elaborate. "What of your family?"

"I married once. Sadly, it didn't work out. I then turned my attention to the city. That's where it would've remained had I not taken in Varum."

"Did something happen to his family?"

"That is not my story to tell," he stated gently.

She dipped her head. "Of course. I understand. I shouldn't have pried."

"It's natural. You want to know about Varum as much as he wants to know about you."

"All he wants is what I know about the Masters."

Nirav's smile widened. "Is that what you think?"

"Trust me, that's all he wants."

"Let me tell you something about him that you don't know," Nirav said as he leaned forward, bracing his arms on his knees. "He has never, not once, broken a single rule or order given to him by his family, me, or this city. Has never pushed boundaries. Never even toed the line. Until you."

Kalyani wasn't sure what to do with that. How did one respond to such a statement? *Thank you* seemed wrong. *I'm sorry* might be better, but it wasn't as if she had done anything. In the end, she opted to remain silent.

Nirav sighed as he sat back, his hands sliding along his thighs. "What do you see when you look at him?"

"A cold, unyielding elf."

"Why cold?"

She frowned, considering the question. "He keeps his emotions in check. Never displays them."

"Never?" Nirav asked with the quirk of a brow.

Since Nirav knew Varum better than she did, she decided not to answer that. "I understand why he brought me here, and I realize that he wants to keep the Masters away from his people, but I want to go home."

"He gave his word. He'll keep it. Of that, you can be certain."

Kalyani glanced to the side at the glass of water. It looked inviting, but she wasn't quite up to testing things out yet. "Did anything I divulged help?"

"In matters such as these, the more knowledge gained—however inconsequential someone might believe it is—is power. It also helps to know that there are those standing against the Masters."

"I told Varum to come back with me so he can talk to my friends."

Nirav shook his head, the sadness he felt written all over his face. "He won't. Not because he doesn't want to gather more information, but because it isn't our way."

"You went to the surface. You walked among us."

"Because I had no choice. A Sea Elf is sent to the Conclave every five years to serve as a representative. I spent years away from my people, longing for the day I could return." He looked away as he paused. "When I came home, it was to suspicion and distrust."

Kalyani saw the sorrow in his eyes and was angry on his behalf. "You did what you had to do. Surely, everyone knew that."

His smile was back in place, though not as bright as before. "Things are never so cut and dried as we would like. My time spent on land changed me. There is no way someone can spend that much time away and not be altered in some way. But that was long ago."

Maybe in years, but she knew Nirav still felt the sting of his people's reaction to him.

"I shared that," he continued, "to help you understand the lengths a Sea Elf will go to not be on land."

She glanced down at her hands folded over her stomach. "Dark Elves come up from the Below. Shouldn't it be as simple for your race?"

"As you've seen firsthand, our world is vastly different from others."

There was a hidden meaning there. Kalyani was sure of it, but she couldn't figure out what it might be. "I don't know much about the rest of our realm. I've never ventured farther than my village. I can't tell you what it's like to walk the streets of Rannora or even Belanore. I grew up far from all of that. I have seen Sea Elves from shore. It was just a glimpse, mind you, but I've seen them."

"How often?" he asked, his gaze intense as he stared.

She shrugged. "Here and there."

"Where exactly is your village?"

Kalyani hesitated, though she wasn't sure why. She was willing to bring Varum to her home. What was the difference between that and telling Nirav where it was?

"Did any of the Sea Elves come out of the water?" he asked.

"Not that I saw."

Nirav turned his head away, his brow furrowed. "I wonder if those were the same elves that Varum followed. They could be meeting the Masters. I need to find Varum."

Kalyani could do nothing as he rose and stalked out of the room and through the front door.

18

Somewhere in the Amrata Ocean

Wind pushed against the sails, sending the ship cutting through the dark blue water. Mist sprayed as the vessel rose and dipped with each wave. An azure sky met indigo ocean as far as the eye could see in every direction. Arya had never felt as small or insignificant as she did in that moment.

She blinked against the bright sun that burned her eyes and swung her head to the side, where her mate stood at the helm. Jai stood tall and straight, his hands on the wheel and feet braced apart as he stared ahead, a look of utter contentment on his handsome face. He knew every inch of the ship. He knew how she would react, as if the vessel and he were one being.

Jai was born to be here. On the water, commanding a ship and riding the waves. She had known he missed it, but he hadn't said a word. When the business with the Masters was finished, they would set sail on this vessel, charting the seas for as long as he wished. They could travel at night and sleep during the day.

It wasn't as if she had a family who would miss her now. Besides, she couldn't be an agent for the CCD forever. It was a good plan, and one she knew Jai would approve of.

Suddenly, his gaze met hers. His smile widened, his expression softening as it always did when he looked her way. She headed to him when he motioned her over. As she approached, he let go of the wheel with one hand and slid her between him and the helm, molding his front to her back. Arya leaned back against him and sighed.

"How is your seasickness?" he asked.

Her skin tingled where his warm breath brushed against her ear. "Perfectly in hand."

"Good. Now, tell me why you were staring."

"Can't I look at my gorgeous lover?" she teased and turned her head to glance at him with a smile.

Jai pressed his lips to hers. "You'd better always look."

She sighed and returned her gaze to the horizon.

"You don't have to tell me if you don't want to," he said.

"I was thinking about our future."

He placed one hand on her hip and tugged her closer. "I like the sound of that. What did you come up with?"

"That we should sail around the realm. This is where you belong. Right here at the helm."

Jai was silent for a heartbeat. "Is that what you really want?"

She turned to face him and looped her arms around his neck. Strands of her long, white hair pulled free from her braid to wave around her face. "What I want is a life with you. It doesn't matter where that is or what we're doing."

"Is it any wonder that I fell in love with you?" he asked.

Arya shrugged a shoulder. "Of course not. I'm amazing."

"That you are," he said huskily.

"Does that mean you like the future I've crafted?"

His eyes, a beautiful light gray with beads of silver woven through his irises and deep gray bands encircling it all, held hers. "I love the water. I love being on a ship. But they pale in comparison to what I feel for you. I don't care if I never see either one as long as you're by my side."

"We lost so many years," she began.

He put a finger to her lips. "None of that matters now. We found each other again. We triumphed against our enemy, and we will win against the evil plaguing our land."

She melted into him as he traced her bottom lip with the tip of his finger.

"I survived years of misery and torment to find my way back to you. Nothing could stop me from finding you, and nothing will keep me from having a life with you," he whispered before giving her a soft, lingering kiss.

Arya wanted to stop time and savor the moment for longer, but she knew the instant she felt his body tense that their private time was finished. He looked down at her and stroked her face. Then, he lifted his head and placed both hands on the helm.

She turned to face forward. "We've reached the spot, haven't we?"

"Aye. Hold the wheel," he bade.

She grabbed the helm just as he released it. Jai hurried down the steps and called out instructions to Rohan and Farah as he climbed up the rigging. Arya followed him with her eyes, but the blinding sun made it unbearable, giving her no choice but to look away. Jai was hurting, too, but like everything else, he never complained.

It wasn't long before the sails were lowered and tied off. She waited to hear him give the command to lower the anchor, and was surprised when it didn't come. Rohan frantically stalked around the edge of the ship, looking over the side into the water as if expecting Kalyani to suddenly pop up.

Rohan made a complete lap before he halted, his hands on the railing as his chin dropped to his chest. "I knew we wouldn't find anything. But still, I hoped."

Jai scaled the rigging once more and shielded his eyes with his hand as he scanned the area. "These are the coordinates the stones gave Yasmin. The currents would've taken anything away that was left over."

"Left over?" Farah asked.

Arya said what no one else would. "Animals."

"The sloop was headed westward," Jai said.

They all followed the direction of his finger. There was nothing more than water in that direction, at least from what Arya could see. Except that was the same direction they had come from after escaping Mortham and stealing the ship.

She swiveled her head back to Jai to find him watching her. When they had swum out of that cave, she had hoped it would be the last time she saw that place. But deep inside, she had known they would return one day.

"Rohan!"

Farah's shout pulled Arya's gaze away in time to hear a splash as Rohan dove into the water.

"Bloody hell," Jai said. "I'll follow him."

Arya rushed to the side just as Jai climbed out onto the rigging and plunged into the waves.

"We have to find Kalyani," Farah said, her gaze locked on the water. "He won't survive otherwise."

"We'll find her."

It wasn't in Arya's nature to make false promises, and even though she hoped they would locate Kalyani, she couldn't shake the feeling that things wouldn't go as planned. They had all been lucky so far. Eventually, that luck would run out.

The vessel started to turn as it got caught in a current. Arya returned to the helm and caught the spinning wheel to hold it straight. Each second felt like an eternity as they waited for Jai and Rohan to surface.

"They're back," Farah shouted as she raced down the ship to lower the ladder over the side.

Rohan was the first to climb up. Farah wrapped her arms around him the instant his feet were on the deck. Arya stared at the rope holding the ladder, waiting to see Jai. She released the breath she had been holding when she spotted his hand, quickly followed by his head. She looped a rope around the helm to keep it in place and made her way to him.

Water dripped from his clothes as he met her halfway. He was out of breath, his white hair slicked back against his head as he shook it. Of course, there had been nothing to find. Kalyani had been here too many hours ago.

"How far down did you go?" Rohan asked.

Jai turned to face him. "As far as I could. I caught a glimpse of the bottom before I had to get air."

"Anything look like an elven city?" Farah asked.

Jai shook his head. "There could have been, but I could only see about twenty feet before me. The deeper you go, the darker it gets."

"I couldn't dive as deep as I'd hoped." Rohan leaned against the side of the ship. "Look around. Kalyani could be anywhere. I may never find her."

Arya grabbed Jai's hand, needing something to hold on to. "She's alive, and she's not with the Masters. Those are two things we can be happy about."

"I should be pleased about that. But I'm not." Rohan straightened and walked to the stairs that would take him down to the sleeping quarters.

Farah patted Jai's arm in thanks and followed Rohan.

Arya waited until they were alone before turning to Jai. "Did you really not see anything?"

"Being down there is worse than a human walking in our world. It's not just the currents and the animals. It's the fact that I can't move properly. Or breathe. If we're going to find Kalyani, we need a Sea Elf to do it."

19

Kalyani sipped on the water, and it tasted so sweet and refreshing that it took everything in her not to gulp it down. But she didn't want to get sick again, so she took it slow. She waited for Nirav to return as she pulled apart tiny pieces of the soft bread he'd left her. Before long, it was gone, as was the water. She waited to see how her stomach would react.

Finally, she decided it was time to get up. She craved a long soak in the tub. Her legs were wobbly when she tested them, and she was far weaker than she had thought, but she made it to the tub without issue. Even her stomach seemed settled.

The hot water did wonders to rejuvenate her as she washed off the effects of her sickness. No matter what she did, the ends of her hair ended up getting wet, but she didn't have the will to care. Once her fingers and toes started to wrinkle, she decided it was time to get out.

By the time she'd dried off and dressed, she was worn out. Kalyani eyed the bed, but she decided to attempt to sit up instead.

If she lay down, she was liable to go to sleep again. She shuffled into the living area and sank onto the sofa. Her gaze landed on the place where Varum had sat. She touched her hair, remembering how he had held it away from her face.

It wasn't something she would have expected from him. Nor was how he had carried her to bed. It almost warmed her heart—except for the fact that all he wanted from her was information. Of course, he would do whatever was needed to keep her healthy so he could get it. Just as she'd started warming to him, she was reminded of why she was in the city against her will.

Kalyani leaned back into the cushion. She longed to hear the waves crashing against the shore, to see the sun rising on the horizon. To run in the sand, bask in the moonlight, and sit with her friends as they ate together.

There was nothing for her to do here but sit and stare at a wall. She didn't like being confined. Her search yesterday had proven that there wasn't a way for her to get out of Varum's home without his or Nirav's help—and neither seemed ready to do that. But if she stayed cooped up too much longer, she just might lose her mind.

Her stomach growled. She pushed to her feet and went in search of more bread. Thankfully, Nirav had left the loaf out on the table. She tore off a piece and put a bite in her mouth as she made her way back to the couch.

Kalyani had just sat when the door flew open. It banged against the opposite wall, and Varum strode toward her angrily. She got to her feet, ready to ask what was wrong, when he was suddenly before her, his hand wrapped around her neck as he drove her backward until she hit a wall. She dropped the bread and gripped his wrist, meeting his gaze. There was very little pressure on her neck, but the threat was clear.

"How many times must I ask?" he ground out, his nostrils flaring. "How many times are you going to withhold information?"

If she weren't so weak from being sick, she'd punch him in the gut. Or kick him. As it was, she didn't think the attempt would do anything but irritate him more. Which was fine, because she was furious. She parted her lips to speak, but he cut her off.

"Don't you dare say you have no idea what I'm talking about," he said, leaning down so that their faces nearly touched.

She simply stared at him. When he slightly squeezed her throat, she narrowed her eyes.

"Speak," he demanded in a dangerously low voice.

"Are you sure? Because you interrupted me last time."

Dark blue sparked in his iridescent blue eyes. "Kalyani," he warned.

"You can't seriously be upset because I said I saw Sea Elves. That has nothing to do with the Masters."

"You don't know that."

"Neither do you!"

He started to say something when his gaze suddenly dropped to her mouth. For a second, her anger dissipated as she realized how close he was. She searched his face for the rage that had been creased into his features, but it was nowhere to be found.

The longer he stared at her lips, the more she struggled to breathe. She didn't understand why she reacted like this. Especially to someone who had firmly planted themselves in the *foe* column.

He was the enemy. And her captor.

But also, her savior.

The elf kept confusing her with his actions. His hand was around her throat. She felt his strength in the fingers encircling her neck. He could snap it with a thought or send a blast of magic into her. Yet his fingers didn't squeeze. He crowded her against a wall, but he hadn't hurt her, even when the thought had clearly crossed his mind. This constant back-and-forth, of not knowing if he was friend or foe, was driving her nuts. And so was staying here twiddling her thumbs, waiting to be released so she could return to her family.

Her gaze lingered on the faint lines around his eyes. She became aware of the heat of his palm against her throat, of the complete control he had over his emotions. There was no way to determine what he might be thinking. Not until she surprised him.

"Kiss me or kill me," she demanded. "But do something."

20

He shouldn't have gotten this close to her. Shouldn't notice the way her chest heaved or how outrage made her brown eyes sparkle. He certainly shouldn't have noticed the nearness of her mouth. But once Varum had, he couldn't look away.

The wrath that had sent him to find her had evaporated once he had her pinned between the wall and himself. This petite human confounded him. He didn't know whether to shake her or shield her. From the moment he had seen her swimming to the boat, he had been captivated by her to the point where he had broken his people's highest law.

He didn't want to find her appealing or feel attraction for her. If he could turn those emotions off, he would do it in a heartbeat. But the longer he stared at her lips, the more those feelings grew and expanded, until he was actually thinking about kissing her.

"Kiss me or kill me. But do something."

Her words cut through the haze, and his gaze jerked to hers.

While her voice had held conviction, her eyes told a different story. Within the brown depths, he saw her uneasiness—and interest. But it was the rapid beat of her pulse against his fingers that told him it wasn't fear that had driven her to lay down such a demand.

It was curiosity.

He found it difficult not to return to staring at that amazing mouth of hers. What would she do if he kissed her? Would she shove him away?

Would she return the kiss?

He was so tempted to find out that he almost gave in to the driving need. *Almost.*

Grudgingly, he straightened. That's when he noticed her hands wound around his wrist. He had been so intent on getting answers —and then being near her—that he hadn't realized her hands were on him. The moment he released her, he knew she would loosen her grip. And for some reason, he didn't want that.

There was no fear in her eyes now. Only defiance. Even in her weakened state, Kalyani refused to be cowed. He wondered if all humans were like her, or if she was an anomaly. He had never been interested in encountering one of her species. However, he was beginning to think he had done himself a great disservice.

Varum relaxed his fingers and began to withdraw his hand. Just as he expected, she released him immediately, leaving his skin prickling with awareness. He dropped his arm to his side, aware that he was still too close to her with thoughts of kisses turning over in his mind.

"So, you can get angry," she said, breaking the silence.

He took two steps back and clasped his hands behind him before curling them into fists. "You say that as if you're surprised."

"I am. You seem made of stone."

If only that were true. It would've made the past bearable. "I owe you an apology. I had no right to put my hands on you."

Apprehension creased her brow. "Anger, and now you're apologizing? That is unexpected."

Why couldn't she just accept that he was sorry? Why did she have to make it into something more? He turned on his heel and walked into the living area. Varum saw the door partially open and regretted allowing his fury to consume him. He should've made sure the door was shut behind him at the very least.

He braced his hand on the door once it was locked and pictured Kalyani's lips. Why did she have to say *kiss*?

"It wasn't on purpose," she said behind him. "If you had only asked, I would've told you that at the beginning."

It took a moment for him to realize she was talking about seeing the Sea Elves, not about kissing. He wanted that word out of his head. More importantly, he wanted to stop thinking about kissing her.

Varum let his hand slide from the door down to his side before facing her. She stood about four steps from him, her expression unreadable. Usually, her thoughts and feelings flashed in her eyes. He didn't like not knowing what she was thinking. "Tell me now."

For a long minute, she studied him. Then she drew in a breath and released it as she crossed her arms over her chest. "I didn't connect spotting the Sea Elves from shore as being part of the Masters. That's why I didn't say anything."

Nirav had said the same thing to him. Why had he gotten so angry then? Why had he stormed out of his office and come straight home to confront her? Just remembering listening to Nirav had Varum's chest tightening as if a band had been wrapped around him. But it was the sharp spike of fear that had eclipsed everything else.

At the time, he had believed it was fear for his people. Now, he wasn't so sure.

"You don't believe me."

He motioned to the sofa. "I do. Please, sit. You're still weak."

For once, she didn't argue. He claimed his couch after she had lowered herself onto hers. They stared at each other as an awkward silence stretched.

"I just saw heads pop up out of the water," she said as she looked away. "I never spoke to them. They disappeared almost immediately anyway."

"Would you be able to recognize them if you saw them again?"

She shook her head, then lifted her gaze to him. "You think the two at the sloop were the same ones?"

"I'm trying to figure that out."

"As I said, I only got a glimpse of them from shore. It could very well have been the same elves, but I can't say for certain. I tried to swim out to them, but they were long gone."

He grunted as he began to relax. "I doubt it. They were likely hiding."

"You can do that?"

"The sea is our home. I imagine there are places you can hide on land."

She twisted her lips. "Good point."

He looked at her throat, trying to see if he had left any marks on her, but her hair was in the way. "Did I...did I hurt you?"

Immediately, she touched her neck. "Nay."

"I am sorry. I won't put my hands on you again without permission."

"To be honest, that display was impressive. A little frightening, but impressive."

He blinked, unsure he had heard her correctly.

"Oh," she said and bent to retrieve something off the floor. She straightened with a mangled piece of bread in hand. "I wondered what'd happened to this."

Varum was on his feet in the next second. "I'll dispose of it," he said, holding out his hand.

She hesitated before placing it on his palm, and to his regret, seemed to make a point *not* to touch him. He walked into the kitchen and threw the bread in the bin. As he turned back, he found his eyes going directly to the back of her head. Then, with a sigh, he found a plate and put another slice of bread on it before pouring some water into a glass and bringing both to her.

"Thank you," she murmured.

Varum should return to work, but he found he didn't want to. He took a seat again. "Are you feeling better?"

"I am. Whatever Nirav gave me seems to have done the trick."

"He's always been like that. If there was a problem I couldn't solve, Nirav had an answer."

She tore off small bits of bread and ate them slowly. "He told me about being sent to the Conclave for five years."

"It's a duty no one wants."

"Because of how everyone treats those sent away?"

Varum nodded. "There are still those who don't fully trust him, despite him being back for over two decades."

"You don't have that problem."

"I think because he was a family friend."

She tucked her legs up and shifted onto one hip. "He had you and your family, then?"

The answer to that would only lead to more questions Varum never liked to think about. "Nirav is likable and charming. He's kind and generous to his friends, but he isn't an elf you want as an enemy. That's why they chose him to go ashore. The Assembly knew he wouldn't be swayed from his duty. And they knew he would return."

"How were they so sure?"

"He was in love with my mother."

21

Kalyani halted mid-chew. "I'm sorry. Did you just say Nirav was in love with your mother?"

"I did," Varum replied with a smile.

"Did your father know?"

He nodded.

"I, ah, I think I'm confused. I thought you said that you lived with Nirav."

"I did."

The more she tried to put the puzzle of his past together, the more confused she became.

Varum chuckled as he glanced down. "I know it sounds strange. Nirav and my father were close friends. When Nirav learned that Dad was interested, he kept his feelings a secret. It was only after my parents wed that Dad confronted him about it. Nirav admitted that he loved her."

"Did they remain friends?"

"Aye. Close friends for a long time, actually."

Kalyani tried to imagine how she would feel if she learned that one of her friends was in love with the same man she was. She wasn't sure she would take it so well. "What did your mum do?"

"I don't think anyone ever told her."

"Is everyone still close?"

The slight tightening around Varum's mouth told her that she'd asked the wrong thing. She was trying to find a way to backtrack or change the subject when he spoke.

"You were right earlier. I could have taken you anywhere to heal you." He twisted his lips and sighed. "I saw you as the answer to all our problems, I suppose. Not only did you know exactly who those on the sloop were, but you also didn't hesitate to attack them. I assumed you knew more than I, and I took advantage of your weakened state."

She lowered her hand to her leg, the last bite of bread forgotten. "Nirav said you never break the rules."

"Don't ask me why I did this time. I can't answer it. I wish I could, because then Nirav would stop asking me."

"There had to be something that pushed you to do something so out of character."

He flashed a halfhearted smile. "Maybe it was seeing you fight."

"I hope it wasn't seeing me injured."

"That probably played a part in it."

Kalyani set the plate on the cushion next to her. "I don't want to be a victim in anyone's eyes. Not my brother's, not yours. Not anyone's."

"I can't imagine anyone calling you a victim."

It was as close to a compliment as she was likely to get. His words spread warmth inside her, and she wasn't sure why that made her feel as good as it did. She stared at him, once more unsure if he was friend or foe. The elf she had thought was cold as stone might just have feelings, after all.

A sharp rap on the door made Varum look away first. She started to rise to go to his room, but he motioned for her to remain as he stood and walked to the door.

"Who is it?" he asked.

"Nirav," came the reply.

Varum unlocked the door and cracked it open to make sure it was only Nirav before stepping aside and allowing his friend to enter. Nirav slipped inside with a strap slung over his shoulder attached to a tube.

A smile split Nirav's face when he saw her. "I'm happy to see you up and about." He glanced at her empty plate. "And eating."

"It's slow, but I'm feeling better," she said, unable to hold back her grin at his pleasure.

Nirav looked between her and Varum and rubbed his hands. "You left in such a rush, I was unsure what I might find when I arrived."

Varum scratched his jaw. "Kalyani explained everything."

"Any chance you could recognize the elves?" Nirav asked her, his brows raised eagerly.

Kalyani shook her head. "I'm sorry, I don't think I can."

"Could you tell if they were male or female?" Varum asked.

She thought back to the fleeting look she had gotten and finally shook her head. "I wouldn't feel right making a guess. The sighting was that quick."

"But you're sure it was a Sea Elf," Nirav asked.

"I am."

Nirav walked to sit next to her and placed the cylinder at his feet. "I've been thinking, ever since you first told me about the sighting, that the elves could've come from anywhere. My immediate assumption was that they were from Tarangarh, but there are other cities."

"How many?" Kalyani asked.

Varum walked to his sofa and sat. "Five."

There were five more cities beneath the water. She wondered how many others knew that. It must not be a secret if Varum shared the information so nonchalantly.

"I would need to know the location of your village to determine if there is a city nearby," Nirav said.

She shrugged helplessly. "I wouldn't even know how to describe where it is."

"I thought you might say that," Nirav said. He reached for the cylinder and opened it. "That's why I stopped by my place and grabbed a couple of maps, just in case. That's why it took me so long to get back here."

Kalyani glanced at Varum to find him watching her. It had never dawned on her that she might be in this predicament, so she had never thought to ask if she shouldn't tell potential allies of their location. She would have to make the decision on her own.

Nirav rolled out a map on the coffee table as she scooted to the edge of the couch, and Varum placed objects on the corners to hold it open. Kalyani looked over the map, surprised to see such a detailed drawing of the shoreline. She dropped to her knees on the floor and leaned close as she oriented herself with the map.

From a distance, she had seen the giant elven faces carved into the plateau with their mouths open to let water flow. From what Farah had told her, the carvings ran the entire length of the mesa. Kalyani had never gotten close enough to make out the exact features of the carvings, but she knew to find the last one that faced the ocean.

From there, she traced her finger along the shore, looking for anything on the map that looked familiar. She was about to give up when she spotted the slight indent of the shoreline where she had grown up.

Nothing on the map designated the location, but she knew it all the same. To think that the village she had lived in for the majority of her life lay right there, hidden from all. Her ancestors had chosen that location because it was secluded and difficult to reach. She and Rohan might have left it, but their younger sister and many other villagers still called it home.

She had offered for Varum to follow her home to talk to Rohan and the others. How was that any different than pointing out a spot on a map? It wasn't. But she still couldn't shake off the feeling that she was making the wrong choice.

Kalyani realized how quiet it was and sat back, aware of the two elves watching her. She reached for her water to take a drink and buy some time to think of a reply.

"We have no designs on your people," Varum said. "I've given you no reason to trust me, but I speak the truth."

Nirav nodded, sighing. "Whatever we discuss stays between us three. I merely need an area."

"Are there many cities so close to Shecrish's shore?" she asked.

Varum braced his forearms on his knees. "Nay."

"It's all right. I shouldn't have pressed you." Nirav moved aside one of the placeholders to start rolling up the map, when she put her hand on it. His gaze jerked to her.

Kalyani's heart was pounding as she slowly moved her finger and pointed to the spot. "There."

Nirav replaced the weight and squinted as he leaned forward for a closer look. She removed her hand when he gently tapped it. He stared at the map for several tense minutes before looking up at Varum.

"What is it?" she asked when neither said anything.

Varum tapped a spot northeast of the shoreline, far out into the water. "This is the closest city."

"Would a Sea Elf swim that far?" she asked.

Nirav shrugged. "Depends. We've been known to do that."

"Is there anything special about your city?" Varum asked.

"Village," she corrected. "And not really. We're small and secluded. It was built only for humans."

Varum quirked a brow. "Really?"

"Interesting," Nirav replied. "I wondered if there would be places like that."

"Why would there be?" Varum asked.

Kalyani shifted into a cross-legged seat. "Because elves notoriously abuse and use us because we don't have magic."

"I saw that firsthand during my time on land," Nirav said. "I had forgotten about it until you said something."

She was incensed that he would say such a thing, but then she remembered that Sea Elves didn't mingle with humans at all. They probably never even thought about her race. It was hard to stay angry at someone for something they didn't take part in.

"You've really not been around elves?" Varum asked.

She gave an exasperated shake of her head. "You didn't believe me?"

"Not about that."

"Until Rohan brought Farah to Siguk, I had only seen elves from a distance."

Nirav caught her gaze. "How did you keep hidden?"

"The way our village is built into the side of the plateau keeps us concealed."

Varum grunted in approval. "That was smart."

"I still wonder what made Sea Elves show themselves," Nirav said, more to himself than Varum or her.

She went back to studying the map until she found her new home—Serenia. It was north, where the mountains reached the water. If Siguk had been secluded, Serenia was isolated.

"If that's where you live, then you swam an incredible distance to the sloop," Varum said.

Kalyani shook her head. "I don't live there anymore. Rohan and the others decided to live away from anyone since they're being hunted by the Masters, and I joined them, intending to do my part."

"Your brother allowed that?" Varum questioned.

She didn't care for the disapproval she saw in his eyes. "I didn't give him a choice. I can be somewhat stubborn."

Nirav settled more comfortably on the cushion. "I'm sure Rohan thought having you close would keep you out of trouble."

A lot of good that did. Kalyani was in a heap of trouble. There would be time to make it up to her brother. She would make sure of it.

"Where did you swim from, then?" Varum asked.

She had been anxious about sharing Siguk's location. No way would she tell him where Serenia was.

"The shoreline is rather long," Nirav said. "They could've relocated anywhere."

Varum shook his head and pointed toward the northernmost part of Shecrish's shoreline. "They're hiding. No way they would go south when there isn't much to keep them concealed. They went north."

Kalyani swallowed, the sound loud to her ears. She didn't know how he had figured that out. Did he know the shoreline? It made sense that he might, even if he didn't go onto the land.

"Am I right?" he asked her.

She hesitated, but given his smile, that was answer enough. It was gone in a flash when he took a closer look at where she had swum from. His gaze snapped to her, fury sparking in his iridescent eyes.

"Do you know what could've happened to you swimming alone that far?" Varum demanded. "I'm not talking about just the animals. I'm talking about other Sea Elves. And even storms. Anything could've happened to you."

"You sound like Rohan."

"Apparently, he didn't do a good enough job of reminding you of the dangers," Varum stated.

Nirav looked up from the map, his eyes filled with distress. "Surely, you must have known you went far beyond the shore."

Kalyani was suddenly uncomfortable, as if she were about to get reprimanded. Not even Rohan made her feel so small and ashamed. "I lose track when I'm in the water."

ozens of questions filled Varum's mind and nearly fell from his tongue. He managed to hold them back, only because now wasn't the time to delve into that. Kalyani was being cagey enough about where she lived. She wouldn't divulge anything personal now.

"Have you noticed those two elves, or others, while you were swimming?" Nirav asked.

She shook her head and nervously took a drink of water.

"That doesn't mean they didn't see you." Varum met Nirav's gaze. "They could've followed her to shore."

Nirav pulled a face. "That's what I was thinking. And they breached the surface to see her."

Varum slid his gaze to Kalyani.

"That means they know where the others live." Kalyani used the table to get to her feet. "I need to warn Rohan."

Nirav lifted his face to her. "It may already be too late."

"I refuse to believe that. You both promised to release me. I need to get home. Now," she implored.

Varum caught her gaze and tried to reassure her. "We will."

"When?" she pressed.

Nirav pulled out another map and unrolled it, laying it on top of the first. Varum watched Kalyani study it. She was smart. It wouldn't take her long to realize it was a map of the trench.

"I've been considering how to get you out," Nirav said. His lips flattened briefly as he sighed. "It isn't going to be easy."

Varum pointed to a location on the right. "What about here?"

"The currents shifted three days ago. You'll never be able to swim through that carrying Kalyani," Nirav said.

Varum nodded. "Right. I forgot. It's a good thing I didn't try to come through that way."

"What about here?" Nirav asked and tapped a location to the south.

That was no good either. "Additional sentries are patrolling there because of an increase in *shalorin*. What about here?"

Nirav gave a quick shake of his head. "That would take you too close to Assembly Hall."

"Then I go back the way I brought Kalyani in."

Nirav sat back and released a breath. "We've already established that it's too out in the open."

"That only leaves one option," Varum said.

Kalyani looked between them. "I take it by your expressions that it isn't a good choice."

"There are considerable dangers," Nirav said.

Varum stared at the map, tracing the direction he would need to swim with his eyes. "I've taken that route before."

"Not carrying someone while using your magic. You barely

made it home, taking one of the easiest routes. You won't make it to shore using this one," Nirav replied.

Kalyani dropped onto the sofa. "What do you mean he nearly didn't make it?"

"It was nothing," Varum stated.

At the same time, Nirav said, "The cost of using his magic to keep you from being crushed by the pressure sapped his strength. Had both of you been out any longer, you'd both have died."

"Oh," she mumbled in shock as she flattened her hands together before holding them between her knees. She clearly had no idea it had been that close for both of them.

Varum squeezed the bridge of his nose with his thumb and forefinger. "Kalyani needs to get home, and we need to get her out of the city. The sooner, the better. I understand the dangers."

"I don't think you do," Nirav replied, his voice clipped with worry. "It's a miracle you reached the city in the first place."

Fear bracketed Kalyani's mouth as she asked, "Are you telling me I can't leave?"

"I got you here. I'll get you home," Varum promised.

Nirav slammed his hand on the table and lifted silvery white eyes to Varum. "Wait until the currents shift again. You can swim inside them then, and they'll spit you out safely on the other side of the trench."

"How long until they change?" she asked.

Varum dropped his head. It was the safer option for him, but also for Kalyani. The sight of her distress in wanting to return to her family made him think of all the times he'd waited for his parents to come for him in his youth.

"How long?" Kalyani repeated.

Varum lifted his head and met her gaze. "Three weeks."

She deflated, as if every last bit of hope had been sucked out of her. "Oh."

One word, whispered in a voice filled with despair. And yet that one word wrecked him. He never should've brought her to the city. It was the first time he had made such an error, and the impact continued to ripple outward. How many more would be affected by that one choice? He was almost afraid to find out.

"We leave tonight," Varum stated.

Nirav straightened and started to speak, his face mottled with anger, but he held his tongue when Varum cut him a look.

"I can't ask you to risk your life like that," Kalyani said.

Varum shrugged. "You're not asking me to do anything. Besides, I'm responsible for you being here. I gave you my word that I would release you once you gave me everything on the Masters. I'm merely holding up my end of the bargain."

"This is reckless, Varum." Nirav shook his head in disgust. "You're never so careless."

"I'm righting a wrong." He hoped Nirav would leave it at that, because there wasn't anything else to say on the matter. Varum returned his attention to the map. "I've been thinking about how the Masters are using ships to move some of the abducted. It would help if we knew where they were taking them. Maybe after I return Kalyani, I'll do some looking around."

Nirav pushed back to sit straight against the cushions. "What about your job?"

"I'll take a few days' leave."

"Varum—"

"Enough. I'm doing this," Varum announced. "Help us or don't but stop trying to change my mind."

Nirav dipped his chin in defeat. "I'll cover for you here, then.

There is a better map that shows that area of the trench. I'll go get it now."

Varum stared at the floor once his friend had left. It never felt good to fight with Nirav. It occurred so rarely that Varum was always left shaken by it.

"Is it as dangerous as Nirav says?"

For a moment, he had forgotten that Kalyani was in the room. Varum looked her way and nodded. "It is, but I've swum it before."

"Not using your magic to protect someone, though."

"You don't need to worry. I'll get us through."

She looked around nervously. "What exactly is dangerous about it?"

"The trench is wide, as well as deep. Right now, we're along one wall of it. There are coral outcroppings and rock formations. The area we're going to is a narrow section known for its rapidly changing currents that move alongside each other. If we get caught in one, it could toss us against the coral."

"And?" she pressed.

He shouldn't have been surprised that she would want to know everything. "*Shalorin* call that area home."

"*Shalorin*?" she asked with a frown.

"They're serpent creatures that live within the coral. They're very aggressive and highly toxic. One bite can kill."

Her dark eyes widened. "We'll be dodging currents and *shalorin*?"

"I will be."

"And what will I be doing? Won't it help if I'm swimming, too?"

Varum shook his head. "I need to be able to swim without worrying about you."

"Surely, you aren't actually thinking about carrying me?"

"I am."

Her mouth fell open in shock. "That's ridiculous. I'm a good swimmer."

"Maybe. But you've never faced these currents or the *shalorin*. Not to mention, my magic will be surrounding you. It's easier if you're against me."

"That's going to make it harder for you."

He found his gaze drawn to a curl brushing her jawline. "I can do it."

"Would the other way be better? The one three weeks from now?"

"A tad easier, aye."

She pressed her lips together and looked away. "Three weeks."

"There's no need for you to wait. You need to return, and the longer you're here, the greater the chance you'll be discovered."

Varum opened the door after Nirav knocked and announced himself. His friend rolled up the other two maps before laying out the new one. The three of them leaned over the table, peering at the detailed drawing of that section of the trench.

"Where are we coming from?" Kalyani asked.

Nirav tapped on the map. "We're here. The eastern, outermost building of the city."

"This may be a silly question, but why can't we just swim up?" she asked.

Varum braced his hands on the coffee table. "It isn't silly. You have no way of knowing that Tarangarh is heavily patrolled, especially the area directly above us."

"Since you two can't take that route, Varum will swim you both along the wall, angled toward the surface for a period before he'll need to dive several meters to get around the dangerous currents," Nirav said. "Those currents aren't easy to navigate, and they change in a blink."

Kalyani's frown was deepening as Nirav spoke. "How will we tell where the currents are?"

"I'll be able to see them," Varum said.

She tilted her head to the side. "You can see them?"

"It is something all Sea Elves can do. How do you think we navigate in the water so well?" Nirav asked. "Anyway, he'll have to go under the strongest section and then swim between them in order to get to the gap in the rocks. The problem then becomes the *shalorin*. They live among the coral and are fed by what the current brings to them."

Kalyani tucked her hair behind her ear. "And once we get through that? Are we safe?"

Nirav shot her a halfhearted smile. "The worst part will be over, but Varum will still need to swim through the trench."

"And all the while, I'm just supposed to sit there and let you do all the work?" Kalyani asked him.

Varum looked up from the map. "You are. When we get a safe distance away, where I know the sentries won't see us, I'll head toward the surface. Once the pressure is safe for you, I'll withdraw my magic and let you swim on your own."

"Then I'll take you to my brother. But that means you'll have to come onto land."

Varum hadn't thought about that. It would be his first time stepping onto soil while breathing air. If Nirav could do it for five years, he could manage it for a few hours. "Do you think your friends will talk to me?"

"They will after I assure them that you aren't with the Masters."

Nirav rubbed a hand along the back of his neck. "They'll be cautious, and Rohan will likely take offense that you took his sister."

"I'll plead my case," Varum said. "If that's all, we need to prepare."

Nirav climbed to his feet. "Are you sure I can't talk you out of this?"

"You worry too much. I'll be back before you know it," Varum said and clapped his friend on the shoulder.

"What about you?" Nirav asked Kalyani as he turned to her. "How are you feeling?"

She gave him a warm smile. "Much better."

Varum was concerned that she was still weak, but he would be doing most of the swimming anyway. He watched her talking to Nirav, his gaze drawn to her mouth. He'd had the opportunity to kiss her, and he had let it slip through his fingers.

It was foolish for him to wonder what her lips tasted like. She was a human and not allowed in Tarangarh. It wasn't as if they could ever have any kind of relationship. Whatever reckless behavior had led him to bring her here was coming to an end. He'd take the information he got on the Masters and ensure that his people were safe.

Maybe one day, Kalyani's face would fade from his memories.

23

Reader Temple

Incense smoke floated through the air like ribbons dancing in the wind, leaving the room heavy with the scents of heated honey and clean air after a rain. Savita had hoped that burning the hardened, amber-gold resin of the *solleaf* tree would ease the tension she hadn't been able to shake. But not even her favorite incense worked today.

She rose, ignoring the fresh cup of tea she had just poured, and walked to her dressing table. Her fingers trailed along the top before she sank onto the stool and stared at herself in the mirror. The first time she had drawn the gold sun on her forehead, marking her as a Reader, had been a day of celebration and joy.

Readers were warned never to ask the runes about their future, but of course, all of them did. The runes hadn't given her any answers about her own life, but they had warned her about Esha's.

Now, her sister was mated to a Dragon King and living among them, far from Shecrish. Where did that leave her?

Savita picked up the small brush with the pointed bristles and, with meticulous care, dipped it into the bottle of gold paint before drawing a thin line from the outer corner of each eye to her temple. Once that was done, she cleaned the brush and set it aside before finding the larger one and marking each collarbone with five gold dots.

Only after the second brush was clean and carefully stored with the others did she cap the bottle of paint. She glided her hands down each side of her head from the part of her tawny hair down the middle, ensuring that not a single strand that fell to the middle of her back was out of place. With a sigh, she stood and straightened the long, flowing, white sleeveless gown that was the uniform of the Readers. The only color came from the golden belt at her waist and the golden stole she diligently draped over each arm, adjusting it so the ends reached the hem of her dress.

Winter was upon Shecrish. No matter how large the fire in the hearth was, it never fully chased away the chill. The land slept during the cold months, slumbering through the snow and ice. How she wished she could join in. Her heart was heavy, and she wasn't sure why.

She turned her head toward the table where she had laid out the square black cloth from her last reading. She hadn't touched the runes after they fell from her hands the night before. Before she realized it, she stood in front of the table, looking down at the runes. The message was still the same.

He's coming.

They could be warning her about anyone. The fact that their message was so ambiguous only made her worry grow. It had upset her so much that she had left the runes and promptly gone to bed. But there hadn't been any sleep. She had tossed and turned all night, her brain sorting through people and conversations, trying to glean who it might be.

Savita gathered all twenty-eight of the white runes with their gold markings and cupped them in her hands. "I need to know more. A face. A name. Something," she implored. "You've never let me down. Help me in my quest to best the Masters."

She closed her eyes and held the runes close to her before extending her arms and releasing her hands. The runes clattered against the cloth and scattered before coming to rest. Her mouth fell open when she read the same message.

He's coming.

"Who?" she begged.

A sharp rap against her door interrupted the reading. She closed her eyes and dropped her head back for a heartbeat. She could ignore whoever it was. No one would force their way inside. Besides, she wasn't in the mood for company.

Another knock came, and her eyes went to the runes. Could it be who they predicted? She turned her head to the door and stared at it as if she could see through the thick plank of wood. The third knock got her moving. She put her hand on the knob but hesitated as a tremor of warning ran down her spine. Savita yanked open the door and found herself staring at a Star Elf. She was instantly drawn to the deep purple of his eyes. His gaze was intense and bold. Still.

"I've been looking for you," he said.

The hair on her body stood on end as his voice brushed against her senses, low and even—a vibration that lingered in the air long after the words were gone. Each word landed like a strike of flint

—controlled, deliberate, and threaded with something she couldn't name. Not charm. Not authority. Something older, quieter.

Her fingers tightened on the door as she debated whether to slam it in his face. This stranger spelled danger in every way, but she couldn't look away from his mesmerizing gaze. His presence filled the room, and he hadn't even taken a step inside.

He bowed his head, breaking their eye contact. The top portion of his long, silver hair was fastened at the back of his head, the ends falling forward over his shoulders. He remained in the bow, waiting. It was a sign of respect that she hadn't seen in some time.

"Rise," she bade.

He slowly straightened, giving her time to take in his features. Sharp cheekbones sat high and stern with a defined chin. The angle of his jaw was almost architectural, as though sculpted for precision rather than softness. His mouth was a contradiction. The upper lip was firm and controlled. The lower, just full enough to betray the softness. It wasn't a handsome face. It was one of predatory beauty. A type of elegance that was impossible to forget.

He was lean and tall. His shoulders broad, his posture straight. He exuded a quiet confidence. Elegant, sharp, and timeless. Every movement was measured. Controlled. Tempered like steel, folded to create the sharpest blade.

She found herself gazing into his purple eyes once more. Their stillness was hypnotic, and she found herself wondering what thoughts might be going through his mind. There was restraint in every inch of him, which was why her heart missed a beat at the sight of the slight curve of his lips—as if he knew she liked what she saw.

"Why have you sought me out?" she demanded.

His smile grew at her icy tone. "Allow me inside, and I'll tell you."

This was a pivotal moment. She could shut the door and forget him. She'd never see him again with that kind of reaction. If she allowed him inside, there would be no turning back. No matter what had brought him to her door, no matter what he shared, she could never erase it. She thought about the runes' message and the request she'd made. Was he the one they had alerted her about? Could he be someone who could help her against the Masters?

Savita pushed the door wide and dropped her arm to her side. He walked past her with a quiet certainty. She turned with him as the faint shimmer of his tunic caught the sunlight. Clothing always told a story, but his wasn't so easy to discern. His clothing was neither rich nor humble. Layers of silk and fine cotton in indigo, deep pewter, and silver covered him, without being ornamental. As if every thread and fold had been chosen with purpose.

He stopped next to her table of runes. She closed the door and watched as he looked over the stones. After a moment, he looked around her rooms before finally turning to face her. Even from across the space, she felt the silence surrounding him.

"Do you know who I am?" he asked.

His words—measured, low, and unfathomably calm—filled the space between them. "Should I?"

"I thought the runes might have told you."

She glanced at the table, preferring not to confirm or deny anything. "Who are you?"

"Someone who can help."

"With what?"

Those amazing lips of his curved slightly again. "I wondered if I would like this banter between us. I confess, I do."

His reply took her aback, leaving her wordless.

He issued a soft snort. "You aren't at all what I expected."

"Is that a compliment?"

"It is."

She tried to look away from his gaze but found she couldn't. "Who are you?"

"Someone who can help."

"You've already said that. Tell me what you want to help with."

His smile vanished as he took a step toward her. "The problem you're attempting to solve."

"I'm afraid you'll have to be more specific."

"You don't want me to do that."

Silence lengthened between them. Savita had stood before many individuals who wielded power and control like weapons, but they paled in comparison to the elf before her. He was something altogether different, and it both frightened and thrilled her.

He took another step closer. "This is a one-time offer. I won't extend it again."

"I would be the greatest kind of fool to accept whatever it is you're proposing without knowing specifics."

"It's prudent of you to be wary," he replied.

She lifted her foot, ready to walk toward him, and only stopped herself at the last second. "And still, you tell me nothing."

"I've told you a great deal."

Savita lifted a brow. "Is that so?"

He took another step. "It is. Would you feel better if you read the runes?"

"Is that why you came here? For a reading? I don't do that."

"I did not," he said with a single shake of his head. "There's no need to read what I already know."

She was surprised by his statement, only to realize that another Reader must have looked into his life. "Since you won't tell me your name or the reason you've offered to help, I must ask you to leave."

"That's a pity. I took you for someone much smarter than that."

His gaze moved over her shoulder as he headed toward the door. The absence of his intense attention made it feel as if a shadow had swallowed her. Yet it was also a relief since her lungs loosened enough for her to breathe.

She told herself not to move as he headed toward her, but her eyes wouldn't obey. Then he halted beside her, so close his arm brushed her shoulder. She turned her head to meet his gaze and was consumed by it. The color wasn't simply a dark purple. His eyes were a violet so deep it bordered on darkness with faint strands of luminous lavender within.

"You need to be careful," he warned.

"Did the Mas—?"

"Savita," he said over her, eyes narrowed dangerously. "Don't speak of them."

She faced him then. "Who are you?"

He sighed and looked toward the door. "I already told you. I came to help."

"Why should I trust you?"

"You shouldn't trust anyone." He glanced at her, a subtle smile playing at one corner of his mouth.

Was she a fool to consider hearing him out? Maybe. But then she had asked the runes for help. "Why do you want to help me? You could go to anyone."

"I could." He looked at her. "But I chose you."

"Why?"

He shrugged, his lips twisting. "Call it a hunch."

"This could be a trap."

"It could be. Or I could be the one person who could tip the scales in your favor."

She walked to the runes and gathered them once more before dropping them. She stared down at the answer for a long time.

"What did they tell you?" he asked.

Savita looked his way. "I accept your offer."

24

It was really happening. She was going home. Kalyani could barely contain her excitement. Just when she had thought she might never see her brother again, Varum had proven he was an elf of his word. Maybe he did deserve to be in the *friend* column, after all.

She wanted to leave right that minute, but there were preparations to make. Nirav left to get something, and Varum departed a short while later, saying he had to wrap up a few things. That left her alone again. Kalyani looked around Varum's home with different eyes now. It was no longer a prison but an extension of him.

Her time in Tarangarh had been brief, and she hadn't seen much of the city, but she had learned a lot about the Sea Elves. She found herself standing in front of the shelves, eyeing the trinkets and books. There was a beautiful seashell with vibrant colors, sitting in the middle of one shelf. It was the largest one she had ever laid eyes on. She tried to imagine where Varum might have found it and what made him cherish it enough to display it on his shelves. Try as she might, she couldn't see the elf she knew carrying such a thing to his home. It made her want to know the story behind it.

Maybe even know more about the elf, too.

The longer she looked, the more she realized it might have been a gift. That instantly brought Tanira to mind. She hadn't seen the female, but Kalyani suspected she was probably stunning. An elf like Varum wouldn't be with anyone else.

"As if I know him." Kalyani snorted.

Her thoughts shifted to when his hand had been wrapped around her throat, and his face a breath from hers. She was back there in an instant, pressed against the wall, the ends of his blue-black hair resting against her as the long strands fell over his shoulders. His anger had been palpable, and while his initial appearance had ignited a spark of fear at first, it had quickly dissipated when he didn't hurt her.

Instead, he had stared at her mouth for so long that it made her acutely aware of her lips—and what it might be like to have *his* pressed against hers. The yearning to know the feel of his mouth was so overwhelming that she had begun to hope he would kiss her as she had challenged.

Instead, he released her.

The quick way he had moved away was a reminder that she was a human—something Sea Elves abhorred. Why would Varum even consider kissing her? He had made it clear from the beginning that the only thing he wanted from her was information.

She wrapped her arms around herself and turned. Her gaze landed on the wall in his bedroom, where she had stood trapped between it and Varum. If she had been bolder, she might have pulled his head down and kissed him herself. She was bold in many aspects of her life, but when it came to romance, she had always felt unsteady. As if the ground she walked on was waiting to trip her. The fear of rejection was too great to attempt such a gesture.

Her attraction was a moot point anyway. It wasn't as if there could ever be anything between them. She couldn't remain in the city, and he wouldn't leave the water. Yet she couldn't shake off the sadness of knowing she would never see Varum again.

She snorted. How ridiculous. He was cold and aloof. Detached. She couldn't hold on to those thoughts, though, as she recalled how he had gently held her hair and wiped her face when she was sick, or the way he had carried her to bed. Perhaps he wasn't as stony as she believed.

"It doesn't matter," she whispered. "I shouldn't care. I don't care. I don't."

Who cared if he was risking his life to get her home? He was the one who had dragged her to the city without her permission in the first place. He should put his life on the line.

Kalyani closed her eyes and turned her head away. The thought of him getting injured just so she could go home didn't sit well. Did she wait, then? That was three more weeks of Rohan being distressed and time spent hiding in Varum's home, hoping no one discovered her presence. Three more weeks of being near him.

There was no guarantee that waiting meant either of them would stay out of danger either. The mere fact that Varum had brought her to the city had made both of them a threat to everyone else. If she remained even an hour more, there was a chance that Varum and Nirav would be caught aiding her and their lives taken. It was best if she left Tarangarh as soon as possible.

The sound of the handle clicking had her eyes snapping open as she whirled to face the door as it swung open, and Varum filled the entryway. He paused when his gaze landed on her. For a heartbeat, they stared at each other.

"Everything all right?" he asked.

She nodded and attempted a smile. "Of course."

"You're eager to get home, I suppose." He shut and locked the door behind him.

"I'm more concerned about Rohan. It will take me some time to make up for what I've done to him."

Varum slowly walked to the coffee table. "He'll forgive you once he sees you."

"I'm not sure I should be forgiven so easily. I did the one thing he asked me not to do."

"If you hadn't, I wouldn't have met you."

Why did her heart skip a beat at those words? Then she recalled that it was about the Masters, not her. "Rohan and the others will be able to give you more details about the Masters."

He dropped the map in the tube and faced her. "You think I'm talking about the information. Of course," he murmured as he looked away. "I did say that repeatedly." His gaze slid back to her. He stared at her for a long moment and then said, "I meant I wouldn't have met *you*."

Once more, her heart skipped a beat. She found it difficult to breathe as she stared into his eyes. "I'm just a human."

"You're not *just* anything."

Why was he saying such things? Did he know that she clung to each word as if it were life itself?

"Kalyani," he said, taking a step toward her. "I have no right to ask, especially with how I've treated you, but...will you tell me about your gi—"

The last word was drowned out by loud knocking. Then Nirav shouted through the door, "Varum, are you home? Don't leave us waiting out here."

"Us?" Kalyani mouthed to Varum.

His lips flattened as he motioned for her to get into the bedroom. He followed her and grasped the handle of the door. Just before he closed it, he put a finger to his lips. She looked around the room, wondering if she should hide. The sounds of voices drew her to the door as her curiosity got the best of her. It was easy to pick up Nirav's voice, but his laugh sounded strained, nervous, even. She realized why in the next heartbeat when she heard the soft, slightly seductive feminine voice.

"Leaving work early isn't your style, Varum," Tanira said.

Kalyani dropped her forehead against the wall and sighed. She wouldn't be able to return home as long as Tanira was here.

"I explained to her that I asked you to take the afternoon," Nirav replied with another forced laugh.

The long stretch of silence made Kalyani want to crack open the door and get a look at Varum's face. Not that he let his emotions show. She turned her head to the side and pressed her ear toward the door.

"What brings you here?" Varum finally asked.

Kalyani was disappointed that there was no frustration or annoyance in his tone. In fact, he was being spectacularly polite. And that irritated her. He should be shooing Tanira out, not being nice.

"You sure don't make it easy on a gal," Tanira purred. "You may have given up on us, but I haven't."

Nirav was quick to say, "That isn't the case at all. Sometimes, these things just don't work out."

"Perhaps I should've played hard to get instead of pursuing Varum as hard as I did."

Varum said, "You can have anyone. Why do you want me?"

Kalyani rolled her eyes. She knew exactly why Tanira wanted him. Because *he* didn't chase *her* as others likely did.

"Do you really need to ask that?" Tanira snorted. "Come, Varum. You know I love you. You're putting off the inevitable."

"Is my future already decided, then?"

Kalyani winced at the hard edge in his voice. Tanira's comment hadn't sat well, and Kalyani didn't blame him one bit.

"Of course. The moment I chose you for my future husband," Tanira replied. There was rustling, and then she said, "Join me on the sofa like you used to."

Nirav cleared his throat too loudly. "We were actually on our way out."

"Where are you going? Perhaps I'll join you," Tanira said.

"Maybe next time," Nirav told her. "I've not spent quality time with Varum in a while, and I'd like him all to myself today."

"I hope whatever you two have planned is within the city," Tanira said.

Varum's voice was deceptively calm when he asked, "Why?"

"I went looking for you at your office and saw the report you were writing," the female began.

"You snooped through my things?" Varum demanded, his words low and deadly.

There was no mistaking the barely leashed rage in his voice this time. Kalyani almost felt sorry for Tanira.

"It was going to my father anyway. What's the big deal?" Tanira asked.

Kalyani imagined the reply was accompanied by a shrug.

"That was an invasion of privacy," Nirav stated indignantly.

Tanira barked a laugh. "You two need to lighten up. I merely informed my father of the report before Varum handed it over. How is that an invasion of privacy?"

"You went into my office and dug around on my desk," Varum answered. "I know that, because the report wasn't on top. It was in a drawer."

"If you would just open up to me, I wouldn't have to go digging to find out anything," Tanira snapped. "Why are you always shutting me out? I'm trying to help you."

Kalyani was practically plastered against the door, trying to hear every word. The longer the silence stretched, the more she longed to see the reactions of those in the room. Except she couldn't. She had to stay behind the door. Which was proving more difficult than she expected.

Varum released a breath. "We're no longer together."

"You shut me out before you ended things. If you would just let me in, you would see how great we could be," Tanira pleaded.

"Why did you take the report to Arvind?" Varum asked, changing the subject.

"It seemed important."

Nirav said, "That wasn't your place, Tanira."

"Nor was the report finished," Varum added. "I had other things I wanted to include."

Tanira made a sound in the back of her throat. "So, write another one with the new additions."

"You're missing the point," Varum replied.

The fact that Varum's voice rose slightly told Kalyani just how incensed he was. She couldn't blame him either. She didn't know whether Tanira was purposefully being dense or if she really was that clueless, but neither benefited her. Or Kalyani.

"You're really upset?" Tanira asked, then huffed loudly. "Your report got the attention you wanted. More patrols have been added all around the city. No one will be getting in or out without being seen."

Kalyani jerked back from the door, unable to believe what she had just heard. Her reunion with Rohan was slipping through her fingers.

Disbelief churned within Varum as he stared at Tanira. Did she know about Kalyani? Had she turned in his report early to get the patrols in place so he couldn't take the human home? Or was it merely a coincidence?

"I think it's time for you to leave," Nirav told Tanira as he opened the door.

She raised a brow before swinging her gaze to Varum. He knew by her look that she'd expected him to take her side. He didn't know why he had for as long as he had, but he was done. With her, and whatever it was she wanted them to be.

"Please go," he bade.

Tanira gaped at him. "Are you really telling me to leave?"

"I think it's for the best, before I say something we'll both regret."

She slammed her hands down on the sofa before shooting to her feet. "I think it's too late for that."

Varum watched as she stormed out of his home. Nirav softly

closed the door behind her before turning to the bedroom. Varum dropped his chin to his chest. He wasn't looking forward to informing Kalyani that she wouldn't be going home. He didn't want to see the disappointment in her eyes or the sadness that would etch itself into her face.

Nirav walked to him and said in a low voice, "I'll tell her."

"Nay," Varum said, grabbing his friend before he could walk away. "I will. I'm responsible."

"This isn't your fault."

"Isn't it? I'm the one who brought her here. I'm the one who didn't hide the report well enough."

Nirav shot him a stern look. "That isn't on you. Tanira had no business being in your office."

"What's done is done." Varum turned to the bedroom. He wished he didn't have to be the one to crush Kalyani's hope, but there was no getting around it. "I can't change it. I can only try to make sure what happens next is to Kalyani's benefit."

"How are you going to do that?"

Varum shrugged. "I wish I knew."

"Let me know what I can do."

"You've done more than enough already," Varum said as he looked at Nirav. "It's best if you stay away from us from now on, in case something happens. I don't want you linked to me."

Nirav snorted as he grabbed the cylinder of maps and slung it over his shoulder. "Too damn bad. I'm linked, and I'm just fine with that. Do what you need to do here. I'm going to make sure Tanira doesn't double back and return." He paused and looked at the bedroom again. "Be gentle."

Varum locked the front door once Nirav was gone and then made his way to the bedroom. He lifted his hand but paused. They had been so close to getting Kalyani home. He sighed before lightly rapping his knuckles against the wood. The seconds stretched as he waited for a response. Finally, he opened the door and peeked inside to find her standing in front of the window, giving him a view of her profile.

She stood stoically, her arms crossed. He wanted to wrap his arms around her and...and what, exactly? They weren't friends. They were barely past enemies. He shook his head, unsure of what he was thinking. Ever since he'd met her, rational thought had deserted him.

"You don't need to say anything," she said. "I heard it all."

He winced at the acceptance in her voice. It felt as if fate were conspiring against them, and while he hated to see her miserable, he was surprised to find that he was glad she was staying. Varum pushed the door wide and walked toward her.

He was two steps from her when he realized that he was actually thinking about comforting her and halted. "I'm sorry. I had no idea that Tanira would go through my desk."

"She's desperate for your attention. Of course, she's going to do whatever it takes to help you." Kalyani swiveled her head to him. "Surely, you know that."

"We're over. She should stop."

Her gaze returned to the window. "As long as she has hope, she won't stop. She loves you."

"She loves what she can't have. That's all it is."

"Maybe."

He shifted his feet, growing more uncomfortable the longer the conversation continued. He'd thought he would find Kalyani in tears, begging him to take her home. He should've known better. She was unlike anyone he had ever met before. "Why are we talking about her?"

"Because there's no reason to talk about leaving. We both know that isn't happening."

"Today. The patrols will eventually lighten."

She dropped her arms and faced him. "You wanted the patrols to ensure the safety of your people. You must have done a good job of explaining the threat the Masters posed, and if it's as good as I think it is, those patrols won't stop until the Masters are defeated."

He didn't want to worry about someone finding Kalyani. He'd made a mistake, and he was trying to rectify it. If everyone would just get out of his way. "I'll find a way to get you home. I gave you my word," he said.

Her smile was fleeting. "Is there somewhere else I can hide until then? I'm sure you would like your home to yourself again."

"You're not going anywhere."

Even he was surprised by the force of his words.

She briefly lowered her gaze to the floor. "Go back to work. If you keep leaving, you'll draw suspicion. That won't be good for either of us."

"I'm not leaving you in this state."

"What state? What can I possibly do?" she asked, her anger deepening with every word. "Stalk into the bathroom? Maybe stomp my feet as I go into the kitchen?"

Varum fisted his hands, so he didn't reach for her. He was the last one she wanted touching her. "I'll fix this."

She started to walk past him when he suddenly clasped her arm to stop her. Their gazes met, and the sadness he had dreaded seeing was clear in her dark eyes. But it was the despair he glimpsed that was like a sucker punch to his gut.

"I gave you my word. I'll keep it," he promised.

"Why do you care what I think?"

He couldn't tell her it was because he was overwhelmed by emotion, or that the sight of her in such torment was not only distressing, but also actually painful for him. He couldn't tell her that he had the urge to enfold her in his arms and keep the world at bay. So, he gave her the only excuse he had, which was not only believable but true. "If they find you, we'll both die."

"Right." She nodded and looked away. Then she pulled from his grasp and walked out.

He watched her leave, knowing that somehow, he had said the wrong thing, but not understanding how to fix it. Varum rubbed his forehead, trying to think of a solution to the problem. He needed to see the patrols for himself. There was always a way through any obstacle if one looked hard enough.

He should return to his office as Kalyani suggested and find out all he could. Perhaps even schedule a meeting with the Tidewarden himself. Arvind might see him. Varum looked out the door to see Kalyani sitting on the couch, staring at nothing. All of that could wait until tomorrow. She had spent enough time alone.

Varum walked to stand beside her and waited for her to look at him. "I don't spend a lot of time here, so there isn't much to do, but if you'll tell me what you like, I can get it."

"You really don't need to do that. I'm fine."

"We both know that's a lie."

She slid to the side until she was lying down, one arm bent under her head. "It's been a really long time since I've had my hopes up so high, only to get them yanked away. Let me sit in it for a bit. I'll be fine after that."

"One of my neighbors sings. I'm surprised you've not heard him already. He's loud, but he's also very good."

"Why are you telling me this?"

Varum sat across from her on the other sofa. "Did you know that Sea Elves are masters of song and dance?"

She blinked before sitting up. "What?"

"It isn't something we share with outsiders."

"All Sea Elves?"

He knew what she was asking, even before she posed the question. It had been there in her brown eyes. He chuckled softly. "Aye."

"Do you dance?"

"Once. Long ago."

She braced a hand on the cushion and leaned on it. "Do you sing?"

"Once. Long ago."

"You don't now?"

He gave a slow shake of his head.

"That makes me sad," she said.

Varum sat back, hiding his smile. He liked her interest in him. "Why?"

"Because it means that something happened to make you stop."

It had, in fact. He was usually careful about what he divulged, so no one could make those connections. Why wasn't he being that vigilant with her?

"I can see by your expression that I'm right," she replied.

He looked away, wondering how she seemed to read him so easily. "I told you about my neighbor because it will be entertainment. I can't take you out and show you the city, but you'll be one of the few humans who will hear our song."

"You don't have to be so nice to me. I'm not going to crumble because of a little disappointment. I'm stronger than that."

"I know. I noticed that the first time I saw you. What caused you to be so strong? Does Rohan not take care of you?"

She shifted around to get comfortable. "Rohan is brave, fearless, and formidable. He takes care of everyone. To the detriment of himself, actually."

"I meant no disrespect," Varum said as he held up his hands in surrender.

"Our father was the leader of the Siguks—my people. He was fair, just, and respected. When our mother died, it hit him hard, and he was never the same. Rohan picked up a lot of the slack, and I pitched in when needed. Then Dad became ill, and I took care of him while Rohan stepped into the leadership role. He never wanted that position, but he did what had to be done. With both of our attention focused elsewhere, our younger sister, Lata, started acting out. It got worse after Dad died. Rohan struggled to fill our father's shoes as our leader, and I resented him."

Varum frowned. "Why?"

"For being the leader. For not seeing the ways I could help him. And for curbing my swimming."

That caught Varum's attention. He'd been waiting for her to talk about that. "What do you mean?"

"My love of the water always scared Dad. He tried to keep me out of it, and when that didn't work, he limited my time in it. I thought Rohan would be better. And he was, to an extent. But I always saw that same fear in his eyes when we were in the water together."

"What kind of fear?"

She shrugged. "The kind that said if I went out too far, I'd never return."

He could imagine exactly what Rohan was going through now. Varum was part of the reason, too.

"And in all of that was Lata." Kalyani twisted her lips. "She's much younger than Rohan and me, and she rebelled against everything and everyone after Dad died. She lived with Rohan, but they fought constantly, so he asked me if she could live with me. I believe he thought she might listen to me better. That wasn't the case at all. We actually fought more than she and Rohan did. She bounced back and forth between us, pushing against every boundary Rohan set up."

"Then she was taken."

Kalyani sighed. "Rohan became a man possessed. Over half of our village had been abducted, and he carried the burden of that responsibility on his own."

"He found Lata, though."

"He did."

"Where is she now?"

"With the others in Siguk. She wasn't happy about not joining us in Serenia—what we called our new hideaway home—but she understands the dangers more than most. She did a lot of growing up in the time she was gone, and she's seen how evil the world can be."

"Everything worked out for your family. That doesn't always happen."

Kalyani released a soft breath. "For a little while, we were happy. Until I could no longer ignore the waves and swam too far."

It was the perfect time for him to ask about her gills, but Varum hesitated. She was talking about herself, and he was curious to hear more. Perhaps if he didn't push, she might tell him on her own.

"The water is a lure," she said. "Each wave is like a knock, and every time it rolls back, it's like it's calling me to it. And I can't stay away, no matter how hard I try."

"You were made for it."

She hesitated before nodding. "So much so that it's sometimes hard to leave it."

26

Kalyani didn't know what possessed her to reveal such intimate facts to Varum. Was it loneliness? It could be hopelessness. Whatever the reason, it had felt good to get the words out. She couldn't hold his gaze, though. There was something different in his eyes now, something almost...vulnerable. It was the exact opposite of what she had come to know him to be, and she wasn't sure what to do with it. So, she looked away, pretending she hadn't seen anything.

"I don't know why I told you that." She needed to change the subject. What could she say? What safe topic could remove the embarrassment engulfing her?

"I'm glad you did."

She kept her gaze on the floor, suddenly more nervous than she'd ever been in his presence.

"You shared something personal. So, I will, too." Varum paused. "I have a complicated relationship with my parents.

Actually, that's a lie. I don't have *any* kind of relationship with them."

Her gaze jerked to him, utterly taken aback by his words.

"Don't worry. They're not in Tarangarh. They left the city—and me—years ago."

She couldn't fathom what she was hearing. Surely, that couldn't be the whole story. Nirav spoke so highly of Varum and how he never got into trouble. There had to be a good reason his parents would abandon him, though for the life of her, she couldn't find a single one. "I don't know what to say, other than I'm sorry you went through that."

"There's no need to apologize. You didn't do it."

"Is that when Nirav stepped in to raise you?"

Varum drew in a deep breath, glanced down, and nodded. "I call him friend, and on occasion, family, but the truth is that he was more of a father to me than mine ever was. I was young, but old enough to know what was happening. Nirav tried to lessen the blow of the truth, but it couldn't be concealed for long."

She wondered what kind of people could so easily discard their child. Varum tried to hide the pain, and he did a decent job of it, but she saw past the mask he wore. Or maybe it was just that she wanted to believe she did.

"My abandonment made others believe there was something wrong with me," he continued. "It's one of the reasons I've not advanced further in my station. That never bothered me, but it has always infuriated Nirav. He was ostracized after his time on land, and he got more of that after taking me in."

That explained why the two were as close as they were. It also made her heart ache for both of them. Neither had asked for their circumstances, but both were shouldering the fallout as only the strong and determined could. She had seen the same with Rohan, which made it easy to spot in others.

Varum shook his head. "Don't pity me. I would rather claim Nirav as my father than the man who holds that title."

"You haven't seen them since they...?" She trailed off, not wanting to say the word.

"Left?" he offered, then shook his head. "They returned once three years ago. They wanted to speak to me, but I had no interest. Nirav met with them. I thought he might urge me to visit with them, but he didn't. He's never pushed me one way or the other. He's always let me make my own decisions, and that was no different. He respected my choice not to talk to them. Once they understood that I had no interest in them, they left."

Kalyani had the urge to go sit by him and give him a hug to comfort him. "I'm not sure I could've stayed away. I'm too curious. I would have wanted to know why they suddenly wanted to talk to me, and I'd likely have asked why they left."

"They left the city because my father saw an opportunity to wield more power and influence elsewhere. Tarangarh is isolated, but other cities are nearer to each other. Each has its own Assembly, but they also have a regional hierarchy. That's what my father was aiming for. And he got it."

"That doesn't mean he can't have a family."

Varum shrugged. "It was Mum who wanted a child. He never did. She claimed me while he was away, and he tried to accept me. His image would've been tarnished had he returned me."

"And it wasn't when he abandoned you?" she asked, outraged.

"I was old enough that it made it seem as if I were the one at fault. As if my remaining with him would end his political career."

Kalyani hoped she never saw either of Varum's parents,

because she had a few choice words she wanted to say to them. "How could your mum let you go so easily?"

"I neither know nor care. For a short time, I wanted to know, but I soon realized that it didn't make any difference. Their actions told the story."

It was a lie. She could see it plainly in his eyes. He longed for the reason, but she wouldn't call him out on it. That wound was old and deep. It had scarred over some, but it would never fully heal. Not until he got the answers he said he didn't want.

"The only one I truly trust is Nirav," Varum stated.

She nodded, understanding more about him in those few words than she had gleaned in the hours she had spent with him. "I hope you understand that what your parents did isn't about you. It's about them."

He flashed her a quick smile. "Nirav told me the same thing."

"But you don't believe it, do you?"

Of course, he didn't. Neither would she in that situation. He had been abandoned as a child, and he would always believe that he wasn't good enough. Wasn't lovable enough. Or wonder what he had done wrong. No wonder he always followed the rules. He never wanted anyone to say that he had done something wrong ever again.

One side of his lips lifted in a quick smile. "I accepted my life and put such things in the past."

He might claim that, but one look in his iridescent blue eyes and anyone could see the pain he fought—and failed—to hide. Could a society that applauded song and dance really be so petty as to shun a child into adulthood for something the parents did? Obviously.

Except not everyone did.

"You said you were snubbed, but that wasn't by everyone. Tanira doesn't seem to care about your past."

Varum snorted a laugh as he briefly looked at the ceiling. "I thought you already had her figured out."

"I'm just trying to untangle everything."

"There's not much to it. Her father is Arvind, the Tidewarden. He's the head of the Assembly and holds the most power and sway of anyone in the city. Their family is also affluent. She was given everything she ever wanted. No one has ever refused her anything."

Kalyani really needed to get a look at this elf. "You did."

"Eventually." He rubbed the back of his neck. "She's determined. I'll give her that. Once Tanira sets her sights on something, she's relentless until it's finally hers."

"I take it others have pursued her?"

"I doubt anyone would turn her away. I'm fairly certain even Nirav would bend to her will. He finds her quite beautiful."

For some reason, that irked Kalyani.

Varum blew out a breath. "I gave in to her, thinking that once she had me, the novelty would wear off. But it didn't. Things went slowly at first because her father wasn't pleased that she had chosen me. I thought for sure that would put an end to it, but she won him over. The next thing I knew, I was going to dinners at their home."

"I'm sure that gave your career a boost."

"Somewhat, I suppose. I declined his offer to move me to another division. I didn't want any favors from him because I had no intention of staying with Tanira. That's when I broke things off."

Kalyani raised her brows. "How did that go?"

"About as badly as you can imagine. As I said, she's used to getting her way. And she said she loved me."

"She won't stop coming for you."

He threw up his hands in frustration. "I can't make it any clearer than I already have."

"Her showing up here twice should tell you that she's not going to give up."

"Then what do I do?"

Kalyani picked at a piece of invisible lint on her clothes. "You're asking the wrong person."

"You're a female. You seem to know what she's going to do."

"It isn't as if I've been in this kind of situation."

He lifted one shoulder in a shrug and held her gaze. "You never had to dissuade a suitor?"

There hadn't been anyone serious. Ever. Though she was loath to tell Varum that. It made her sound pathetic. Yet she couldn't come up with a believable excuse, and she didn't want to lie. So, she told the truth. "Nay."

"You really don't have a lover waiting for you?"

By the stars, why did he have to say that word? It drew her gaze to his mouth and had her mind contemplating kissing him again. She tried to swallow, but her mouth was dry. "I do not."

"I find that hard to believe."

She tore her gaze from him. It was suddenly hot in the room. She gathered her hair in her hands to get it off her neck.

"I didn't mean to make you uncomfortable," he said.

"It's fine." It wasn't, but she didn't want to admit to that either. How did they end up on this subject, and how did she get off it?

Varum drew in a sharp breath and released it. "It seems I owe you another apology. I'm sorry for stepping over the line and asking such a personal question."

"There's nothing to apologize for."

"Then why won't you look at me?"

If only he hadn't said it in that soft voice, she might have been able to deny him. As it was, she was powerless against him. It took her a few tries, but she was eventually able to look him in the eye again.

The moment their gazes met, she felt something shift between them. Some unnamed sensation that once exposed wouldn't so easily vanish. She released her hair and folded her hands in her lap, yet the word *lover* kept repeating in her head, eventually sounding like an endearment.

"You told me to kiss you or kill you, but the mention of a lover embarrasses you." Varum's grin was slow. "You are a contradiction."

"I know I'm difficult."

"You aren't difficult. You're a contradiction," he corrected gently. "Just when I think I have you figured out, you say or do something I don't expect."

She shifted slightly while clearing her throat. Was that a compliment?

The question must have shown on her face because he smiled and said, "Take the compliment. Few people surprise me."

"Thank you," she murmured, still unsettled by his words.

"I mean it, though."

She shot him a puzzled look. "About?"

"That I find it hard to believe someone hasn't claimed you."

Kalyani took instant exception to that. "I'm not something to be owned."

"Nay, I can see that."

Was that humor she spotted in his eyes? She narrowed hers while trying to decipher the elf before her.

"What are the men like in your village?"

"They're...men."

Varum pushed to his feet and walked to the kitchen, where he got out two glasses and a bottle. He set the glasses on the coffee table between them and opened the bottle, pouring a finger of a faintly glowing blue liquid into each glass. "Is Rohan preventing you from marrying? Or is it that no one has caught your eye?"

"I thought we were talking about your problem with Tanira. Why are we discussing me?"

He flashed her a smile. "You're much more interesting."

27

The more self-conscious Kalyani became, the more Varum wanted to know about her. She was—by far—the most interesting person he had ever met. Now, he wished he had kissed her when she challenged him. Would she be fiery and fierce, or would she be shy and nervous as she was now? He really wanted to find out.

If Tanira hadn't stopped by, he and Kalyani would be on their way to the surface, and he never would've gotten to know this side of her. The danger of her being in the city had increased, though. He wasn't sure whether to be grateful to Tanira or not.

"I'm very boring," Kalyani stated.

"Surely, you've traded with others who would allow you to venture to other villages."

She shook her head of dark curls. "The men went, not the women. We did have some traders come to us, though."

"It's no wonder you sought refuge in the water," he mused.

Her gaze quickly darted to the side before returning to him. "That isn't why I swim."

"Then why?"

"Because there's an entire world beneath the surface that's a part of Zora yet different. It's like I've stepped into another realm. The plants, the animals, the very essence of the ocean that feels both vast and small at the same time."

He nodded, understanding exactly how she felt. It was why he never wanted to leave the water—and why so many Sea Elves refused to allow outsiders into their home.

"The water feels like home," Kalyani said. "I'm more myself when I'm swimming."

"Yet you miss the sky."

A wistful look came over her face. "Underwater is striking, but there is much beauty on land, as well. The soft glow of a sunrise or the sky lit up in the brilliant colors of a sunset. A clear blue sky or one filled with gray clouds right before a storm. There are the skies with the big, puffy clouds that drift lazily past, and the clouds that seem as if some god stretched them from one horizon to the other. Then there's the night sky with its blanket of stars and the moon above." She paused and laughed softly. "It seems I've lived my life either looking up at the sky or looking down into the water."

"I've never seen the sky. I've never ventured close enough to the surface to get a glimpse."

"You're missing out," she replied.

For the first time, Varum thought he very well might be. He leaned forward and grasped a glass before handing it to her. "It's *lumara* nectar. Careful, though. It's deceptively strong."

She sniffed it. "What's it made out of?"

"Coral sap and sweet kelp sugar. A warmth lingers after you swallow, and it'll spread throughout your body."

A look of interest flashed on her face before she took a sip. He watched her mouth against the glass. The sight of her tongue peeking out to lick her lips sent a surge of desire straight to his cock.

"This is good," she said.

He grabbed his glass and sat back. "Take it slow. It'll hit you hard."

"Do I look pitiful enough that you felt the need for liquor?"

"Aye," he lied.

She shot him a smile. "What are the odds that I'll get to leave the city?"

"You'll leave. Alive. I promise."

"You can't promise something like that."

He tossed back the drink and leaned forward to refill it. "I can, and I do."

"I won't hold you to it."

"I'll figure out the patrol schedule. There are always cracks in things. I'll find it, and we'll get you home."

She took another sip. "Hmm."

"You don't believe me, do you?"

"I was just thinking that I'm intruding on your living space."

The thought of her being anywhere but in his home was like a cold hand of steel wrapped around his chest. "You aren't. Besides, I'm responsible for you."

"Now you sound like my brother," she said with a grin.

He certainly didn't want to be her brother with the way he kept thinking about her mouth. "I imagine sitting here with nothing to do isn't exactly fun."

"Not really."

"What do you do in Serenia?"

She took another drink and scrunched her face in thought. "I fish, cook, gather herbs, clean, and do whatever else needs to be done."

"You do a lot."

"Everyone pitches in."

He watched as she finished the *lumara* nectar. "Want more?"

"Please," she said eagerly.

Varum gave her another finger's worth and added more to his own glass before sitting back. Her embarrassment from earlier was gone, and she was once more relaxed. He almost broached the subject of lovers again just to see if she would get flustered.

"I can clean and cook for you while I'm here," she offered.

"That won't be necessary."

Her shoulders slumped. "I have to do something. Sitting around will make me go daft."

"I'll find you something, but you don't need to take care of my things."

"Why not? I'm living here, too—at least for the moment."

He downed more of the nectar and waited for the warmth to spread through him. "You aren't my maid. I'll find you something," he said again.

"Is Tanira pretty?"

Varum was startled by the quick change in subject. "She is."

"Why don't you want to be with her?"

"She asked the same thing."

"What was your answer?"

He propped a foot on the table. "I explained that I didn't love her, and that I couldn't see a future with her."

"She's an elf everyone wants, yet you don't."

"If the feelings aren't there, they aren't there. You can't force yourself to care for someone."

She nodded and started to tilt to the side. He rose to help her, but she caught herself in time and chuckled. Varum sat down, but he remained on the edge of the cushion.

"Ah, but when the feelings are there, they're sometimes obvious to everyone but the two involved," Kalyani said.

He set aside his empty glass. "You speak from experience?"

"I do," she said, slurring her words slightly. "Rohan tried to act all tough with Farah at first, but then he would suddenly be gentle with her. He claims he didn't fall for her until they went on their adventure, but I think he was already under her spell as he tended to her injury."

Varum was beginning to feel that he and Rohan had a lot in common. He inwardly grimaced at the direction of his thoughts. What good would it do for him to find Kalyani attractive? They were from two different worlds, and there was no compromise for either of them. She couldn't live in his, and he couldn't live in hers. Then again, no one said that just because he took someone to his bed, he had to spend the rest of his life with them. He pressed the heels of his hands to his eyes and struggled to turn his thoughts away from her as a lover.

"I know why she wants you. And it isn't because you didn't go after her."

His head snapped up to see Kalyani's face flushed from the alcohol.

She unfurled her legs, so her feet were on the floor, before she carefully placed her empty glass on the table. "It's hot."

"That's the nectar."

She nodded, waving her hand in front of her face.

"What were you going to say?" he pressed.

"What?" she asked, her brow furrowed in a frown.

He grinned, realizing she was drunk. "You said you know why Tanira wants me."

"Have you looked in the mirror? You're gorgeous."

He could only stare at her. Did she really think that?"

"It's more than that, though," she added. "It's you."

"What's that supposed to mean?" he asked when she didn't elaborate.

She braced her hands on either side of herself and closed her eyes, her face lifted to the ceiling. "You have this...thing."

"A...thing?"

She nodded exaggeratedly. "Aye. A thing. It makes you stand out from others."

"I have no idea what you're talking about, and I don't think you do either. The nectar has gotten to you."

Her eyes opened, and she shot him a scathing look. "I do, too, know what I'm talking about. You're..." She waved a hand up and down at him. "That."

He grinned. "I guess I am. Thank you for pointing it out." He rose and walked to her. "I think it's time you went to bed."

"It's not time."

She didn't fight him when he gathered her into his arms. "You can't see the sky, remember? You don't know what time it is."

"That's right," she murmured and rested her head on his shoulder.

He stood there, cradling her in his arms. He liked the feeling of her against him, but he liked her head on him even more. "I should've limited you to one glass."

"You're honorable, kind, and generous."

Varum was startled by her words. They had been mumbled but were distinct enough that he heard them.

She flung her arm around his neck. "You have a...a...presence others lack."

He held her tighter. Nirav always gave him compliments, but that was what a parental figure was supposed to do. Kalyani wasn't beholden to him, and she was drunk. Truth usually sprouted from the lips of those in their cups, so he knew she meant what she said.

And she would never know just how much those words meant to him.

Varum made his way into the bedroom, but he didn't set her on the bed immediately. If he did, he'd have to release her, and he wasn't quite ready for that. He could get into bed with her. If for only a little while. She would never have to know.

As much as that appealed to him, he couldn't do that to Kalyani. He had disrupted her life by bringing her to the city. He didn't want to make things worse by abusing her trust when she was most vulnerable. Nay, he wanted to earn that trust. He wanted to be the elf that she believed him to be.

Everything he thought he knew about humans had been wrong. Kalyani had opened his eyes to another side of her race. Her spirit, her courage. Even her compassion. She was extraordinary.

He laid her on the bed, and the minute he did, she rolled away from him onto her side. He straightened, but he didn't leave. Unable to help himself, he touched the silken strands of her hair. A curl wrapped around his finger as if holding him captive, and he had to wonder if he wasn't already spellbound by her.

Varum extracted his finger and then pulled the covers over her. He couldn't climb into bed with her, and he couldn't leave her, so he did the only thing he could. He walked to the window and opened the lattice to watch the patrols. Varum counted the elves and the number of times they made a round while searching for weaknesses.

Kalyani would go home. He would make sure she made it out of the trench, even if it was the last thing he did.

28

Varum rubbed his chest. The tightening wouldn't loosen, no matter how long he stood at the window. There was also his knotted stomach. But the worst was the fear with its icy fingers sinking into his back. And the culprit?

Kalyani.

He turned to look at her. She was sleeping soundly, thanks to the nectar. If he thought he could achieve that kind of rest, he'd chug the entire bottle. But he knew if he did, the sleep he'd get would be filled with variations of Kalyani captured by his people.

No matter how many times he thought back to when he first saw her, he couldn't pinpoint when or why he had thought it best to bring her to the city. It was as if he'd lost his mind for that space in time. He hadn't just pushed against the rules. He had busted through them as if they were nothing. The repercussions would be extreme, and he was prepared to accept them— for himself. He didn't want any kind of blowback on Kalyani.

She was innocent in everything. Not that anyone would listen to him. It was why she had to leave. The sooner, the better. Because every minute she stayed, it put her more in danger. He didn't want to carry the weight of her death for a single second. He wouldn't be able to bear it.

His feet carried him to the bed, and before he knew it, he was standing beside her. He ran his eyes over her face and the wild curls that seemed to have a life of their own. His hand lifted, fingers outstretched to stroke her cheek, but he stopped himself and dropped his arm to his side.

Would she have found a way to free herself from the chains had he left her that day? What might he have found if he had brought her to shore? Why had he risked both their lives just to have her in the city? Had he seen something during that brief battle that triggered the thought of sneaking her into his home?

He wondered if he would ever learn the answers. Maybe they would only confuse him more. He should be studying the patrols, but he couldn't seem to stay away from her. He walked a treacherous road. The more he was with her, the more she fascinated him.

And the more he wanted to know.

She wasn't his. Could never *be* his. So where did this sudden ache come from? Why did he yearn to hold her, to feel the length of her body against his? Why did he feel...everything now, after years of nothing?

It was futile to allow himself to think about what it might be like to run his thumb along her bottom lip. It was pointless to wonder how sweet her kiss would taste. It was hopeless to speculate about a night in her arms. The trajectory of his life had been cemented the moment his parents discarded him.

He started to turn away, but he froze, shock running through him. His heart thudded against his ribs as he slowly turned his head and looked down to see her fingers gripping his hand. His gaze jerked to her face, but her eyes were still closed. Did she know he was the one she grabbed?

Varum stared down at their hands, immobile. He lightly caressed his thumb over her fingers, marveling at the contrast of his blueish-green skin against the brown of hers. There was no webbing between her fingers or toes, no points to her ears, yet she belonged in the water like any Sea Elf.

"Who are you?" he whispered.

He should return to the window and his study of the patrols, but Varum carefully sat on the edge of the bed with his back against the headboard. The minute she released his hand, he would leave. Until then, he would enjoy the time she granted him.

It wasn't long before he stretched out one leg on the bed to get more comfortable. Ten minutes later, he had both legs up with his ankles crossed. Just as he was settling in, Kalyani rolled onto her back, still clutching his hand. He rested his head against the headboard and closed his eyes, his mind going over the few patrols he had seen to look for weak spots. He needed to know all the patrols to get the complete picture. The truth was, he was surprised that the Assembly had agreed to the patrols, merely from his incomplete report. There had to be something else afoot that he didn't know about. Finding out more would be next to impossible.

Nirav might have better luck. Even Tanira would know before he did. He didn't want to go to her, but he might have no choice. She wouldn't give up the intel for free, though. She would want something in exchange. He would give Tanira whatever she wanted if it meant Kalyani could go home. He was the one who should have to pay for his mistakes.

The guards patrolling the area outside his home were more frequent than he had anticipated. They swam in teams of three. If every area of the city had such patrols, that meant they were using every guard on rotation. It was a good way to keep the city safe for a short period of time, but it wasn't sustainable.

Was this a show of force? Had there been a threat from the Masters already? Or was this to hold others within Tarangarh?

Varum sighed, hating that there were always more questions than answers. He was thinking about how much magic it would take for him to carry Kalyani out of the trench while shielding her from the pressure when she rolled toward him again. He peeled his eyes open to look down at her, just as her head moved from the pillow to his leg.

For several minutes, he did nothing but watch her. Then he lightly stroked the fingers of his free hand over her head. She must have been terrified being taken from her home and confined, but she had put on a brave face. The only time he'd witnessed a crack was when she couldn't see the sky to know what time it was.

Shouldn't she have yelled at him? Railed about being kidnapped and held against her will? Surely, she should've cried. Maybe she had when he hadn't been around. She hadn't wanted to show any weakness. The lone human far beneath the water in a city that would gladly execute her before she had a chance to speak.

He couldn't believe he had made such a blunder in bringing her to Tarangarh. It was no wonder his parents had left him behind. Perhaps they saw the mistakes he would make and thought it prudent to distance themselves from him.

Varum grimaced as he thought about Nirav. He didn't want his friend to get tangled up in all of this, but if Varum picked a fight,

Nirav would know something was up. He never should've gone to him about Kalyani in the first place. But they were too close. No matter how loudly or vehemently Nirav declared his innocence, no one would believe him.

Had he just condemned two people to death? Varum squeezed his eyes closed as the truth hit him. The only way to save both Kalyani and Nirav was to get her out of the city and back with her people. It didn't matter how many scenarios he pictured in his head. In each, he got caught by patrols.

The only way to bypass that was to wait until they slacked off. A week, at most. Seven days of leaving Kalyani alone. Seven nights of lying awake, thinking about her while listing out the many reasons he couldn't have her.

A human and a Sea Elf weren't compatible. Sea Elves weren't even well-matched with other elves. But a human? That was like trying to force a bird to live underwater. It wasn't feasible. Facts didn't lie. And yet, it saddened him.

Kalyani had brought fire into his dull life. She'd forced him to see just how dismal his existence was. And what had he done for her? Not much. That would change, though. He had a problem to solve, and he was an expert at sorting through difficult situations.

Varum slowly scooted down while adjusting her head until she was resting on his chest. He stared at her face, watching to see if she woke, readying an excuse if she did. But she slept the sleep of the dead. He put one hand behind his head and lightly rested the other on her shoulder.

"What am I doing?" he whispered.

He should be putting distance between them, not settling her on his chest for the night. It didn't matter what logic his brain gave. His body refused to move.

Nirav stalked into his home, slamming the door behind him as he made his way into his office. He tucked the maps back into their slots and put away the tubes before rubbing his hands together and facing the shelves of books. Some of the volumes had been handed down through six generations of his family.

He would pass them on to Varum. At one time, he had been desperate for a wife and children, but fate hadn't delivered that to him. Instead, he had been gifted Varum. And right now, Varum needed him.

Nirav walked to the first bookshelf and ran his finger along the spines. He grasped a tome and flipped through the pages, scanning for any mention of humans. When he found none, he replaced that book and moved to another, then another, and then another.

Somewhere in the many records that had been passed down and added to over the generations, there had to be some mention of humans with gills. He wanted to know how Kalyani had them. And now that she was staying a little longer, he might get the chance to learn the truth. Of course, her remaining also put her and Varum in danger. Nirav had favors he could call in, and he intended to use them if anything happened. He would die before he let anything happen to Varum, and it was clear that Varum would do anything to protect Kalyani.

Nirav looked up from the page he was scanning. He wondered if Varum was aware of how he had come to care about Kalyani in such a short period.

"Or maybe I'm seeing something I want to be there but isn't," he mused.

Varum had given his word to Kalyani, which meant Varum

would hold true to it. It was up to Nirav to see that all of them came out of this alive. He replaced the book and stretched his arm high above him to grasp another. After flipping through the pages, he stopped and hurriedly flipped back a few when he caught the word *human*.

It took him reading two pages before he found it. The paragraph led him to another book. He carried it to his desk and began skimming chapter by chapter, hope fading each time when he didn't get the answers he was looking for.

After three more books, he poured himself a drink and stared at the manuscripts before him. They had never let him down before. Maybe he was searching for the wrong thing. Perhaps he needed to try a different approach.

Nirav tossed down the liquor and set aside the glass before going back to the books.

29

Kalyani yawned as she rolled onto her back. What was she doing in Varum's bed again? Had she climbed into it? She sat up at the thought and immediately clutched her head as it began to pound. She groaned as she remembered drinking the nectar the night before. Varum had warned her that it hit hard, and he hadn't been wrong. She'd only had two glasses.

At least she *thought* it was only two. Truth be told, she couldn't remember much of that night after the first glass. She held her head and looked around the room for him. To her relief, he was nowhere in sight.

"Oh, my head," she murmured. "I'm never drinking that again."

Her mouth felt as if it had been stuffed with a rag. She needed water, but that meant moving. She wasn't sure what was worse: staying there with a dry mouth or attempting to walk. Kalyani cautiously moved the covers aside and climbed out of bed. She carefully made her way into the kitchen and poured a glass of water.

She drained it and then refilled it to take to the table. Once she was seated, she propped her head in her hand and closed her eyes. The pounding subsided a little, but not enough for her liking. After she'd finished the second glass of water, she decided a bath would make her feel better.

Relaxing in the hot water had a positive effect, though it didn't erase her headache completely. Kalyani reclined in the tub and moved her legs and hands as if she were swimming. It had been days since she had been in the water, but she hadn't felt the ache in her chest that she normally did when she stayed away. Was it because she was already in the water? Surely, that couldn't be the case. She might be far below the surface, but she was still looking at it much as she did from shore.

Had Varum done something to her that would ease the longing she had for the water? It might not have been intentional. Or could it have been? The Sea Elves didn't want to share their world with anyone, not even other races of their kind. Why would they be okay with her?

Her stomach sank at the thought. Varum had asked many questions about her swimming. So had Nirav, now that she thought about it. But what did it matter if she liked to swim? It wasn't as if she would ever be able to dive deep enough to find any of their cities. She wasn't a threat.

Kalyani climbed out of the tub, no longer able to relax. She dried off as the water drained and then dressed. The house was empty again, leaving her to move about and search through things as she wanted. She walked to the shelves in the living area and looked over the objects and books there again.

She chose one of them and flipped through the pages, but it was in a language she couldn't read. She returned the book to its place and sighed as she turned around. There really was nothing for her to do. She didn't know when Varum had left, so she didn't know when he would return. That left her hours to do nothing but sit idly with her thoughts.

Kalyani trudged to the sofa and sat. She stared at the spot Varum usually occupied and tried to recall her missing memories from the night before. She really hoped she hadn't said something stupid or insensitive. It wasn't as if she was new to alcohol, but she hadn't ever had so much that she couldn't remember things.

Strangely, she didn't worry that Varum had harmed her in any way. Which was odd. She should fear that, shouldn't she? It wasn't as if she knew him very well. He was a stranger and her jailor. Actually, she didn't know what he was. The more she discovered about him, the more confused she became.

"So, maybe drinking wasn't the smartest thing I could've done," she mumbled.

She'd been feeling sorry for herself and depressed at not being able to go home. *Anything* could've happened in that missing time. Yet she had to admit that Varum hadn't tried to harm her, other than when he grabbed her neck. And even then, he hadn't used any force. There had been plenty of opportunities for him to hurt her, and he hadn't. Why would he wait until she was drunk? He wouldn't.

Though she wasn't sure how she was so positive about that.

Kalyani couldn't sit there and let her thoughts go round and round. She needed something to do to help with her boredom and the headache. She walked to his room and set about making the bed. He didn't scatter things about, so there wasn't much to pick up or straighten. Once she found a cloth, she wiped down every-thing in his room and the bathing area before moving into the main rooms.

She took her time, carefully lifting an item to dust it, and then the area around it before replacing it in the exact same spot. Even then, she was finished all too soon. The pounding of her head had diminished significantly, and she used that time to get something to eat.

The pantry had been restocked, but she wasn't sure when. She shrugged and looked through the unrecognizable items. Not being able to read the labels made it even more difficult. She settled on bread and a jar of what looked like jelly that smelled delicious.

She set everything out on the table and tested the jelly. It was like an explosion of flavor in her mouth. She quickly slathered a large helping of it on the bread and devoured two pieces. It wasn't that she minded eating alone. It was that she was alone. She couldn't even say that it was quiet, because it wasn't. The sounds of the water and the life within it were a kind of background noise like the waves rolling onto shore.

Why then did she feel so lonely? The waves had always given her a kind of comfort. Even when she first woke in Tarangarh, the sounds of the ocean had been enjoyable. Now, it was a reminder of being a prisoner, of being an outsider in a world where everyone hated her simply because she was human.

Kalyani cleaned up and found herself back on the sofa. How many more days did she have like this? She didn't think she could handle even another hour, much less days. She dropped her head into her hands and felt tears prick her eyes.

The jiggle of the door's handle snapped her head up. She stared at it with her heart in her throat. Varum wouldn't jiggle the knob.

He would just walk in. Did that mean someone was trying to break in?

"Varum?" a soft voice called through the door.

It was a voice Kalyani recognized.

She slowly pushed to her feet as Tanira twisted the handle again. Kalyani took a step back. What was the elf doing? Was Tanira really trying to break into Varum's home? Right on the heels of that question was the realization that if she did, Kalyani would be caught.

Panic built quickly, turning her blood to ice as she frantically looked around for a place to hide. She could fit beneath the sofa, but she would be visible. Same with the dining table. The bedroom was her best choice. It would also be the first place she looked if she were searching for someone.

The handle twisted again, harder this time. Varum's magic should hold, but what if it didn't? What if Tanira busted in and found her? Kalyani's life would be over. Or would it? Tanira wanted Varum. Would she really turn him in for harboring Kalyani?

None of this should be happening. She would be back with her family now if Tanira hadn't meddled. And now, the elf was doing it again. Neither Nirav nor Varum was there to run interference. Kalyani would have to deal with this on her own. She didn't want to die in Tarangarh. She refused.

She dashed into the bedroom and bent to look under the bed, but there was no place to hide. She checked in the bathing area before scanning the room. Her gaze landed on the armoire that held his clothes. She hurried to it and yanked open one of the doors.

Her hope dwindled when she saw there were mostly shelves.

She shoved aside some clothes and climbed into the armoire by lying on her side with her knees drawn up to her chest. She stretched out her fingers to grab the doors and pulled them closed, even as the jiggling of the handle grew louder and more forceful. Tanira was going to bust her way in, one way or another.

Kalyani was doubly glad that Varum had closed the lattice over the windows so Tanira couldn't get in that way. Kalyani wished she had some way to contact Varum to get him here. She squeezed her eyes shut as if that would shut out the sounds of Tanira attempting to break in. Kalyani didn't know how much time had passed before she got a cramp in her hip, and then her feet went to sleep.

Belatedly, she realized that she didn't hear the handle being jiggled. Did that mean Tanira had given up? Or did she get in? Kalyani could've kicked herself for not paying attention. She wanted to stretch out her legs, but she didn't dare come out of hiding until she knew for sure that it was only her and Varum.

Time ticked by. Eventually, she dozed. Until a bright light woke her. She held up her hand to shield her eyes as she blinked them open.

"What are you doing?"

The sound of Varum's voice instantly eased the tension in her muscles. She dropped her hand and took the first easy breath she had taken in hours.

"Are you going to answer me?" he demanded.

She nodded and moved one of her cramped legs to get out, except her body didn't work properly, and she tumbled out. But she didn't hit the floor. Instead, she found herself in his arms. She looked up into his face, creased with worry.

"Are you hurt?" he asked in a soft voice.

Kalyani licked her lips. "Just stiff. I should be fine once I walk around."

He stood and lifted her to set her on her feet, but he didn't immediately release her. Instead, he held her until he was sure she could stand on her own.

"Thank you," she murmured and stretched her back.

"I'm waiting for an explanation."

She cut her eyes to see him standing with his feet apart, arms crossed over his chest. It wasn't anger she saw, but concern. Kalyani glanced back at the wardrobe and tried to imagine what it must have been like to find her there. "I hid."

"Why?"

Her head swiveled back to him. "Someone tried to break in."

His entire demeanor changed as his worry shifted to outrage. "What?"

She tried to take a step back, but he held her firmly. "Someone tr—"

"I heard you," he bit out. "I'm just…trying to understand." His brows snapped together. "Are you certain?"

"She was jiggling the handle."

"She?"

When most people were angry, they yelled, spewing words with emotion like flames. Not Varum. He became as frigid and unforgiving as winter. His eyes went still and dark like a bottomless lake. His voice softened, but the steel in his words carried his fury. Yet it was his body that told the biggest story. He was motionless, like a predator ready to pounce on its next meal.

"She?" he asked again.

Kalyani nodded once. "It was Tanira. I heard her call out your name."

His gaze shifted to the side. She debated whether to step away from him, but in his present mood, she decided it was safer to stay where she was.

"How long was she here?"

Kalyani shrugged. "I'm not sure. It felt like a long time, but I can't say for certain."

"You believed she would break through my magic."

It wasn't a question but a statement. Kalyani found his unusual gaze locked on her once more. "She seemed determined to get in."

"Then I need to have a word with her." He dropped his hands and took two steps back. "This won't happen again."

30

Anger burned like charred fingers scraping along his veins as he stalked through the corridors. Varum could barely contain his fury, it burned so hot. The image of Kalyani curled into a tight ball, her hands over her ears, kept flashing in his mind.

When he first entered his home, he hadn't been too concerned about not seeing her immediately. But it became clear after a quick search that she was gone. Panic had taken hold, leaving him both breathless and terrified that she had left him. That's what kept going through his mind.

She had left.

Without a farewell.

It was only when he looked at the window to see the lattice still in place that he knew Kalyani hadn't gone anywhere. His next thought had been that someone had taken her. But that wasn't right either, because his magic had been in place when he returned.

And if she hadn't left, and no one had found her, that only left one option—she was still in his home.

Varum had torn up his flat then, opening cabinets, looking under the bed, and behind every door. The wardrobe had been the last place he checked. His knees had almost buckled at the sight of her. Right on the heels of relief was shock, followed closely by alarm. He'd had to stop himself from reaching for her. He hadn't been sure if she was merely sleeping or if she was dead until her eyes fluttered open. Once he learned why she had been hiding, all he could think about was finding Tanira.

The only way to appease his outrage was if he busted into her home and gave her a piece of his mind. He knew exactly what he would say to her. He'd throw off all the confines society dictated and tell her everything he had kept to himself. How many times had he swallowed the words that had been on his tongue? How many times had he stayed silent for her sake?

Too damn many.

He heard someone calling his name, but he ignored them and kept walking. What happened to Kalyani would not happen again. He had put her through too much already. It wasn't right that she should be so terrified.

She never should've been in that situation to begin with. If only he had been thinking clearly the day he'd seen her. No matter how much he wished, he couldn't turn back the clock. All he could do now was keep Kalyani safe until he found a way to get her out of the city and back with her family.

Varum slowed his steps as his anger began to cool, and he could look at the situation with a clear head. As much as he wanted to let Tanira know he knew she had tried to break into his home, he couldn't. She could have known he was at work and wanted a look inside. If he accused her of attempting to break in, she would know someone was inside.

Even if she wasn't aware that he was at his desk, she would want to know why he hadn't answered the door. Either way, he would end up being the one answering questions, and that wasn't what he wanted.

The only way to stop Tanira from returning to his home was to sever any and all ties between them once and for all. Varum had thought he'd already done that, but it seemed she wasn't willing to let go. She would once he finished with her.

He had calmed enough by the time he stood outside her door that he knew he wouldn't do anything reckless to put Kalyani or Nirav in danger. Just before he knocked, he turned his head to the side and spotted the house he had spent the first four years of his life in. Someone else lived there now, so he hadn't been back inside. Nor would he set foot in that residence again.

Varum took a breath and used the bell pull to announce his presence. Within moments, the door opened to reveal one of their servants. They showed Varum inside and asked him to wait in the front room. He stood, staring at one of the paintings without actually seeing it. The swish of Tanira's clothing announced her presence before she entered the room. It gave him enough time to prepare.

"Varum! How exciting that you're paying me a visit," she said.

He turned to face her and greeted her with a slight bow of his head. "This isn't a social call."

"I know it isn't about business, so what else could it be?" She walked to a divan and sat before patting the spot next to her.

It was something she had always done, and it always got on his nerves.

"Are you hungry? Thirsty? I'll ring for some snacks," Tanira stated.

"I'm fine," he interjected before she could reach for the small bell on the table beside her.

She froze and then lowered her arm to her lap. This time, when she turned her attention to him, she took a good look. "Has something happened?"

He was glad he had calmed down, because he would've fallen right into her trap. She suspected he was here about her trying to get into his home. As much as he wanted to address it, he wouldn't. Just one more thing for him to swallow, but it was the last time.

"Not at all," he replied. "After your visit, I thought it prudent for us to talk."

"About?"

He glanced at the floor and sighed. "You know what."

"I'm afraid I don't," she stated, playing ignorant. "You're going to have to spell it out for me."

"About us."

She flashed him a bright smile. "I knew you hadn't given up on us."

"That's just it. I've moved on. You led me to believe when I ended things that you understood it was over."

Tanira waved away his words. "You were confused. You'll come around."

"I won't."

"Stop!" she shouted as she shot to her feet. She closed the distance between them until they were nearly toe-to-toe. Then she whispered, "Don't say another word. It might get back to my father."

Varum quirked a brow. "I don't care if he knows."

"I do," she replied in another hushed whisper, her hands fisted at her sides. "Don't you understand I'm trying to save you?"

"Save me? From what?"

Tanira rolled her eyes. "You can't be that ignorant."

"It looks like I am. Spell it out," he demanded.

Her nostrils flared as she glared at him. "If you want to rise from your current social standing, you need me. Having me as your wife will elevate you to where you should've been all along if your parents..."

She trailed off, but he didn't need her to finish. Varum knew exactly what she was about to say. They were the same words Nirav had said countless times.

"I don't care about raising my station," he told her.

Tanira's eyes widened as she took a stumbling step back. "Why not?"

He snorted a derisive laugh as he looked away. "The fact that you have to ask tells me you know nothing about me."

"I know you deserve more than an office tucked away in a dark corner. I know you deserve for others to stop looking down on you for what your parents did to *you*."

Varum's gaze slid back to her, shocked by her words.

Tanira licked her lips. "I know you deserve a better life."

"I appreciate your offer, but I'm fine."

"You aren't," she insisted. "When do you smile? Laugh?"

He tilted his head. "You think that by us marrying, I'll suddenly start smiling and laughing?"

"Aye," she replied confidently.

"That isn't how love works."

"It will," she insisted. "I love you enough for the both of us. Given time, you'll come to love me, too."

Varum glanced at the ceiling. Of all the things he'd thought Tanira might say, it wasn't this. "You should be with someone who loves you just as much as you love them."

"But I want you."

"I'm not someone who can love. Not in the way you want or need. No amount of wealth or social standing will remove the stain upon me. I accepted that long ago. I work to keep the city safe, and that's enough."

It was her turn to roll her eyes. "That's a lie, and we both know it. Why not take the opportunity I'm giving you? Am I so bad?"

He gently grasped her shoulders and looked into her silvery white eyes. "You're sought after by everyone in the city. Stop wasting your time with me. I'll only give you heartache." Varum stepped back and let his hands fall to his sides. "I'm not worth it."

"You really don't want me?" she asked in a small voice. Her brow was furrowed in disbelief. "I know I chased you, but I thought you were just playing hard to get."

"I'm sorry if I led you on, but there is no future for us," he stated, his voice firm but kind.

A tear rolled out of the corner of her eye onto her cheek. "I can be whoever you want me to be. Just tell me who you want."

"I want you to be who you are. Don't change for me or anyone else. Be true to yourself as you always have."

She grabbed his arm when he started to walk past. He gently removed it and bowed his head before walking out. Only time would tell if he'd gotten through to Tanira. He wasn't comfortable leaving Kalyani alone while they waited for a time to get her out of the city. Varum didn't want to ask Nirav for more, but the only other option was for him to stay with Kalyani. He would lose his position, as lowly as it was.

If he wasn't in the offices, he wouldn't stay abreast of what was happening with the patrols. That meant he couldn't quit. He halted, conflicted about what to do. Every direction he turned put someone in danger. He had already made a huge mistake. He didn't want to add another on top of it.

Varum backtracked and took one of the hallways to Nirav's.

"I know that look," Nirav said after he opened the door. "What happened?"

Varum hesitated. "I don't want to ask, but I need your help."

"How many times have I told you I will always have your back?"

"And if this ends in your death?" Varum whispered.

Nirav grinned and motioned him inside. "Then it does. Death finds us all eventually. Wipe the bleak look off your face and tell me what happened."

It didn't take long for Varum to explain what had occurred. The anger he thought he had under control rose again as he described how he'd found Kalyani.

"How is she?" Nirav asked.

Varum blew out a breath as he sank into a chair. "She was fine when I left her, but I'd like to get back soon."

"Of course. Like you, I'm not sure if Tanira will heed your words. I'll stay with Kalyani until we can get her home."

"It's asking a lot," Varum began.

Nirav held up a hand. "There isn't anything you can ask me that would be too much. Ever."

"Thank you."

"Is there anything else?"

Varum should've known he wouldn't get anything past his friend. "Listening to Tanira made me wonder why I stayed in Tarangarh."

"We should've left when you were young."

"You asked. I'm the one who wanted to stay." Because he had hoped that his parents might return.

Nirav drew in a breath and released it. "Let's deal with one issue at a time. First up, keeping Kalyani safe. I'll stay with her when you aren't there."

"Meanwhile, I'll figure out a way to get her out."

"We'll figure out a way," Nirav corrected. "Come. Let's get to your place and check on her."

31

No matter how Kalyani tried, she couldn't relax. She had wanted to call Varum back, to run and cling to him so he would stay, but he had left before she had the chance. She had stared at the door long after it closed behind him, counting the seconds until his return.

She had known fear before. It wasn't an emotion someone grew accustomed to. No matter how many times it found her, it always burrowed deep and stayed long after the event was over.

The same was true now. She couldn't shake off the apprehension, couldn't dispel the worry. She looked back at the wardrobe and contemplated climbing back in. Her feet even took a tentative step forward, but she realized it wouldn't save her if someone came looking. Nothing—and no one, not even Varum—could stop them if they came for her.

Kalyani turned her attention to the window as she moved closer to it. The lattice was still closed, but she could see through the spaces to the water beyond. She didn't want to die, but if her choice was being hauled out of Varum's home by force to be executed, she would rather take her chances in the water. Even if she were crushed to death, it would be better than whatever might befall her at the hands of those who despised her kind.

She wanted to hate Varum for bringing her here, but she couldn't. Because if their places were reversed, she likely would've done the same thing. Not too long ago, she had been that desperate to find Lata. If she'd had even a hint that a Sea Elf could help her, she would've found a way to find one. So, how could she be angry at Varum for doing what he thought was necessary?

"Where does that leave me?" she whispered.

She put a hand against the lattice. If it weren't there, could she really go through and take her chances of being crushed? She peered up, trying to see how deep they were, but just as before, she couldn't see anything but varying shades of dark blue.

For so long, the wonders of the ocean had lulled her into the water. She had frolicked and played, uncaring of how worried Rohan became. She had always known she would return. Nothing in the water scared her.

At least, that was how it used to be.

Now, she was terrified of everything. The water was just out of reach, yet she didn't want to swim. If she somehow came out of this with her life, she might never get back into the ocean again. Her entire life had been in that one location. Even moving to Serenia had only been up the beach. There was an entire world out there, waiting to be seen. Fear of the unknown and obligation had kept her by Rohan's side.

Even he had left with Farah and saw Shecrish. What had she done? Swum. Ignored promises of staying close to shore. And for what? To be trapped in a place that seemed waiting to snuff out her life.

The doorknob rattled, yanking her out of her thoughts. Kalyani spun and hurried to plaster herself against the wall behind the bedroom door. She gazed at the wardrobe, wishing she had gotten back inside.

She listened as the front door swung open, but no one made a sound. Her ears strained to hear Varum's voice call out to let her know it was him. Her blood was rushing so loudly that it drowned out everything else.

Suddenly, the door she was hiding behind was yanked away from her. She gasped even as her gaze landed on Varum.

"Why didn't you answer?" he asked breathlessly. "I've been calling your name."

Had he? She hadn't heard anything. She tried to swallow, but even that was difficult.

Varum blew out a breath and nodded as if gathering himself. "You're pale. We brought food. A good meal will help."

She belatedly realized that his hand was wrapped around her wrist. How had she missed how big his hands were? How long his fingers were. Her wrist looked as fragile as a twig in his grasp. She stared down at his blue skin that was so different from hers. They were opposites in every way, yet somehow, she trusted him. It hadn't been intentional. But somehow, it just...happened.

"Kalyani?"

Her name was a caress that fell from his lips. She lifted her gaze to meet his. Time slowed as they stared at each other, lost in the moment and whatever held them. He took a step closer. That one movement made her stomach quiver, and heat spread through her. Then his beautiful eyes dropped to her mouth.

"Is everything all right?" Nirav asked as he pushed against the door.

Varum reached out with his free hand and kept the door from opening any wider. "I found her. We'll be out momentarily."

"Oh. Right," Nirav said with a chuckle.

She struggled to breathe as Varum continued to stare at her lips. She was just about to make the same demand as before when he suddenly released her and backed up several steps.

"Answer next time, please. I was worried," he stated. "Now, come. Nirav is waiting for us."

She watched him walk from the room. It seemed he was always walking away from her lately. Or maybe she was just clingy. She tended to do that when she was scared. But this wasn't a situation where she could cling to anyone. She needed to keep her worries to herself. It wouldn't do to let anyone know just how troubled she was about the situation.

Kalyani followed Varum into the living area to see him and Nirav at the table, setting out food. Nirav flashed a bright smile when he saw her. She found herself returning it as he hurried her over and sat her down. Varum put a plate of food in front of her. Both he and Nirav seemed relaxed, like nothing of concern was happening. If that was how they wanted it, she could follow along.

Nirav kept the conversation flowing as she picked at her food. She didn't recognize any of it, but it smelled amazing. And she was hungry. Once she finally gave it a try, she realized how delicious it was. She stuffed her face while Nirav told stories about Varum growing up.

She watched the two of them together and how easy they were in each other's company. Nirav laughed and smiled often, and she saw Varum smile for the first time. It wasn't a grin, but a wide, happy smile that made the corners of his eyes crinkle. It changed his entire face from handsome to blindingly gorgeous.

The more she listened to them, the more she realized they were decent individuals. How could a society reject a boy because his parents abandoned him? How was that the child's fault and not the parents'?

It also wasn't right that they'd spurned Nirav for his five years on land. It wasn't as if he had volunteered to go. He had been chosen.

Neither man had picked their path, but fate had brought them together, giving each of them the family they both desperately needed. What the Sea Elf society shunned had become her gain. Not that she could call Nirav and Varum friends, but they were protecting her. That was more than anyone else here would do.

"Why did you two remain in Tarangarh?" she asked. The moment she spoke the words, she realized she had not only said them aloud but had interrupted a conversation. "I'm sorry. I shouldn't have pried."

Nirav's smile was soft as he looked at her. "I thought about leaving when I first returned, but the city has always been my home. Of course, I didn't realize how difficult it would be to settle back into my old life. I hadn't been back long before Varum needed me."

She glanced at Varum, but his gaze was on the table, his face unreadable.

"And," Nirav continued, "we talked about leaving every now and again. Varum wished to remain, and his life had been disrupted so badly already that I couldn't refuse."

"Would it have been any different anywhere else?" Varum asked.

Nirav sighed. "Maybe. It's hard to say."

"We should've left," Varum said.

Surprise spread across Nirav's face.

Varum looked up and met his friend's gaze. "I think it's time we both start fresh. Away from Tarangarh." His head swung to Kalyani. "Once I have her back home, I don't plan on returning. I stayed for too long."

She searched Varum's eyes, but she wasn't sure what emotion she saw there.

He sucked in a breath and looked at Nirav. "It's time. For both of us."

"Where are you going?"

One corner of Varum's lips curved upward. "I don't know. Why don't you choose?"

"Well," Nirav said as he blinked, his brow furrowing, "the ocean is vast. We could go anywhere."

"Visit the Dragon Kings," she said.

Both men's heads swiveled to her.

"The dragons are a myth," Nirav said.

Kalyani wrinkled her nose, wondering if she should tell them everything. Then she shrugged. She had already spoken about the Kings. She might as well finish it. "They aren't, actually. It wasn't that long ago that Kendrick, a Dragon King, was chasing something that had killed a bunch of dragons. They said it was invisible, but some could see it. I don't know," she said with a shrug. "But it brought Kendrick across the border into Shecrish. He teamed up with Esha, an Asavori Ranger, and Dain to find it."

"Dain again?" Varum grumbled.

Nirav quirked a brow in question.

"That Dark Elf is in every story she tells," Varum answered.

Nirav chuckled and motioned for her to continue.

Kalyani wiped her mouth with a napkin to cover her smile. "I don't think I ever heard the entire story, but I know that Esha and Kendrick fell in love."

"A dragon and an elf?" Nirav asked with a frown. "How is that even possible?"

"I left out a crucial detail. The Dragon Kings can shift from human to dragon at will. Esha went to live with him, though she still meets Savita on occasion. At least, that's what Dain says."

Varum rolled his eyes at the mention of Dain.

"Savita?" Nirav asked.

"Oh," Kalyani said, realizing her mistake. "She's a Reader. Esha's sister."

Varum sat up. "You know a Reader?"

"I've not met her personally, but some of the others have. Arya, Jai, and Dain have seen Kendrick shift into his dragon form, too."

"There really are dragons, then?" Nirav asked, his voice a shocked whisper.

She nodded. "Apparently, quite a few. The elves almost started a war. The Conclave learned about Kendrick and attempted to retaliate, but the way Dain tells it, it was the Dragon Kings' show of force that stopped anything from going further."

"You make it sound as if the dragons would welcome us," Varum said.

Kalyani shrugged as she looked between them. "Why wouldn't they? They've accepted Esha."

"But no one is supposed to cross the border into Idrias," Nirav reminded her.

She sighed and twisted her lips. "Do the borders extend all the way out into the water?"

"Nay," Varum and Nirav replied in unison.

Nirav looked to Varum. "We could go see, and actually surface for once. I'd like to get a glimpse of a dragon. Maybe Kalyani could ask Dain to facilitate a meeting with Kendrick."

Varum shot them a dark look before surging to his feet and stalking away, leaving her and Nirav to laugh. After the terror of that morning, she hadn't thought she would be able to smile for a long time. Yet here she was, laughing.

32

Varum would be happy if he never heard Dain's name again. He hadn't met the elf, but he hated him. Kalyani's laughter trailed behind him. The sound eased some of the tension in his body. When had something so minor become so important? Had it happened suddenly, or was it something that had occurred so slowly he didn't notice?

He refused to come home again and be unable to find her. Twice now, he'd felt an emptiness, a sort of bleakness that had grasped him like the icy hands of a specter when he hadn't been able to find her. His thoughts took him to finding her behind the door. His chest tightened as he thought about how close he had come to pressing his lips to hers.

The door of his home closed behind him, cutting off her laughs. Nirav would keep her occupied so she didn't have time to think about Tanira trying to get in. Varum wasn't so sure he would be able to keep his thoughts from straying for the rest of the day.

He was more motivated than ever now to find a way for Kalyani to leave Tarangarh.

He strode into his office and pulled out the maps of the trench. He knew the ins and outs of the city as well as anyone. He knew its weaknesses and strengths. Somehow, somewhere, in all that knowledge, was the path to freedom for Kalyani. And if he was lucky, redemption for his colossal lapse in judgment.

Rohan would never forgive him, but Varum wouldn't ask that of her brother. Getting her home safely was the least he could do under the circumstances. No matter what it took, no matter how arduous it was, he would get Kalyani home.

Varum put thoughts of the Masters aside as he pored over map after map and studied logs of the currents. He tracked the distance from the trench to shore and looked over the migration patterns of dangerous marine life. He checked the shipping lanes the Sea Elves had taken note of to find the safest, quickest route.

The problem was that there wasn't one. Each path posed a different danger. The greatest was getting out of the trench. He found it hard to believe that with as much time as Kalyani spent in the water, that she hadn't encountered any Sea Elves. That didn't mean they hadn't seen her, however. He'd have to swim some distance behind her to ensure that no one tried to attack her.

He tossed down the pen and leaned back in his chair, closing his eyes. He wished to return home and tell her that he was taking her that evening, but the patrols were still too numerous for them to pass unnoticed. They had no choice but to wait.

Varum sighed and leaned his forearms on his desk, staring at the map once more. They needed a distraction. Something that took everyone's attention elsewhere. He suddenly sat up, a smile pulling at his lips as an idea took root.

"The next Assembly," he murmured.

It would occur in three days. The vast majority of the city would be in attendance. The timing could work. He chuckled as the tightness around his chest lessened. There was enough time for him to get things in order. He hoped it would be enough for Nirav, too.

Varum looked around his cramped office with its tiny desk littered with papers. He could walk out now. Few would notice his absence now that Tanira wouldn't look for him. There were details he needed to iron out with both Kalyani and Nirav anyway.

He pushed to his feet to leave when the Tidewarden rounded the corner. Varum met Arvind's bluish-black eyes. The elf had never been pleased at their involvement, and while Arvind had never outright admonished Varum because it would've hurt Tanira, the Tidewarden had made it clear he thought his daughter could do better.

Handsome and charming, Arvind wielded his power carefully —and exactly. He was never showy, preferring to be deliberate and calculating in every action he took and with each decision made. So, the fact that he was there was not something Varum dismissed.

Varum dipped his head to the elder official. "My lord. What brings you to my office?"

"Your report." Arvind looked around the office as he strolled casually inside. "Why did you send it through Tanira?"

"I didn't. I wasn't finished with it. However, she found it and made the decision to bring it to you without telling me."

Arvind's brows shot up as he clasped his hands behind his back. "She told me you asked her to bring it to me personally. Are you calling my daughter a liar?"

"I'm merely explaining what happened."

"Those are carefully chosen words."

Varum held the elder elf's gaze, not bothering to say anything else.

Arvind suddenly inhaled quickly. "I'm sure you've noticed that I added new patrols and increased the guards."

"I did."

"You don't seem thankful."

Varum eyed the Tidewarden as he wondered about the elf's anger. Could it be because he'd contradicted Tanira's account? Nay. It was something more. Unease made Varum's stomach clench. There was no way Arvind knew about Kalyani. If he did, he wouldn't be holding back.

It wouldn't do Varum any good to get into any kind of debate with him. He didn't want Arvind's attention on him now that he was leaving. The fact that the Tidewarden was there made Varum rethink things.

"I'm grateful, my lord. One of the requests I made in the report was to have additional patrols to keep our city and its occupants safe."

"You should've come to me right after you found the two elves helping the Masters."

Ah. That was why he had come. Varum bowed his head in deference. "As I explained, I was still compiling my report. I wanted to make sure I had everything included."

"There is more?"

"I'm still investigating."

Arvind looked away as he nodded. "Is that why you've not spent as much time in here as usual?"

Wariness stole over Varum. Was he being followed? Arvind had taken note of his absence, and that wasn't a good sign. Then again, Varum had become suspicious of everyone after sneaking Kalyani into his home. It wouldn't hurt to be cautious, however. "It is."

"How are you doing that within the city? Shouldn't you be out finding more boats?"

Varum frowned while studying Arvind's face. The Tidewarden swung his head around and met Varum's gaze with an expectant expression. He needed to get out of the city, but with Kalyani. There was no way he'd be able to do that if Arvind sent him out on a mission. It made Varum wonder again if Arvind knew about her. Was this some kind of test?

Or worse, a trap?

"I've been looking over shipping lane records," Varum said as he pointed to the ledger on his desk. "We've not paid much attention to what the other races are doing, but that could hold the key since they're obviously transporting those abducted via boats."

Arvind cut his gaze to the ledger. "It doesn't look like there's much in there."

"There isn't. Yet. I wanted to find some way of locating the two Sea Elves I saw, but so far, I've been unsuccessful."

Arvind grunted as he looked at the items on the desk before lifting his gaze to Varum. "It's easy for someone to hide in Tarangarh. Your report didn't give much of a description of either elf, other than that they were male."

"There was a lot happening at that time."

"It's hard to believe that anyone in my city would join the Masters."

Varum had expected such a comment. It was one of the reasons he had put as much detail as he had into the report. He couldn't help but wonder—once more—exactly why Arvind was here. Maybe it was time for him to do a bit of testing himself. "Yet rumors of them have spread even to us. How? Unless someone is involved with them."

"Surely, you aren't accusing me."

"Of course not," Varum stated. "We know very little about the Masters or the organization, other than that they are kidnapping people. Those shackled on the boat were human, but what happens when all the humans have been taken? They've already began taking elves above."

Arvind shook his head once. "Humans are the weaker ones. It makes sense they would be targeted."

Varum was disgusted by the words. Had he thought the same before Kalyani? Had he looked down upon her kind with the same sort of disdain? "That doesn't make what is happening to them right."

"This isn't about right or wrong. It is about keeping Sea Elves safe," Arvind said. "I've reached out to the other Tidewardens to see if they've gathered any information. "

"I'm happy to know that you're taking this so seriously."

Arvind's eyes narrowed. "I need proof. So far, I only have your account. There were no other witnesses."

There were, but Varum couldn't bring Kalyani into things. "What if none of the other cities have had any dealings with the Masters?"

"That means you'll have worried for nothing."

"I sincerely hope you're correct."

Arvind issued a snort. "At any rate, you no longer need to concern yourself with this issue. I've given it to someone else."

Varum wasn't surprised by the move, but it still brought a rise of anger from within him. He told himself it didn't matter, that he was leaving Tarangarh. Now, Arvind had made it even easier to say goodbye to the city.

"As you wish," Varum said with a bow of his head.

"I heard you visited my house today."

Varum sighed. Maybe now they could get to the real reason for the Tidewarden's visit. "I needed a word with Tanira to clear up something."

Fury tightened Arvind's face. "It had better not have been about reuniting. I know that is what my daughter wants, but I refuse to have someone like you married to her."

"Someone like me?" Varum had heard those words his entire life, but somehow, they infuriated him now. "You mean someone who goes above and beyond for the city? Someone who is loyal and dependable?"

"You know exactly what I mean," Arvind replied icily.

Varum snorted while barely reining in his fury. "I do, indeed."

"Good. I'm glad to see we're of like mind."

"Hardly." Varum walked around the desk and out of his office without looking back. If he stayed, he'd likely say something he would later regret. As it was, he was carrying a huge regret already. There wasn't room for any more.

He made his way home, his thoughts filled with Kalyani and how to get her home. As he neared, he heard the faint sounds of a song coming from his neighbor. Varum paused to listen to the elf's haunting voice, but it wasn't the words that stopped him. It was wondering what Kalyani thought of the music.

Varum trudged to the door, his hand on the knob as his magic unlocked it. Just as he was about to open the door, he pictured her face from earlier when he found her hiding. The relief in her gaze had sent a bolt of something electric through him. But it was the sight of her lips that had undone him.

33

Flamefall

Savita walked through the row of tents as she made her way to the forest. She wanted to lift her skirts and run, but that would bring too much attention. Her heart pumped furiously as her gaze darted around. She knew each of the Asavori Rangers personally. It was hard not to after being stationed with them for so many years, but things had been different since Esha left with Kendrick.

Though it wasn't the Dragon King that had Savita on alert. She wanted to say it was the unnamed Star Elf who had visited her, but it wasn't him either. Her pace quickened as she reached the trees and altered her destination to the edge of the mesa. The Rangers on guard duty in the trees would see her, but she often made this trek, so nothing would seem out of the ordinary.

She needed to appear as if everything was normal, even though it wasn't. Her fingers wrapped around the rune pouch tied to her belt. Their warning had sent her early to her meeting with Dain.

Her journey to reach the carved elven faces seemed to take much longer than usual. She heard the roar of the waterfall before she broke the tree line and headed to the steps that led down to the ground. At one time, she had come here simply to watch the water flow out of the mouth of the great carved faces before tumbling into the pool below. Things had been simple back then.

They were far from that now.

She reached the steep steps and grasped her skirts to begin the grueling descent. Savita glanced toward her meeting spot with Dain, even though she couldn't see him. He always remained hidden until she arrived. Most times, Esha and Kendrick joined them at the border. It gave her a chance to talk to her sister so they could keep each other updated. But not this time.

Those meetings might need to be put on hold. The Star Elf's visit—and his warning—had caused Savita to worry that she was being watched. As far as she knew, no Reader had been abducted, but that didn't mean the Masters would steer clear of them altogether.

Her foot slipped on a wet stone, causing her to tilt to the side as she hurried to regain her balance. Her arms pinwheeled, and her heart jumped into her throat. Gold magic surged from her palms as she steadied herself. She stood there, breathing heavily for several moments, before she continued down the never-ending steps.

When her feet finally touched grass, she had to fight not to break into a run. The area was open. The only place for someone to hide was by ducking down in the waist-high grass. She glanced to the side across the border into Idrias. It was too dark for her to make out any dragons. How she wished Kendrick and Esha were coming. She couldn't shake the feeling that she might need their help tonight.

"Don't come, Dain," she whispered. "Don't come tonight."

The night was still, the air heavy with the scent of approaching rain. Even the double moons were hidden behind thick, slow-moving clouds. It was the kind of night meant for terror and pain. A night of death.

She clutched the bag of runes again. Had her message reached Dain in time? There was no way to know. Nor could she allow him to greet the night alone. Never had she imagined she would call a Dark Elf a friend, but that's exactly what he was. He had done more in the fight against the Masters than anyone. It made sense that they would focus everything on him now.

The soft stirring of the wind tugged a strand of hair against her face. Shadows parted before her to allow Dain to step out. He met her gaze and halted mid-stride. A quick frown furrowed his brow before it vanished.

"*Run*," she mouthed.

But it was already too late.

Dark Elves poured out of the shadows to surround them. She gathered her magic as Dain drew his sword. Black magic swirled around his hand before rolling down the blade, making the metal gleam like onyx. He swung the weapon in a wide arc as elves attacked, sending out a blast of magic that slammed into them and sent them flying backward.

Savita tossed a bolt of gold magic and quickly spun in the other direction. Her skirts whirled around her before tangling against her legs. She lunged, pelting the nearest Dark with magic. Out of the corner of her eye, she saw one of them leap toward her, a blade aimed at her head. She leaned to the side and rotated slightly, watching the sword pierce the air where she had been.

She dropped to a knee and swung out her leg to trip her attacker before spinning back to her feet and sending out a blast wave of magic. There was a grunt of pain behind her, and she glanced over her shoulder to see Dain take a double hit of magic and a blade to his left arm. She took a step to help him, but was struck in the back of her knee. It brought her to the ground, and she used the momentum to roll and come up on her feet, magic already aimed.

It didn't matter how many shots she fired. There were too many Dark Elves for her and Dain to take on alone. She had used up too much of her magic and was tiring quickly. The only way for her to recharge was with the sun, and that was hours away.

"Go!" Dain shouted at her.

But there was nowhere for her to go. She gathered the last of her power, putting everything she had into it. It was her only chance to get her and Dain free. All they needed was a moment. Then he could get them out with his shadows.

Her arms shook from the effort. It wouldn't be enough, but she still had to try. Suddenly, a Dark came at her, his hand filled with magic, aimed at her face. She tried to get out of the way, but her limbs were sluggish. Suddenly, someone was beside her. A hand covered her face as they turned her against a hard chest. They spun her, and she saw a flash of purple magic between their fingers.

She clung to the individual just to stay on her feet. One arm now held her against a hard chest as he shifted. She tried to look around the broad shoulders at Dain, but she was being moved around, too, as if they were dancing.

Savita called to her magic. There was still a little left within her. She attempted to push away from him to use it, but the arm tightened around her, preventing her from leaving. The next thing she knew, she was being cradled in strong arms. She looked back and saw Dain down on one knee, still fighting.

"Stop. I can't leave him," she said, slamming her fist against a solid shoulder. When the individual didn't halt, she hit him harder. "I said stop."

She was lowered onto something, and she found herself looking into the Star Elf's face.

"How bad are your injuries?" he asked as he scanned her body.

Savita shoved his hands away and got to her feet. "What are you doing? Dain needs help."

"You can't help him," he said as he stood to look down at her.

"But you can."

The Star Elf snorted. "Why would I do that?"

"He's a friend."

A muscle in the elf's jaw clenched. He peeled back his lips as if to speak, but whirled around and raced back to Dain. Savita tried to make out movement in the dark, but the night had abruptly settled into silence again. She should go to Dain herself and do what she could. She tried to move her foot, but her limbs wouldn't listen. Her gown was sliced in places and covered in blood and burns from the battle.

Blood trickled over the top of her hand, running down a finger before dripping to the ground. Even with the warning from the runes, she had been ill-prepared. She had thought the alarm was for Dain alone, but now she wondered if it had also been for her. The Dark had kept coming at her.

She reached for the bag of runes, but it was no longer attached to her belt. Panic filled her as she dropped to the ground and began searching with her hands.

"What are you doing?"

She didn't bother to look up at the Star Elf as she crawled to another area. "My bag of runes."

"We need to go."

She shook her head and then looked to where Dain had been. "Where's Dain?"

"Gone. Just as we need to be."

"I'm not leaving without my runes." Savita mustered the last of her strength to get to her feet. She managed two steps before she felt him behind her.

And then, everything went dark.

Dain gasped for breath as he sat precariously on a limb high in a tree. Pain stole his breath and made it challenging to think straight. Warm blood trickled in thick ribbons down his body from multiple strikes. He needed to get to Sundar so he could be healed, but the Star Elf was too far away. Dain dropped his head back against the bark. He wouldn't make it back to Serenia in the shape he was in. He might make it to Durga's, though. It would be close, but if he stayed in the tree, he would either die from blood loss or the attackers finding him.

He had no idea where Savita was. One moment, she was there. The next, she was gone. He hoped she got out. Maybe she'd run across the border and was now with the Dragon Kings. He hadn't thought of going there himself, but it was too late now.

"Once more," he told himself. "I just need to make one more jump."

Durga would help him. Even if she wasn't home, her servants would know what to do. But he was so tired. He closed his eyes. It would be so easy to just let go. To give up on...everything and everyone. He could stop fighting, stop hiding. Stop the torment that had been his life.

Reva's face suddenly filled his mind. She smiled at him, her warm brown eyes shining with amusement. She was the only light in a world that had been filled with darkness. She was the only one who made him want to stay alive.

He swallowed, his heart aching at the mere thought of her. His body was weakening fast. There was no time to delay. He opened his eyes and lifted the hand he held against his side to see it covered in blood.

"Don't you dare give up."

He frowned at the sound of Reva's voice. She couldn't be here. He knew it was a hallucination, and yet he still scanned the area around him for her.

"You can't stay here. You have to go. Now."

The only one who could make him move was Reva. Dain clung to her words, even as he gathered his shadows and focused on Durga's house. He lost his grip on the shadows, and all too soon, was spat out of them. His knees buckled, and he fell to the ground. Every breath felt like a dozen blades scraping the insides of his lungs. Each beat of his heart sent more blood pumping out of his wounds.

He looked up and found himself in an alley behind a building —and nowhere near Durga's. The pain beat a steady rhythm, chasing away everything else. He had missed his mark getting to Durga's. There was nowhere else close he could go.

In his need for comfort, he thought of Reva and let her face fill his mind again. He regretted...everything with her. He'd had opportunities to say the things he felt, but he'd been too much of a coward. Instead, he had kept them bottled inside, choosing to remain silent. Alone. He was forever alone. Those around him were always in danger. How could he bring her into that? She was too precious for such things.

"The Dain I know wouldn't give up."

Maybe it was his time. Everyone died. He had escaped it too many times in the past. Eventually, it caught up to everyone. He'd always known he would die in battle. He had accepted that long ago. But he really didn't want to breathe his last breath in the filth of the street.

Dain strained to push up onto his hands and knees. He sat back on his haunches to look for a place to crawl to when he realized that he was close to The Crossing. Could he make it to Sidiq's storage room? He wasn't sure he should even try. If nothing else, he had to let someone know what had happened to him and Savita. At least Dain wouldn't die on the street, and Sidiq could get word to Durga.

Dain reached for his shadows, but nothing happened. He tried again, but they still wouldn't answer. He reached down, grasping for the last dregs of his magic. He couldn't even manage a smile when the shadows reluctantly enveloped him.

Reva was coming out of the storage room when she heard a loud crash from within. She recoiled at the sound and glanced around, but no one in the pub seemed to have heard it over the loud din of conversation. She hesitated before slipping back inside the room, wondering if she had accidentally tipped something over.

She carefully moved around the room, looking for what had caused the crash. She saw the broken bits of barrels and crates. Amid all of that was a boot. Her eyes followed the boot to the leg. The moment she recognized the distinctive long, black coat, she rushed forward.

"Dain!" she cried when she saw him lying on his back, unmoving, his clothes torn and bloodied.

She put a finger under his nose to make sure he was still breathing before jumping up and running to get Sidiq. The Dark Elf owner of the pub saw her before she reached him. He came out from behind the bar, and she grabbed his sleeve and pulled him into the storage room. To Dain.

Sidiq slung Dain over his shoulder before he turned to her and said, "I'll be back."

"He'll be okay, though, right?"

Sidiq's lips flattened. "I don't know."

The shadows took both elves, leaving Reva alone.

34

The first notes of music halted the words from Kalyani's mouth, but it was the divine voice that took her breath away. She couldn't understand the words, but she didn't need to in order to experience the longing and soul-crushing ache of the tune itself. She heard it in the poignant melody and the evocative voice that sang it as if his very heart had been shattered.

She forgot the conversation, forgot she wasn't alone. She forgot everything and gave herself over to the emotional song. Kalyani closed her eyes and allowed every note to fill her. She rode the highs and lows of the music until it felt as if it had melded into her very essence. She wiped away a tear as the last note finally faded, and silence followed.

The world felt somehow diminished once the elf stopped singing. She longed for more, yet at the same time, she yearned to curl into a ball and release a torrent of tears. Kalyani opened her eyes and tried to remember her talk with Nirav to pick up the conversation, but she couldn't think of anything but the song.

"Ah," Nirav said with a sigh. "That one always gets me."

"What was it?" she asked.

"A love song."

Her head whipped to the side at the sound of Varum's voice. Their eyes met, held.

"A sad love song," Nirav corrected. "It's about a Sea Elf and a—"

"The lover he couldn't have," Varum said over him.

There was something different about Varum, but Kalyani couldn't put her finger on what.

"Something happened," Nirav said.

Varum sighed and nodded. "I had a visit from Arvind."

"The Tidewarden?" Nirav frowned as he glanced at the floor. "Why?"

"To let me know I'm no longer to investigate the Masters or anyone involved with them. He's handed it off to someone else."

Kalyani was outraged on Varum's behalf. "That's wrong. You did all the work."

"That's how things go, unfortunately. Varum and others do the initial work, and someone else gets the credit. It's how it has always been," Nirav explained.

She shook her head. "That doesn't make it right."

"I don't care," Varum said, just as Nirav was about to speak. He walked to the chair and sat. "I spent the day going over maps for currents and shipping lanes to find the best route to get Kalyani home."

Nirav quirked a brow. "Does that mean you found one, even with the patrols?"

"It does."

Elation surged through her. "Really?"

A small smile curved Varum's lips when he looked her way. "Really. I was leaving my office for the last time when Arvind entered."

"What do you mean by last time?" she asked.

Varum's gaze lowered to the floor. "We'll leave in three days' time. I planned to spend that time getting everything sorted. Since I'm not returning, there's no use doing any work. Besides," he stated as he looked up at her, "there are things I need to do before we leave."

Kalyani's smile melted when he saw the way Nirav was staring at Varum. Something more was going on, and neither man wanted to speak of it in front of her. She almost pushed to see if she could discover what it was, but she decided it might be better if she didn't know.

"Then I should also prepare," Nirav replied as he got to his feet.

Varum stood so that the two faced each other. "You don't have to."

"I've long said there is nothing here for either of us. You're also going to need my help."

"And they would go straight to you when they realize I'm gone." Varum twisted his lips. "There's no way to untangle you from my mistake."

Nirav clapped him on the shoulder and grinned. "Our fates have been entangled for years, and I'm glad of it. I have plans this evening. Let's talk tomorrow." He looked at Kalyani and bowed to her. "It was a pleasure, my dear."

"Thank you for staying with me today," she told Nirav with a smile.

She rose to her feet as Varum walked Nirav to the door and

shut it behind the older elf. Varum stayed there with his hand on the knob for several beats before finally turning to face her.

"Did anything else happen?" she asked.

He gave a small shake of his head. "Nothing of consequence. I told you it was a treat when my neighbor sings."

She let him change the subject, even as she wanted to press because she knew there was more. "It was an incredible song. The music was unbelievable, but his voice is…"

"I know."

"Do all of you sound like that?"

There was a slight hesitation before Varum said, "They might sound pleasing, but he's exceptional."

"I thought all Sea Elves had the gift."

"I don't want to talk about singing or dancing," he said.

His expression was unreadable again, as if he had shut the door on his emotions so she couldn't see what he was thinking or feeling. "What do you want to talk about?"

"Things I shouldn't want."

There was something in the words. Something she knew she was supposed to understand. She knew what she wanted those words to mean, but she wasn't sure they did. If she was leaving in three days, why would she want to find out?

He stood still as stone, his gaze locked on her. "Aren't you going to ask?"

"I'm not sure if I should."

They were treading precariously close to things that couldn't be taken back. She didn't belong in his world, and he couldn't be in hers. It didn't matter how much she might have come to like him, or how her eyes looked for him, even if he wasn't there.

Silence stretched as a quick frown furrowed his brow. "Are you saying you don't want to know?"

Could he really want her? Did she dare allow herself to imagine such a thing? And what if he did say it was her? Was it better to know his kiss and never have it again, or to never know it at all?

She thought about earlier when she had believed he might kiss her. She had craved it, longed for it, and nearly pulled his head down to press her mouth to his. He couldn't tease her like this and have her ignore it. She wasn't strong enough to withstand his pull.

"Do I tell you who occupies my every thought?" he asked as he took a slow step toward her. "Do I tell you about the dreams I have?"

Her heart was beating so fast she thought it might jump out of her chest at any moment. He continued toward her with measured steps as if expecting her to dart away. Where would she go? She had been caught long before she acknowledged it.

Then he was in front of her, his body so close she could feel his warmth.

"Do I say how I've thought about kissing her since the moment she ordered me to kiss or kill her?" he asked in a husky whisper.

He had flung open the door and showed her his hunger, his yearning.

Chills raced over her skin as she stared into his iridescent blue eyes. All she had to do was take a step away and put an end to this madness. But she couldn't. Maybe he had been out of his mind when he brought her to Tarangarh, or perhaps it was fated that she should be here. None of that mattered now.

"Do I?" he asked.

Her reply would cement whatever came next. There was no taking it back, no forgetting. And no regrets.

"Nay," she replied.

Pain flashed across his face as he slammed the door shut again. He took a step back and looked away. "I understand."

"I want you to show me."

His head swiveled back to her. He searched her face for several tense moments before he faced her fully and closed the distance between them. There were no more words as one of his large hands cupped the back of her head, and he slowly lowered his lips, pressing them to hers in a long, lingering kiss.

Desire unfurled like the petals of a flower, igniting something fervent and primal. It slid through her, heating her blood. She gasped for breath as he lifted his head. Her eyes opened, briefly meeting his. The need she saw there made her stomach flutter.

His other hand rested on her lower back as he pulled her against him a heartbeat before he kissed her again. She grabbed him as his tongue swept past her lips to tangle with hers. He deepened the kiss, molding her body to his until she no longer knew where she ended and he began.

The kiss was charged, fiery. Uninhibited.

He poured everything into each kiss—and demanded she give the same in return. Every sweep of his tongue, every touch of his lips, tightened the desire that had settled low in her belly. Her hands roamed over his back and shoulders, feeling the thick sinew beneath her palms.

The feel of his arousal against her stomach sent heat flooding through her. Without his mouth leaving hers, he guided her until she was against the wall. Her nipples hardened, and her breasts swelled as she ached for his touch. With every fiery kiss, she fell more and more under his spell. She didn't just want him anymore. She *needed* him. He was the only one who could fulfill the ache inside her. The only one who could ease the need he had ignited.

She shoved against his shoulders, spinning him until he was the one against the wall. Their lips broke apart briefly as their gazes met. He let out a growl and seized her lips once more. Then he lifted her off her feet. She wrapped her legs around his waist while his lips traced hot, hungry kisses along her jaw and down her throat.

Her head lolled to the side as she slid her fingers into the cool strands of his hair. How could she have ever considered not kissing him? He had awakened something within her that had been buried. Or maybe it had just been waiting for him. A fire raged now. The inferno engulfed her, and his kisses stirred the flames. He had begun it, and only he could end it.

"Kalyani."

The sound of her name on his lips made chills race over her body. She lifted her head to look at him. Desire blazed in his beautiful eyes as clear as a full moon. He wasn't hiding it. It was as if he wanted her to see. She touched his face, marveling at the stunning specimen before her.

"You need to tell me now if you want to stop. If I keep going, I won't be able to," he said.

She answered with a kiss, and a moan rumbled in his chest as he strode into the bedroom.

35

Varum couldn't stop kissing her. He was afraid that if he did, Kalyani would vanish from his arms. He hadn't intended to give in to his need to taste her lips, but when he saw how moved she was by his neighbor's song, the last thread of his will snapped.

From then on, all he could think about was her.

The moment she sank against him after their lips touched, he was utterly, completely hers. Each sigh, whimper, and moan she made drove him wild. Her hands were a torture all their own as she stroked and caressed him, leaving a trail of heat everywhere she touched. But it was her fingers in his hair, her nails softly scraping against his scalp, that nearly sent him over the edge.

He'd thought to only take one kiss—one quick touch of their lips. But he had made the mistake of looking into her eyes. Need smoldered as bright as the moon. The promise he had made to himself to back away had disintegrated instantly. She hadn't taken the chance he'd given her to end it, and he was glad she hadn't.

Varum stopped beside the bed as he ended the kiss and looked into her dark eyes. She unlocked her ankles and allowed her legs to drop. He then let her gradually slide down his body until her feet touched the floor. His gaze dropped to find her lips swollen from their kisses. He lightly touched her cheek, and she leaned her face against his hand.

He unfastened a button of her tunic. When she didn't stop him, he moved to the next, and then the next. He gathered the hem of the garment in his hands and slowly tugged it upward. She raised her arms so he could pull it over her head. It dropped from his hand, forgotten as she began to unbutton his. He could do nothing but watch as her fingers nimbly worked until she rose on her tiptoes to push his tunic over his shoulders and off.

Her lips parted as she flattened her hands on his chest and smoothed them over his shoulders and down his arms. His balls tightened with need. His cock ached to be inside her, to have their bodies sliding against each other. But he would not rush this.

His hand shook as he ran his finger along the waistband of her pants. She sucked in a breath when he slid a digit between her body and the fabric. Her fingers dug into his waist, her body tense, waiting for his next move. He held her gaze as he loosened the fastening.

The pulse at her neck beat rapidly when he slid both hands around her waist and pushed her pants down. He slowly dropped to one knee as he tugged the fabric down her legs bit by bit until they puddled around her ankles. He then gently lifted first one foot and then the other, before shoving the trousers away.

He had barely gotten to his feet before she moved so close their bodies were almost touching. He stared at the top of her head as her hands came to rest on his waist. His breath lodged in his throat when she slid a finger into the band of his trousers as he had done to her. Varum fisted his hands to keep from reaching for her.

She lazily skimmed the digit across his skin, leaving a hot trail in its wake. His cock jumped each time she got close. All the while, her warm breath fanned his chest. Then she lifted her head. Their gazes clashed once more as she unbuttoned his pants. He watched as she lowered to her knees and pushed his trousers down. Varum stepped out of them at the same time he pulled her to her feet.

Before he could reach for her thin layers of underwear, she was already removing the panties. He swallowed hard and divested himself of his undergarments. Then she tugged off the rest of his clothes. For several moments, he could do nothing but stare at her beautiful body. Her curves begged to be caressed, from her breasts to her dark nipples that pebbled beneath his gaze.

He rested his palms on the swells of her hips and caressed upward to the indent of her waist, then higher until his hands were just below her breasts. She stroked upward from his wrists to his shoulders. Varum's control was quickly evaporating now that they were skin to skin, but he wanted to savor every second.

He wrapped an arm around her before gently settling her on the bed. He followed, leaning over while braced on his hands. She tugged him down so that he settled between her legs. A small smile played upon her lips before she pressed her mouth to his. He groaned as their tongues tangled.

A moan escaped Kalyani at the feel of his delicious weight. She wound her arms around him, her hands on his back as he deepened the kiss. The fire he had begun was slowly becoming an inferno. She rocked against his hard length, helpless against the need throbbing at her core. He shifted to the side so he could caress a hand down her body and up the inside of her thigh.

She tensed as he neared her sex, waiting for his touch. His touch was light as he stroked over her center once, twice. Then he slid a finger between her labia. She groaned and shifted her hips forward. He applied just the right amount of pressure as he circled her clit. Kalyani wrenched her mouth from his and cried out from the exquisite pleasure that bloomed outward.

It was too much, and yet, it wasn't enough. She clutched at his arm, her desire steadily building. She felt his breath against her nipple a heartbeat before his lips wrapped around the peak and he suckled. Need shot from her breast to her sex, making it throb. As if sensing what she needed, Varum slid a finger inside her. She gasped, her back arching. Then he began to slowly move his finger in and out of her while continuing his assault on her breast.

She was close to climaxing already. The feel of him, the smell. The taste. He overwhelmed her senses, becoming the center of everything. He worked her body as if they had been lovers for years, and she was powerless to do anything but bask in the pleasure.

He would never get enough of her. Varum knew it after their first kiss, but it was confirmed once they were skin to skin. Her soft cries, seductive moans, and the way her body undulated...it was as if she had been made for him and him alone.

"Please," she begged.

He glanced at her face as he shifted his attention to her other nipple. He swirled his tongue around the peak while adding a second finger inside her. She was unbelievably wet. And he needed a taste.

Varum slid down her body and spread her legs wider as he settled between them. He looked up to find she had lifted her head to watch him. He grinned, holding her gaze as he dipped his head and licked her.

She groaned as her head fell back. He issued a satisfied moan as his tongue found her clit and began to mercilessly tease it. He didn't relent until she was writhing on the bed. He paused to slide his fingers inside her once more, and then he returned his attention to her swollen nub.

Desire tightened with every flick of his tongue and stroke of his fingers. Kalyani fisted her hands in the covers as he brought her ever closer to the edge. He had coaxed her there twice already, but backed off just before she climaxed. Her entire body shook with the need for release.

"P-pl-please," she begged.

His fingers kept a steady rhythm as his tongue flicked faster. Her body tensed, seeking the release. Then, she was hurtled over the edge as white-hot pleasure engulfed her. Shudder after shudder racked her body until he finally lifted his head and withdrew his fingers. She cracked open her eyes to see Varum rising up on his hands and knees, desire darkening his gaze.

She didn't have time for words as he flipped her onto her stomach and grabbed her hips, pulling her to him. He set her on her hands and knees and ran his hands down her back and over her arse.

"I've longed for this moment," he rasped.

She swallowed hard, knowing exactly what he meant. Kalyani looked over her shoulder at him, but his gaze was on her back. His jaw was clenched, his body taut. Then he met her eyes. She couldn't name what passed between them, nor did she try. It was bigger than them, bigger than the moment.

He leaned forward as the head of his cock rubbed against her sensitive sex. She moaned and dropped her head, eager to feel him within her. She didn't have to wait long. He pushed between her folds and slid inside. He went slowly, giving her body time to adjust to his size until he filled her fully.

Then, he began to move.

Varum gripped her hips as he moved with short, slow thrusts. The slick walls of her sex gripped him tightly. He wouldn't last long at this rate. The sight of her dark curls falling over one shoulder, and her soft cries filling the room, was almost too much.

He grabbed a handful of her hair and turned her head to the side so he could see her face. She was breathing heavily, and her eyes were glazed with pleasure. He released her and began to thrust hard and deep. She moaned in response. Soon, their bodies were slick with sweat.

She shouted his name right before her body clamped around him. He felt the tremors that ran through her body from the climax, and they sent him to his own orgasm. He thrust deep inside her and shuddered as his seed spilled into her.

He didn't know how long they stayed locked in that position before he came to. Varum slowly pulled out of her, and she collapsed onto her side, breathing heavily. He curled around her and shifted his arm under her head.

Neither said anything as they lay in the aftermath of their union. He didn't know what to say. Nothing had ever felt so right and amazing, but even as he admitted that, he knew there couldn't be anything between them.

Tormented lovers.

Just like the song his neighbor had sung. Was he following the footsteps of that Sea Elf who had fallen for a human? Varum wanted to deny it, but he couldn't quite muster the energy to even think such a thought. Maybe giving in to his desire had been wrong. Kalyani was leaving in just a few days. Still, he wouldn't take it back, even if he could.

He tightened his arm around her, and she snuggled back against him. Things had already been complicated between them. This only muddled it more. There was no way to untangle his emotions. All he could give her now was safe passage home. And he would, no matter what he had to do.

Varum lifted his head to look down at her and discovered that she was asleep. He grinned before kissing her temple. As he lay his head down, he made a list of what needed to be done over the next two days. He didn't want to return to work. He'd rather stay with Kalyani, but he didn't want any undue attention cast his way either. That meant he'd have to go back in, at least for one more day.

So many things could go wrong between now and then. While he couldn't think of every scenario, he should contemplate the worst and get prepared for those, at least. He had gotten Kalyani into the city without incident, and he was determined to get her out the same way. No one would expect a human, especially if he put her in a bag so no one could see. She might not like that, but it would only be for a short time. And Nirav had a sack that was big enough.

Varum smiled as he realized that was the answer that had been plaguing him from the beginning. Even if the patrols saw him, they wouldn't stop him.

"It's perfect," he murmured as he closed his eyes.

36

Flamefall

Hiding among the Asavori Rangers was as problematic as One had known it would be. He should leave, yet he lingered, waiting for Savita to wake when he should have been far away by now. He had taken a huge chance by interfering in the battle. His cover could've been blown. But when he saw the Dark attacking Savita, he acted without thought.

It had been a mistake to go to her. She wouldn't trust him until he gave up some answers, and he had no intention of doing that. Which meant they would forever be at an impasse. It was time for him to find an alternative.

He was about to turn away when movement out of the corner of his eye stopped him. He swiveled his head toward the tent and saw Savita rushing out. She hastily scanned the area as she clutched the bag of runes in one hand. Was she looking for him?

Did she know he was the one who found the runes for her? Or was it Dain she sought?

One watched the Rangers hastily surround Savita. Within moments, they rushed toward the edge of the mesa, leaving Savita behind—no doubt looking for proof of the battle. They wouldn't find any. He had removed any trace—for his sake. He hadn't spent years setting things up, only for it to crumble now.

His gaze returned to Savita to find her facing his way. No matter how hard she scanned the brush, she wouldn't find him. He wondered if she knew he had wiped the paint from her face yet. Her injuries had been severe. He didn't know if she had been aware of how many wounds she'd sustained. It was almost as if the Dark had been aiming for her eyes. There had been a lot of blood to clean up after he'd healed her, but he hadn't needed to remove all the paint. He still wasn't sure why he had done it.

That simple action had confirmed that he needed to choose someone else to partner with. Others were fighting against the Masters, though none had done as much damage as the Reader and her friends. They were the best choices. He could approach Arya again. He had helped her before. Dain might be more willing to listen now, too—if the Dark Elf survived the attack. He hadn't looked in good shape the last time One saw him.

Savita was the optimal choice since she could use the runes to convince the others, but that wouldn't work now. He had intervened. He never should've gone to the meeting place to begin with. It had been by happenstance that he had overheard that there would be a surprise attack against Dain and Savita. He'd told himself to keep to his search for Gita, but somehow, he'd found himself in that grassy field.

He had hoped Savita wouldn't come, but he caught sight of her white robes coming down the mesa's steps. He'd even contemplated stopping her so she couldn't reach the meeting point, but he hadn't. And just as he had suspected, the runes must have told her what was coming since she tried to warn Dain.

It didn't do much good. Too many Dark had been waiting for them. Dain was a warrior used to battle, but the Reader wasn't. Still, One had been surprised that she'd managed to hold her own for as long as she had. Perhaps she had gained some skills from her time with the Rangers. She might have actually held them off if her magic hadn't run out.

He rubbed his chest, thinking about how his heart had dropped to his feet the first time a blast of magic had cut her cheek. Before he knew it, he was at her side. It had been foolish and reckless. And something he had never done before.

He hadn't spent years calculating and planning to get to this point, only to let it all slip away now. There could be no mistakes, no miscalculations. No missteps. Not when he was so close to getting everything he wanted. As perfect as the Reader might have originally been, she was becoming a nuisance now. And just like everything else that got in his way, he cut it out of his life.

With one final look at Savita, One slipped away.

The Crossing

Reva was at the pub before dawn, waiting for Sidiq. He hadn't returned the night before, which meant she had spent the night wondering if Dain had survived. Every time she closed her eyes to sleep, she saw images of Dain lying lifelessly, covered in blood. It had made getting rest impossible.

She opened the tavern and set about getting things ready for the day, hoping that having something to occupy her time would keep her from worrying. It didn't. Every sound had her head snapping up, searching for Sidiq or Dain, and each time, she was disappointed. She half-expected Arya or Jai to drop by, but with every hour that passed, she came to realize they must already know that Dain had been injured. Or they were also wounded and unable to do anything.

Reva had no way of contacting anyone to get news. How was she supposed to get through the day? The not-knowing led her to imagine all sorts of things, and that only twisted her stomach into tighter knots.

She tried to force a smile when the first customers entered, but she gave up on that quickly. She was short-tempered and sullen enough that she eventually set up behind the bar and let the other staff tend to the tables. That helped, but it didn't keep her away from all the patrons. Fortunately, Sidiq wasn't much of a talker, so their regular customers didn't expect her to be chatty.

It wasn't until she had to go into the storeroom that she realized Sidiq *had* returned to the pub sometime during the night, since everything was cleaned up. There wasn't a scrap of spilled liquor, a splinter of wood, or a drop of blood anywhere. It was as if Dain crashing into the room had never happened. If she hadn't seen it with her own eyes, she wouldn't think it'd actually happened.

She looked at the spot where she'd found Dain, staring for a long time. He and the others toyed with danger on a daily basis. Sidiq knew that. He was the one who had urged her not to get involved. Sidiq was nothing if not careful. Of course, he would've returned to clean up any evidence that Dain had been there. But the fact that Sidiq was still absent said that he was taking care of Dain.

"He'd better be," she murmured.

She would never forgive Sidiq if he didn't make sure Dain got to a Healer. If only she had been able to go with them. However, she was a mere human that magic had no effect on. It wasn't as if she could do anything to save Dain. But he had been there for her in her hour of need. He'd come out of nowhere and swept her up in his shadows, taking her to safety. No one had ever done that for her before. No one had ever cared if she was safe or cared for. But he had.

He'd walked her home and had even gotten new locks for her door. He'd given her purpose by letting her collect intel for him.

Then, he'd taken it all away.

She didn't know what she had done wrong. She had asked, but he'd never told her. Reva had thought when she spoke to Arya last that she might be able to help Dain by passing information on to her, but Arya hadn't returned to the pub. And Sidiq had refused to get word to either Arya or Dain.

It was as if everyone was trying to stop her from doing her part. She had been kidnapped like so many others. Why shouldn't she do whatever she could to help? It might not be much, but something was better than just sitting by.

Was it because she was human? Or because magic had no effect on her?

What was it that made her such an awful individual?

She swiped at a tear that'd dropped onto her cheek. There was no forgetting about the Masters or their nefarious deeds. Reva had seen some of them for herself, and she wasn't going to simply stand by and let others put their lives on the line. She might be what some would call weak because she was human, but she could still contribute.

Reva took a deep breath and wiped her face to erase any evidence of tears, then whirled around. She had a pub to run until Sidiq got back.

Somewhere in the Below

Sidiq tossed away another blood-soaked bandage, adding to the growing pile, and stared down at Dain, who had yet to regain consciousness. He needed to get word to Arya, but he was afraid that if he left Dain, he wouldn't be alive when he returned. The short period he had returned to The Crossing during the night to clean up had almost cost Dain his life.

But nothing Sidiq had done was helping. If Dain didn't get help soon, he would die—no matter if Sidiq remained next to him or not.

He had been out of the intelligence game for too long to know who to trust anymore. Not to mention, there were the Masters. Sidiq didn't want to accidentally take Dain to an enemy. Nor did he know where Arya might be.

Sidiq ran a hand down his face. Dain was a skilled warrior. It would've taken a large number of individuals to land so many blows. Sidiq got to his feet and looked around the small cavern he used to hide in after many dangerous missions for the CCD.

"Why did you come to the pub?" he asked Dain. "You could've

gone anywhere. Why my place? Was it because of her? Did you want her to tend to you?"

He knew the question was irrational, but it kept replaying in his head.

"I should leave you here to die. That's the only way Reva will be safe. Your very existence puts her at risk." Sidiq blew out an irritated breath. "I see her looking for you. At least you've kept to your promise and stayed away. That's the only reason I'm going to help you."

There were only two places Sidiq dared to take him. One was too far away. The other was potentially the end for both him and Dain. He had to do something, though, because he'd never be able to face Reva again if he didn't attempt to help Dain.

Sidiq bent and sat Dain up before slinging him over his shoulder again. Then he gathered his shadows and took a chance based on a passing comment Dain had made months ago. Even after Sidiq arrived at his destination, he contemplated leaving, but the feel of Dain's blood dripping onto his hand propelled him into action.

He slowly parted the shadows until he caught sight of the large desk and the female Wood Elf sitting there, her gaze locked in his direction.

"Who are you, and what are you doing in my office?" she demanded.

Sidiq let the shadows drop so he could look Durga in the eye. Her mouth dropped open, and she jerked to her feet at the sight of Dain.

She hurried around the desk to them. "Set him down," she urged.

Sidiq dropped to a knee and laid Dain on the floor. Durga stared at him for a long minute, taking in his injuries.

"Don't move," she ordered Sidiq. "I'll be right back."

Before he could reply, she was out of the office. Within moments, she returned, carrying towels, then dropped to the floor on the other side of Dain.

"Help is coming," she told Dain as she pressed the towels into his wounds. She looked up at Sidiq. "What happened?"

He shrugged. "I don't know. I found him like this in my storeroom."

"Don't you dare die on me, Dain," Durga stated in a firm voice. "We've too much to do yet."

37

Kalyani woke to find herself looking across the pillow at Varum. He slept peacefully, his breathing deep and even. Her fingers itched to touch his face and smooth his hair from his forehead. Her body was still pleasantly sated from the pleasure they had shared. It was crazy to think that they had slept together when, just hours earlier, she hadn't been sure if he was friend or foe.

Yet he was risking everything to get her home. Much had been left unsaid the previous night, but there was no need to push him. He had years of suffering that he was finally coming to terms with. That would be difficult on its own. What was worse was that she was the cause of him leaving a city he was clearly devoted to. If there were a way for her to escape on her own, she would do it. Rohan had always called her reckless, but even she knew her limits.

She had been happy for Varum to shoulder the blame for bringing her to Tarangarh before, but now, knowing what she did, that seemed like such a trivial point. She couldn't identify when things had changed for her—or even why—but they had.

Her gaze roamed from his face to his bare chest. She rested her hand atop his arm that lay between them. The sight of her tan skin against the bluish-green of his reminded her of their many differences. Yet it wasn't the differences she saw. It was the similarities.

That arm didn't belong to a Sea Elf. It belonged to someone who had held her, kissed her. Pleasured her. A male whose passionate touch had made her melt. Whose desire had enflamed hers. She had felt cherished and worshipped in his arms.

There would never be another who could touch her like that.

Emotion surged within her. Unable to help herself, she softly laid a hand on his cheek. The last thing she should do is allow her feelings to become entangled with him, but it seemed that was out of her hands now. For so long, she had dreamed of encountering a Sea Elf. Varum had given her her dream and so much more.

She had gotten to live in their city, taste their food, have conversations, and hear their song. How many other humans could boast such a thing? Her life had been mostly dull, except for when she was in the water. Her time with Varum would make everything else pale in comparison.

How could she go back to her old life? How could she ever swim in the ocean again and not search for him? How could she ever think about anyone but him? Already, her heart ached for what she longed for—what could never be.

She smoothed her thumb across his cheekbone, marveling that he had chosen her. His eyes slowly opened and met hers. He smiled softly and covered her hand with his. Then he brought her palm to his mouth and pressed a kiss to it before tucking it against his chest over his heart.

"I was afraid to wake. I thought it might've all been a dream," he said.

She found herself grinning, swept up in the pleasant aura that enveloped them. "It wasn't a dream."

"This complicates things."

"Maybe, but I don't care."

He tightened his fingers over her hand. "Me, neither. Though I should."

"What if I stayed?"

He gently moved a curl away from her cheek. "I thought about that as I held you while you slept. As tempting as that is—and it *is* tempting—I won't do that to you."

"It would be my choice."

"You've barely been able to stand being locked in here without seeing the sky for a couple of days."

She turned her hand, so their fingers were linked. "I'd get through it."

"You wouldn't, and we both know that."

Kalyani sighed as the truth of their situation settled around her. "It isn't fair that I should find you, only to have to say goodbye."

"I know."

"I want to stay, but if I remain, you'd continually be worried about me being discovered. Nor could I handle the thought of you getting hurt." She managed a half-smile. "That means we need to make the most of the time we have together."

He nodded as he inhaled. "What should we do, then?"

"I'd like to stay right here forever."

"Then we stay in bed."

"What about work? I thought you needed to keep up appearances."

Varum twisted his lips. "Right. I suppose I should, but there's still time before I have to leave."

"How can you tell?"

"I just know." He tucked a strand of hair behind her ear and let his finger linger against the skin there. "Will you finally tell me?"

She frowned at him. "Tell you what?"

"Your secret."

"My secret?" she repeated as fear cut through her like a blade. "What do you mean?"

He sighed as his expression fell. "Never mind. I shouldn't have pushed."

"Wait," she said as she clenched his hand. "It isn't that I don't want to tell you, it's just that I've never actually said the words aloud."

"You can trust me. No matter what, I will protect you."

Kalyani glanced down, trying to find some courage. It should be easy to tell him. He was a Sea Elf, after all. She licked her lips and tried to swallow, but her mouth was dry. All she had to do was say a few words. It wasn't that big of a deal. She couldn't understand why she was so scared.

"I've kept it a secret from everyone because it made me different. My parents, and then Rohan, were always so worried about me that I didn't want to make things worse. I thought I could pretend that I was like everyone else."

Varum rubbed his thumb across her hand, silently encouraging her to continue.

She finally managed to swallow. "I think something calls me out into the water."

"What do you mean?" he asked, frowning. "You said you felt a pull toward it."

"It's more than that. It's almost as if I wasn't meant to be on land."

His frown deepened. "I don't understand."

"Neither do I." She looked away, pulling up those memories. "The first time I heard it was when I had just begun to walk. I remember the sound clearly. It wasn't quite a song or the wind, but something altogether different. I knew it was the water, and I raced toward it. Rohan thinks I didn't get into the sea, but I did. The moment I dove under the water, I felt a connection to something. Dad swam after me and managed to catch me. I fought him, screaming to keep swimming as he hauled me back to shore. He always believed I would die if I went too far from shore, but I knew that I'd find something else."

"What?"

Her gaze slid back to Varum. "I don't know. I heard the sound a lot when I was younger, but it came less and less as I got older, until it stopped altogether a few years ago. I saw how desperate my family was to keep me with them, and I grew scared of going out too far and leaving them behind."

"You never told them?"

"I couldn't. I tried telling Rohan a couple of times, but I could never get the words out."

Varum lightly tapped the skin behind her ear. "What about this?"

She reached back and felt the area. "What about it?"

His brows drew together. "You really don't know, do you?"

"Know what?" When he hesitated, she grabbed his wrist. "Tell me. Please."

"How do you stay under for so long?"

She found his question odd since he had asked her that before. "I told you. I can hold my breath for a long time."

"You don't hold your breath."

"I do."

He briefly closed his eyes, a look of sadness softening his features. "You might start off that way, but your body changes."

"Changes?" He was beginning to scare her now. "I think I'd know if my body changed."

"Not if you weren't aware or couldn't see it."

She started to pull away, but he held her in place.

"I thought you hadn't told me because you didn't trust me," he said. "Now, I believe you don't know."

"Know what?" The words came out as a strangled whisper.

Varum's hand moved to her cheek. "I know your body changes because I witnessed it myself. It was one of the reasons I brought you to Tarangarh. The place I touched behind your ear? It changes into gills like the Sea Elves have."

Kalyani jerked back as she sat up and felt behind both ears, but there was nothing but smooth skin.

"There's nothing for you to feel now," Varum said as he pushed himself upright. "They vanished once I brought you out of the water."

That couldn't be right. She would know if something like that happened, wouldn't she? She shook her head. "I hold my breath. I know I hold my breath. That's all."

"Of course," Varum said as he tenderly grasped her wrists and lowered her arms so he could hold both her hands in his. "I must have been mistaken."

He was lying. She couldn't call him out on it because that

would mean she had to face what he claimed, and she couldn't. If she did, she would have to admit that she was as different from her family as she had always suspected. But she wasn't a Sea Elf either. What was she if she wasn't human or an elf?

Varum cupped her face, forcing her to look in his eyes. "Let's forget I said anything."

She nodded and let him enfold her in his embrace. Kalyani wound her arms around his neck. She needed to change the subject and quickly, lest her thoughts remain on the topic. She sat back and grinned. "I'm starving."

"Ah," he said as he climbed out of bed and reached for her, setting her on her feet beside him. "I did wear you out last night."

"Exactly. I need to refuel," she said and flashed him a smile.

He took her hand and led her into the kitchen before nudging her to the table. "Sit. I'll make us something."

Kalyani sat in the chair and gave his nude body an appreciative look. "Are you working a full day?"

"I'll go in for a short time and make it look like I'm working. There are a couple of other maps I'd like to look at to double-check my calculations."

"You aren't worried about getting caught?"

He glanced at her over his shoulder. "I look at maps all the time, so nothing will seem out of the ordinary. I'll stop at Nirav's when I leave there." Varum suddenly froze and looked at her. "I forgot. Nirav will spend the day with you."

"I'll be fine. I promise."

"I'd rather he be with you. Just in case."

Kalyani stood and walked to press her naked body to his back. "Too much needs to be done. I can handle a couple of more days on my own. Besides, you talked to Tanira, so she won't be back. I don't have anything to worry about."

"I don't know," he hedged.

"I would tell you if I were uncomfortable alone."

He sighed and patted the arm she had around him. "The trip to Nirav's will be quick."

"Is there anything here you'd like me to pack up for you?"

"For what?"

She leaned to the side to look at him. "To bring with you. There must be something from your home you'd like to take to your new one."

He looked around his home for a long minute before shaking his head. "I plan on leaving everything."

Kalyani had worried that he was leaving because of her, but maybe she had been wrong. Maybe he really was finally breaking free of the city to start anew. It wouldn't be with her, but she hoped he found somewhere to live a long, happy life.

38

Varum didn't want to leave Kalyani. He couldn't explain the feeling of impending doom, no matter how he tried to rationalize it. He chalked it up to being overly cautious after Tanira's exploits the day before. Yet as he made his way to his office, the urge to turn back grew stronger with every step he took.

He couldn't stop thinking about her reaction when he spoke about the gills. The shock that'd slackened her face had been real. He hadn't had the heart to push when she denied it so strongly. She really hadn't known about breathing underwater.

When he reached the Assembly Hall, he halted. The pull to return to Kalyani was so strong that he actually took a step backward, as if some unknown force had grabbed him from behind. He looked around as he dragged in a lungful of air. Something was wrong. Dreadfully wrong. He spun around at the same time he heard someone calling his name. Varum looked to the side to see

Nirav hurrying over. The unease that churned in Varum's gut only grew when he spotted his friend's tense expression.

"I'm glad I caught you," Nirav said in a low voice when he reached him.

Varum noted the way the older elf's gaze darted about suspiciously. "What's going on?"

"I don't know, but I don't think you should go to your office."

"Why?"

Nirav grabbed his arm and began leading him toward Varum's. "I heard someone's office was being raided."

"What has that to do with me?"

"Maybe nothing, but I don't want to take any chances. I think we should leave with Kalyani right now."

Varum halted and jerked his arm from Nirav's grasp. "We're not ready. It would put her in danger."

"Then we can get ready within a few hours." Nirav leaned close. "I don't have a good feeling."

Neither did Varum. "If something was going to happen to me, it would've been last night when Arvind paid me a visit."

"Maybe."

"He doesn't hesitate. Ever."

Nirav blew out a breath. "I can't get anyone to tell me what's going on. I'd rather be safe."

"All right," Varum agreed, no longer able to ignore the growing worry. "We move the plans up. Bring the large sack we use when we go hunting. It'll be perfect for Kalyani to hide in."

Nirav nodded, then his expression tightened as his gaze moved over Varum's shoulder. Varum turned and spotted a group of spear-wielding soldiers headed straight for them. They weren't just any elves. They were the elite squadron assigned to the Tidewarden.

"Get to Kalyani," Varum whispered over his shoulder.

He didn't look to see if Nirav left. He knew his friend would take care of Kalyani. Varum looked around at the stone-faced soldiers quickly surrounding him. A growing crowd gathered around them to see what was going on, but all he could think about was Nirav getting to Kalyani.

"Come with us," one of the soldiers demanded.

There were too many people watching for Varum to try to escape. That was likely why the soldiers had found him outside of his home. The best thing would be for him to go with them and see what was going on. The only thing he had done wrong was bring Kalyani into the city, and there was no way anyone knew about that. Arvind was likely just putting on a show.

Varum nodded to the squad leader. Then, in unison, all eight soldiers turned to the side to retrace their steps. Varum walked in the middle of the group, but they didn't take him to the Tidewarden's office. Instead, they led him to the detention center. He buried the dread that filled him. He had spent his life learning to hide his feelings, and he was a master at it. No one would know the depths of his worry—or his fear.

The soldiers guided him into an empty room. As he turned around, the door shut behind him. He fought against the urge to rush toward it and yank it open, but he kept himself rooted to the spot. He wouldn't do or say anything until he found out why he was being detained. Varum stood in the middle of the room and stared at the door, waiting. Someone would interrogate him. All he had to do was bide his time until he learned what was going on.

There were no windows in the room, but he still didn't drop his guard. He was glad he had left home. Otherwise, the soldiers would've gone there and found Kalyani. At least she was safe. No matter what, Nirav would get her out of the city. He would remedy Varum's lapse in judgment. Though could Varum still call it that after their night together?

What they had shared, the emotions that had engulfed him, felt as if the gods had bestowed a gift upon him. One that he never would've discovered if he hadn't brought Kalyani into the city. He'd learned a great deal from her in a short time. She had erased the things he had erroneously believed about humans. He saw them through her eyes now, and he was forever changed because of it.

The door suddenly opened, snapping him from his thoughts. Just as Varum had expected, it was Arvind who strolled in. The Tidewarden stared at him for a long moment before quietly closing the door and leaning back against it with his arms crossed over his chest.

"I've expected to bring you here for many years," Arvind said.

Varum quirked a brow. "Have you? And here I thought you were a fair elf."

"My duty is to this city, above and beyond my personal beliefs."

"Since all I've ever done is serve Tarangarh, I know I've done nothing to warrant being detained."

Arvind snorted as he disdainfully raked his eyes over Varum. "You have no idea how embarrassed I was to have my beloved daughter chase after you while you ignored her, and then, you had the gall to rebuff her love. Nothing I said could dissuade her from you."

"Shouldn't you be glad we're no longer dating?"

"Your presence has left a stain on my family that can never be washed away."

Varum had heard such words before. Normally, he let them roll away, but he was tired of allowing others to make such remarks. "You wouldn't think that way had my parents remained."

"But they didn't. Because of *you*," Arvind stated.

"Blame me all you want. I know the truth. And so do they. Why don't we skip this little scene and move on to what you really brought me here for, so I can go home?"

Arvind dropped his arms as he pushed away from the wall. "Home? You're never leaving here again."

That ominous feeling from before barreled into Varum tenfold. He fought to stay on his feet as the room spun.

"You're being charged with treason for colluding with the Masters to bring about the downfall of Tarangarh."

Varum gaped at him and fisted his hands in outrage. "You know I'm not a part of that. I wrote the damn report!"

"You were seen helping to secure abductees in a sloop," Arvind said over him. "You will have a trial, as is our way, but the end result will be the same. Death or imprisonment for the rest of your life."

Varum took a step forward, Kalyani's name on his lips as Arvind walked out, slamming the door with a finality that brought Varum to his knees.

39

Everything felt empty once Varum left. Kalyani wandered around his home, wondering about his being able to walk away without bringing anything. That wasn't exactly true. He was bringing Nirav, and he could be considered the most important thing in Varum's life. She smiled, thinking about the stories Nirav had shared about Varum. The older elf might not have been the one who had welcomed Varum as a father, but he had ended up being that in the end.

"Varum probably came out better for it," she murmured.

Kalyani felt as if she should be doing something besides sitting around. Varum and Nirav were doing their parts, but she had nothing to do. It was just as maddening as it had been waiting for Rohan and Farah. She wanted to be in the action, regardless of how dangerous it was. It was her home—her world—too, and she had a right to defend it how she saw fit.

She sighed and plopped onto the sofa. This wasn't exactly the same, though. She was hiding in order to stay alive. It bothered her that a race could hate as deeply as the Sea Elves did. They didn't just hate humans, either. That's what she couldn't quite wrap her head around. Each elven race had something special. Why did the Sea Elves believe themselves above all others?

Varum's words from earlier returned. She touched the skin behind her ear, but just as before, there was nothing there. The quick way he had let her change the subject told her he had decided not to push the issue. She was grateful, because she wasn't ready to think about such a thing.

But what if she did? What if she contemplated it even for one minute?

Kalyani drew her knees up to her chest and wrapped her arms around her legs. She closed her eyes and tried to imagine being in the water, the currents moving around her.

The door suddenly burst open, splintered wood and fragments of coral flying through the air. She raised her arms to shield her head and dove to the floor between the sofa and the coffee table. Her ears rang from the explosion as debris rained around her. Rough hands grabbed her and dragged her up. She blinked to get her eyes to come into focus and found herself surrounded by a number of armed elves wearing uniforms.

Her heart skipped a beat as she gazed at all the faces registering shock and anger at the sight of her. That's when it hit her that she had been discovered. She scanned the area around her for Varum and Nirav, but they were nowhere to be found.

"Bring her," barked a deep voice.

A bag was yanked over Kalyani's head, and she was unceremoniously hauled from Varum's home. She had no idea where they were taking her, but she knew it wouldn't be good. Varum had warned her what would happen if she were caught. Was she going to her death right now?

If they'd found her, that meant they would go after Varum. She fought wildly against the elves holding either side of her.

"Wait!" she screamed. "Please, wait!"

Something slammed into the back of her neck, and everything went black.

Nirav ducked into a hallway as he heard Kalyani's voice. He watched the patrol cart her now-unconscious body out of Varum's home. Nirav briefly closed his eyes. He had to let Varum know before he found out from someone else.

If he hadn't been taken by the soldiers.

Nirav worried that Varum was out of his reach. If both Kalyani and Varum had been taken, it wouldn't be long before soldiers came for him, too. He was their only chance at getting out of Tarangarh alive, which meant he had to stay one step ahead of everyone. It would be easier if he knew what was going on, but he didn't have that luxury. And that meant he would have to piece it together bit by bit.

It was a good thing he had set up different stations around the city with supplies for just such an occasion.

He waited until he knew the guards were gone and then set out to the nearest location that housed a change of clothes and some weapons. He'd learned a lot during his time on land, and it was all about to be put to use.

40

No one returned, and the more time that ticked by, the more frantic Varum became. He stared at the door Arvind had exited from, afraid to move lest he lose the slim thread of control he still possessed. He didn't know whether Kalyani was okay or if Nirav had been detained like him. And the not-knowing was driving him insane.

Which was exactly what Arvind wanted.

Outwardly, Varum appeared calm and unworried. But inwardly, he was bellowing in rage, eager to get his hands on someone to show them just how incensed he was. It wouldn't do him any good, though. If he wanted to get out of this and make sure Nirav wasn't dragged in and no one found Kalyani, he had to remain composed.

When everything was over, when he walked free, he would show Arvind and everyone else just what he was made of. But not until he was cleared of these ridiculous charges.

He knew their justice system well. There was clear evidence

that he had nothing to do with the Masters. Except...he couldn't use that evidence because it was Kalyani. All the proof he had gathered was either stories from her or his firsthand accounts. For the first time, it dawned on him that he might not get out. No wonder Arvind had been so confident.

"No one will tell me anything."

Nirav's words from earlier came back to him. They were intentionally keeping Nirav in the dark so he couldn't help. Or was it because they planned to implicate him, as well? Varum's stomach clenched as dread filled him. Arvind was wrapping things up nicely. Did that mean he was involved with the Masters?

Varum staggered backward until he ran into the wall. He sagged against it as he began to fit everything together. He had suspected some inside the city were aiding the Masters, but he hadn't been able to investigate. Even if he had, he wouldn't have started with Arvind. Whatever his personal feelings toward Varum, he'd always led the city. It seemed he had fooled everyone.

Had Tanira taken the unfinished report to Arvind to help Varum or to protect her father? The more Varum thought about it, the more he suspected it was the latter. They had gotten their hands on the report to see just how much he knew. That's why Arvind gave the investigation to someone else—someone aligned with him and the Masters, to ensure they were never exposed.

Varum couldn't believe he had been that close to the Masters' allies without realizing it. He had stepped right into a trap, which put both Nirav and Kalyani in danger. Nirav would do the right thing and get her out of the city immediately. He'd take her and never look back. Because there was no way Varum was getting free.

How many others within the city were involved in the Masters?

Was it a few? Or was it more? Varum would never know, nor would anyone else. Elves would begin to go missing, like everywhere else. Nirav needed to get Kalyani back to her brother so Rohan and his friends could stop the Masters before they destroyed more lives.

He looked down at his hands that had held Kalyani just hours before. Varum had never been happier. He'd accepted that they couldn't be together, but he had believed he'd get to see her one more time. Everything had been taken from him again. He had dared to take something bright and shiny and good for himself, and he was being punished for it.

The creak of the door opening drew his gaze. A dozen guards filed inside, creating a wall on either side of him. He stared at the opening in the door as three more soldiers strode in. The tallest remained at the door, eyeing Varum as only someone in charge could. The other two approached. They grabbed his arms and heaved him away from the wall.

"Your trial is about to begin," the commander stated.

Varum didn't fight them as they walked him out of the room and through the building. The twelve guards marched in line, continuing along the wall. They didn't take him into one of the courtrooms, however. Instead, they directed him toward the arena. Foreboding slid down his spine like icy fingers. The closer they got to the doors, the louder the crowd noise became.

The leader threw open the doors and entered ahead of them. Varum knew the moment the crowd saw him, as the din began to quiet. They hadn't bound his hands, but they probably didn't think they needed to with so many soldiers surrounding him. The grip of the two guards holding him was firm, but that wouldn't deter him if he saw a way out.

They came to a halt in the middle of the arena, so Varum stared across to the upper balcony where Arvind sat with his wife on his left and Tanira on his right. Behind him were his closest supporters. Varum took a good look at everyone there. He never wanted to forget their faces since they were all likely part of the Masters.

This wasn't a trial. There was no way Arvind would allow him to remain alive. Varum might be able to convince someone of the truth, but that would only complicate matters. Nay, this was merely a formality for the planned execution.

The speaker's voice rose clear and strong as he said, "The trial of treason against Currentspeaker Varum will commence."

Varum didn't hear the rest of what was said. He chose to focus on the one thing that had brought true happiness into his life. Kalyani.

Shock hurtled through Tanira as she watched Varum being led into the arena. Her father hadn't told her why he had called a city Assembly, and when she had pressed, he had yelled at her, demanding she follow his orders. It had stunned her because he had never before raised his voice to her.

She swallowed nervously and glanced at her father, who was smiling confidently. She slid her gaze back to Varum and noted the guards surrounding him: her father's elite force. But the two soldiers holding Varum caused her to frown. Her heart started racing as she listened to the litany of crimes Varum was being accused of. She grabbed the arms of her chair and started to rise when her father's hand clamped painfully on top of her wrist, holding her in place.

She swung her head to him, wincing in pain. "I brought you the report he wrote. You know he isn't with the Masters."

"You will not rise from your seat," her father replied. His eyes bored into her, filled with anger and a threat. "You will not make a sound. You will not do *anything* that brings attention to you."

"What are you doing?" she whispered.

He returned his attention to Varum. "I'm securing things."

"What does that mean?"

"All you need to know is that you'll be protected."

Tanira looked at her father's hand still clasped on her arm. She slowly relaxed her fingers and eased her body. Only then did his grip loosen. Still, he kept his hand on her. She couldn't shake the thought that she was as trapped there as Varum was in the arena. Her gaze swung back to him as he stood tall and still in the middle of the room.

He had always hidden his emotions. It made him difficult to read. It was why so many people kept away from him. But she had witnessed his gentle side. There was so much more to Varum than anyone gave him credit for. He might look calm, but she suspected he was anything but.

She loved her father, but she also loved Varum. He was innocent of the charges. She was sure of it. She didn't know why her father was falsely accusing him, but she intended to find out. And then she would discover a way to free Varum.

"Tell me," her father said as he leaned toward her and lowered his voice. "Just how well do you know Varum?"

"I know he's innocent," she replied.

Her father turned his head to look at her. "I'm only saying this once. You're my daughter, and I will protect you. But you need to remember your part in this. Family comes first."

This was a side of her dad she had never seen before, and it frightened her. She didn't know or recognize the elf staring at her now. If he wanted her to play a part, then she would. After all, she had studied Varum well enough to know how to do it. Tanira bowed her head in acceptance.

"Good. Now, I ask again. How well do you know Varum?"

She glanced at the elf she had loved for years. The elf she had expected to marry. "I know him as well as he has allowed me to. Why?"

"You've been to his place recently."

"I have. I told you I've not given up on us."

"Did you know?"

She sucked in a breath as his fingers dug into her arm. There was no point in trying to pull away, not with the grip he had. She met her father's gaze. "Did I know what?"

"It doesn't matter if you did. No one will know that you were there."

Tanira was about to ask what he meant when she saw another of the arena doors open and more soldiers enter.

Pain radiated from Kalyani's neck to her shoulders and along her arms as well as down her back. She didn't know what had struck her, but it had definitely left a mark. She tried to keep her feet under her as they cruelly dragged her, but her limbs refused to work properly. The bag over her head kept her from seeing anything, further disorienting her.

She didn't know how long she had been hauled around before she heard the growing clamor of voices. She bit her lip to keep from asking any questions. It wasn't as if they would tell her anything, anyway.

Her feet got tangled, and she started to fall, but the hands holding her yanked her upright. She cried out from the pain of their grip, which only made them clutch her harder. The noise suddenly became deafening. She could tell that they were no longer in the corridor, and by the sound of it, she was somewhere she didn't want to be. She didn't know how they had found her, but she hoped Varum and Nirav were safe.

Finally, they halted upon a raised platform. She tried to calm her breathing as she fought to get her bearings. Then, the hood was abruptly yanked from her head. She blinked and turned her head away at the bright lights. There was an audible gasp before everything went silent.

Kalyani could hear her own ragged breaths as she blinked to get accustomed to the bright lights. She noticed the guards surrounding her first. They faced her, spears pointed in her direction as if she were some threat.

She looked beyond the soldiers to the tiered seats on stepped rows that rose from the ground in a semicircle. She glanced up to the domed ceiling overhead that held back the ocean. She lowered her gaze to the center of the auditorium, where a large, opulent section of seating caught her attention. It was obviously meant for someone important. She spotted the male Sea Elf around Nirav's age sitting in an ornate chair in the middle of the front row. On his left side was a female Sea Elf—likely his wife. And on the other, sat another stunningly beautiful female. There were also others in the box, and all were staring at her.

Kalyani looked around at the thousands of faces ogling her. She curled her fingers into a fist, wishing she could disappear into the floor. She could feel the hatred from the many eyes glaring at her. And as they did, the noise of renewed conversations began to rise.

She wouldn't show them any fear. No matter what they said or did, she would keep what dignity she could. Varum's warning about how painful her death would be returned. Hopefully, he wouldn't be there to see it.

A noise from the side drew her gaze. She looked over to find another set of soldiers lined up in the middle of the arena. But it was the sight of Varum held between them that sucked the breath from her body. She took a small step when her eyes met Varum's. The point of a spear pricked her stomach, causing her to release a gasp of pain.

She jerked away and covered the spot as blood dripped from the cut, and a loud roar filled the auditorium. She looked at Varum to see him fighting like a man possessed to get past the guards. They struck him repeatedly with both magic and blades, but he didn't slow. His clothes were torn, and his blood drawn, again and again. Tears coursed down her face as she watched him eventually be taken down by eight elves until he was pinned to the ground on his stomach with his arms stretched out to the sides.

But even then, he didn't take his eyes off her.

Varum felt his shoulder being pulled from its socket, but he didn't care. He had to get to Kalyani. More weight pressed onto his back, restraining him and pushing him against the floor. Other hands grabbed his legs, pinning him. Then someone firmly planted a foot on his temple, keeping his head turned to the side. That was fine by him. He needed to see Kalyani anyway.

The shocked crowd was getting louder by the moment. He knew what was coming for her, and he kept fighting to get free. He might not be able to save her from death, but he at least wanted to be beside her. She shouldn't have to face what was coming on her own when he was the one who had put her life in danger.

His heart clutched painfully. Just that morning, he had woken beside her. He should've gotten her out of the city already. Nay, that wasn't right. He never should've brought her here to begin with. Varum struggled again.

The foot on his head pressed into him harder. "You'd do well to keep still."

The voice wasn't familiar, but it wouldn't matter if it was. No one would stop him from reaching Kalyani. He gathered magic in his hands and readied to release it. A sharp pain in his upper back stopped him in his tracks. Something warm and wet slowly slid down his back and soaked into his tunic.

"I warned you," the voice stated.

Varum seethed. The bastard would be the first one he killed when he got free. He might be dying that day, but he would take as many enemies with him as he could. Varum fought to get another look at Kalyani, but the guards around her had shifted and blocked his view. The fear he had seen in her eyes broke him. He had promised to keep her safe and get her home, and he had failed on both accounts.

He attempted to inch over to see her face. The wound on his back throbbed as more blood gushed, but the foot on his head kept him in place. He stilled when he spotted her bare feet. They hadn't even put shoes on her. But why would they? They believed humans were lowly beings not worth the time. He was ashamed that, for most of his life, he had thought the same. She had changed his perspective. Nay, that wasn't true. She had changed *him*. All of him.

And what had he done for her? He'd abducted her, kept her locked in his home, and allowed her to be captured. The final blow would be her death. His eyes burned with tears when it hit him that he would be forced to watch them take her life. A tear ran out of his eye, over his nose, and onto his cheek.

"Kalyani," he whispered.

The foot ground into his cheek and temple. Dimly, he heard

the speaker talking. Fury coursed through him when they called her a *disgusting human*. He yanked on his arm and kicked, but the guards had a firm hold on him.

Finally, the speaker stopped talking. The crushing weight atop Varum made him fight for breath. He gathered magic in his hands once more, but they noticed immediately. The soldiers forced his hands into fists and restrained them. He was quickly running out of options.

Varum stilled when he heard the speaker call the Tidewarden's name. He couldn't see Arvind, but he could tell when the elf stood because the crowd quieted again. A heartbeat later, Arvind's voice filled the arena.

"Human, you have violated our most sacred law and entered our city uninvited. How do you plead?"

Varum shifted his head as far as he could to see Kalyani. She was strong and confident, going up against those working for the Masters. She hadn't cared if she was injured. This was far from battle. He knew she was afraid, and it killed him that she was alone.

Kalyani couldn't see the face of the elf who questioned her. He stood in the box and was dressed as an important figure, but that didn't sway her. Her heart pounded so hard and loud, she thought it might give out before they could deliver a verdict of death. It would be nice to take away their need to execute her.

She drew in a breath. "Does it matter what answer I give?" She was pleasantly surprised by how strong her voice sounded. With the way she trembled, she'd thought for sure it would come out as a strangled whisper.

There was another gasp from the masses. Kalyani didn't take her eyes off the elf questioning her. He had already sentenced her to death. This show was merely a formality for those watching. The fact that they'd brought Varum told her that much. She hadn't yet figured out if this was just about her, or if the Tidewarden intended to take his anger out on Varum, too. She might not be able to do much, but she would do what she could to save both Nirav and Varum.

"You don't seem to care that your life is in my hands," the Tidewarden stated.

"We both know you've already decided my fate. I don't know why you would ask such a question. If I say I knew I came uninvited, you will cite that I deliberately went against your laws and demand my immediate death. If I say I had no idea I needed to be invited, you will declare that my ignorance doesn't justify my actions and call for my immediate death."

Kalyani wanted to glance at Varum, but she didn't dare. Everyone had seen how he had tried to get to her once he saw her. It was all a part of the display being put on by those in charge. She had been discovered in Varum's home, which automatically connected them.

"Then, perhaps, you'll share *how* you found Tarangarh," the elf asked asked. "Our city is hidden."

She shrugged. "Not as well as you might think."

The crowd noise rose at her statement—some with disbelief, and others with outrage. The Tidewarden had wanted to shock everyone. Well, two could play that game.

He walked closer to the platform railing. His long, turquoise and white robes drew the eye. "There's no way you found the trench on your own, much less Tarangarh. Who brought you here? Was it Varum?"

"Who is that?" she asked.

"You're claiming not to know the elf whose house we found you in?"

Kalyani almost dared a glance at Varum, but she stopped herself in time. "I am. I had no idea where I was. I've been in and out of several places since I arrived. How else do you explain how I got these clothes?"

Once more, her comments sparked conversation among those in attendance. Even from a distance, she felt the elf in charge's hateful glare. Everyone here underestimated humans. She was just using that to her benefit.

"There's no way."

Kalyani lifted her chin as she kept her gaze on the Tidewarden. "You keep saying I'm not able to do these things, and yet, here I am."

"Humans cannot swim to these depths!"

She lifted her arms. "I'm standing before you now, saying that I can."

Varum couldn't believe what Kalyani was doing. Every time he tried to speak up, the crowd drowned out his words. He knew what she was doing, but it was futile. Arvind was too smart to have made any errors. As brave as she was, it wouldn't do anything but anger Arvind and bring about her death even quicker.

Nirav hadn't been dragged out with them. That could only

mean he had managed to evade the guards so far. Arvind would have the city thoroughly searched. Even if Nirav could get away, he wouldn't. He would stay and attempt to reach Varum. It would all be in vain, though. Neither he nor Kalyani was getting out of this alive.

"You lie!" Arvind shouted at her.

To her credit, Kalyani kept her voice even when she said, "I have no reason to lie. I've always been an exceptional swimmer."

"Then explain how you can breathe underwater."

Varum closed his eyes at Arvind's demand. He couldn't imagine how she would answer after she'd vehemently denied having gills.

"I was hoping the Sea Elves could tell me," she said. "Why do you think I sought you out?"

Arvind slammed his hand atop the railing. "Even if you could swim to these depths and somehow breathe underwater, you wouldn't have been able to navigate the currents or find the entrance."

"You're right. I wouldn't be able to do that on my own."

Varum's eyes snapped open. He waited for her to say his name.

Instead, she said, "I saw a couple of Sea Elves and followed them. They never looked behind them, so it was pretty simple."

He stared at her foot, the only thing he could see of her, and wished he could wrap his arms around her. She was quick with her answers. Not that they would spare his life. She was just making things worse for herself.

Tanira looked from the human to her father's back. She had lost sight of Varum when the soldiers took him to the ground the moment he caught sight of the woman. She thought back to when she'd visited Varum last. He had seemed more anxious than usual with her being in his home.

She went back over that encounter carefully. Then she compared it to his visit, where he had put an end to them permanently. He had been different both times. Still aloof, but there had been a subtle shift. Did it have something to do with the human?

Tanira recalled trying to get into Varum's and frowned. Had she been able to get through his magic and unlock the door, would she have found the human? Varum had called on her hours after she attempted to break in. She hadn't thought much about it then, but now, the coincidence was too clear to overlook.

The woman was trying to steer things away from Varum, and she was doing an admirable job. Tanira might even believe her if she didn't know Varum as well as she did. He wouldn't have tried to get away from the guards if it had been her in the human's spot. Someone had finally broken through his walls. Tanira had always thought it would be her. Instead, it had been the woman on trial now.

Tanira looked at her father again. He was too involved with the interrogation to pay attention to her. It might be her only chance to get away. She glanced at her mother, but even she was caught up in this mockery of a trial. Tanira was used to moving about as she pleased. No one but her father would stop her. At least, that's what she hoped.

She got to her feet and headed out of the box. Tanira didn't breathe until she was out of the arena. It wouldn't take long for her father to notice she was missing. She had to act fast.

42

Nirav stood at the back of the arena, watching the hearing unfold. He arrived after Kalyani had been brought in, but he had heard everyone's reaction at the sight of her. Panic set in until he finally located Varum beneath the pile of guards.

Soldiers were stationed everywhere, and only their interest in observing the proceedings allowed him to sneak in. He had changed into more humble clothing and wrapped a scarf around his head, but if anyone looked closely or stopped him, he would be discovered.

The plan to reach Kalyani and Varum before they were taken into the arena was gone. Even if Nirav had an army to storm the building, he wouldn't be able to get to them. Kalyani would likely be executed right there in front of others. Varum, however, would be taken away. Arvind wouldn't let him live. His execution would be a big event. That would give Nirav time to find a way to free Varum.

Nirav grinned as he listened to Kalyani hold her own against Arvind. She was doing better than anyone else in that situation, but it wouldn't last long. Arvind didn't do anything unless he had a plan. It didn't matter how well-spoken she was or how strong her answers to his questions were. Her life became forfeit the moment they busted into Varum's home and found her. It was too bad, too. He liked her.

And so had Varum.

For the first time, Nirav had seen Varum begin to let himself feel something. What little progress Varum had made would be eradicated with Kalyani's death. In truth, Nirav feared he might lose Varum forever.

Nirav slowly backed through the crowd and slipped out the doorway without being noticed. He headed down the corridor to the holding cells, where he expected Varum to be brought eventually. It would be a good place for him to hide and wait while he planned their escape.

He turned the corner and ducked his head when he spotted some soldiers headed his way. But it was too late. They had seen him.

"Hold up!" one hollered.

Nirav halted and waited for them to approach. He kept his gaze lowered as he took stock of how many were around him. If he surprised the two guards in an attack, he might be able to get away.

"There you are," came a feminine voice he recognized.

He frowned as he looked down at a pair of stylish sandals he had seen Tanira wear. Her hand touched his arm, and he swung his head to her.

"I have him. He's one of my servants who snuck out to get a look at the proceedings," she said.

Nirav watched her smile and chat with the soldiers before they walked away.

Once they were gone, she spun around so they faced the same direction and nudged him forward. "Come on."

"Where are we going?" he whispered.

"To save Varum and the human," she said in a low voice. "Unless you were headed somewhere else."

Nirav glanced behind him to make sure no one followed. "What are you doing, Tanira?"

"Isn't it obvious? I'm helping."

He stopped and pulled away from her. "You do realize it's your father leading the trial."

"I do. And before you ask, I know exactly what I'm doing. Do you want my help or not? As you saw back there, my participation can be very beneficial."

It was true that she'd be able to turn any soldiers interested in him away, but there had to be a catch. "Why?"

"Believe it or not, I love Varum. I want to help." Her face fell as she hastily looked away. "If I had known what Dad was going to do when I gave him that report, I never would've done it. The man I know as my father never would've done any of this or talked to me as he just did."

"You're also helping Kalyani."

Tanira pressed her lips together as she swung her gaze back to him. "I know. Varum cares about her. I knew it the instant I saw his reaction when he spotted her."

"And you're okay with that?"

"Far from it. But, like I said, I love him. Now, are you coming or not?" she said before she started walking again.

Nirav hurried to catch up. "Do you have a plan?"

"Nay. I was hoping you did."

"I'm getting one for Varum."

Tanira glanced at him. "What about the human?"

"Do you really think Arvind will allow her to leave the arena?"

"It's the first time an outsider has breached the city. He'll make an example of her."

Nirav sighed. "That's what I feared. If they don't take Varum out before that, I'm not sure what he'll do."

"Then we need to be prepared."

"Admit that it was Varum who brought you to Tarangarh!" the elf in charge bellowed.

It was the third time he had tried to make her say as much, and Kalyani was tired of it. "I told you how I came to be here."

"You're lying!"

She was, and she would continue to do so until her last breath. If there was even the smallest hope that she could save Varum's life, she would do whatever she had to do.

The male put his hands on his hips as he glared at her. "Did you really expect to leave without us discovering you?"

"I did, in fact. Had you been even an hour later, I wouldn't have been there."

"Why an hour?" he pressed.

She shrugged. "It was an expression. It wasn't as if I was

keeping time. It's difficult to know the hour without the sun or moon."

"If you came to figure out how you can breathe underwater, then why didn't you approach any of us?"

"I observed." It wasn't a good answer, but it was all her rattled brain could come up with. He was leading her in circles. She might have stood against him at the start, but she wouldn't be able to keep it up for much longer, as evidenced by her latest response.

He chuckled. "You observed. There's no way someone didn't see you."

"You'd be amazed at the places a person can hide and listen."

"So, you have information."

Kalyani inwardly winced, wishing she could take back the words. "Listen long enough anywhere, and you'll pick up things."

"Are you working for the Masters? Is that why you're here?"

The minute he brought up the Masters, Kalyani knew what he intended. Cold fury simmered in her veins. She couldn't relay information about finding the sloop with the abducted humans, since that was in Varum's report and would link them. She would have to think of something else.

"One of the reasons I'm here is to escape them. The kidnappings are happening all over Shecrish. I had hoped it would be safe here. But I did overhear talk of a group in the city aiding the Masters."

Just as she expected, her words caused a ripple of unease to move through the crowd. She bit back a smile and waited.

"There have been no links to the Masters here," he declared loudly. "And there never will be."

Kalyani desperately wanted to bring up the report Varum had written, but again, she couldn't.

"It is more likely that you were sent here to spy on us and bring information back to the Masters so they can begin taking my people," he retorted.

She shook her head, no longer able to hold back her anger. "Humans are being abducted. We don't work with the Masters. That's what your kind does."

Varum had never felt so helpless or powerless as he did while listening to Kalyani's interrogation. He couldn't interject or give his side. Each time he tried, the foot on his face dug in harder. The sole was smashing his cheek into his teeth, slicing the inside of it until blood filled his mouth.

He couldn't talk, couldn't move, or use his magic. He was useless. And he had no one to blame but himself. Kalyani's death would be on his conscience. He had dragged her here. Had refused to take her home because it was a little too dangerous. Now look where she was.

Maybe his parents had been right to leave him. They must have seen the kind of carnage he was capable of leaving in his wake, all for the sake of saving a city that had never wanted him.

He saw Kalyani curl her toes inward. She knew what awaited her, and she stood fighting. He owed her that, at the very least. Varum might not be able to use his voice or his magic at the moment, but he would as soon as he got everyone off him. He just needed a small diversion.

"You stand in the face of every resident in Tarangarh with your insolence," Arvind retorted. "You should be begging for your life."

"Since when is it a crime to enter a city?" Kalyani asked.

Varum smiled through watery eyes. Until the last, she was playing innocent to protect him.

"I'm giving you one last chance to tell me who brought you into the city," Arvind said.

Kalyani wondered how Rohan would've fared if he had been standing in her place. He likely would've had better answers that would've saved himself and Varum. She had done the best she could, but even she had to admit it hadn't been great.

All the years she had kept her true self from her family, and for what? Because she had been afraid of how they would react? They would never have turned away from her. She had kept silent because *she* hadn't wanted to learn the truth. Varum had tried to tell her, but she had brushed his words off and changed the subject.

She nodded at the elf in charge. "I've repeatedly told you how I got into the city. I didn't know it was an offense to enter. However, I did go into others' homes and take their clothing. I'm sure, like in any other city, I will need to pay for those crimes."

"Offense? Crime?" He snorted a laugh. "You honestly have no idea how serious this is, do you?"

Oh, she knew, but she had to pretend not to. Besides, she wanted it spelled out for everyone watching. There had to be others in the crowd like Varum and Nirav. Those who disagreed with such a barbaric practice. Not that she expected that to stop her death, but it might get people talking after she was gone. It might even spare Varum.

And that would make everything worth it.

"I suppose I don't. What will it be? Two years? Five years?" she asked as the building went silent.

"Death."

The word echoed in the arena. She felt every eye on her. Varum was watching, but she wouldn't look at him, no matter how much she wanted to see his incredible eyes again.

She sighed dramatically. "Well, that's excessive."

Kalyani's remark and everyone's response were just the diversion Varum needed. He kicked one foot free and rolled onto a hip, dislodging those piled atop him. Then he was on his feet. He didn't go to Kalyani. He headed straight for the one person who had begun all of this—Arvind.

He made it four steps before the guards grabbed him again. Varum locked eyes with Arvind. They stared at each other, hate growing with every second that passed. Arvind suspected Varum, but without Kalyani admitting it, there was no proof.

"Toss her out!" Arvind said and pointed.

Varum jerked his head around to see Kalyani being hauled off the platform and dragged toward the back window. She wasn't fighting them. In fact, it looked as if she had given up. He met her gaze before she looked away.

It was then that his heart broke.

43

Everyone and everything died. It was a fact of life that couldn't be ignored or dismissed. Kalyani had always expected to be an old woman with plenty of wrinkles and gray hair when she finally passed on. Yet she was being hurled toward her end much earlier than expected—and there was nothing she could do about it.

When her gaze met Varum's, time slowed for a heartbeat. All the things she had wanted to do and say but had been too afraid to, filled her with regret. Yet the cold, reserved elf who usually kept a tight rein on his emotions had disappeared. Except it wasn't warmth and affection reflected in his eyes. It was fear.

For her.

And that broke her as nothing else could.

The elves dragging her farther from Varum came to a stop and jerked her to her feet. She shook uncontrollably as blood rushed loudly in her ears. Thousands might be ogling her, but the only one who mattered, the only one she sought, was Varum.

Kalyani struggled to keep her knees from giving out. Death loomed over her like a black cloud waiting to burst. She could practically feel the cold fingers of the afterlife reaching for her. It was bad enough that Varum was being forced to watch her die. She couldn't dissolve into tears. She would greet the end with her back straight and her head held high. Maybe it would help lighten the guilt he would insist on carrying.

All the lies she had so blatantly told moments earlier would be revealed the moment they tossed her into the water. Would the pressure kill her instantly? She hoped the pain didn't last long. She wasn't ready to die. There were so many things she hadn't done. Yet she didn't blame Varum. If she hadn't been unconscious when he found her, she likely would've begged him to take her with him. One way or another, she would've ended up in this exact position.

It was too bad she wouldn't have the chance to tell Varum that. Another regret was Rohan. Her brother would never know what had become of her. She'd never meant to hurt him in such a way. Hopefully, Farah would be able to help him eventually accept that she wasn't returning.

The speaker from earlier began listing her offenses again, as if that were necessary. She dared another glance at Varum to find him still watching her. He needed to look away. The longer he stared at her, the more it seemed as if they knew each other.

She hoped he wouldn't try something stupid like attempting to save her. There was no stopping what was about to happen now. Things were in motion. Her life was over, but there was still a chance for him.

A subtle melody caught her attention. It was faint, nothing but the barest of whispers, but she couldn't ignore it. Her mind emptied as she sought to hear more of the tune she hadn't heard in years. The notes and harmonies swirled in and around her, gradually taking away her fear. No one else seemed to hear it, which surprised her. Could it be that only her ears detected it?

She shot the guards a furtive glance to make sure their attention was elsewhere, then pulled out of their grasp. The two who had been holding her, swung their heads to her as she took a step backward.

Out of the corner of her eye, she saw Varum lunge in her direction. She couldn't look at him again, or she would lose her nerve. During that momentary waver, the music became louder. It filled her mind and body, the beats resonating through her until she didn't know where it ended and she began.

She took another step backward. The pull of the song was too strong to resist.

"What is she doing?" Tanira asked.

Nirav jerked his head to her to find her staring out a window toward the auditorium. She had brought them into a private room with a view of the back of the arena. They couldn't hear what was going on, but they could see everything.

"Who?" he asked.

"The human."

"Kalyani?" Nirav rushed to stand beside Tanira, his mouth going lax when he saw Kalyani backing toward the *nehras*. "She's going to step through on her own."

Tanira's gaze slid to him. "Why would she do that? She should be fighting to live."

"She's saving Varum."

"How does that help him?"

Nirav smiled sadly. "I knew something was developing between them."

"How is that helping him?" Tanira repeated, louder this time.

"Varum managed to get the soldiers off him. He did it with the intent of reaching her, and Kalyani knew that. She intends to plunge into the water before he can do anything that implicates him. Her actions will stun everyone and keep them from noticing Varum's reaction."

Tanira's head slowly turned back to the window. "How long has she been at Varum's?"

"A few days."

"And they developed feelings that quickly?"

Nirav nodded once. "It happens that way sometimes."

"Eventually, my father will notice his reaction." Tanira sighed and faced Nirav. "We need to get to Varum before then."

"We can't. The plan I have is for when they return him to the holding cells."

Tanira gathered her long, blue-black hair at the back of her head and wound it into a knot. "We won't have time for that. Listen and do exactly as I say."

Kalyani felt the soft compression of the window behind her. The song filling her ears was so loud that she heard nothing else. Not the crowd, not the speaker. Not even the beating of her own heart.

She took one more step backward and felt the viscous material of the *nehras* cling to her an instant before it spat her out into the water. For a heartbeat, nothing happened. She saw the faces of those on the other side of the *nehras* staring at her, dumbfounded. She was going to be fine. The pressure wasn't going to kill her. That was all she got before agony tore through her, ripping along her skin as if someone were peeling it from her muscles.

Her body spasmed as her mind screamed for her to swim to the surface, but she couldn't move. She was being compressed on all sides. The pressure of the water crushed her bones and squashed her lungs. And yet, the pain within was even worse.

Something was expanding outward. The moment her bones were flattened, they reformed. The push and pull felt as if she were being torn in half. There was nothing but endless pain and anguish. She had no voice to scream, no tears to cry. She was suspended, her body neither whole nor broken but something in between. No longer could she control her limbs. All she could do was endure the torment that ripped skin from muscle and cartilage from bone, and then back again, over and over.

Varum watched helplessly as Kalyani writhed in the water just out of reach on the other side of the *nehras*. The pain contorting her face stole his breath. He tried to wrench free of the soldiers, but they resorted to magic to keep him contained.

He bellowed her name, but no one heard him as everyone shouted and pointed once she had stepped through the window. No one—least of all him—had expected her to take her own life. He was witnessing it, but his mind still couldn't grasp the nightmare unfolding before him.

"What is that?" a guard murmured.

Varum leaned to the side as he attempted to see what the soldier was talking about. The guards that had surrounded Kalyani were lined up in front of the *nehras*, watching, making it difficult for anyone else to see. Then Kalyani began to slowly float upward. Varum blinked in disbelief when he saw currents shooting from all directions to surround her. They swarmed in, moving in alternating courses as if holding Kalyani in place.

Her hair swirled around her, hiding her face like a veil. The currents quickened their pace as bubbles rose from the churning water, blanketing her until she was completely covered. He shook his head, refusing to believe that she was gone that easily.

Emotion filled his chest as tears overflowed his eyes and ran down his cheeks. His beautiful, stubborn Kalyani was no more. He had failed to protect her, failed to keep his promises. He had thought to gain answers from her, but he had only brought her to her doom. Just as he was about to look away, a flash of yellow caught his eye. Then another. And another.

Then, as suddenly as the currents had formed around her, they slowed. The bubbles soon dissipated, revealing Kalyani curled into a ball. One by one, the currents moved away, and as they did, they grabbed her wrists and ankles to stretch out her body.

All the air left Varum's lungs as shockwaves rippled through the auditorium at the sight before them.

Kalyani opened her eyes and looked at the deep blue water above her. She had no idea how long she had been adrift in the pain. It was gone now, but so was the melody. She moved the fingers of her right hand and turned her head to look at it. Her arms were floating out to the sides as strands of her hair drifted around her face.

She became aware of lights around her and focused her gaze past her fingers to them. They looked like the lights of Tarangarh. Was her spirit trapped there? To forever see Varum's world but never be a part of it?

Kalyani looked at her hand again and, for the first time, noticed something yellowish on the back of it. She bent her arm, pulling her hand closer for a better look. Shock reverberated through her as she realized the color she had seen was small scales. They ranged from bright yellow to bronze, with hints of orange and even red. A quick look at her other hand showed the same scale pattern.

A closer inspection of her arms had her noticing that the elven clothes Varum had given her were gone. Her arms were bare, save for more of the scales near her shoulders. She touched her chest and found more scales skating along her collarbones. Her breasts were held by a fitted band of shimmering scales, the same mix of yellow, orange, and red. Then she looked lower.

She no longer had legs, but rather a tail with long, flowing, yellow fins. Kalyani touched the scales of her tail in disbelief. The body she knew was gone, and in its place was someone different. Nay. Some*thing* different.

Slowly, she lifted her eyes and looked through the *nehras*, meeting Varum's gaze. Shock slackened his face as it did all those watching her. She had thought she would die by stepping out of the arena, but it seemed fate had other ideas.

She was exquisite. Varum had thought her beautiful as a human, but seeing Kalyani in her true form left him speechless. He couldn't stop looking at her beautiful scales or the yellow highlights that now streaked her curls. She even had a smattering of scales at her temples that faded into her hair.

As astonished as every Sea Elf in attendance was, none seemed more shaken than Kalyani at her transformation. The moment their eyes met, he knew he had to get to her. Varum tried to take a step but was quickly held in place.

"I want her captured!" Arvind shouted.

Panic seized Varum. He caught Kalyani's gaze again and mouthed, *Run!* She hesitated before flicking her tail and darting away faster than he had seen any Sea Elf move. The arena erupted in pandemonium as soldiers dove through the *nehras*, and residents hurried back to their homes. Varum fought to stay in his place until she faded from sight. Only then did he allow the guards to drag him back to the doors they had entered through.

They tossed him into the first open cell they reached before rushing off. He leaned back against the wall and slowly slid down onto his haunches. He sighed, a smile curving his lips. Kalyani was alive, and if she could stay out of the soldiers' clutches, she might stay that way.

His head turned toward the entrance at the sound of the lock grinding as the bolt was slid back. Then, the heavy door opened to reveal Tanira.

She waved him over. "Come on."

"Why would I go with you?"

"We don't have time. Nirav went to help Kalyani. I'm here to get you out. Now, are you coming or not?"

Varum jumped to his feet and crossed the room in two strides. She put her finger to her lips and motioned for him to follow her.

44

Kalyani zipped through the water with barely any movement of her tail. She saw the currents and somehow knew the direction of each. She knew which were the fastest and which were the slowest. She knew which ones to steer clear of and which were favored by certain animals. The sea had always been beautiful, but she saw it with different eyes now. Clearer eyes.

She moved through the trench with ease and stayed close to the wall, darting in and out of the coral to hide from Tarangarh's soldiers. The Tidewarden wanted her dead. He hadn't gotten that, but that didn't mean he would leave her be now.

Kalyani ducked beneath an arched formation and jerked to a halt when Nirav swam in front of her. He motioned for her to follow and took off. She had to force herself to swim slower as she trailed him to a small cave in the trench wall. Moments after they ducked inside, a group of soldiers swam past.

She tried to leave, but Nirav tugged her back. She wished they could talk, but she had never asked how Sea Elves communicated underwater. Maybe they didn't. She wasn't sure if she could, seeing as she didn't even know what she was.

Kalyani caught Nirav staring at her with a blend of awe and curiosity. She didn't blame him. She couldn't quite get over her transformation either. It had saved her life, but what troubled her was that she didn't know if it was permanent. Would she ever be able to return to land again? The sea had always been special to her, but she wasn't ready to give up walking along the shore with Rohan either.

Finally, Nirav gave her the okay to venture out. She followed him out of the trench, and when she would've headed straight to the surface, he nudged her to continue along with him. She saw why a few minutes later when she noticed more soldiers.

Nirav kept them in darker water. He swam slower than she would have liked, but it allowed them to dart out of the way when they spotted guards. They traveled a vast distance before he finally brought them to the surface.

"I don't know how long we have," he said as soon as her head was clear.

She looked at the night sky and the double moons overhead. "Where are we?"

"Probably an hour's swim east to shore. I tried to get you as close to your home as I could."

"They'll keep looking for me, won't they?"

He nodded. "Arvind won't give up."

"What about you and Varum?"

"Tanira is helping Varum get out of the city. I'll meet up with him soon. Don't worry about us."

She got excited at the prospect of seeing Varum again. Still, as quickly as that emotion arrived, it brought with it the realization that Varum and Nirav needed to get as far away as possible. "Do you think she can really get him out?"

"I have faith in her."

"Where will you go?"

Nirav looked around and shrugged. "I don't know yet."

"When you see him, will you tell him…?"

"What would you like me to tell him?" Nirav asked when she didn't finish.

Kalyani blew out a breath. "Tell him I'm grateful for everything."

"Is that all you want me to say?" he asked with a knowing look.

She nodded and tried to smile. "Thank you for all you've done for me."

"Is there anything else?"

The things she wanted to say shouldn't be given through a third party. She wanted to tell Varum directly. Kalyani shook her head.

Nirav sighed. "Good luck."

"You, too."

He gave her a smile before diving beneath the waves. Kalyani slipped beneath the surface to see him heading back toward the trench. She turned east and started swimming.

Varum was taking a risk by trusting Tanira, but he had already been caught. If she was setting him up, then he wasn't losing anything he hadn't already. Then again, if she was helping, he might just be able to find Kalyani.

He thought he knew the city, but Tanira took him through doorways and along corridors he hadn't known existed. She ducked them into rooms when they heard others coming, and she even managed to hide them when they heard Arvind's voice demanding to know where Kalyani was.

"If your father finds out what you've done, he won't be happy," Varum said.

Tanira shrugged and looked down at her bruised left arm. "The man beside me today wasn't the father I've known. I don't know who he was, but I didn't like him or the things he did. I'm scared of what he's done."

"What do you mean?"

Her nose wrinkled as she led him back into the hallway. "I think he's aligned with the Masters."

"I'm pretty sure he is. I figured you already knew."

"I didn't," she told him and glanced his way. "I swear. He told me today that as long as I played my part, I'd be protected."

Varum didn't like the sound of that. "Why don't you come with me? You won't be safe here now."

"Someone has to stay and fight. No one will suspect me."

"You don't know what you're getting into."

She flashed him a bright smile. "I won't be alone. I'll have you and Nirav helping me."

"What?"

"Nirav and I already set things up. I'll be the eyes and ears within Tarangarh, while you and he will keep track of the Masters elsewhere."

Varum shook his head as he chuckled. "Sounds like something Nirav would do. There's a lot of risk involved, you know."

She stopped in front of a door and faced him. "As I said, no one will suspect me. I'll make sure of it. Nirav set up a meeting place and time. Hopefully, I'll have something for you by then. Right now, you need to get clear of the city and the guards. Nirav said to meet at the designated spot. He said you'd know what that meant."

"I do." Varum eyed the woman he had thought a nuisance for months. "Thank you."

"I saw how you looked at Kalyani. I wanted to be the one you looked at that way, but I'm not."

He glanced at the floor. "I didn't expect you to help us."

"Who knows? If Dad hadn't spoken to me the way he did, I might have let my jealousy come through and taken it out on Kalyani."

"But you didn't."

She smiled sadly, her eyes brimming with unshed tears. "Whatever you may think of me and how I pursued you, I did it because I love you."

"I'm sorry I wasn't the one for you."

"I'll find him," she said. "Don't worry about me."

He touched her arm. "Watch your back."

"I will. Take this door and follow the corridor to the left. You'll come to a room where you can slip out a window. Head straight down to the trench wall. There's a path to swim that will lead you into the open ocean."

Kalyani had always loved to swim, but now, it was as if she could bend the water to her will. Every movement felt instinctive and effortless, as though the sea anticipated her intent. There was power flowing from a new strength within her now. The long, fluid form where her legs should have been propelled her forward with a grace she had never known. Each sweep sent her gliding through the water, fast and sure.

The underwater world was sharper. More brilliant than ever. Even the colors were richer. The sounds of the water, the calls of the creatures, and the distant hum of the deep all reached her with startling clarity.

She reached Serenia in record time and made her way into the cove, swimming into shallow waters. She peeked above the surface and looked at the cluster of huts that made up their community. No one patrolled the beach, but it was late. She tried to swim closer, but her tail bumped the ocean floor.

Kalyani didn't know what would happen if she tried to leave the water, but she had to see Rohan. There was no point in scaring anyone. Besides, what would she tell them about her new appearance? She hadn't really had time to digest what had happened herself. There was no better time for that than the present, while she was alone.

She swam to one of the rocks and climbed up on it to bask in the night air. Once she was completely out of the water, she reached behind her ear and touched the skin there to find three slits. Her gills.

The moonlight reflected on the scales of her tail, creating an array of striking colors. She raised her face to the moon and stared at the stars she hadn't seen in days. There had been a moment, not so long ago, that she had believed she might never see the sky again. Now, that panic had been replaced by a deep melancholy at leaving Varum.

She had never really fit in with humans, but she hadn't fit with the elves either. Her body might have changed, but that didn't mean it made it easier for her to find a place. How could there be when she had never seen anyone like her before? Maybe she was destined to always be just outside of everything.

A long sigh fell from her lips. She should be thinking about the scales and the tail that now replaced her legs, but her mind was filled with thoughts of Varum and whether he had gotten to safety.

"Kalyani?"

Her head whipped around at the sound of Rohan's voice. She smiled as tears spilled onto her cheeks at the sight of him. He stood on the shore, the waves breaking against his boots as he stared at her as if she were an illusion. Then his eyes dropped to her tail. She braced herself for his reaction, but he strode into the water and threw his arms around her.

"I've been so worried," he said as he held her tightly.

She buried her face in his neck and finally released the torrent of tears she hadn't dared before. He didn't ask any questions, simply let her cry until there were no more tears.

He leaned back and cupped her face, forcing her to look at him. "Whenever you're ready to tell me what happened, I'm here."

She nodded, sniffing.

"Do you, ah, have to stay in the water now?"

"I don't know."

Rohan gently tucked a lock of hair behind her ear. "Want me to stay with you?"

"I'd rather go to my hut. Except..." She trailed off and looked down at her tail.

"Then I'll carry you."

He gathered her in his arms before she could reply. As he turned them toward shore, Kalyani saw the rest of their group standing to the side. They would want to know where she had been, and they needed to know. But not now. Things were too raw and painful. She needed time to think over everything.

Rohan set her down on her bed and dropped onto his haunches. "Are you hungry?"

"Not now."

"Do you want me to stay with you?"

She shook her head. "I'd like to be alone for a little while."

"I'll be outside if you need anything. Just holler."

"Thank you."

He straightened and leaned down to kiss her forehead. She watched as he walked out and closed the door. Kalyani lay her head on the pillow as the rhythmic sound of the waves crashing onto shore filled her ears.

45

Three weeks later

Rohan glanced to the side when he heard Farah come up beside him. He briefly met her gaze before swinging his back to the shoreline where his sister stood. It had taken Kalyani three days before she had finally opened up and told him everything. The sadness that had filled her eyes the night he'd found her on the rocks had only deepened as the days passed.

"Has there been any change?" Farah asked.

He shook his head. "None. She continues to stand by the water without letting a single wave touch her feet."

"Still no sign of Varum?"

"None." Rohan swallowed and faced her. "Have Arya and Jai returned yet?"

Farah's downcast expression matched the melancholy that had settled over Serenia. "Only just. Dain's wounds are taking longer than usual to heal. Durga thinks some kind of poison was used on him."

"Has he regained consciousness at least?"

"Not yet."

Rohan glanced at the sky. "So, we have no idea what happened to him."

"It was the Masters. We know that."

"We don't know specifics."

Farah laced her hand with his. "Dain is alive. He'll pull through."

"Things have been too quiet with the Masters for too long. I don't have a good feeling."

"None of us does. I'm tired of being on the defensive. I'd like to attack them first for a change. I thought our strikes were making an impact, but I'm not sure anymore. I'm scared that all of this has been for naught."

Rohan pulled her against him and wrapped his arms around her as he rested his cheek against her head. "All we can do is keep fighting."

"I know. I shouldn't give in to such fears."

It was the same apprehension he had. How could he blame her for such feelings? "We'll win," he vowed.

They had to.

Kalyani stared out at the horizon, where the late-afternoon sky met the deep blue of the ocean. Every day that passed without Varum weighed on her like a mountain. Nirav had been so sure that Varum would get free, and she had believed him. She wondered if Tanira hadn't gotten Varum out in time. Or, worse, that Varum had decided not to seek her out.

They'd only had the one night together, and there had been no promises of anything more. Besides, both of them had acknowledged that neither could live in the other's world. There was no way they could be anything more than two people whose lives had briefly entangled. She wanted to accept that fact, but her aching heart refused.

Nothing felt right anymore. Food tasted bland and refused to settle comfortably when she did manage to get anything down. Sleep was as distant as the horizon. She was desperate to slumber in hopes of finding Varum in her dreams, but even that had been denied to her.

She curled her toes in the warm sand. It had only taken an hour after Rohan carried her into her hut before the scales faded and her legs returned. Yet she hadn't gone back into the water. For the first time in her life, she was scared of it. Scared of not discovering what she was, of encountering more Sea Elves. And scared that if she did return to the ocean, she would spend the rest of her life searching for Varum.

So, she stayed on shore and firmly chose a place to fit in. No song lured her into the waves anymore. Nor did she feel the pull of the water as she once had. Had her turning into...whatever she had solved it? Or had something else happened? Perhaps she should be more concerned, but she couldn't muster up a single fretful thought.

Kalyani was thankful that everyone at Serenia left her alone. She had only wanted to tell the story once, so she'd made Rohan gather everyone. Once she finished, she answered every question they posed. And no one had brought up Varum's name since. They were careful when she was around to talk about anything but her time away.

She sat with them at every meal, even if she couldn't eat. And each time, she felt her brother's eyes on her. He had urged her to eat only once before Farah had quietly admonished him. After that, he was silent. But his look said everything—even if she refused to meet his gaze.

Yasmin said that she would eventually shake off the pain. That sometime in the months ahead, she would wake up and realize that the ache wasn't as bad as it had been. Kalyani couldn't imagine such a time. Not with the agony that filled her chest. She had been in such a hurry to return home, but she would do anything for one more minute with Varum. One more look at him.

"I don't know what gods are listening, but I beg you to hear my plea. Let Varum and Nirav be safe and free," she whispered. "Please let Varum find happiness, wherever that may be."

She dropped her arms and turned away, slowly making her way back to her hut.

46

Varum kept his arm looped around Nirav as he swam. The wound Nirav had sustained needed proper care, but it was difficult with the groups of Sea Elves tracking them. Varum had purposely kept from finding Kalyani so he wouldn't bring danger to her. At least that had been his plan. Things had changed when Nirav fell unconscious the night before.

He adjusted his grip on Nirav and kept going. There was no time to stop to rest or eat. Nirav was worsening with every hour. And as it was, Varum wasn't sure he would reach Kalyani in time. He wasn't even sure going to her was the answer. The fact was, he didn't know what to do.

Enemies surrounded him everywhere he turned. He couldn't go back to Tarangarh. None of the other cities would take them in either. He and Nirav had been hiding for weeks. Several times, they had nearly been caught. He was running out of time. After everything Nirav had done for him, he had to do whatever he could to save him. Varum prayed that he did enough to shake off those tracking him so he wouldn't lead them to Kalyani.

He spotted one of the fast currents and swam into it, letting it do most of the work as it shot him and Nirav forward. Varum allowed himself a brief respite. He wanted to check the bandage on Nirav's wound, but the current was too volatile.

Varum rode the current for as long as he could before tightening his hold on Nirav and swimming out of it. His fatigued muscles strained at being used once more. He gritted his teeth through the pain. The shoreline was in sight now. He glanced behind him, his gaze searching the blue for any signs of Sea Elves —or Kalyani's yellow scales. There was no sign of either, however.

The shallow water eventually forced him to stand and let his head break the surface. He only rose up enough to scan the shoreline. It was dark, but no one was guarding the beach. He slowly turned his head and spotted what appeared to be houses of some kind. They looked crude in nature, but they blended into the forested mountain landscape.

He had followed Nirav's directions, which meant this had to be where Kalyani resided. Even if it wasn't, Varum had to get Nirav out of the water. The elves tracking them would never think to look on land. Varum shifted Nirav onto his back and looped his friend's arms around his neck, then straightened and walked out of the ocean onto land.

His feet sank into the wet sand as he carried Nirav. Once he was safely out of the water, he dropped onto his knees and released Nirav. Varum caught him before he fell and gently laid him down. Only to still at the cold press of steel against his throat.

"You'd better have a good explanation for being here," a voice stated behind him.

Varum slowly sat back on his haunches and raised his arms. He thought about asking for Kalyani, but decided against it. Instead, he remained silent. The blade never wavered against his skin as the male walked around him. To Varum's shock, he found himself staring into the face of a Dark Elf.

"I'm waiting for a reply," the male said.

Varum looked into the Dark's light gray eyes. "You didn't ask a question."

"Then let me," a feminine voice said behind him. "Why are you here?"

Was it another Dark? Kalyani had said she knew three. Dain, of course, because she was forever saying his name. And of the others, one had been a female named Arya. He wasn't sure of the male's name.

"Answer her," the male said as he pressed the blade into Varum's skin until a bead of blood ran down his neck.

"Let him up."

Varum frowned at the sound of the third voice. He didn't recognize it, but it seemed as if the female knew him. Instantly, the Dark removed the sword and sheathed it. Varum looked behind him to see a female Dark, and beyond her, a woman with long, black hair who watched him.

He climbed to his feet and faced her. "Do you know me?"

"I've been expecting you. It took you long enough to get here."

Uncertainty flooded him as he frowned. He could only see a partial view of her face, but she wasn't Kalyani. He had no idea who the human was. "What are you talking about?"

"There will be time enough for answers. For now, let us see to your friend."

Varum looked toward Nirav, but he was gone, as were the two Dark.

"Don't worry," the woman said as his head swung back to her. "He's safe. We'll tend to him while you deal with other things."

Varum took a step toward her as she walked away. A heartbeat later, he noticed a Sun Elf moving away from a tree and falling into step beside her. Varum hesitated, his mind reeling. He scanned the beach and noticed the gritty feel of sand as it stuck to him. He became aware of the rhythmic roll of the waves onto shore. His gaze was pulled to the water as he saw the light from the double moons reflected in the rippling waves.

It held him spellbound. The sights, the sounds, even the scent of salt hanging heavy in the air—all of it created a scene that would forever be stamped onto his soul. The drawings Nirav had shown him of life outside of the sea dimmed in comparison to experiencing it himself.

Now, he fully understood why Kalyani had been so desperate to see the sky. Varum didn't know what he liked more. The moons or the stars. And if this was the night sky, he couldn't wait to see it all during the day.

He sighed as the ache in his heart deepened. He had hoped she would be in the water, waiting, the moment he swam into the cove. At the very least, he had thought she would be on the beach. He wasn't sure how many days had passed since she'd swum away from Tarangarh. Maybe she had forgotten him. Or it could be that the memories of her time there were too painful, and she didn't want any part of him.

The only reason he had managed to survive up to that point was the thought of seeing her again. That was all he needed. One look at her. He wouldn't ask for more. He wouldn't even speak to her. It would be enough to know that she had made it back to her brother and was safe. If he wanted to learn where she was, he needed to ask.

Varum steeled himself and turned to follow where the Sun Elf and woman had gone. He took two steps and looked up, his gaze colliding with Kalyani's, where she stood a short distance away. It was as if the gods had heard his heartfelt plea. His breath caught when the moonlight shone on familiar curls.

A storm of emotions burst inside him, swirling and tangling until he thought he might break into pieces. And yet, even in that onslaught, there was a thread of relief that she was, indeed, home and very much alive.

Then she was running toward him, her body colliding with his. Varum wrapped his arms around her and held her tightly. He felt her shaking as she sobbed. His own tears traced down his cheeks and ran into her hair. This wasn't a dream. She wasn't a figment of his imagination. She was real.

"Where have you been?" she asked, her voice cracking.

He cupped the back of her head, not wanting to ever let her go. "Trying to get to you."

"You're here now." She sniffed, her fingers digging into his back as she held on tight. "I thought you might have had a change of heart."

"Never," he whispered.

Kalyani had thought all her tears had dried up, but the sight of Varum had brought them all back. She knew she was holding him too tightly, but she didn't care. She had spent too many days without him.

"You must be tired."

His only response was a grunt.

She tried to lean back to look at him, but he didn't loosen his arms.

"Not yet," he murmured.

Unwilling to move herself, Kalyani gave in to his request. She was content to be in his arms and feel his warmth once more. There was so much she needed to tell him, but she had time now. She smiled through the tears drying on her cheeks.

Suddenly, all his weight fell on her. She stumbled backward in an effort to stay upright, but she eventually dropped to her knees as panic seized her. It took everything she had to keep him against her. "Varum," she called.

His arms dropped lifelessly from her, and his head lolled to the side.

"Varum! Wake up," she cried frantically.

But there was no response to her pleas.

"Rohan!" she screamed as she tried to lift Varum's head to see his face.

In seconds, her brother was beside her. "What happened?" Rohan asked as he pulled Varum back to lay on the ground.

Kalyani crawled to Varum's side and took one of his hands as she searched his face. "I don't know. We were talking, and then he collapsed."

When Rohan remained quiet, she tore her eyes from Varum to her brother. "What is it?" she demanded.

Rohan slowly lifted his bloodied hand to show her.

"Nay," Kalyani said with a shake of her head, refusing to believe what she was seeing.

Before she knew it, Jai and Ravi were there. It was Ravi who pried her hands from Varum as Jai's shadows swallowed them. The run from the beach to the hut seemed to go on forever, the sand sucking at her feet as if trying to halt her progress.

When she finally burst inside, Rohan, Jai, and Farah had already cut away Varum's tunic and rolled him onto his stomach. She skidded to a halt at the sight of the injuries on his back. Kalyani looked down at her hands, which were stained red. He hadn't said anything about being wounded. How she must have hurt him when she'd held him and dug her fingers into him.

"Kalyani!"

She jerked, her gaze going to her brother.

Sweat streaked Rohan's face, and Varum's blood seemed to be on everyone and everything. "I need you to put pressure here."

She hurried to her brother and replaced his blood-soaked hands where they were on Varum's back. Time ceased to exist as Rohan barked orders to those around him to stop both Varum's and Nirav's bleeding. Both had multiple injuries on the fronts and backs of their bodies. It was chaos within the small hut as everyone worked tirelessly to stabilize both Varum and Nirav. There was no time to rest or think about anything but saving them both.

Sunlight streamed through the shutters when Rohan finally dropped onto a stool. Kalyani stood in a daze, staring at the blood-soaked bandages littering the floor. Neither Nirav nor Varum had woken during the long dark hours of the night. Several times, she had put her finger beneath Varum's nose to make sure he was still breathing.

"I've done all I can do," Rohan said. He lifted his head to her, exhaustion in every line of his face. "All we can do now is wait."

Farah was immediately by his side. "Come, love. You need to rest."

Kalyani watched the two of them leave. When Yasmin started cleaning up, she stopped her. "I'll take care of it."

"You've been here just as long as we have," Jai said.

Kalyani glanced at Varum. "I'm staying anyway, so I'll clean up."

"We'll help," Arya insisted.

Ravi shot her a quick smile. "It'll go quicker if we all help. Then, we can all rest."

She had no choice but to admit defeat. The cleanup went more quickly with their help, and true to their word, the two couples left soon afterward. Kalyani then pulled up a stool to sit next to Varum's bed and look across at Nirav.

47

Varum opened his eyes to a bright light. He blinked against the harshness and turned his head to get away from it. A dull pain pressed on him and spread throughout his body. He dragged in a ragged breath as his gaze landed on Kalyani. She sat on a stool, bent over so that her head rested on one arm while her other hand held his.

For a long moment, he did nothing but stare at her, taking in the sunlight streaking through the open window to land on her curls. He watched the wind gently lift strands, allowing him to witness the red and copper colors in her hair that he had never noticed before. As if they could only be seen in the sun.

He reached his free arm over his body, biting back a moan of pain at the pull he felt in his back, just so he could smooth some hair away from her eyes. In the moonlight, Kalyani was captivating. But in the sunlight, she was ravishing. Whether in the depths of the ocean, hiding in his home, covered in yellow scales, standing in the moonlight, or sleeping in the sun, she was the most beautiful thing he had ever seen.

His finger skimmed her cheekbone before caressing her temple. He didn't even mind the pain since he was touching her. Varum smiled as he lowered his arm to his side. Her eyes fluttered open before their gazes met.

She immediately sat up. "You're awake."

"It seems so."

He followed her gaze as she glanced over her shoulder and spotted Nirav in another bed, still resting.

"I should get Rohan," she said.

Varum stopped her by tightening his fingers on her hand and refusing to let go. "Not yet."

"You scared me last night. Why didn't you tell me you were wounded?"

"I didn't know that I was."

Her brow furrowed in disbelief. "How could you not know? Do you have any idea how many injuries you had? Rohan spent most of the night tending to them."

"I didn't feel anything. There wasn't time while trying to stop Nirav's bleeding and getting to you without being caught."

"Don't do that to me again," she said and looked away.

He rubbed his thumb over the back of her hand. "I won't."

The door opened before he could say more. Varum eyed the man and the Wood Elf who strode inside. He and Rohan looked each other up and down. Rohan was exactly as Kalyani had described him.

Varum started to sit up. Kalyani tried to keep him down, but he gently pulled her hand away. She shot him a dark look while helping him up. He had to grit his teeth against the shooting pain every movement cost him.

"You shouldn't be up," Rohan said from the foot of the bed.

Varum waited until the worst of the pain had passed before turning his head to meet Rohan's light green eyes. "Thank you for seeing to both Nirav and me. Kalyani spoke highly of your skills in healing."

"Even humans have their uses," Rohan stated.

Beside him, Farah elbowed Rohan's ribs, while Kalyani narrowed her eyes at him.

Varum touched Kalyani's arm. "He has a right to his anger."

"You're still injured. He should save it," she argued.

Varum couldn't help but smile. After all, she was taking up for him. His grin faded as he remembered why he was here in the first place. He sighed before returning his gaze to Rohan. "I wronged both you and Kalyani by taking her to Tarangarh without her permission. I put her life in danger."

"You had a good reason," Kalyani said.

Varum shook his head. "I disagree."

"It doesn't matter. I've already forgiven you."

He touched her face, amazed, once again, at her willingness to let go of the past and look ahead. Had he been able to do that, his life could have been much different. "It does matter. And while I have offered my apology to you already, this one is for Rohan." Varum looked at her brother. "I'm sincerely sorry for the suffering you went through, wondering where Kalyani had gone."

"You think words can fix things?" Rohan asked in a tight voice.

"I do not, but the words are owed. I intend to follow them with actions."

Rohan grunted. "Is that so?"

"Enough," Farah chastised Rohan as she tossed her long, red braid over her shoulder. "He's still recovering."

"If he can sit up, he can have a discussion," Rohan stated.

Kalyani rolled her eyes. "You call this a discussion? You're intentionally needling him."

"I deserve it," Varum interjected.

Rohan pointed to him as he looked between Kalyani and Farah. "See? Even he agrees."

Farah tugged Rohan's arm down and gave him a pointed look. After a moment, Rohan released a loud sigh and looked away, but he didn't say more. Farah then turned her hazel eyes to Varum. "As you may have guessed, Kalyani told us what happened while she was with you. We all worried that you and Nirav might not have made it out. Please, stay for as long as you like."

"We didn't come empty-handed," Varum said.

Rohan quirked a dark brow. "Meaning?"

"Meaning, that while Nirav and I were evading the soldiers, we were also gathering information."

Farah shoved Rohan toward the door and told Varum, "We can't wait to hear it."

"What are you doing?" Rohan asked her as he fought to stay in place.

Varum watched the couple exchange looks before Rohan sighed loudly, obediently turned toward the door, and walked out. Farah lifted a hand to him and Kalyani as she followed Rohan.

"I'm sorry about that," Kalyani said. "Rohan can be a bit much sometimes."

Varum slid his gaze to her. "He's protecting his family. I don't blame him. I'm surprised he left so easily."

"That's because it was Farah," Kalyani said with a smile. "She's good for him. Really good for him. He smiles now. And laughs. He would do anything for her."

Varum knew the feeling well. Each time he remembered the sight of the soldiers leading Kalyani into the arena, he was overcome with fear and anger again. "Do you think you can ever forgive me?"

"For what?" she asked, tilting her head to the side.

"I promised to protect you."

Her lips curved into a smile. "You did. What happened wasn't your fault."

"It's solely mine. You wouldn't have been in that mess had I not brought you there."

"I thought we already talked about this."

He tried to shift to ease the throbbing of his wounds, but nothing lessened his pain. Besides, the ache of his injuries was nothing compared to that of his heart. "You could've died."

"I could have, but I didn't. Neither of us did."

"Do you have any idea how scared I was when you walked through the *nehras*?" He winced as his heart clutched. Despite her fear, she had taken the upper hand and stepped into the water herself. It had been an incredibly brave act. Yet it would haunt him for the rest of his days. "I couldn't get to you."

She glanced down before covering his hand with hers. "Why do you think I did it? I saw you struggling, and I didn't want you to get hurt."

"Me?" he asked, shock rolling through him. "You were thinking about me when you were about to die?"

"Of course."

He searched her face, seeing the truth reflected in her eyes. "You should've been worried about yourself."

"I was trying to save you. I thought my life was already over, and I wanted to do whatever I could...for you."

Varum followed the tear that rolled down her cheek. He gently brushed it away with his thumb.

Kalyani sniffed and wiped her other cheek. "Did Tanira really get you out?"

"Aye." He lowered his arm and curled his fingers as he fought the urge to pull her against him. "There were passages I didn't know about that she used to guide me out. She intends to remain in the city and gather intel on the Masters and her father."

"That's going to be dangerous."

He flattened his hands on his thighs. "She's made up her mind. Tanira always was stubborn, but from what I saw and what Nirav told me, she's found something to turn her attention to. She'll be a great asset."

"As long as she doesn't get caught."

"It's a risk we all take while fighting against the Masters."

Kalyani nodded and turned her head away.

Varum studied her profile. The scales along her temples and on the backs of her hands were gone. She was once again in the simple, bleached gray garments he had first found her wearing. The clothes covered her collarbones as well as her arms, making it difficult to know if there was any trace of the scales there.

"You can ask," she suddenly said. "I know you want to."

"It seems like something you don't want to talk about."

She swung her head back to him. "It isn't that. It's just...I don't know the answers. I've tried to find them for Rohan's sake. He found me...like that."

Varum could imagine Rohan's shock, but it had likely dimmed at the knowledge that she was home.

"Do you remember when I told you that I used to hear music coming from the sea?" she asked.

He nodded, watching as she fidgeted nervously while refusing to look him in the eye.

"I heard it again as I was dragged toward the *nehras*." She paused and met his gaze. "The fear that had gripped me so fiercely faded. I became calm. Relaxed, even. That was how I was able to go into the water myself."

"Did it hurt?" His voice was a broken whisper.

She inhaled deeply and slowly released it as she nodded. "It was more painful than anything I've ever experienced before. I thought I was being crushed by the water. I had no idea what was happening. It felt as if it lasted for hours."

"It was over fairly quickly."

"Really?" she asked with a slight frown before shrugging. "Once the pain stopped, I saw the changes."

He looked at her legs. "That change allowed you to get away."

"It did."

"Can you change at will?"

She tucked her feet out of sight. "I don't know."

"What does that mean?"

"It means I've not been back in the water since Rohan carried me out. It took some time, but I eventually returned to normal."

Now, he understood why she was hesitant to look at him. "It's normal to be scared about such a change. It's also probably good that you didn't go back into the water. Patrols are everywhere, looking for you, as well as Nirav and me. And," he said when her gaze darted away again. "How do you know that you aren't meant to be both this version and that one?"

"It never happened before. What if I can't get my legs back?"

"What if you can? What if you were meant to become exactly that? It doesn't matter if you have two legs or that stunning tail, you are beautiful."

Slowly, she looked at him once more.

He smiled as he took her hand. "You should've seen yourself after you transformed. Those yellow scales stood out like a beam of sunlight in the darkest parts of the deep. You were so magnificent that you took my breath away. I thought I needed to save you, but it turned out you were able to save yourself."

"I didn't do anything."

"I disagree. From the moment I first saw you, you've set aside worry about your own safety to help others. Even locked away in my home, your thoughts were on Rohan. You're braver than you realize."

She glanced down at their joined hands. "You said you would never leave the ocean."

"That was before I fell for you. All I've been able to think about has been you and getting here as quickly as I could. I know what life is without you, and I don't want to spend another day apart. I don't care if we're in the sea or on land. As long as I have you by my side, I can face anything. I..." He swallowed and tried again. "I love you."

"That was hard for you to say."

He shook his head, holding her gaze. "Only because I've never spoken the words before. And...I wanted to convey the truth of them to you—the one I cherish above all others. The one who means more to me than anyone. My beloved."

"No one has ever called me such." She brought his hand up to her cheek and leaned her head into it. "I understand how you feel. I don't know when I began to love you, and it doesn't matter. You claimed my heart. I want to greet every rise of the sun and moons with you. I want to experience every moment of life with you." She pressed her lips into his palm. "I love you."

Varum had never known he could experience such happiness. Even the pain of his wounds barely registered as he pulled her against him and slid his fingers into the tangle of her curls.

"It's about time," Nirav said in a gravelly voice.

Varum met his friend's gaze as Kalyani pulled out of his arms and spun around. He and Nirav exchanged a smile while she fussed over him before rushing out to get Rohan.

"Grip her tightly and never let go," Nirav said.

Varum grinned as he watched Kalyani run back inside. "I intend to."

EPILOGUE

Three days later...

"The rumors are true, then," Arya murmured as their group sat around a fire on the beach. "They're building a new Shaldorn in the ocean."

Nirav grunted in pain as he stretched out his legs and leaned back against a log. "It's heavily guarded, too."

"We barely got away," Varum added.

Kalyani frowned at Nirav and then Varum. "You shouldn't have been so reckless."

"If they hadn't, we wouldn't have that information," Ravi said.

She cut her eyes to him, but she knew the Sun Elf had a point.

"Not everyone visiting will be a Sea Elf. How are members going to get in?" Yasmin asked.

Varum rotated his shoulder, testing his wound. "They're building a tunnel that connects it to a small island nearby. It'll be the only way in or out for everyone but Sea Elves."

"Did you happen to see a Moon Elf female?" Yaz asked.

Nirav shook his head. "There are only Sea Elves constructing it."

"The original Shaldorn was nearly impossible to get into or out of. This one will be even harder," Ravi murmured.

Varum grinned. "Good thing you have us."

"If I was them, I'd make it so the tunnel collapsed," Jai interjected.

Farah stirred the fire with a stick. "I was thinking the same thing."

"We're all at a disadvantage in the water," Arya said.

Kalyani looked out at the waves. She wouldn't let Nirav and Varum go by themselves. She would return to the sea and accept whether she changed again. Either way, she would do what needed to be done. "Then we find an advantage."

"We need to let Durga know, and I'd like to check to see if Dain has regained consciousness," Arya said as she got to her feet.

Jai stood with her and turned his gray eyes to first Varum and then Nirav. "You two should prepare. Durga will want to meet you."

Then they were gone.

Kalyani slipped her hand into Varum's. "I'll be going with you."

"Why would you need to do that?" Rohan demanded.

Farah rolled her eyes. "Sometimes, my love, you can be so dense."

"What?" Rohan asked her. "It isn't as if Varum won't return."

Kalyani exchanged a look with Varum. "We don't want to be apart. Besides, I want to see Rannora."

"Then it's settled," Varum said before Rohan could speak. "We go together."

Kalyani leaned to the side and rested her head on his shoulder. Rohan put on a show, but she had seen him and Varum talking and laughing together. Their bond might take some time to grow. She didn't mind, though. Both Varum and Nirav had a place in their growing family.

Varum leaned his head against hers as they listened to Farah telling a story about the first time Rohan tried to run across the tree limbs. Kalyani smiled, having heard the story before, but it made Nirav and Varum laugh.

The moment was one that everyone sitting around the fire treasured, because each of them knew just how precious time was when standing against the Masters' evil.

Durga glared down at Dain, who had yet to wake. The two Healers she had rotated to heal his injuries said he should've woken already. The fact that he hadn't made her worry that the poison used on him had done more damage than even the Star Elves could heal.

"You've been lying there for long enough," she told Dain. "It's time to open your eyes and tell me what happened. I need to know who attacked you."

She looked over at what was left of his favorite coat. Most of the blood had been cleaned away, and skilled artisans had mended the numerous rips, tears, and burns caused during the battle. She had rushed everyone, wanting to ensure it was ready for him when he woke.

The coat had been saved, but his armor hadn't been. He would likely be upset about that. Dain had few things he treasured. His coat, armor, and sword were it. She was having specially designed armor made for him now. It should be ready later that day.

All someone had to do was look at Dain's face to know that he was a survivor. When others would crumble or break, he kept going. He didn't know how to give in or give up. It was why she knew that he would eventually open his eyes. There was still work to be done.

There was a soft knock on the door, and Durga turned toward it as it cracked open to reveal one of her servants. "Arya and Jai have arrived."

Durga nodded and glanced back at Dain. She had decided to keep him in her home. It was heavily fortified with both magic and guards. Yet only a handful knew the Dark was here. She had never trusted easily before, but now, she didn't trust anyone except for Dain and those who fought with him.

She strode out of the room. Jai and Arya wouldn't have returned so quickly if they didn't have information. One day, she would have what she needed to bring down the Masters for good. She might be fighting the battles behind the scenes, but that was how she got things done. She was just as willing to put her life on the line as Dain and the others were. And it would take attacks aimed at the Masters from different sides to end them.

The door closed softly with a click as Dain opened his eyes.

Thank you for reading **BURNING SEA**. I hope you enjoyed Varum and Kalyani's story, because I fell hard for them and the incredible Sea Elf world.

If you want more Elven Kingdom stories, I'm pleased to announce that **DARK RUIN** is up next in the series.

BUY DARK RUIN NOW
at www.DonnaGrant.com

* * *

If you love the elves, you'll love the next Dark Universe book set in the Dragon King series, **DRAGON SIEGED**.

BUY DRAGON SIEGED NOW
at www.DonnaGrant.com

To find out when new books release
SIGN UP FOR MY NEWSLETTER today at
https://www.tinyurl.com/DonnaGrantNews

Join my Facebook group, Donna Grant Groupies, for exclusive giveaways and sneak peeks of future books.
https://bit.ly/DGGroupies

Keep reading for a glimpse of DARK RUIN and DRAGON
SIEGED ...

GLIMPSE AT DARK RUIN

ELVEN KINGDOMS, BOOK 6

New York Times and *USA Today* best-selling author Donna Grant continues her acclaimed Elven Kingdoms series with *Dark Ruin*, a captivating new installment coming soon.

BUY DARK RUIN NOW
at www.DonnaGrant.com

DRAGON SIEGED, DRAGON KINGS, BOOK 11

She is the one thing no Dragon King can survive…and the only woman he can't resist.

Fedra is the end of magic. A living void that devours power—feared, hunted, and locked away for centuries. Now she's free.

And she's come for the dragons who took everything from her.

Marcus is a Dragon King. Ancient. Unrivaled. Nothing has ever threatened him.

Until her.

Because the closer he gets, the faster his magic unravels.

He knows what she is. Knows exactly what she intends to do. Which is why he should walk away.

But he can't.

Not when every glance lingers too long. Not when every touch pulls him closer to ruin.

Staying away would save him.

Wanting her may be the end of him.

And when vengeance collides with desire, he'll have to choose—stand with his kind...or take the one woman who will destroy them all.

New York Times and _USA Today_ bestselling author Donna Grant delivers a gripping story of vengeance, forbidden desire, and impossible choices in the latest installment of her electrifying Dragon Kings series.

BUY DRAGON SIEGED NOW
at www.DonnaGrant.com

Keep reading for an excerpt of DRAGON SIEGED ...

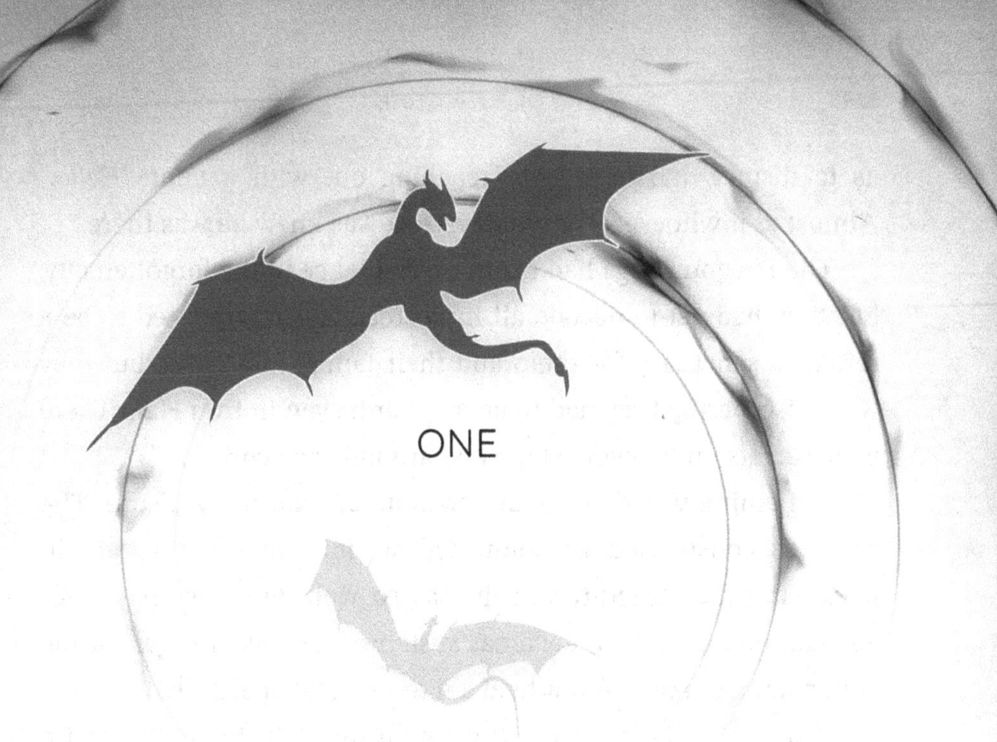

ONE

Iron Hall

The ancient corridors were quiet and still as Marcus soundlessly walked through the underground city. It had been three days since he'd first heard the plaintive whisper of his name drifting to him like a ghost's caress. That should have been enough to keep him from the atrium, but he couldn't resist the draw to that place. It was as if someone—some*thing*—had latched onto his soul and called for him.

He hadn't been the only one to sense that something was off. Constantine had used magic to block the long, caved-in hallway connected to the atrium. That was the only thing preventing Marcus from striding down it now. He couldn't make up his mind if he was thankful that Con had taken such drastic actions or not.

When Marcus first heard the whisper, it had taken him aback. He'd thought he had just imagined the voice. He even went so far as to dismiss it. Yet it kept reaching out with a faint *"Hello."* Almost as if whoever—or whatever—it was knew he was there.

The Dragon Kings had taken up residence in the forgotten city, but they had yet to decode all its secrets. It was supposed to be a refuge, a sanctuary for them and their family and allies, but they were discovering they had to be on guard, even in Iron Hall. There were secrets under every stone and around each corner.

Something was down that corridor. Of that, he was sure. The city was constructed in connected sections in order to aid in preserving the structure and it was so well designed that, after abandonment, while a few areas sustained damage, the rest of the city remained intact. But it held a flaw—a fatal one, at that.

If struck at the right locations with the right force, the entire city could be ravaged within seconds.

That was the case with one of the halls attached to the atrium, and the very reason he was there. *His* main flaw was becoming so engrossed in his work that everything else faded away. Hector had vanished only steps away without Marcus realizing it, simply because he had been too intent on repairing the city to be aware of what was happening. It was only *after* Hector disappeared that Marcus discovered that the city was in danger. Luckily, they'd found Hector, and Iron Hall had been saved—barely.

Marcus rubbed his forehead, inwardly berating himself for his lack of attention. He hadn't always been this way. He had been through so many changes over his very long life that he no longer tried to think about the past. The one thing he knew for certain was that nothing stayed the same. Pain dulled. Anger could be quashed. Even the sharp ache of loss eventually became blunted.

But the Dragon King he'd been had died the day he helped to send his clan from Earth.

His feet slowed as flashes from that day flickered in his mind. He stopped in the silence of the hallway and looked down it. The light from the wall torches reached his boots, shining upon them like a halo. As bright as the light was, it barely reached his knees while the rest of him stood in darkness.

All he had to do was take half a step forward and he would be in the light, but it seemed as if the hand of fate had stopped him there to show him that nothing he did would ever completely shake off the darkness that had enveloped him that long-ago day.

How naive he had once been to think that becoming a Dragon King would solve everything. He, like so many other Kings, had reached for the position without a second's hesitation. How could they not, if the magic had seen into their hearts and chosen them? It meant that each and every one of them was worthy of holding the position.

It wasn't that Marcus thought his duties as a King would be easy. Rather, he assumed that he would know what to do in every situation. How bold and arrogant of him. How confident and utterly foolhardy.

Then the world he'd known and loved had gone up in flames, taking everything he held dear in one fell swoop. He, along with the rest of the Kings, had been plunged into a nightmare that some were *still* living in, even after countless millennia.

One didn't simply wake from something like that without deep, lasting wounds. The scars might be hidden from the world, but they were there all the same. Inflamed and festering day by day. Even if they scabbed over, something would always chafe the lesion, irritating it until it bled once again.

It was a cycle he couldn't seem to get out of.

And he had stopped trying.

Long after the dragons had been sent away and the Kings finally emerged from Dreagan, Marcus had found himself in a world he didn't recognize. Learning how to coexist with humans while hiding who he really was and pretending not to want to unleash a torrent of dragon fire on the world had been one of his greatest trials. It had taken a tremendous amount of effort to calm his ire, and he only managed that by finding the things that gave him joy—building and planning.

He had designed and erected every structure on Dreagan, from their home to the many distillery buildings. And then he'd come to Zora to build Cairnkeep, a manor for the capital on the dragon's land. Soon after, they discovered Iron Hall, and he'd found himself here to help repair the city.

The dragons on Zora barely tolerated the Kings and refused to abide *any* humans on their land, regardless of whether the Kings brought them. The dragons were descendants of those from Earth, so it was understandable how their aversion to humans would grow. Iron Hall was perfect for the Kings, their mates, and the children and other magical beings needing a place to hide. It was large enough that over half of it was situated under dragon land, with the other half on the human side.

Marcus looked down the corridor, his superior vision letting him see clearly into the darkness. Each time he thought of the atrium and the voice, he remembered the cold hand of terror that had gripped him. He wanted to find who the voice belonged to but also worried about what the revelation might mean.

He stepped out of the light and into the darkness, putting his back to the wall and closing his eyes. The last time he had been so restless was the day he'd lost his clan. Something was down that hallway. Con wanted more time, but for what? The only way to see what awaited everyone—and called out to him—was to go down there and investigate.

Marcus turned his head to the side, raising his eyelids. The voice had called him by name. Did it know him? Could it see him? Why *him*, of all the Kings?

Or had it called others by name, too?

After all, he hadn't been the only one to hear it. Evander had, as well. Ryder had walked halfway down the corridor, and while he had felt the same sinister threat, he hadn't said anything about voices. Marcus wanted to know if others had heard their names being called, but he was hesitant to ask. If they hadn't, they might think he was losing his mind. If they *had*, Con would be even more adamant about waiting.

Marcus looked down at his jeans, tee, and thick-soled boots. He hadn't worn a suit in weeks. His love of designing and constructing eventually evolved into a highly successful business that brought in considerable assets for the Kings. Though nothing surpassed the profits of their whisky, Dreagan. It hadn't been difficult to clear his schedule to come to Zora. He wouldn't have cared what he had to do to see the dragons again.

After he had stepped through the Fae doorway onto Zora and heard the dragons, he'd lifted his gaze to the sky to see them. Being on a different planet and away from the Dragon Kings had changed many things for the dragons. They no longer remained in clans designated by color. They intermingled in life and with their mates. There were dragons of mixed colors now, and they were a spectacular sight to behold.

Whatever homecoming he had expected from the Lavenders was hastily dispelled. The only thing that had kept the Kings together and slogging through the endless years on Earth was the hope that they would find the dragons again someday. Perhaps they should've expected the dragons to have centuries of built-up anger and resentment.

Just one more of the Kings' failings.

He blew out a breath and straightened as he pushed away from the wall. Once more, he wandered the city as he did every night. His patrol rotation had finished hours ago, but he didn't bother returning to his chamber. He never stayed there for long. Dragons didn't need sleep, and he couldn't stand to be idle. They'd taken him off the guard rotation at the borders after he and Ryder ventured into the caved-in hall and lost time.

Marcus didn't want anyone in the hallway. Each time someone got close, he had the overwhelming impulse to stop them—at whatever cost. And he couldn't explain why. Ryder had also felt the impulse, which made sense, since they had walked the corridor together. Strangely, however, Evander had felt it, too, and he *hadn't* been with them. Or had he? Perhaps Evander had been there, and none of them could remember.

Marcus had gone over and over it in his head without discovering a solution. And there wouldn't be one until someone went to the other end of the hallway and discovered what was there. The caved-in corridor was unlike the others fanning out from the atrium, almost as if it had been constructed for a special purpose. But why just the one hall? Then again, the entire city had yet to be mapped. There *could* be other areas like it that they hadn't found yet.

Were the builders the same ones who had brought the tech they'd discovered in the corridor that had stumped even Ryder? Each King had a special skill. For Ryder, it was any and all tech. But he had said that it was unlike anything he had ever seen before. That same piece of tech had transported Hector thousands of miles away from Iron Hall to Highvale, an island only accessible to those with magic.

Minutes ticked by as Marcus stalked down the hallways, moving about the maze of the city from one floor to another while keeping clear of others making their rounds. Some of the walls were adorned with murals, but he didn't see them. His mind was too full of the current problems plaguing the Kings.

When he came to a passageway crossing, he paused and looked down one side, then the other. After a moment, he looked ahead. He should continue forward. It would take him on another loop of the city before bringing him to a set of stairs where he could go down a level. Instead, he turned right.

His heart rate increased with the first step, yet he didn't stop. He kept walking, even though he knew he should turn back. He didn't stop until he stood at the atrium's entrance and gazed at the stunning domed ceiling and the starry blue middle of the six-pointed white star. He tried to take a deep breath, but it felt as if an unseen hand had wrapped around his chest and squeezed.

It didn't matter how many times he saw it. He always stood in awe of the vestibule. Each of the star's points on the dome correlated with a hallway that branched off. The symmetry was perfect, the design flawless—as was all of Iron Hall. But the atrium was uniquely special. The builders placed great significance on the area, and someone only did that if it was important.

He lowered his gaze to the corridor across from him and looked down it to the rock that blocked the section, preventing him from seeing farther. Had this area been constructed to highlight whatever was on the other side? Marcus needed to know the answer. It would haunt him unless he figured it out.

Con had put up the barrier to keep everyone out. As King of Dragon Kings, Con was the largest and strongest of all dragons. And his word was law. It could be weeks or months before Marcus talked him into reopening the area. There was no way he could wait that long.

He glared at the atrium's wide opening, where the barrier began. He hadn't heard the voice in hours. Was Con's magic keeping it from reaching him? Would Marcus hear it again if he got closer to the corridor? He lifted a hand, ready to try and bust through Con's magic. It was such a shocking move that he froze, wondering at his thoughts.

If anyone knew he was there, they would start watching everything he did. His gaze landed on the table and the numerous plans there—some spread out on the surface, and others rolled and stacked in a box on the floor. His work was there. He needed it. Maybe he could use it as an excuse to go against Con's order.

Suddenly, the sound of whistling reached him. Marcus frowned as he took half a step closer and peered into the atrium. Shock rolled through him when he spotted Teo, the young lad Hector had brought from Highvale, reclining in the doorway of one of the halls, whistling as he tossed something long and slender into the air and caught it.

"What are you doing?" Marcus demanded.

Teo startled, bolting upright, his bright blue eyes widening when they turned to Marcus. "Am I not supposed to be in here?"

"Nay, you're no'."

"Um...perhaps there should be a sign or something so others don't just wander in," Teo said with a nervous grin only an over-confident youngster on the verge of adolescence could muster.

Marcus narrowed his eyes as he looked from the skinny eleven-year-old with his mop of dark, wavy hair to Con's barricade. "Did you no' feel the barrier?"

"Barrier?" Teo asked as he jumped to his feet and walked over. "I felt something brush against me when I went through."

"Are you telling me that you walked through a wall of bloody dragon magic without any effects?" Marcus asked in disbelief.

Teo went still, his eyes bugging out and his face paling. "Nope. I would definitely not say that."

"Do you know what you are, lad?" Marcus asked softly as he studied him.

"I...um..." Teo licked his lips and shook his head as his gaze darted away. "I do not."

The lad could see the Kings as dragons, even though they walked around in human form. And now, apparently, not even Con's magic had much effect on him. "If you want to find out, I'm sure we can help with that."

"I'll think about it."

Teo obviously wasn't sure what to make of Marcus, which made two of them. "What are you doing out of bed?"

"Can't sleep. I miss the sound of the ocean," Teo answered.

"You should've told one of us. We can make it so that sound fills your room."

Teo grinned. "The way you Kings use magic is effortless. I wish I could do that."

Marcus was about to call him out of the atrium when he looked at the caved-in hallway once more. He strained his ears, listening for that wispy voice saying his name. "Do you hear anything?"

"I hear *you*," Teo answered, looking at Marcus as if he were daft.

Maybe he was.

Marcus met the boy's blue eyes. "Do you hear a whisper? Perhaps someone asking for help?"

Teo slowly shook his head while his brow furrowed.

"Come on out," Marcus said with a sigh. "Let's get you back to your chamber, and I'll make sure the ocean puts you to sleep."

***

BUY DRAGON SIEGED NOW
at www.DonnaGrant.com

ABOUT THE AUTHOR

New York Times and *USA Today* bestselling author Donna Grant® has been praised for her "totally addictive" and "unique and sensual" stories.

She's written more than one hundred novels spanning multiple genres of romance including the bestselling Dragon Kings® series that features a thrilling combination of Druids, Fae, and immortal Highlanders who are dark, dangerous, and irresistible. She lives in Texas with her dog and a cat.

www.DonnaGrant.com
www.MotherofDragonsBooks.com

facebook.com/AuthorDonnaGrant
instagram.com/dgauthor
tiktok.com/@donnagrant_author
bookbub.com/authors/donna-grant
goodreads.com/donna_grant
pinterest.com/donnagrant1